RETURNING
TO NO
APPLAUSE

RETURNING TO NO APPLAUSE

Only More of the Same

PALT

Podium

*To Mamma and Pappa, who both gave me life,
and to Ida, who gave me passion,
and to all of my RRL readers, who gave me direction,
especially Earl, who gave me heart.
And also to my buddy Mark.*

Published in 2022 by Podium Publishing, ULC
www.podiumaudio.com

Podium

RETURNING
TO NO
APPLAUSE

THE PORTAL THAT TOOK HIM BACK HOME

He had only been a soldier for a year, but he turned fifteen last Yuletide. He had only been a child for two years, but even then he knew what War of the North was. There was nobody ignorant of that rampant force.

Now he saw that creature, that *man* separating a dozen of his fellow soldiers into neat halves. The upper bodies didn't remain, the faces didn't remain, and their souls had left the moment they heard who their opponent was. Few things in this world were a death sentence, but War was one of them. He had consumed and destroyed countless armies. Slaughtered thousands. His armor was red, and his mind was surely no different.

Gerald slung his too-light body behind a broken boulder, hearing only barely how a misfired arrow whizzed past his dirtied face. It had been fired by an ally, but right now he was alone.

The smell of blood and flesh and iron forced its way into his nostrils, making him buckle over again, clutching at his face with his gloved hands. All he had was his leather armor. Way back before they had gotten there, before they had come face-to-face with death, he'd carried a spear. Not that he missed it. At this moment, weapon or not, his chances of survival remained zero.

There was another flash of noise and smell. He squeezed his eyes shut. It smelled like arsenic and charcoal. It sounded like a bubbling, fleshy pyre.

They had brought two wizards, hadn't they? Just two. No, that wasn't fair . . . A *whole two*. A few of the important soldiers and officers had been rubbed with some sort of brew, an ointment to hide their scent or give them strength. It didn't help now. That man, after all, that was what he was—neither dragon nor werewolf—had seen them coming. Wind on their back, he smelled them coming. Bared his fangs. Face hidden by a helmet, body welded to his armor, he swung that slab of iron as if it weighed nothing. And when people came too close for the sword, he didn't hesitate to simply tear them apart with his bare hands.

Gerald had hidden himself not long after. Now . . . Now, he was sure not many remained. The crunch that had rung out mere seconds before, followed by the fizzle of magic being snuffed out, proved that even their wizards had been slaughtered. Not that it changed much.

A whimper escaped his sore throat. The air was so dry. It should have been wet. He could smell the blood. He could see it, too. The ground was muddy. Muddy like a hundred horses had gone through. Muddy like a dozen wars had been fought in that very spot. Gerald shifted uncomfortably, trying to control his thin, wheezing breaths, but when he pressed his hands into the mud only to find the ground just beneath it being made up completely of something hard and soft and *bony* . . .

"—*Hiik!*" He really couldn't help it.

The area beyond the boulder gave a sound. Wet splashes, the soft mud hiding the cracking and breaking of bones just beneath. Such heavy steps, covered with armor ten times heavier than what Gerald's officer bore. Only one person on this battlefield wore such armor, and when the boy realized that, he knew it was over. He looked up, just above the small boulder hiding him only barely, and there he was, rearing up like the most hideous of titans, that blood-red helmet of War. The glint of an eye could only barely be seen through the single slit in the red helmet, shining like a lone star in a red sky.

And in that moment, Gerald knew he would not survive the day.

. . . Until the sound of something else made him look elsewhere, beyond the looming death before him. A soft, friendly hum. It had a warm color, too. Welcoming, like a mother's embrace. Gerald's mother had never been too close to him, but if she had been . . . she'd feel like that large, swirling pool of mana did. It was so inviting. It smelt like homemade food and a bakery shop. Unafraid, he stood up. He didn't even look at the physical embodiment of human war before him. War himself turned around, looked at the portal, and started walking. As did Gerald. Soldier and death walked side-by-side toward the portal.

Out of the corner of his eye, Gerald could see others. His fellow soldiers, people he had known for months or days or minutes. All moving toward the portal. Their eyes were hazy, smiles speckled their faces, and he was sure his facial expression was no different. He wondered for a moment if War was smiling as well.

For a second, they all stood around the portal. The swirling sinkhole in the ground. It was magical; he knew that.

The first man stepped into it. Another followed, and soon Gerald had followed too, War coming along.

They dropped down into what seemed to be a cave, lit throughout by dim magical torches. They all stood there, a mere two dozen soldiers and the man who had ended their allies. With the portal gone, swallowed by the ground, there was nothing that kept the soldiers from attempting to avenge their fallen brothers or War from continuing his rampage. They turned on him and he on them.

Gerald knew better than his brothers did. He threw himself away from the carnage before it even began. In a mere minute they were slain, some turned to red pulp, others sliced in half. All unmistakably dead.

In a corner of the cave—the cave that felt so distant and unreal that he couldn't possibly believe it existed anywhere in the world—Gerald curled up with his back against the cold, wet wall. War wasn't in a hurry. He approached slowly, his massive broadsword scraping against the ground, the unneeded shield resting lazily in his other hand. That star-gaze of an eye fell on Gerald again. Something seemed to flip in the boy's mind. He calmed down. He accepted it. This wouldn't be too bad. An honorable death. Death in war. His father would surely gain a pretty penny. If he was to go out, this would be—

"%&¤ /(> %=(*"?"

A voice. The language spoken was foreign, of a kind that he had never heard before. It sounded vaguely Germanic, but he didn't understand it one bit. It was faint, too. Just down the hall. Not there. Not yet. Soon.

War's head turned, moving away from Gerald. Something in his movement seemed less stiff than before, more *alive*. Confused. That was it. The way he turned away fully and left Gerald where he was. Acting as though Gerald wasn't a threat, which he wasn't. He knew that. So, why did Gerald stand up? Why, when War moved toward the hallway and the voices, why did he choose to follow?

And when those strangely dressed people appeared, why did he take a step back?

They were all speaking that weird language, but even more so, they were all weirdly dressed. Their hairdos were alien as well, unlike anything he had ever seen. The women were far too pretty, much like spirits, and the men had disturbing looks in their eyes. Could what they wore even be called armor? It seemed more like thick pieces of cloth, nothing metallic to be seen. Most of them held conventional weapons, but two in the back carried what seemed like deformed lightning rods.

"#¤¤ &/)#!" one shouted, raising their weapon. Another laid their eyes on the two dozen dead. They seemed horrified, beyond the usual. Most people back in the Yungland Empire had seen at least a few dead in their life. Then again, Gerald knew exactly how they felt. This was carnage beyond the regular.

The moment the odd people charged at War, they found themselves in the same position as Gerald's now-dead brothers of the battlefield. In mere moments, they were either dead or dying, and Gerald couldn't muster any more disgust or apprehension. No more. He'd seen enough.

The only thing surprising now was to see War bend down before one of the dying. He held her dainty hand in his armored hand, staining it with the blood of thousands. She spoke words that Gerald couldn't understand, and then she died. War stood up again and looked about, his eyes never falling on Gerald. He decapitated the few people left alive, and then, just as his shoulders started to fall, they both heard that sound again. The humming drone that had lured them the first time. War didn't hesitate to move toward it, and Gerald, who no longer had anything left to lose, followed him at a moderate distance.

It wasn't the same portal. It was vertical instead of horizontal and was much paler. Not as inviting, but far more so than death. They entered.

It was true. He'd known it. They spoke English, his mother tongue. Not German, not Chinese, not French, not anything like that. English. A dead language.

But it wasn't dead on Earth.

What lay before Kreig was not the desolate land of mud and bones that he had been constantly warring on for thirty years ever since he escaped his captors. That ever-fighting place where he had been the winner only because he wasn't dead. It wasn't that forever-red sky, it wasn't the corpse-littered ground, and it wasn't the otherworld anymore.

What lay before him was a sprawling cityscape. Tall buildings, taller than the tallest wizard's tower, rose toward the sky like grasping fingers. The sky was blue and clear, and the faintest lines of things Kreig remembered to be airplanes crisscrossed the sky. It was nostalgic. After all these years.

He was home.

PART I

RETURNING
TO
EARTH

CHAPTER 1

A COLD WELCOME

Cold, fresh air met his lips and he breathed easy.

What could he do but remove his helmet? He'd been wearing it for so long . . . It was no longer the pristine white that it had been before everything went wrong. No, it was a tainted red, much like the rest of his armor. Soon, he'd remove that as well. He was home, after all. What need did he have for armor back here?

The gentle breeze caressed his bare face. It was the same as it had been since he was thirty-seven; a result of gaining the highest level in the Faith skill. Immortality. Eternal youth. If you could call thirty-seven "young."

That didn't matter, though. Nothing did anymore.

How had he gotten home? Why had he been returned only now? That wasn't important. After all, he was home!

That soldier trailing by his side like a meek house mouse didn't matter either. Nor did the man right in front of him, what with the glasses and slicked-back hair and suit and terrified expression. The people behind him were unimportant too. And the officers on standby in the back even more so.

They were all in the middle of a street—what seemed like a large crossroad. Behind him, the portal closed with a dull mumble. Until, in only a minute, all that remained in the crossroad was him, the speckled suit, the party—very similar in age and dress to those that were inside the cave—and the five police vehicles. Cars. Those were cars. He hadn't seen one of those since he had been summoned to the otherworld. Ah, there was also the little soldier behind him, but to Kreig, he was more unimportant than the worms in the ground.

"Who, what—" the speckled suit stammered. He had a weak voice. A whimper. For some reason, he seemed completely broken, tears on the verge of falling from his dark eyes.

"Step back, Thomas! We'll deal with this!" a yellow-haired kid in the armored group shouted, bearing his spear in a way that could only be described as amateur. Kreig habitually glanced above the boy's head.

Human, Lv. 38

Pathetic. A boy like that shouldn't be holding a weapon. Even then, Kreig wouldn't hesitate to end his life. Earth or not, he was always prepared to defeat his enemies.

"N—no, wait, David, don't attack him!" the speckled suit called out. If it hadn't been in English, if it hadn't been in Kreig's mother tongue, he would not have hesitated. "Just . . . hold on. We need to— He hasn't attacked, see?"

The boy shook his head, burrowing his frenzied eyes into Kreig's. "You—you can see his level too, can't you?!" Or, rather, the way he couldn't see it. Kreig knew this fact well. It was impossible for a boy of level thirty-eight to see the level of a man at 999+. Kreig knew how it worked. What he didn't know was how in the world a man on Earth could have a level of thirty-eight without being a murderer of dozens and how this man could see levels. It suggested things that Kreig didn't even want to imagine.

"I . . . I understand that, and that's exactly why we won't attack. Please— please remove your weapons."

"But, sir!"

"*Remove them!*" the speckled suit shouted, never taking his eyes off of Kreig. Kreig, in turn, didn't take his eyes off the speckled suit. There was a faint solidarity between them. Somehow, they understood each other's intentions. The speckled suit didn't want a battle, and Kreig . . . Kreig honestly wouldn't mind fighting another battle. He'd fought so many wars that fighting in another one was just a chore. Though he'd rather it didn't happen on Earth. "Sir . . . Do you . . . Do you understand me?"

Kreig looked down at him. Such a short man. All men had become short after Kreig became strong. "Yes." After all, he did.

English was a dead language, but through his prayers, he had kept it alive in his heart. "Is—is that so . . ." The speckled suit smiled a thin, uncertain smile. Then he mumbled something that Kreig wouldn't have been able to catch if his senses weren't inhuman. "Holy shit, it can speak English . . ." With that said, he tried to give a more robust smile, but it was obviously strained. "Will—sir, if you will, could you please come with us to the station?"

The station. The police station?

". . . Yes," Kreig said. He agreed. It was all he could do, really. He hadn't planned on ever returning. After all these years, he had long since forgotten the fantasy of returning to Earth—of what he'd do if it happened.

And now that he *had* returned . . . all he could do was go along with what was happening.

The speckled suit seemed surprised. "You—you will? That's, uh, great! Just follow me to the car, and—" And at this moment, the speckled suit noticed the soldier timidly hiding behind Kreig. "Hello? Will you also follow? Please?"

The soldier seemed surprised at being called out to. "*Is— Are you talking to me? I can't understand, please . . .*" The soldier spoke in German. He must have been from the Empire, then. The mere thought made Kreig's blood boil in that familiar manner, but he suppressed it. There on Earth, he might as well forget his prior grudges.

"Is that— Did he just speak in German?" The speckled suit turned around to face the police and the party behind him. "Um—sirs! Anybody— Does anyone here speak German? Please—"

Kreig couldn't bother. He turned toward the soldier, who shrank visibly under his gaze, like a rabbit trying to meld with the floor. "*Come along.*" And that was all Kreig had to say.

The soldier, meek as he was, followed him.

The speckled suit looked at him, looked at the soldier, and understood the facts of the matter. "Is he your subordinate or something?" Kreig shook his head gently. "Um, okay, just . . . come here, and—" The speckled suit led Kreig and his follower toward one of the many police cars lined up specifically to halt traffic. The party that had been standing outside the portal followed at a distance while the police took several steps back at their approach. The speckled suit opened one of the police cars. "H—here. Get in, please."

And that Kreig did, though with no little amount of apprehension. This thing, this car . . . it mildly frightened him. The last time he'd been in so much as a carriage was—well, it was the last time he'd been captured.

Though it didn't matter now. He sat in the left backseat and the soldier was seated on the other side.

A deeply reluctant pair of police officers was seated in the front of the car. They seemed more than uncomfortable, but once the car got started, the uncomfortable one was Kreig. And surely the soldier as well. After all, the loud beetle went at extremely quick speeds, was very loud, and only seemed a tad bit more modern than the cars Kreig could remember from his youth.

He'd been gone for 130 years. Surely, the cars should have gotten a bit more modern by now. Then again, the skyline was the same, the language wasn't exceptionally altered (he'd seen how the German that the Imperials spoke slowly grew both more simplified and further complex over all these years), and apart from the people who could see levels, not much was different. At all.

Might it be . . . that he hadn't been gone long at all?

Had all these years been a mere blip in time back on Earth? For some reason, the thought made him unhappy. It should have done the opposite. No time had passed. The world hadn't changed. He was different, as altered as one could be, but the world . . . the world had barely even turned.

It disgusted him.

A snarl found its way onto Kreig's face, and he only barely noticed how the soldier tried to press himself farther into the car door on his side. If there were anybody in this car who was more uncomfortable than Kreig, even more uncomfortable than the police officers, it was the soldier. Kreig wasn't sure if he should have killed him earlier. But it didn't matter.

Outside the window, the world whizzed by. People walked the streets like normal, wearing the same clothes as normal and acting in the same way as normal. Everything was normal except for him.

His muscles were the same as before. His body was still that of a thirty-seven-year-old man. Not a seventeen-year-old kid, like when he'd been summoned.

Something there was very strange, but Kreig figured he wouldn't be getting answers until they reached the station.

Until they got there, neither the police officers nor Kreig nor the soldier had so much as attempted to say anything. It made sense, in a way. People usually didn't want to talk to Kreig after he tried to kill them, and that was especially so after he killed their friends and comrades. It seemed to make them dislike him, which was a rather natural thing to do. Nowadays, Kreig couldn't imagine there was anybody who actually liked him.

They reached the station. There were a few people who seemed to have been waiting for them. Namely, a few people wielding weapons and a couple of police officers in more subdued uniforms. Each seemed just a tad more nervous than they had to be.

They opened the car door for him, and as soon as he exited the vehicle, a pair of cuffs was placed on him.

Purely by instinct, he flicked his wrists to either side, causing the cuffs to snap and break. The armored man who had tried to put them on him froze in place, staring at Kreig's wrists. "Um. Uh. Sir, we, er, we need you to w—wear cuffs. For safety reasons." All right. He couldn't disagree with that. If it meant being accepted . . . Kreig stuck his arms out again, showing that he accepted being cuffed. Despite how disgustingly nostalgic it felt.

The armored man gave a pleading look to a police officer, who ran up and replaced the broken cuffs with a fresh pair. The timid soldier was also given a pair, and the two were led inside the station, a gaggle of armored people following them at every turn.

At the end of a hallway, Kreig and the soldier parted, with a single armored man following the soldier while the rest continued following Kreig. Kreig didn't mind this arrangement, and he figured the soldier didn't mind it either.

While Kreig was led to the highest-security holding cell, the soldier was instead brought to an interrogation room.

Good thing many interrogators were bilingual.

CHAPTER 2

WHERE ARE YOU FROM?

All right, is this the guy?" Adam asked as he stepped into the glass-walled interrogation room. The officer on the other side of the glass who had just finished securing the otherworlder to the table nodded stiffly. As Adam took a seat before the otherworlder, the officer exited the room, leaving him alone with the guy. "You speak German, don't you?"

The soldier seemed startled. "You understand my tongue? This world . . . is unlike my own. Am I to assume that the gods have moved me?"

"—I'll take that as a yes, buddy. Now, I just want you to understand that we're not your enemy, all right? Whatever happened to your friends in the portal is unimportant. The party we sent in *had* to act that way; otherwise, they would have been killed instead. After all, the only way to escape a portal is to defeat the things that come from the opposing world. Though those things aren't usually human," Adam explained confidently. He didn't actually *have* to explain how the portals worked to this guy, but to build up some trust, he had to speak a little truth.

The guy simply stared at him. "I do not fear your people."

That was . . . an odd thing to say. Surely, since only two of theirs came out of the portal, they must have lost a fair few. ". . . Is that so. What's your name?"

"Gerald Speerhalter," he answered. ". . . Truly, is this another world?"

Adam didn't answer. "How many others did you enter with? You have to have at least five creatures to enter. That's how it works. What happened to your friends?"

Gerald was not a tanned man. He was pale. Pasty and thin, and he had a child's face, and in that moment, it suddenly seemed so much older. So much paler. "They . . . they were defeated. By War. Three thousand soldiers . . . Two dozen went into the whirlhole. Only I came out. You even brought him here. You brought War into this very building."

Adam leaned closer to the bulletproof glass window that separated him from Gerald. "Who do you mean?"

"War," he said in a whisper. "War of the North. One of the Four." The boy, so much younger than he should have been, shivered. A white sheen covered his brow and Adam realized that he was dirty. His armor was covered in mud and something else, even darker. A child soldier. The thought made his insides twist up into a knot, but he had to continue. He nodded. "The man you brought to this building, together with me. He is not a human. He has killed thousands—too many armies to count. A nation . . . crumbled. He cannot be kept here. Like Famine of the East, like Pestilence of the West, like Death of the South . . . He will destroy."

And in all the mumbled, confusing words that Gerald spoke, a single line stood out to Adam. Something he recognized. Something he could understand.

Famine of the East.

It had attacked like a raging maelstrom. Before they understood how the portals worked, before any truly strong Fighters had appeared, *Famine* emerged. It came from one of the portals. It squeezed its body out of it like a molting maggot escaping a cocoon. It brought death and starvation upon an entire city, and after nothing else worked, the only way to defeat it had been to destroy it. Completely and utterly. It had only barely died from two nuclear warheads. That was Famine of the East.

War of the North. If Gerald spoke the truth, if the man that had exited the portal that spawned in the Fielder's Cross was truly War of the North . . .

It could very well spell the end of the city as a whole.

Adam rose from his seat and left Gerald where he was. He had to tell someone, *anyone* about this.

An officer looked up from the paper in his hands. "What's your name?"

"Kreig . . . Wiedermann."

"Age?"

He had no reason to lie. "147."

". . . That so?"

". . ."

Kreig had no idea what the need for all this security was. Not only had they brought him down exactly two staircases, but they had also placed him in a cell with the thickest glass he'd ever seen. It was likely supposed to be a defense of some sort, but Kreig knew he could crack it with the slightest touch. The specially reinforced cuffs they'd placed on his hands just cemented that fact.

And then they sat an interrogating officer of some sort in front of him. They hadn't gotten very far, but he could already tell that the officer didn't like him much. "—Now, apart from the fact that you don't look a day over forty, people don't live that long. Not even otherworlders like you."

". . . Otherworlder?" Kreig asked, his voice as dull and monotone as it could be. His face was no more expressive, a fact that seemed to really get to the interrogating officer.

"—Yes, see, ya came from a portal that connects this world, called *Earth*, with your world. And since you came from the other world, that makes you an otherworlder," the interrogating officer helpfully explained. Then he leaned back in his chair, blowing out a nasal sigh. "See, we know either you or that soldier kid killed our Fighters. But that ain't a crime. Whatever happens in those portals *stays* in those portals, but bein' an otherworlder . . . Now, *that* we can keep you here for."

A simplistic threat. "I'm not an otherworlder."

A scoff dangled on the officer's lips. "Hah! Really, now? All right, let's hear it. Give me your wittiest quip."

"I am of this Earth."

". . . You're shitting me. Really? That's your excuse? All right . . . What's your social security number, Mr. Earthling?" the interrogating officer asked with a smirk that Kreig wanted to remove from his face.

"I cannot remember," Kreig answered honestly. Though, even without that, he was sure he could prove his identity somehow. There was, after all, one question he still had. ". . . What year is it?"

For a moment, the interrogating officer clearly considered not answering. "It's 2020. What's it to you?"

2020. Ten years. He'd been gone for ten years.

. . . Someone must have noticed. Someone must have understood that he had gone missing, and, as one would do on Earth, they must have filed a missing-person report. One that must exist within the police registry. Kreig hoped they had it, that this would work. "Kreig Wiedermann. 2010. Missing people."

The interrogating officer looked him up and down. Clearly wonder-ing if he should humor the otherworlder or not. In the end, he turned to one of his nearby officers, barked an order at him, and crossed his arms. "I won't believe it. There's no way in hell you went to the other world ten years ago and only returned now. It'd be ludicrous! And from what I've heard, you're supposed to be some sort of high-profile otherworlder, too! Prime to be moved to the Other Island. Even if you're really an Earthling to begin with, it's not as though we can just let you go! You get that, right?"

Kreig couldn't answer. He clenched his jaw and considered his options. He didn't want to mess this up. If he made an enemy of the government and killed people there, he wouldn't be able to just escape.

He was home, wasn't he? So, why was it so different?

The subordinate officer returned, speaking into his superior's ear. The interrogating officer's face changed at a moment's notice. "Is that so . . . Really, now? I see . . . Dismissed." He turned back to Kreig. "Ten years ago, a teenager by the name of Kreig Wiedermann was reported missing by his family. Now . . . how come you, an otherworlder, knew of this?"

Kreig really shouldn't have had to explain that part. "I am him."

"So you say. I suppose you have no real evidence of why that migh—"

"*SIR!*" The door burst open, revealing the form of a man Kreig didn't recognize in the least. He seemed lower in rank than the man in front of him, who had turned to look at the intruder with an annoyed stare. "Sorry for the intrusion, sir! I need to speak with the otherworlder as well as you!"

"Right. So? Go ahead, Adam. I'm not stopping you."

"Uh? Huh? Oh, um. Okay!" Adam stomped through the hall and over to Kreig's cell. Their eyes met, and for some odd reason, this man, Adam, stared at him with a crumb of the same fear as almost everyone else did, apart from this man in front of him. He seemed to hold the same fear as most everyone back in the otherworld did. "You . . . Are you . . . *War of the North?*"

Kreig drew a blank.

Kreig could remember gaining many titles during his years in that hellscape. Holy Guardian, Prisoner, Captain of the Royal Guard, Royal Missionary, Fugitive, Prisoner again . . . It wouldn't surprise him if he'd been bestowed with yet another ill-fitting nickname. Though calling him-self War . . . No, he wouldn't like that. Not at all.

Adam seemed as confused as Kreig felt. "You—you're not? Wait, no, that isn't . . ." The man backed into a wall, eyebrows furrowed. ". . . Wait, hold on, um, sir . . . Is it possible that you can check your status?"

Kreig wasn't sure where Adam got that idea from. If anybody back in the otherworld asked that of him, he would've been somewhat scandalized. That is, if he'd been about fifty years younger. After all, the only ones who could see their status, the only ones who could make use of skills, were advocates of the Holy Order of White Roots. Sure, only few of the people of that long-dead religion could see the statues, but in modern times, they were considered the most unholy of heretics.

Nevertheless . . . There, things might be different. Furthermore, the Holy Order *did* teach their followers that honesty was a virtue. "Yes." He had no reason to disagree.

Divine Human, Lv. 999+

Guardian of Sacred Walls

War of the North, Survivor, Fugitive

Purge of the Holy (X), Devotion (X), Shine of Divine Light (X), Warrior's Breath (X), Undeath (X), Dragon's Perception (X), Holy Swordsmanship (X), Wings of a Dove (X)

. . . There it was. *War of the North*.

"What do you see?" Adam asked, leaning in closer to Kreig's glass cage. A bold move for someone so visibly frightened.

Kreig glanced at Adam. The truth was that Kreig hadn't checked his status in thirty years. After all, when you're constantly fighting people and monsters and armies, stopping to check your status wasn't very optimal. Then again, he wasn't surprised by what he saw. Though, as odd as it was, he could never remember seeing anybody else with a level of 999+. The closest he'd seen was an arrogant dragon who had challenged him with a level of 800. The strongest human he'd seen had a mere 400. "Nothing new."

Adam stared at Kreig. "You know . . . on the way here, I met an officer who told me something very interesting. Are you really from Earth?" Kreig didn't answer, but his silence was enough of an answer. "Really, now? I don't suppose you've got a family? Brother, sister . . . mother and father?"

Kreig's eyes widened. Family. A brother and a sister. He . . . he *did* have those, didn't he? Yes. He did. A mother who made food and a father who worked, and . . . and a brother and a sister. He couldn't recall their voices. Their faces felt as blurry and distant as how he looked when he was summoned, and, if he was completely honest, he couldn't even recall their names. But he knew he had them. People he cared for.

He hadn't met them in 130 years, but in all the worlds he had been to, they were the only ones alive that he could possibly care for. ". . . I do."

Adam grinned. "Would you like to meet them?"

Of course. There was only a single answer to that question. And yet, Kreig hesitated to speak it. Something in Adam's smile made him feel unsure. As if to agree would be to submit himself to their will. Though, in all his years, had he ever not submitted to the will of another? ". . . Yes."

Adam silently pumped his fist before leaning in to whisper something into the ear of his superior. The man turned to him, and they exchanged a series of whispers that Kreig was privy to on account of his extremely well-honed senses.

"Adam, we can't let him meet his family."

"I understand, but this is our golden ticket! Whatever his level is, he's clearly still human! Despite what the other recovered otherworlder said. With this . . ."

"As far as we know, he might be trying to fool us. We can't know for sure whether he cares for his family or not or if he's willing to follow directives to meet them. It's too risky. The best bet so far is to either try to nudge him back into the other world or to do him like they did Famine."

". . . Before we make any such decision, can we at least make him give us his card?"

The first interrogator turned back to Kreig, his face hard and stoic. Then he removed one of many white cards out of a pocket on his shirt. It was blank and the approximate size of a business card. Although there was no slit for him to put it in to give it to Kreig, he was able to place it in a small box which could then be turned over to Kreig's side. Kreig took it from inside the box and held it up to his face. White and clear. ". . . Sir, will you please remove your gloves?"

Right, Kreig was still wearing his full set of armor, bar the helmet. Carefully, with the honed skill of a seasoned knight, he removed the gauntlets and placed them on the floor before grabbing the business card again.

The white card suddenly gave a light shine before abruptly blackening, the few spots not turning black and remaining white displaying what seemed to be Kreig's status.

"And now place it back in the box." Kreig hesitated. He hadn't been thinking much until now. If he let these people know how strong he was, what would happen then? How would they handle him if they knew what he could do? Would they still let him meet his family? Could he yet return to his life? The card weighed heavy in his hands. He should just destroy it. He had a lot of skills. Purge of the Holy could encapsulate anything in a white fire that destroyed it fully, leaving only snow behind. They wouldn't see him destroy it. "If you want to meet your family, I suggest you do as asked."

Kreig glanced up. Met the eyes of his captor and savior. He placed the little card in the box. Unlike the societies in that damn hellscape of a world, he could remember those in his homeworld being far less corrupt. Less morally repugnant.

Forgiving and honorable. Or so he hoped.

The officer looked over the card, showed it to Adam, and then looked at it again.

He fished another blank card out of his shirt pocket. "Here, do it again."

Now that Kreig knew how to do it, the process took much less time and effort than before, and his hesitation was far less than the first time around. Within a minute, the officer had the little card in his hand, looking at it like a loving and happy husband might look at divorce papers and a restraining order. "Yeah. Okay. All right. Henceforth, we will be acting under the assumption that what you tell us is the truth, the full truth, and nothing but the truth. Unless you agree to this, our nation and, by extension, *your nation* will have no choice but to deem you an enemy of the people. How do you speak?"

That was . . . a bit of a mouthful. An enemy of the people, huh? It was not the first time he'd be a fugitive, but . . . Honestly speaking, that period of his too-long life had been one of the worst. He couldn't imagine doing it all over again.

He just wanted peace and quiet. To meet his family and live his life again. He wondered how his little sister was doing. She was young; he remembered that. Now she must almost be an adult. Maybe she'd even gotten married? As for his brother . . . A hard worker. An adult by now. And his parents . . . Had they gotten old? It was the duty of a child to care for their parents, and to just leave them alone for ten years . . . He almost felt ashamed. Yes, he had much to do. And none of those things included making a mess. Not declaring war, not harming anybody . . . He'd cooperate. "I agree."

The officer gave a faint smile. "Glad to hear it. Officer Adam, will you get back to interrogating that other otherworlder? Details on what happened before he got here, who he is, what country he works for . . . Anything like that."

"Yes, sir!"

The officer turned back to Kreig. "And as for you, I need you to tell me everything. What happened after you were 'summoned'?"

A simple question to begin with. For the first time in thirty years, Kreig spoke fluently. For the first time in a hundred years, he spoke English without restraint.

CHAPTER 3

BEFORE

He was summoned a few days after his seventeenth birthday, alongside four of his classmates. At the mention of his former comrades, the interrogating officer perked up, seemingly in both mild apprehension and hope. Kreig quickly informed him that these people had died long since. The officer grumbled something about it being a great tragedy before asking for their names so that he could send out a report to the victim's families. Kreig obliged, though he noted rather unhappily that the officer didn't seem to consider Kreig's loss of innocence to be a tragedy of any kind.

Then the officer asked how they died. That took him back. Back to before he became a warrior, before he took a life, and before he became a man.

"Huh? What's this?" Kreig was the third person summoned, but the others appeared soon after. They all rose from within one of five marble caskets, finding themselves inside a pristine white church filled to the brim with holy figures and peasants crying and weeping for the occasion. "Where am I?" A man approached them, dressed in the most extravagant white robes Kreig had ever seen. The church smelled like black mold and burnt pine needles.

A few men dressed in robes began to gather around him, two of them grabbing his arms tightly to hold him in place. A black ball was forced into his mouth and a pair of strong hands clasped his lips shut. He tried to fight or resist, but in the end, all he could do was swallow. It tasted like some kind of mushroom he'd never had before.

The people in the church all spoke a refined, complex English that Kreig barely understood, but with his classmates there, he felt less afraid than he should have been. A priest welcomed them with open arms and a wide grin, telling them to forgive their lack of introduction. They had been summoned by the Holy Order of White Roots as their Bodies. Heroes to fight for their cause. To fight for a god Kreig didn't know and didn't understand. What they had been forcefully fed was a Messiah's Egg. All of them had been given one, and in a few weeks, they would awaken the aptitude to become Oracles of God.

And there was nothing they could do about it.

They were isolated in a small, closed space, stripped of all their belongings, and fed with only wheat and water. Somehow, it was enough. They didn't die. For six days and six nights, they grew closer and they began to slowly accept their new life. Kreig missed his family. Two of the others had reasons not to. Then, on the seventh day, a black mushroom sprouted from Kreig's left hand. Something—everything—told him to eat it. He did.

Awaken

In time, his classmates awoke as well. They saw the system and the system saw them. Once they had all awakened, the Order released them.

These kids, barely children, became soldiers. Fighters in a quest for Divine Truth.

He was a Paladin. Peter was a Priest. Jamie was a Cardinal. Rudy was a Monk. Charlie was a Churchrat. They worked together, trained together, learned together. Together, they came to accept their new lives. Together, they came to accept their new god. Oh, yes, they prayed. There was a skill for that. "Prayer." Really, there was a skill for everything. It was like a game. Kreig learned the sword, and his Swordsmanship skill went up. Peter learned to heal and buff his friends, and his Heal skill went up. It continued.

There were so many heretics in the Alumni Kingdom. So many people called the Holy Order a cult. So many denied them. That wasn't important yet.

They were first sent out to defeat monsters and beasts and things that shouldn't live. A small army would come with them. It was hard to take a life at first, but after fighting enough monsters, he got the hang of it. It was easy. Slash them with the sword, hide behind his shield. Defend his friends. Protect his god.

It was easy.

Until he had to kill humans.

The Order was greedy. No—no, not greedy; it was only desperate to show others the truth. The king wouldn't let them. He protected the heretics, exclaimed that the Holy Order was no longer to be accepted. But that didn't work. The Holy Order had many devoted advocates. And they had the Five

Bodies, too. They were adults now. It had been twenty years at that point. Twenty years of defeating monsters, twenty years of evening prayer, and twenty years of doing everything the Holy Order told him to.

He was thirty-seven. And when he took a life—a human *life—his Faith skill hit the max. It became "Devotion," giving him a sort of eternal youth. He no longer aged. At the moment, he didn't understand that it was a curse.*

The Holy War for the throne of Alumni took five years. Five years of slaughter, five years of putting his faith to the test.

In the end, the Holy Order usurped the throne. Their belief reigned true. Heretics and nonbelievers were executed, and with such a sudden increase in power, the White Pope declared that the Holy Order of White Roots would expand into the nearby nations.

They met a swift and unfair beatdown. Five kingdoms allied, all on the border of the Theocracy of White. In a mere five years, the Theocracy was reduced to ashes. Three of the Five Bodies were killed in the five-year war. Peter was executed. Of all the Five Bodies, only one survived. Kreig was captured and kept in secrecy by the Yungland Empire, one of the major forces in defeating the Theocracy. He was kept neither well nor fairly. The beginning of his capture was fraught with torture and isolation to force him to recant all his former beliefs.

His language, English, had been killed alongside the Holy Order of White Roots. Only he remained. Only he kept English alive; only he praised his god. He prayed. For seven years, he remained in captivity. For seven long years, he prayed and pretended that his faith had left him, when it remained as true as his language. They forced him to learn German. They forced him to kiss the foot of the Empire's lords. They forced him to praise the Emperor.

And after that was all done, he was accepted as a new man. After all, he was broken. There was little in him that remained of the boisterous, loud-mouthed warrior of before.

He became their loyal soldier. He became their loyal officer. He became their loyal captain of the Royal Guard.

Only in his heart did he bear resentment for their treatment of him. For the deaths of his comrades. For their sin of letting him live.

. . . But he didn't live badly. He made a living. He was able to live in his own house. He was able to gain comrades. And, after acting as a captain for long enough, the Empire allowed him the special privilege of forming a monster-combating party, which he gladly did. It reminded him of his old party, his old friends, but he was ready to put it behind him. He'd been

in that world for fifty years. He could forgive, and if he was allowed to, he would happily forget.

He formed a true loyalty. With his party, he grew stronger. He grew to like them, to consider them friends, and they seemed to feel the same about him. They fought in wars for the sake of the Empire. Killed for the sake of the Empire. The only time he spoke English was for his nightly prayer but even then, it was only to keep his faith alive. Not for the sake of the Holy Order.

Things were good. He was comfortable.

That was until the nearby nations became aware of his existence.

It happened out of nowhere, and he wasn't aware of it until his own soldiers tried to attack him—tried to capture him—tried to execute him. The Empire had turned on him the very second public outcry from their allies forced them to. So, he ran. His party fought alongside him and ran with him. They were ready to die to keep him alive.

And they did. One by one, during a period of nine years, they were all killed. In the end, after seventy-nine years in a world he no longer considered home, he gave up. There was nothing for him to live for. Even his own God had abandoned him. He resigned himself to the gallows.

But he was not killed.

Much like so many years before, he was kept in captivity. Though, due to his strength—due to what the Empire considered to be a possible great threat—he was locked beneath everything. There, in a room that had once kept a demonic dragon, he remained, isolated from the world above. There was neither light nor torture. No humans, either. Pure and simple isolation. Alone. In that darkness, the only thing that kept him even slightly sane was his prayer. He trained. He prayed. He chanted. He kept himself moving.

But it was twenty years. Enough to make any man break.

He had forgotten what the sky looked like. He had never been a creative or intelligent man. His mind could not conjure things to keep him busy, things to keep him sane.

In the end, what saved him was the skill "Prayer" reaching the maximum level and evolving into "Shine of Divine Light." He escaped.

But he was nothing.

"—From then on, I have only fought." Somehow, Kreig was surprised he could even remember the names of his former classmates. They had been so young when they were taken. So old when they died. Still, it had been too early. He glanced up at the officer where he sat, slack-jawed with a creased brow.

"Is—is that so . . ."

Silence stretched between them.

"Well, I, er . . ." He scratched the back of his head. "Guess I can just give a little info on what's been happening here in the meanwhile. These past ten years have been . . . pretty turbulent. These damn portals started opening up, and if nobody went in them for around three days or so, monsters and things would come out of it. We've learned how to deal with it, sort of. Mostly because of these people who started popping up. They can see statuses and grow stronger by defeating the monsters in the portals. Fighters, the lot of them. They'd have these randomly assigned jobs that only let them use certain weapons. Weirdly enough, most of them are kids . . . Really weird.

"It's mostly good, but sometimes . . . sometimes, really strong monsters come out of the portals. In most cases, we can see how strong the monsters in the portal are and send in stronger Fighters, but sometimes the Fighters still get defeated. In those cases, we have a backup team just outside, but in cases such as yours . . ." He glanced away. "We've got no choice but to deal with it in some other way."

So, that was how it was. Those people he saw in the cave must have been those Fighters that the officer had talked about. Kreig almost felt a little guilty to have killed them.

Though, by the sound of it, if he hadn't done it, he wouldn't have been able to leave the portal at all.

"May I speak with my family?" Kreig asked. The officer didn't meet his gaze.

". . . At the moment, we cannot allow that. Though, in some time, you will be allowed to. Undoubtedly. Until then, you will be kept elsewhere, as this cell is unfit to contain an otherworlder of your caliber. Not that we have anyplace truly suited to hold you . . ." The officer shrugged self-deprecatingly. *Elsewhere* could really be anywhere. But the thing that Kreig found himself caught up on was a single little detail.

"I'm not an otherworlder."

"Sure, yeah, of course! But at this moment, you've gotta be treated like one, okay? Don't hold it against us; it's only protocol. Listen, I promise you, on my auntie's grave: you *will* meet your family. As long as you don't rebel against us or hurt anybody. You've been through a lot; you told me so yourself. I can't imagine how hard that must have been on you, and sitting here in a cell yet again must remind you of a lot of terrible things. But if you just stick through it . . . one day, you may very well go free," the officer said. The smile on his face almost seemed warm. Friendly.

Kreig hadn't seen a friendly smile in so long. At this moment, he could only glance away and accept it all. "... Of course."

The officer clapped once and stood up. "All right! The transporters will be here within the hour, so what I need you to do is strip off that armor you've got."

Kreig whipped his head around to face the interrogating officer. His armor? This heavy thing that he'd fought through countless wars in? The last remaining artifact of the Holy Order of White Roots? This armor that had saved him from the breath of a dragon, from the pikes of man, from the biting teeth of nature? He was to take it off, put it to the side? Remove his weapons and his shield, too?

"... Please?" the officer asked, testing the waters by giving another nonthreatening smile. How was Kreig to know that he was testing the waters? That he'd realized Kreig's fatal flaw of being unable to say no to a friendly face?

"... All right." His gauntlets were already off, so he just continued up his arms. Carefully, he removed the vambraces, the rerebraces, the couter, the pauldron ... He placed these parts so gingerly upon the ground. The parts may have been red, but many years before, they had been the most pristine and pious white. He had sullied them with his battles, as his battles had sullied him. The breastplate, the placard ... it was heavy. He wasn't sure if a normal man could lift even his gauntlet.

He placed it all on the ground, and when he was done, he stood there. Clothed only in the bare rags that he had escaped from the Empire in. They were tattered, many parts rubbed off and destroyed by his mere movement.

He was almost naked, really.

And the interrogating officer was immediately flustered. "... You've really been fighting in that for—what? Thirty years?" Kreig nodded. "Jesus. Okay, Officer Jenkins, go get him a pair of overalls. Extra large." Kreig had no idea what the officer had run out to fetch, but for some reason, he felt rather excited about it. After all, he hadn't worn new clothes in, what, fifty years? A typical lifetime. And now he'd get to wear new clothes. He just hoped they had his size. He'd always been extraordinarily tall, not to speak of his muscle mass.

While Officer Jenkins hurried out of the room, the interrogating officer turned back to Kreig. He looked him up and down and gave a true, heartfelt sigh. "Geezus."

For some reason, Kreig felt the same.

About five minutes later, far less time than Kreig had expected, Officer Jenkins returned with a large orange thing in tow. He held it folded in his grip, and he seemed a little out of breath. Had he been running? Needless of him. Either way, the interrogating officer swiped it out of Officer Jenkins' grip and stuffed it into the little box that went into Kreig's holding cell. Kreig unfolded it. It was a large jumpsuit, only a few sizes smaller than Kreig. It even had a zipper, something he hadn't seen since his summoning.

With no possible hesitation or wait, Kreig peeled off his rags, finding that many of them had plastered to his body, using dried blood and mud as a gluing agent. God, he was dirty. But now he had a clean jumpsuit to wea—

"No, hold on, Kreig!"

Kreig turned to the interrogating officer. "I can't let you wear that without getting a damn shower. You're crusted in filth! How have you been able to live like that?" Kreig had an answer to that, but he wasn't sure if the interrogating officer would like it. So, instead, he folded the jumpsuit back up. The interrogation officer's eyes scanned Kreig's body. "Yeah, you need a shower. Officer Jenkins, unlock the cell and cuff 'im. I'll take him to the showers." Officer Jenkins seemed like he wanted to object, but a well-placed glare got him to work.

At this point, Kreig had already removed his shirt, so the only thing that kept him from complete nudity was a pair of torn wool trousers. Still, he had no shame. He'd lost that years before.

He was soon led out of the holding cell, cuffed, and guided out of the door with the interrogating officer as his lead.

Outside, they found what seemed to be a young Fighter carrying a fancy-looking spear and wearing modern armor holding guard. The appearance of Kreig set the young Fighter's teeth on edge, and he brandished his spear purely by instinct. "Stand down, Fighter," the interrogating officer said.

"B—but sir—"

"Stand. Down."

Maybe the interrogating officer could sense the murderous intent flowing off of Kreig; maybe he knew that a man such as Kreig would react to violence the same way a wounded animal would, or maybe he was starting to feel genuine compassion for the man. Either way, the Fighter reluctantly followed the order. Though, even as they were leaving, Kreig could feel the Fighter's eyes burning into his back. Eyes of fear. Eyes that knew what he was.

Somehow, the interrogating officer hadn't truly understood that. It was one thing to see a few numbers on a card or to hear a tale of woe and death. It was another to see those three question marks—to see them and know that you faced Death.

He'd felt it himself, after all.

The first time, it had been a dragon. Right in the middle of a grim battlefield. He'd been fighting for the Empire, and back then, he hadn't known that adolescent dragons enjoyed joining human wars just for fun, to see all those people running, forgetting their alliances in the face of death. Like trampling ants. It had been grinning all while it lapped up humans and crunched and mangled their bodies like a great big crushing machine.

But that was long before.

Really, almost everything he remembered was.

"Here's the showers. Be quick, but be thorough. There's shampoo and conditioner over there." The showers were of the combined kind, clearly meant for the use of several people at one time. The floor was covered in beige tiles and encased limestone. Although Kreig no longer knew how to use shampoo or conditioner, he went over and grabbed the two bottles anyway.

And then he took a shower. The warm water washed over him rhythmically. The grime and dirt that had stuck to him like muddy memories of the past slowly passed. Fifty years. The blood in his hair, the dirt in the grooves of his rigid body, the sweat that clung to him like clawed insects, it all went away. He had to carefully scrub a few parts to really get it off, and when he used the shampoo to remove smells as well, he had simply never felt cleaner. Not in 130 years. Like a newborn baby, warm and safe and good. The tension in his muscles seemed to melt off and seep down into the drain. Gone.

He stepped out of the shower, dried off on a towel that Officer Jenkins had reluctantly handed him, and dressed up in the clean jumpsuit.

He was new. Fresh.

As if everything that had happened was just gone. It wasn't gone, he knew that, but all of a sudden . . . it sure felt like it had.

The interrogating offer took a look at his watch and noted that they would arrive shortly. Kreig nodded, almost completely out of it. He didn't even bother to wonder who "they" were. For some reason, he really just wanted to lie down. This new piece of clothing felt light. Light and comfortable. Sleeping would probably feel nice. Since he had Warrior's Breath, the evolved version of the skill Stamina, he no longer needed sleep. But even then, that didn't mean he couldn't sleep at all.

And right now, he really wanted to.

He was led through the halls again, through winding corridors and doors that he had to hunch to go through. And, finally, he was outside again. He liked seeing the sky. It was blue, and he really liked that. And in the middle of that blue, blue sky, something approached.

It hummed like the melody of a massive cricket. A helicopter. That's what it was. Rather large, too. As soon as it came close enough to the ground, a man wearing a full set of actual plate-armor jumped out of it, landing with a clang and a rustle. He flicked the visor of his helmet open, revealing the face of a rather young, gravely confident man. His eyes landed on Kreig before turning to meet the interrogating officer. "This the guy, Sergeant?"

Human, Lv. 343

The interrogating officer didn't hesitate to hand Kreig over to the man Kreig could only assume to be a Fighter of somewhat high class. After all, though his level wasn't much when compared to great beasts like Wyverns or even Two-Legged Drakes, compared to almost every other human, he had a pretty robust level. The man accepted Kreig, and somehow, he didn't seem frightened in the least.

He looked like a man posing with a tiger, full of vapid confidence.

Soon, several other Fighters with levels above 100 (though nobody in the 300 range) stepped out of the helicopter, likely to escort Kreig to wherever they were going. Kreig hadn't felt this important since the last time there was an international manhunt for his head.

The 300-level Fighter handed Kreig over to another Fighter, who led him onto the loud helicopter while he went over to chat with the interrogating officer. Apparently, going by what Kreig could hear, it was mostly a brief summary of who Kreig was, what not to do, and who to hand him to once they got to the Other Island, whatever that was. After hearing the interrogating officer—or, as the 300-level Fighter called him, "Sergeant"— say for the third time that messing with Kreig would be a death sentence, Kreig couldn't bother listening to it anymore and brought his focus back to the helicopter itself.

It was very high-tech, filled with things on the walls and people with big guns and soldiers. Most importantly, a full roster of 100-level Fighters. Was he really that important? Possibly. Though, since he had no intention of being a bother, it really wasn't needed. A handful of smiling faces would've been enough.

They guided him to sit on a seat fastened to the wall, and the second he did, they chained his specially strengthened cuffs to the ground. He didn't mind much, but he really would have liked some manner of freedom. Maybe not holding his sword or shield, but with nothing at all, he felt naked. Hung out. Empty. He was confident in his hand-to-hand skills, but as a Paladin, his greatest strength would always lay in his use of a sword and shield.

The 300-level Fighter said goodbye to the sergeant, entered the helicopter, and shouted for the pilot to lift off. Then he strode up to Kreig and sat down in the empty seat right next to him.

"Hi there, big guy. Fella down there told me your name is Kreig?" he said, leaning in far closer than Kreig was comfortable with. Even then, he didn't respond. For some reason, he felt like responding to that question would only make the situation worse. Not that it wasn't already bad. The last time he'd been this high up in the air was when he'd hopped on that arrogant dragon's back while it took to flight. "It is, isn't it? See, the funny thing is, my name is actually Craig! So, there can only be *one*. Y'see where I'm going with this?"

Now Kreig turned to Craig. He had strangled people before. If he didn't put that much strength in, he could surely restrain himself from snapping the guy's neck.

"Hey, hey! It was a joke! Geez, you really don't have a sense of humor, huh? See, the sergeant went and told me not to stir up anything with you since you're some sort of dangerous guy, but you really don't look like it. Honestly, you look like the kind of guy who'd go around spouting about the power of friendship, hah!" Craig babbled. Kreig could feel himself being lulled to sleep by the drone of Craig's loud, grating voice.

"Um, Craig, maybe you shouldn't tease it?" A cloaked girl sitting just across Kreig and Craig hunched her back shyly as Kreig turned to look at her. Kreig agreed fully with her statement. He didn't like being teased.

"Huh? Nah, nah! We've got two hours of flight! If I don't get to tease someone, I'll just pick a fight instead!" Craig said, ending his little statement with a throaty laugh, the kind you'd expect from a much larger man than Craig. "Hey, Mr. Big-And-Scary, wouldn't you like to hear what happened to your equipment?" Now, that got Kreig's attention. "Thought so! See, they got a bunch of guys in there, but nobody could lift the thing. Not even a glove! So, they're gonna get a bunch of high-level Fighters to lift it, but even then, they doubt they'll be able to get it far."

All right. As long as Kreig would be able to make use of them again, he was happy. Well, maybe not *make use of*, more like *see*. After all, hopefully, he wouldn't need his armor any longer. He just wanted it for nostalgic purposes.

"Ah, but they might also try to melt it down to see what it's made of." The sheer amount of killing intent that exploded from Kreig in that moment was enough to make even Craig a bit woozy. "N—not that they'll actually do it! They're just considering it. Relax, dude!"

After a few seconds of calming himself down, Kreig was indeed able to relax.

"Gee. I'm not sure if you're fun to talk to or not. Like, you barely react. Or, I mean, you *do* react, but not by speaking. Mighty uncool of you."

Maybe if he ignored Craig, he'd stop talking.

". . . Do you think I'll stop talking if you keep ignoring me? Ohohohoh, not so! As my mother can attest to, that is not the case—not at all!"

Shoot.

Two hours of this, the duration of which Craig spent ninety percent talking. Talking and talking and talking. Kreig just wanted to bury his face in his hands, but if he were to make such a movement, he'd snap his chains and be a bother to everyone. So, all he could do was sit wide-legged and stare out of the window on the other side of the helicopter. Silently, he watched how the land turned to sea until, after two hours, he could see land again.

It was a little splotch of gray. A simple gray island, like a large fortress in the middle of the blue sea. It wasn't that big once they got close to it, hardly larger than the Royal Palace of the Empire or even the Grand Dom of the Theocracy.

Still, it was their destination.

CHAPTER 4

A NEW HOME TO REPLACE THE OLD

He knew it was so because that was where they landed. Craig led him out, and Kreig was made aware that they had landed in the middle of a large, empty prison courtyard. And only now that Kreig looked back at the helicopter did he see how the soldier from before exited it as well. He seemed just as startled to see Kreig as Kreig felt seeing him. "Move along, dude; move along," Craig said, ushering Kreig through a sliding door that Kreig had to hunch to fit through.

They walked for a long while. The hallways were all gray and dreary, nothing interesting to look at. Though, once they descended a staircase and entered an elevator, that quickly changed. The gray shifted into a pristine, plastic white that seemed less "prison" and more "high-tech." To Kreig, who hadn't seen a shiny white surface in a hundred years, it felt like he'd stepped onto an alien planet, which he almost had.

Their trek continued farther and farther down, his escorts using codes and fingerprints and eyeball scans to open gradually thickening doors.

It felt suffocating in a way that his old prisons never had. This was something else entirely. A labyrinth of winding hallways, lit by invisible lamps and red blaring lights and nothing else.

Finally, they reached the end of it.

This door, unlike the last two dozen, was dull and metallic. Kreig could tell from a look that this metal wasn't anything ordinary. It was Dragonheart, the toughest metal to be found in the otherworld. As a matter of fact, his armor and weapons—the ones he'd been forced to undress—had been made with a mixture of Dragonheart, White Stone and Hearth. It was made to make the armor lighter than pure Dragonheart while keeping the same strength. This door, on the other hand, didn't seem to be pure Dragonheart, as the metal was extremely precious, but it seemed to have been mixed with several Earth metals to retain the strength and decrease the weight.

Craig did not open this door himself. Instead, he stepped to the side, letting a woman of a far lower level step up to the task. Opening the door required an eyeball scan, a fingerprint scan, a vocal command, and a final code. And when that was done and yet another person had repeated the process, the door finally slid open.

The room inside wasn't very large, although the roof was extremely high. It contained a bed, a toilet, a sink, and a small table and chair. The bare necessities for living, but compared to what Kreig had been given in that sealed room below the Empire's dungeons, it was a luxury.

Compared to what he'd been living off of for the last thirty years, it was divine.

He felt like crying.

He didn't.

"All right, Kreig, welcome to your new home! If you need a book or paper to write on or whatever, we can get it for ya! Though, obviously, we can't let anything leave the facility. You'll receive three meals a day through that hatch over there"—Craig pointed at a solitary hatch in one of the four barren walls—"and if anybody wants to speak with you, that mirror over there can turn into a window." The wall he pointed to this time was made up entirely of a mirror fixture. He couldn't see through it, but he could smell the people on the other side. They smelled like chemicals and soap. "And, finally, if you don't do anything wrong for long enough, you'll not only be allowed to speak and hang around the other otherworlders, you can also meet your family! Ain't that neat?"

Kreig supposed so. The rules were simple. *Don't make a ruckus. Don't do anything wrong.*

Kreig stepped inside his cell. Going by the smell, all walls apart from the mirror wall had some percentage of Dragonheart mixed in. They must have been thinking that it'd be able to keep him secure, though they likely didn't construct this for him specifically. Even then, for now, this would be his home.

Constantly monitored. Never alone. Always observed.

. . . Better than always fighting.

Craig gave a little goodbye wave, and the Dragonheart door slid shut, leaving Kreig alone in his new abode. The bed had a metal frame and only creaked a little when Kreig sat down on it. The covers were soft and welcoming. He wanted to lie down immediately but decided to check out the rest of his room first. The desk was wooden and basic, though not as imperfect as the ones he was used to. He wouldn't need to use the toiletries, and the hatch would remain shut for now.

That left him with the matter of what to do. There were plenty of skills he could try to strengthen, but somehow, he felt that it would be an improper use of his time. No, he'd rather do something more concrete.

He turned to the mirror wall and stared at the most prominent scent spot. "I'd like paper and pencils."

That way, he could do *something* with his time. He wasn't sure exactly what he would do yet, but until he knew and until he received the necessary items, he might as well lie down.

The bed was soft. Softer than the blood-soaked mud. Softer than the stony floor. Softer than anything. A pillow under his head. Although his body was as straight as a board, uncomfortable with this new act, he slowly relaxed. His muscles softened and his bones shifted into their proper places. His eyes fluttered shut. The darkness felt warm and welcoming instead of the usual cool callousness. It felt good. He let the air escape his weary lungs. Slowly, quickly, softly, barely, he slipped into slumber.

Sleep was welcome. Lying down was welcome. He did not dream, but he rested.

In the Empire's dungeon, he slept for singular hours at a time.

Now he slept for a full twelve hours. Never tossing, never turning.

Resting as sweetly as a snake.

When he woke up, he did so to the sound of a metallic shuffle, and he quickly found the cause of it being the hatch on the far wall opening to allow a tray of food to slide through. Kreig stood up, wobbled to the side, wobbled to the other side, found his footing, and took a deep breath. After all, he hadn't slept in many years. It made sense that it'd make him feel a bit off.

That wouldn't keep him from taking a peek at the hatch. He hadn't eaten in a fair few years—though he had taken a bite out of the arrogant dragon, just to see if it did make the eater immortal—and the smell of actual, honest-to-God food was making his mouth water. At the hatch, he found the tray of food. He grabbed it and put it on his desk, where he sat down on the chair.

Whatever the hour was, this was clearly lunch. A bowl of warming stew. A piece of newly baked bread. Some butter and a few individual pieces of greenery. A little cookie.

A balanced meal.

Kreig wolfed it down in mere minutes. The stew was rich and flavorful, the perfect mixture of salty, sweet and savory. The bread was crispy on the outside and fluffy on the inside, and the second he thought of dipping the bread into the stew, he felt like a true genius. The greenery was good, but he couldn't stomach the cookie. It was far too sweet for his tastes, and the second his tongue lapped against the side of it, he recoiled.

He left the cookie on the tray before putting the whole thing back in the hatch. Then he noticed something that he really should have noticed before. In the hatch, to the side of where the tray had been, there was a bundle of paper and a case of pens, a few erasers and a pencil sharpener.

He hummed softly while bringing the lot of it over to the desk.

He unboxed the pencils, sharpened one, picked out a paper, and there he was. Staring at the empty sheet, he wondered what to do. In the end, he placed the sharp pencil against the paper and watched unhappily as the pencil exploded the second he applied any kind of pressure to it. That was a problem. He grabbed another pencil, sharpened it, placed it on the paper, and promptly dropped it. His grip was now too weak to so much as hold it. He increased the pressure slightly. A little more. Slight increments until he could hold it without dropping it or crushing it.

Then he dragged it across the paper. His hands trembled, the line was all crooked, but it was a line. It hadn't gone through the paper; it hadn't *not* left a mark. Progress.

Another line. And another. A triangle! Slowly, with trembling movements, he brought the tip of the pencil to the middle of the triangle. A little bow and two dots. A smiley. Kreig mimicked the smile. Next to the triangle he drew the pencil in a large arc, creating a crooked oval-like circle. He drew a smiley on it as well. Two happy friends. Then, to finish the drawing, he drew two little legs on both the shapes and two little arms, two of which connected to the other with a thicker dot.

They were holding hands. Friendship. Yes, that was good.

Kreig's little smile faltered. He didn't have anyone like that anymore.

He slid the paper to the side and grabbed another blank sheet. Back in the otherworld, papers were rare and expensive, but he knew they were cheap here. Now he drew five circles quickly, one after another, gaining confidence as he went. Two were taller than the three, with the three all being of varying sizes. Then he gave them bodies out of rectangles and stick limbs. All five were holding hands, and once he added wide smiles and hairs, the picture became obvious. A family. Mother, father. Three siblings.

He moved his pencil to just above the second-tallest child. There, he wrote, in the most uncertain and trembling handwriting: *Kreig.*

Above the two parents, he wrote *Mother* and *Father.* Above his siblings, *Brother* and *Sister.* Then he turned the page around. Sure, he hadn't written in years, but he had to do this. He had to relearn this. He set the pencil to the paper and started writing a letter.

It read,

Dear venerable mother and father. And my sister and brother too, whom I love deeper than the Reignian seas.

I have not been well. Time has been long and rough and I cannot help but confess that I have not missed you as of the last hundred years, yet at knowing your lives remain here, I realize now that you are all that I have. So too do I remember scantily the few years I had with you before I was taken to a world much unlike our own. Never did I tell you that I loved you. I regret that now.

Truthfully, there is much I regret, such as never keeping my memory of you alive. Always, I thought of you as an unmovable, unshakable memory, something that would never leave me. It did. Your faces are foreign, your voices the hum of the Earth. If we met on the battlefield, I would have reaped your life, never knowing your worth.

Coming to Earth has been a journey I never intended upon succeeding in, and where I sit, in my endlessly compact isolation, the idea of meeting you is all that keeps me from unhappiness. My chest is light. I hope you will forgive who I have become. What sins I have committed are justified in the eyes of God, but to mortals such as you or I, they remain unacceptable.

I will never hurt you, and I hope that you will not hurt me through your absence.

May the warm hands of God bring us closer soon and may we meet in joy,

Your lonesome son and brother,

Kreig.

He put down his pencil and read through the letter twice. And then he put it to the side. At least his handwriting got better as he reached the end of it. The last time he wrote a letter was in . . . God, it must have been over fifty years before, while he was still running from the Empire. He'd written a letter to one of the lords closest to him, one of the main advocates of his rehabilitation after the Unholy War. In the letter, he had begged for an explanation, if not a simple mercy. Not for him, of course.

For his party.

Whether that letter made it to the lord was still a mystery to him. He almost hoped it hadn't reached the lord; that he hadn't been betrayed by that man as well. Though, of course . . . that was all in the past now.

He folded the paper as neatly as he could, making sure all edges matched perfectly. Then he stood up, wandered over to the hatch, and placed the letter inside. "Give it to my family," he said, turning to where a person stood just beyond the glass. The scent of the person didn't move.

It was good enough for Kreig. He went back to the table and sat down. Hours upon hours of time, and nothing to do with it.

Back in the dungeons of the Empire, he'd spend most of his time praying, something he sadly couldn't do too freely once the skill evolved. Then, martial arts? It would be fun, he had grown to enjoy pure combat as of late, but he was rather sure that doing anything of that nature might alert his captors. The one thing he wanted right now, apart from peace, freedom, and meeting his family was to not alert these people. They were his only way of contacting his family.

Then, something to do with these blank papers. Maybe he should try writing a novel?

. . . No, he'd never been that imaginative. And he wouldn't like to write another letter before his family even received his first one. That'd be terribly impatient.

Something he could do on paper that wasn't writing. Something *fun*.

Ah, of course. How had he been so stupid?

Drawing. Back in the otherworld, he hadn't been able to even give it a shot. Parchment and paper were expensive, and he usually had neither the time nor the urge to so much as try it. As for now . . . He grabbed the pencil again. Without the conscious effort he'd been able to retain before, the pencil again burst into a cloud of carbon and a heap of splinters. He just wasn't very good at this. The people on the other side of the mirror had surely already seen his blunder, but he still wanted to discard the evidence.

So, he shuffled the other broken pencil into the same pile as the freshly broken one, and once he had it all in one pile, he swept it into his open palm.

He held up the pile of splinters and ashes.

Purge of the Holy (X)

He activated one of his many max-leveled skills, watching as the little pile of splinters in his hand burst into white flames that lapped and gnawed at the former pencils. It took exactly two seconds for the entire pile to disappear, the burnt pieces being charred into white snow. The snow melted in his hand. The holy flame could not harm him unless he willed it to, and even then, his defense was way too high for it to actually do him any damage.

Kreig hadn't even picked up another pencil before some unseen speaker resounded.

"Please avoid using supernatural abilities while in custody."

Turning to where the voice had come from, he saw a stereophone of some sort retreating into a hole on the wall. No skills, huh. At least, no flashy skills that the people monitoring him could recognize as such. He could do that.

But his first step to normalcy seemed to be drawing. For some reason, the blank paper didn't look inviting in the least, but he forced himself to get started.

He drew a cat. A dragon. A warrior fighting the two. A princess . . .

Skill gained: Artistry (I)

. . . That was to be expected. As Kreig continued drawing, he mentally summoned the description of the skill.

Artistry (I)
Rank I: Stable hands, smoother lines

Nothing his observers would be able to notice, even though the effect was quickly apparent.

He kept drawing. For several hours at a time, he kept drawing, only stopping to eat. This continued for several days. During this time, his Artistry skill ranked up twice.

Artistry (III)
Rank III: Greater anatomy, perspective, shading
Rank II: Greater color and design
Rank I: Stable hands, smoother lines

The effects had been grandiose, but getting the rank of a skill higher than III was far harder than getting it higher than II, usually taking far greater time, effort, and ingenuity than before. Getting it from IV to V took a minor revelation, and breaking the skill through the Rank V barrier into the evolved form, signified by an X, took something grander. Time wasn't a matter. Transforming the *Faith* skill into *Devotion* had required him to take a life in the name of his religion.

The same philosophy would reign true for Artistry.

A week after being isolated in that hole, hundreds of feet below the ground, Kreig decided to write another letter. He did not know how long he would have to remain there until they trusted him to join the company of others, but until that happened, he was prepared to continue drawing.

His drawings and paintings littered his cell. Some were like the doodles of a child, others truly skillful. He did not have talent, only devotion.

Dearest family, you who I miss so much,

On the back of this letter, you will find a self-portrait. It is unlike how you may remember me, but nowadays there isn't much I see besides my own face. One of the walls in my cell is a mirroring fixture. I look tired. I hadn't realized before that I was so pale. Though virtue is white. Being pale isn't too bad.

How do you look? Have you received my previous letter? I hope you are well. If you are unwell, I promise to make you better. Many of the powers I have gained can help in many ways. If your back is sore, I can heal it. Will you be coming to meet me soon? The authorities have promised to let me meet you if I refrain from causing a mess.

I'm terribly lonely.

I hope that we should meet soon,

Your ever-loving son and brother,

Kreig.

It was shorter than the other letter, but he was saving a lot of things he wanted to say for when they actually met.

Once again, he folded the letter, placed it in the little box, and told his observers that he would like for it to be sent to his family. There was no response.

He could do without a response.

DR. DARIUS FALK'S LOGBOOK ON INMATE KREIG WIEDERMANN'S INCARCERATION ENTRY NR. 3

Head Observer Dr. Darius Falk's Logbook on Inmate Kreig Wiedermann's incarceration Entry Nr. 3, October 5th 2020:

Inmate Wiedermann does not eat mushrooms or fungi of any form. Through the use of an impeccable sense of smell, he is able to instantly understand the contents of a stew. This is applied in several situations, such as to deduce whether or not a seemingly fresh slice of bread is, in reality, carrying the budding spores of various molds. Whenever presented with these, he will state that he does not eat mushrooms and place the contaminated piece of food to the side.

His dislike continues whether or not the food containing fungi has had its scent disguised through natural or supernatural means.

Is it scent or something else?

Further observations: during the three weeks since his first incarceration, apart from a single incident in which an unknown fire power was used to transform two destroyed pencils into snow, Inmate Wiedermann has shown no aggression nor used any destructive powers apart from his physical strength—though even that seems to be unwitting. The only things he has requested have been art supplies and for the two letters he has written to be delivered to his family. The latter request has been denied, though the decision was never made clear to Inmate Wiedermann, over fears of how he may take it.

His artistic abilities have shown a steep increase in quality and quantity as he spends almost all hours of the day drawing. He does not sleep. It is hypothesized that he does not require sleep or food to survive, though he still accepts the food he is given—which, for the record, is the same food that staff here is given (God help the budget). According to the testimony recorded from Inmate Gerald Speerhalter, Inmate ID #442, Inmate Wiedermann—referred to by Inmate Speerhalter as "War"—had neither slept nor eaten for the last thirty years. Despite this, Inmate Speerhalter admitted that his knowledge on the matter was lacking.

As of yet, no further interrogation apart from the general conducted by Sergeant Peter Oxford of the Kreepsville Police Department has occurred in reference to Inmate Wiedermann.

Authorities are as of yet continuing their discussion on the future treatment of Inmate Wiedermann. The consensus so far indicates that Inmate Wiedermann may soon be allowed to interact with the inmates on the Lower Level. The matter of the Wiedermann family is still in discussion, as some fear allowing Inmate Wiedermann to meet them may cause an incident. The media and world as a whole are still in the dark, though the Wiedermann family has been reached out to without any current response.

Personal notes:

I do not believe that Inmate Wiedermann is a bad man. We've all read the accounts—the story Inmate Wiedermann gave of his own life . . . It's enough to make anyone pity him. Although the man is clearly used to a life of isolation, we must not assume that he can remain unbothered by the silence for any longer than one week more. Letting him interact with other prisoners may allow him to grow more stable. However, I must agree that uniting him with his family without any preparation may cause a grand incident that we do not have the budget or manpower to handle.

—*Dr. Darius Falk*

CHAPTER 5

ALL THOSE OTHER OTHERWORLDERS

A week after Dr. Darius Falk wrote his weekly report, it was announced that Kreig would be allowed to mingle with the Lower Level prisoners on the condition that he didn't harm anyone or cause a ruckus in any other way. It was a deal that Kreig was all too happy to accept, though he remained tenacious in asking if his family had received his letters. He received no answer, but his repressed optimism—brought out by his return to Earth—whispered to him that it was surely on the way.

So it was that while drawing a picture of the White Pope in His Divine Memory, Kreig heard the door to his abode slide open, revealing a small crowd of people. At the head of these Fighters and guards stood a familiar face, carrying a pair of oversized cuffs that seemed to cover the hands as well as the wrists of whoever was to wear them.

"Yo, my double!" Craig said, a grin proudly on display. Did they not have any other high-level Fighter that could escort him to wherever they were going? "Dude, don't look at me like that. Fighters of my stature are actually really rare, yanno?"

The most unsettling part of Craig seemed to be his ability to read Kreig's mind, even though Kreig's facial expressions and body language were the human equivalents of a dried fish.

Human, Lv. 122
Human, Lv. 197
Human, Lv. 146

Out of all the Fighters present, only Craig seemed unfazed by the situation. To the others, although they may not have been completely certain of what their escort mission had been in service to, the second they saw Kreig's unlisted level, they must have understood that he was not a normal man, not by far. This wasn't just moving a Lower Level prisoner from one part of the prison to another, this was a matter of national safety. After all, apart from this man, the highest-level otherworlder was only level 287.

A man who roamed the Lower Level.

But this place was beneath that, beyond such meager depths. True isolation, an anomaly in every aspect.

"All right, so, y'see these here cool cuffs? Like, we know you won't do anything wack—at least, we're pretty sure that you won't—but people feel a lot more comfortable when you're in these big cuffs. You get it?" Craig said, fearlessly striding inside Kreig's little abode like a blind mouse walking into the den of an equally deaf tiger. "I'll just put them right here. On the bed." Craig stared at Kreig, who was staring right back at him. "Dude. Just come over here and put them on."

Kreig watched him for a few seconds, his eyes unwillingly landing on the cuffs. Sighing, he heaved his heavy body out of his comically small chair. One of the many drawings littering the floor was moved to the side, but Kreig didn't look at it. He walked over to the bed. Next to Craig, he was absolutely massive.

Craig smiled. "'Kay, so now, you put your hands in these holes. It's like a pair of metal gloves! Or mittens. You won't be able to move your hands in them. Unless you're strong enough to do that? Ah, but these babies cost a lot, so don't do that. Man, knowing those fat cats up top, I'm sure they'd somehow twist it all to be my fault. So, don't ruin them. Yeah?"

Kreig suddenly felt a lot like destroying the cuffs, just to mess up for Craig.

But he didn't want to be a bother. So, he bent his back down, slid his large, callused hands inside the iron mittens, and felt as it locked up and tightened and captured him all on its own. A very impressive piece of machinery that Kreig almost wanted to think was some form of magic. This world was filled with so many things that he didn't understand. Magic he could understand. He was no magician, not by a long shot, but he got the gist of it. It was mostly mushroom-based, anyway, bless those heathens.

As soon as Kreig got the mittens on—which were fastened to each other by an immobile beam that kept his hands constantly together—Craig took a victorious pose, turned to his semi-stunned entourage, and shouted for them to bring the collar.

Kreig was barely able to even so much as wonder what the hell "the collar" was before Craig clasped it around his neck. It was large, thick, and kept Kreig's neck mostly immobile. It had several odd parts to it, but it didn't poke him in any uncomfortable way. Even then, he was so startled by the sudden addition that he almost ripped it off. "Hey, hey, cool it, big guy! It's just another safety thing. If you do something weird, a little mic on the side of it will tell you not to do it. And there's also a tracker, a video camera, a microphone, a chip sensor that'll know how close you are to which inmates . . . It's high-tech! Don't worry about it!"

Somehow, that was able to calm Kreig down enough for him to allow it on him. Though even then, he felt like a shackled dog. Degraded.

It wasn't a good feeling, but it clearly made Craig's entourage calm down, some even sharing nervous smiles and uncertain laughs. If it put those people less on edge, it was likely a good thing. No matter how he felt.

"Okay! Let's get going, my other half! I'm sure you're excited to meet new people, huh?" Craig began leading Kreig out of his cell, and for once, Kreig was genuinely stunned. Nobody had told him anything about meeting other people. All he knew was that the door opened and Craig put him in cuffs. For all he knew, they could have been leading him to some deeper place in this strange building. "You didn't know? Oh, yeah, you're a prisoner. Nobody tells you anything, huh? Maybe it's 'cause you never tell anybody anything back? Heh!"

Craig gave that throaty laugh again, deciding to take the time to rest his arms behind his head, entirely uncaring.

One of his followers took note. "Um, sir, are you sure you should be talking to it like that? Isn't it, I dunno, a prisoner?"

"Huh? Well, yeah, but look at him!" Kreig glared at the follower as she tried to look at him. "Total wuss. Wouldn't hurt a fly." The way the follower flinched and turned away from Kreig assured him that these people understood him a little better than Craig did. "Seriously. Guys who never talk are really weird. Like, if a girl does it, it's super cute, but a guy? Really, Kreig, get your life together. You're embarrassing all us other Craigs!"

It took all of Kreig's remaining will to not slam his mitten-hands down on Craig, an act that would likely have resulted in the boy's death. Such a young man, and yet he had zero survival instincts. It was almost impressive.

Craig, in accordance with his disturbance of the soul, continued chattering like a scalded ape during the entirety of the walk, and every time Kreig started slipping into silent, barely perceptible excitement over the prospect of meeting people, Craig would notice and pull him back out. Kreig could swear that the kid could read minds. Of course, even if he did have such a skill, Kreig's skill Defense of the Soul (X) protected him against any and all mind- or soul-based skills and attacks.

It was a shame that it did nothing to protect him from mental weariness as a direct result of Craig's chattiness. At some point, he'd started gossiping about the possible love life between a Fighter and a prison guard, but Kreig really couldn't handle it.

He was stuck between zoning out and paying as little attention as possible.

"I really think they'd make an adorable couple, but HR keeps insisting that showing any kind of personal weakness in front of the otherworlders could cause a revo— Ah, here we are!"

They stood in front of a metallic door. At this point, they had ascended several staircases and gone up at least two elevators, but even then, Kreig could tell they weren't entirely at the top. Craig stepped up to the door, placed his thumb against a scanner, poked a PIN number into the mounted keypad on the wall, and opened the door. He held it open. None of the Fighters or guards moved, and neither did Kreig.

"Huh? Whatcha waiting for? Get in there, you big lumbering blockhead! If I hold the door open for too long, the guys inside might try to escape!" Craig said, scandalized, nodding for Kreig to enter.

Slightly flustered at his mistake, Kreig entered, noticing rather unhappily how the door closed behind him with a metallic click and whirr that suggested it locked itself. A guard standing by the side of the door on the inside eyed Kreig warily. Kreig eyed him right back before turning to the room as a whole. It was about the size of a normal bar, lit by cold fluorescent lights and populated almost entirely by round tables, randomly littered boxes, and thick books written in all languages except English. Finally, there was a whole gaggle of prisoners.

About a dozen and a half. Most of them sat crowded around the tables, gleefully playing card games that were surely too modern for Kreig to understand. Others simply sat in book circles, quietly reading. The language spoken seemed to mostly be German—the Empire was rather large, after all—though the people around another table spoke French. This pattern repeated in several smaller groups, each speaking another language such as Korean or Afrikaans.

Not a single soul spoke English. Kreig adjusted himself. He had only ever learned English, Mandarin, and German. The people in the Alumni

Kingdom that existed before the Holy Order of White Roots took over spoke Mandarin, while those of the Yungland Empire spoke German.

It was simple.

For a few seconds, Kreig just stood there, staring at this minor collection of people.

Magus Human, Lv. 247

Human, Lv. 190

Human, Lv. 288

Magus Human, Lv. 216

A few turned to look at him. As they turned, others moved as well, until, finally, each of them was looking at him. Most of them were middle-aged and male, though their ethnicities varied. About half had the pointed ears that characterized the Magus Humans, what most would call sorcerers, wizards, and witches. Unlike common belief, these long-eared, blue-eyed, magic-wielding people did not come to exist through the mixing of races or even through the offspring of spirits. They were simply, much like the Oracles of God, created through the consumption of a certain type of mushroom. Unlike the Messiah's Egg, eating these were luckily cause for neither execution nor excommunication.

These people now looked at him, and Kreig was entirely unsure what to say. Should he introduce himself? As whom? Surely one or two in this room knew his identity—surely they must be ready to attack him on sight . . .

"It's Sir Kreig!" one of the sorcerers called out in German, standing up from his seat. Kreig was ready to accept the oncoming beatdown. After all, to the Empire, he was a traitor. A dirty, rotten— *"The Captain of the Royal Guard!"*

Huh?

About three-fourths of the blue-clad prisoners surrounding the German table sprang from their seats, their faces split wide by some of the largest grins Kreig had ever seen. The few other Germans seemed deeply confused but were unable to stop the others, who bolted for Kreig, surrounding him in a matter of seconds. Some were excited enough to let their hands rest on the iron mittens covering his hands; others simply stood there, eyes glittering.

"Sir, sir! It's an honor meeting you! How is the Empire doing? Surely, we've not been invaded by those dastardly Pretzians?"

"Sir royal knight, have seventy years truly passed in our absence? Say it isn't so!"

"I've got a wife and kids; how are they? Have you met them? I must say, sir, though I never became a knight of the Royal Guard, you were always my inspiration! And, Klaus, according to my calculations, it should have been eighty-five years, not some measly seventy!"

"Shut it, Kilian! You've been here longer than I have!"

Ah. So, that was it. Time passed differently between the two worlds and these people . . . they must have been there for too long to have understood Kreig's new status as a fugitive. Or, even worse, as a sort of natural disaster. He'd never considered himself as such, but according to those people who interrogated him a month before, that was what he was.

"Say, sir, you're being awfully quiet. Everything all right?" one of the long-eared fellows asked. Somehow, Kreig had never heard any reports of magicians and wizards going missing. Though entire armies disappearing was a more common occurrence, typically attributed to adolescent dragons or grown drakes goofing around.

Now, this, on the other hand? This was a far more interesting phenomenon.

The people close around him shared a few glances, since Kreig still wasn't responding. One leaned in closer to another and began whispering things. Kreig didn't hesitate to snoop. *"Hey, isn't it odd that the Captain is still alive? If sixty or seventy years have passed, shouldn't he be dead? I mean, maybe they've kept him here for a while, but . . ."*

Kreig didn't like the sound of that. He didn't want to make a mess, and since only three skills or a single forbidden spell could grant some form of immortality, having them suspect him of being a heretic could easily lead to a big mess.

Nevertheless, what eventually caused the mess was not Kreig himself but the single fourth of Imperial citizens still lingering about the Empire's table.

"Hey! Get away from him!" one of them shouted, knocking over his chair as he swiftly rose from it. A few of his fellow Imperials rose as well, carrying equally as conflicted and apprehensive expressions on their faces. All other people in the room were merely watching as it happened. *"That's the guy, that's the heretic bastard knight we told you about!"*

Busted.

One of the many Imperials collected around him turned his way, gave him a sharp, disbelieving look before turning back on the one who had cried wolf. *"Oh, no. Oh, absolutely not. You are not pulling this shit in front of the honorable Captain. And even if he did something like that, who cares?*

Didn't we all agree that former allegiances and wars would be put aside in this world?"

The man on the other side balled his hands into fists. *"What he did isn't something that can be forgiven. Didn't you hear how the keepers spoke the Language of Mold with him out there in the hall? If it was any other heathen cult, it could have been forgiven! But that one—you can't stand on the same side as a sinner of his depth! Why would they even release him from the Basement? The number of seals we put down there . . ."*

Something clicked in Kreig's mind. He'd never seen the names or faces of those who locked him up. He had allowed himself to be sealed up, but those feelings of belonging left him too soon.

Vengeance. Yes, a feeling of freezing cold vengeance took hold of his chest.

For the first time since being surrounded by these filthy Imperials, he moved. He took steady, careful steps toward this man. This man who had kept him locked up for twenty straight years. For once, he put the man's features to mind. His skin was slightly tan, as all Imperials were, and although his eyes were brown, they were significantly lighter than most. Toward the edges of his widening eyes, a golden sheen refracted the light. A crooked eagle nose capped off by a scar was stuck in the middle of his otherwise well-formed face. He was likely a former soldier, perhaps even the chief of one of the guard sections.

He had a strong, large build, though not as large as Kreig's. And when Kreig had come close enough to him, the whole room muffled by a choking silence, this difference in size was all too obvious.

The man looked up at him, his face twitching in a fear that had awakened only now. There was a reason why Kreig wore restraints while everyone else wore nothing but ankle bracelets. There was a reason his jumpsuit was orange instead of their domestic blue.

There was a reason the Empire had sealed Kreig in the deepest dungeon they had, in the Basement where only a lone powerful monster could dwell at a time.

When this man had left with his little army and his little conviction, Kreig had still been kept down there, all safe and secure.

Clearly, he hadn't been willingly released.

He had *escaped.*

"Inmate Wiedermann, refrain from harming your fellow prisoners." A voice spoke on the giant metal collar Kreig wore, and suddenly, life and presence returned to his eyes.

"Ah . . . Sorry." His voice was softer than anybody in the room would have expected. There was an underlying strength to it, but only in the most superficial way. It wasn't hard. It wasn't scruffy. Almost sweet. And that was all that he said. He left the man and lumbered over to an unpopulated table, where he sat down. Alone and unbothered.

Yet the silence that had smothered the whole room was only lifted a full five minutes later. The people who had previously stuck to Kreig now shyly retreated to their seats. Cards were picked back up. And somehow, everyone knew not to talk to the giant in the room. Even those who didn't understand a lick of German knew that this man was not one to be messed with. At least, that was the case for all but one.

The boy hadn't been sitting alone before. In fact, he'd been sitting over with the Imperials, but with his blue eyes and blond hair, he stood out a fair bit. Even then, he spoke his German well enough and he wasn't making a fuss.

That was until he stood up and tiptoed over to Kreig.

"Hi," he said. Kreig blinked at him. "Forgive the intrusion. Have you any objections to my presence? . . . No, I assumed as such," he said, flashing a small, uncertain smile before sitting down. "Surprised, aren't you, my lord? Yes, I would suspect as such. After all, I speak the Language of Mold, don't I? Horrible nickname." Kreig simply stared at him. This man who had not only approached him but done so while speaking English, of all languages. "You must be wondering how they came to accept an anomaly such as myself." The boy glanced over at the other people in the Lower Level with such unbridled fondness that Kreig couldn't help but listen to every word he spoke.

"I arrived before . . . before the Holy War. And the resulting Unholy War. Never in my twenty-four years could I have ever assumed that our religion could commit such atrocities . . . but I knew my new comrades down here would never commit to deceit such as lying to me. I trusted them as I trust them now. Though . . . I must be honest with you, my lord. You, the second of the Five Bodies, the sole survivor of the Holy Order of White Roots, you have been my only hope. The others have accepted me these past ten years, but every time a new one arrives, the stories told of you are only more and more outlandish."

Kreig's eyes softened. ". . . I'm afraid what you've heard is true."

Kreig chose not to elaborate on what parts were true. He didn't want to hear this man recount his days. He'd already done that once on this green Earth, and having to hear it again would only make him more self-conscious. He'd rather avoid it.

The young man looked at him, frowned meekly, and rose once more. Watching the one person in the world who praised the same God leave felt like a betrayal of the soul. But it was necessary. He could not retain such a relationship, where he was referred to only as *my lord.*

For some reason, he hated the thought of being above someone. After all, he did not deserve such a title.

He sat alone for three hours, and then he was brought back to his cell. Craig asked him if he'd had any fun, and Kreig didn't respond. Back in his cell, he spent his time wisely by drawing the people he'd met. One portrait of the former devotee. A sketch of the people crowding around him. A detailed drawing of the man who had previously incarcerated him. For a brief moment, he considered drawing something unsavory about the Imperial who had gotten him stuck down there, but after a few moments of thought, he decided upon another motif.

A round table, a deck of cards, and a bunch of people from all the different tables and ethnicities, including the boy believer and the Imperial, and then, finally, himself. All together. But, somehow, it felt off. The smiles on everyone's faces were wrong and there was no true light in their eyes. He was doing something wrong, something that his Artistry skill wasn't able to fake for him.

Something he had to do himself.

He reinvented his drawing. He had to think, had to add true feelings. There was no warmth and no softness in the painting. But he could add that. A few well-placed strokes added warm colors. The people touched each other in a friendly manner, had their arms on each other's shoulders. People showed different emotions and varying degrees of those. One man was upset at losing, another patting him on the shoulder and laughing. One was concentrating, another peeking at his cards. All of them were happy. The boy believer was happy, the Imperial was happy, and . . . and *he, Kreig,* was happy.

Artistry reached Rank IV

Artistry (IV)

Rank IV: Evoke emotion

Rank III: Greater anatomy, perspective, shading

Rank II: Greater color and design

Rank I: Stable hands, smoother lines

From that day onward, he was given three hours a day to stay in the same room as the other Lower Level prisoners. He didn't talk to them and they didn't talk to him. After a few days, he was allowed to skip out on wearing his iron mittens—though not his collar—and to also bring paper and pencils. At first, nobody paid him any mind, but after he drew the Reignians where they sat laughing and throwing cards at each other, he was soon noticed.

Unlike the harsh backlash he had expected, he was greeted with mildly appreciative smiles and somewhat standoffish looks. And then, one day, the boy believer decided to sit down in front of him and request to have his portrait made. Kreig obliged him, placing just a little more effort into the lines than usual, making sure every detail was right—from the glint in his eye to the quirk in his untethered smile.

He may have been the first, but he certainly wasn't the last. Slowly, shyly, one of the Imperials approached, asking if he could have himself painted as well. Kreig drew as best he could.

That was how it started. They were hesitant at first. After all, Kreig was an impressively intimidating figure, though once he turned his eyes to the paper and moved his pencil with such careful, light strokes, he was almost a different man. When he handed them a little drawing, the slightest smile tugging at his lips, nobody could truly fear him.

They learned to like him.

He changed their minds through art and art alone.

They never accepted him fully. Of course not. He was an unforgivable heathen, after all. But somehow, in that deep place, they learned to understand that he was human just like they were—despite his impious deeds. He was neither one of them nor separate from them.

To the observing researchers—the psychologists trying to understand if he was mentally stable enough for future social interactions—this was enough.

Even then, there were some skeptics pushing for him to interact with the Upper Level prisoners sooner than later. They argued that although allowing him more time with other humans was a generally good thing, if his experience confirmed his belief, he could never be truly accepted by other people, that it might be worse than pure isolation. Being actively isolated by other people could be far more stressful than being passively kept in isolation by superiors or caretakers. Thus, although it was a good thing that he was among people who knew him somewhat, the fact that he wasn't actively friendly with them was a problem they believed wouldn't go away with enough time.

Furthermore, there was the issue of his family. They had been contacted and had rightfully expressed great interest in meeting inmate Kreig

Wiedermann. Despite their excitement, the resident psychologists still wished for there to be more preparations done.

Finally, the two letters inmate Kreig Wiedermann wrote to the Wiedermann household. Until further notice, these would be kept in a safe under the head observer Dr. Darius Falk's jurisdiction. In respect of the sender, they would remain unopened.

Although it might have been odd for the observers to preach privacy, they had all come to agree that inmate Kreig Wiedermann was not only a man to be feared but a man to be respected as well. And not just as a citizen of Earth but also as a human being who deserved what little privacy he asked for.

Things were stable. Kreig was spending his days and nights drawing in more and more ambitious forms, such as oil on canvas. When his ideas finally ran dry after so many paintings, the first place he looked was straight in the eye of Dr. Falk. Or maybe it was his own reflection? No, he was clearly looking right at him. The inmate stared at him for a moment, closed his eyes, and took a deep breath through his nose. Then he opened his eyes again and started painting on his blank canvas.

Dr. Falk was a clever and observant man, but even he was a slave to his human curiosity. "Show me camera Three-C," he said to one of the half-dozen other observers in the room.

"Yes, sir," the man replied, fiddling with a few buttons to make the screen of camera 3C appear like a hologram on one part of the wall-sized mirror fixture they used to observe Inmate Wiedermann. Falk glanced over at the screen. It showed the back of Wiedermann, along with the one-way mirror and, most importantly, the no-longer-empty canvas.

So far, all he had were a few large splotches of color. Something white, something dark brown above the white alongside a gray background. It wasn't much to look at, but as Falk had come to learn during Wiedermann's incarceration, all art began by looking like something foul.

Wiedermann closed his eyes and took a whiff. Then he opened them again and continued painting.

Details soon became more prominent. A firm jawline, a black buzz cut, a pair of striking black eyes like swirling pools of inky velvet, a beige shirt, and a brown vest. A Black man Darius could only recognize as himself. Even that slight pout of the lips his wife told him made him look far too serious was there. Every detail was spot on, and the other observers quickly took notice. A few nervous smiles were exchanged.

"Sir, should I tell him not to use any abilities? This is a bit unprecedented," one of his assistants asked, thumbing the intercom. Darius affixed him with a harsh gaze.

"No, let him continue." Darius crossed his arms. Call it professional curiosity—call it the will of a man who had never been painted before. He wanted to see where this was going, and he wouldn't let any of his coworkers stop it. After all, he wasn't harming anyone, was he? "Let's see if he can finish it."

And he did. The whole painting took a mere two hours, a time that shouldn't have been physically possible for such a large oil painting. But Wiedermann had proved his artistic capabilities on many occasions, which included an unearthly speed that Darius now appreciated.

It really was him. Every detail was right and every inch correct. It was like looking into an honest mirror.

As Wiedermann stood up to place the oil painting somewhere in the room, Darius couldn't help but feel like something was off. The painting was not completed and it certainly wasn't in the right place. Without asking for permission from either one of his associates, he paced over to the intercom, pressed the button, and brought it to his lips. "*Inmate Wiedermann.*" The man in question turned to look at the speaker on the wall. "*Please sign the painting and place it in the hatch.*"

His colleagues were baffled and Darius felt the same. What the hell was he doing? This man was a prisoner of the highest caliber, not some poor artist he could just get a free painting from; that would be—

There was a metallic clank as the hatch opened and closed on Wiedermann's request. His fellow observers turned to look at him.

Darius left the observation room. Usually, they had many lower-level workers who handled the hatch. But even then, it wasn't as though Darius wasn't allowed in there. It was simply that he had never had any reason to go there. Today was a different matter.

He opened the door to the hatch-operating room by thumbprint and keypad. Inside, he found a food elevator going to and from the kitchen, alongside a small furnace just in case Wiedermann were to attempt to pass something foul through the hatch. He never had, but the possibility was always there.

The hatch was on the far side of the room. It was closed and locked now, but mere moments before, it had been unlocked and open. Beside the hatch was the painting. It had no frame, but unlike mere seconds earlier, it now had a signature. Just a little one, *Kreig,* and a little triangle with a line extending from one side beneath it. It looked like a very simplified mushroom, though Darius couldn't fathom why he'd have that as a signature. But that didn't matter.

A mere two days later and the now-framed picture was hung up in the observation room. The cover story was that Darius's wife had a passion for painting, but everyone knew that there was only a single painter in the facility with that level of skill.

And a mere two days after this incident, the decision was made to allow Wiedermann into the Upper Level on account of his improving mental health.

CHAPTER 6

GERALD

Rise and shine, dropout!" Craig shouted the second the Dragonheart door to Kreig's cell slid open. As always, Kreig was sitting by his desk, at this point trying to draw with ink. "Huh? You're not in bed?" Kreig put down his brush. "Hrm. I'll take your silence as a firm *maybe*! Seriously, though. It's like six in the morning! All the other prisoners would have a riot if they were awakened at this hour, you know?"

As always, Kreig did not oblige Craig with an answer, only rising to face him.

Craig, in turn, fetched the iron collar Kreig always had to wear, alongside the mitten-cuffs that Kreig hadn't worn in two weeks. "Yeah, surprise, surprise! Since nobody else has told you anything, I'll go ahead and say right away that we're not headed to the usual meeting place." They weren't? "Nope. We're going to the Upper Level, where they keep all the otherworlders below level 100!" Now, that was . . . unusual.

Kreig was above the highest level visible. All things considered, there was neither rhyme nor reason as to why he should be allowed in the same room as what he personally considered to be regular people.

"Yeah, a bit odd, right? Well, consider it a final test! If you can continue not harming anyone and not doing anything wrong, they'll consider letting you into more, well, regular situations. Like the outside. Or, for example . . ." A competitive grin flashed across Craig's lips. "Your family." Kreig froze where he stood, his hands half-inside the mitten cuffs. "I thought that'd get a reaction outta you. Now get those things on and we'll get going! You've gotta hit the showers, after all!"

Another unexpected detail. Though it did make sense, since he really hadn't showered in two weeks or so, which was the third time they had let him shower. Not that he actually needed to shower at all.

How long had he been there? He knew it was no more than two months. He'd gotten really good at counting the days back beneath the Empire. Now that he compared the two lifestyles, he really couldn't say that this was any worse. He saw people every day and was allowed to draw and paint as he pleased. It wasn't bad.

Though now that they were climbing higher than he'd gone in over a month, he did feel somewhat nervous.

"Oh, also, we haven't informed them of who you are or anything. The only thing that those guys above will know is that you're a new prisoner. Try and get along with them, yeah?" Craig explained things as they walked. It was a bit odd, but Kreig would rather that be the case than what had happened on the Lower Level. If they got to know him before they learned who he was, he might be able to get along with them. Somehow.

The shower that Kreig took was quick and "surface-level," the kind you take before a strenuous exam when you know you *have* to shower but can't bother to remain for too long.

And then it was time. The clock had hit seven in the morning, according to Craig. Apparently, early mornings did nothing to dampen his spirits.

And there they were in front of the back exit to the cafeteria. This exit was one of many used by guards and other people coming or going between the upper and lower levels. There were several hundred Upper Level prisoners, most of them the soldiers of various otherworldly nations. All of the leaders and sorcerers of their platoons had likely ended up in the Lower Level due to their higher level.

They wore red jumpsuits with different, subtle markings to inform the other prisoners of their national affiliation.

Kreig emerged into a room full of these prisoners, each huddled around their tables, eating breakfast foods that they had never had before they came to Earth. Not a single soul turned to look at Kreig, and that was how he liked it. Going by the voices and languages he could hear, the Imperials sat with the Imperials, the Pawinians sat with the Pawinians, and that was how it went. Larger nations had more tables, but even small nations had at least one full table.

The single guard at his side removed the iron mittens from his hands and gave him a nod before wandering away. With that, he was left to his own devices.

Although he no longer held any love for the Empire, he had to admit that these were the only people he could sit with at this moment. Although many higher-level leaders and captains and lords in the Empire knew of Kreig's "betrayal," this wasn't a commonly known or public fact. To the people of the Empire, he was a blank face. As long as he didn't tell them anything.

He stepped up to one of the many tables housing the soldiers of the Empire, waited for them to notice his presence, and affixed them with his gaze. *"Good morning."*

One of the soldiers flew from his seat. *"Y—you!"* The others turned to look at him strangely. The soldier was young, around fifteen, and for some reason, Kreig could swear he recognized him. Those large, white eyes that were assured of death, his trembling lower lip . . . *"War!"* The boy gave a final shriek before turning to his confused comrades. *"He—he's the one I told you about! The monster in our midst—War of the North!"*

One of the other soldiers glanced between the boy and the stunned, silent Kreig. *"Uh. Gerald, this is the guy? This is War of the North, who destroyed your platoon?"*

"Yes!" Gerald said with no trace of hesitation.

The other soldier turned to Kreig. *"Hey. What's your name?"*

"Kreig," Kreig answered swiftly. The soldier stared at him, looked at the other members at the table, and gave a wave for Kreig to sit in an empty spot beside Gerald. *"Thank you,"* Kreig mumbled. He hadn't grabbed any breakfast out of sheer nervousness, but he didn't need any.

Gerald seemed absolutely heartbroken. *"B—but!"*

The soldier almost glared at him. *"You told us that War was a Newtonian. Like the rumors said."*

"W—well, that's . . ."

"Ergo, Kreig here can stay." The soldier looked Kreig up and down. *"Say, is there a reason you're wearing an orange jumpsuit and a . . . collar? The name's Unglaus, by the way."* It was a good question, and Kreig wasn't sure how to answer it. In most cases when Kreig was uncertain how to act, following the words of the scripture was usually the wisest decision. It was written by wise men, and Kreig himself was not wise in the least. Therefore, honesty was a given.

"I was brought up from the Lower Level." No need to elaborate on that one, no siree.

". . . Is that so? Erm. I mean . . . Did they perhaps misjudge your 'level'? Really, we have no idea how they do it. All they need is a guy to look at you

and for you to touch a strange card, and they know how strong you are. Some of our guys have been hypothesizing that they've all eaten a Messiah's Egg, but that makes no sense. Not only is it the most sinful deed of all, but there is no way that those fungi could possibly grow in this weird world. I suppose it only makes sense that their magic artifacts would fail one of these days," Unglaus said with such perfect rationality that even Kreig wondered if that wasn't what had happened.

At this provocation, one of the other members at the table spoke up, presenting a theory that since the Messiah's Egg was a mushroom most foul, it was likely to have invaded this world through spores. Another disagreed, figuring that little white imps might have brought it there.

Yet another believed that the people could not, in fact, see their strength, but that the card alone did the trick. The Messiah's Egg person was just a scare tactic.

In the end, nobody came to an agreement and breakfast was finished without much further ado. Gerald still seemed extremely apprehensive at Kreig's mere presence, but in a certain way, that was to be expected. He *had* killed his entire platoon, after all. Maybe he should apologize? Wasn't it only right to apologize to someone you've wronged? Ah, then again, that might be a bit too much.

And even if he *did* decide to apologize, he would barely even know how to. He'd learned long before that the best way to apologize to someone was through actions and gifts, not words. Regardless, complimentary words always did well too.

Then again, he had no actual reason to apologize, either. And not because he killed them in "self-defense"; no, there was just no reason to try to befriend Gerald at all.

No, there was one reason. A singular reason.

If he made friends, albeit temporary ones, he could prove to the authorities that he was stable enough to be given free rein outside. Perhaps even stable enough to meet his family. That settled it. If he could befriend a man who absolutely hated him, that must prove that he was well enough in the head for his observers.

That left him with the pure physicalities of befriending Gerald.

At the moment, there was no action Kreig could perform that would raise Gerald's opinion of him. Gerald seemed mostly liked by the other prisoners in the Empire group, and they generally sympathized with his plights. He was not treated poorly, and thus Kreig could not intervene to help or save him.

Then, a gift?

Kreig knew many skills that could bless his comrades, but most of them were impermanent, and the two permanent ones he had were extremely flashy, meaning that others would know he did it.

Ah. Of course.

He could paint a picture of the boy.

Kreig nodded to himself and rose from where he'd been sitting, watching as the other soldiers from the Empire played a ball game Kreig had never seen before. They were out in the courtyard where Kreig had first arrived. Until now, Kreig had not attempted to join their game. He had not been invited to join, either.

Kreig wasn't a very approachable man. To most people, when he did something, he seemed to do it with such deliberate intent that nobody could believe he wasn't doing what he fully wanted. Thus, nobody invited him, since they expected his absence to be of his own intent, not from a lack of asking.

And now, Kreig decided to join the game.

"H—huh? War? What are you—um," Gerald muttered as Kreig stepped closer. Apparently, going by how he was the first one to notice Kreig approaching, he must have been keeping an eye on him at all times. Although Kreig had hardly come close to the young boy, Gerald still took a few steps back. He looked Kreig up and down, unwillingly meeting Kreig's eyes. *"I . . . Do you, uh, want to join the game?"*

Kreig nodded.

Gerald gulped, shooting pleading gazes at the other players, who had now quieted down. *"That's . . . Um, if you just, check the rules over there . . . Can—can you read?"* Gerald was pointing at a sign labeled Basketball in several different languages. The rules and explanations were written below in just as many languages, none of them being English.

Kreig almost considered just reading it himself. But then he recognized something in what Gerald had said. An offer to help.

Shaking his head, Kreig tried his best to give Gerald a somewhat-pleading look, though going by the way Gerald flinched and grew a shade paler, it was probably more of a glare than anything.

"Is—is that so? That's . . . um . . ." Gerald said, clearly hesitating on going through with his own offer.

He'd need some sort of push.

A push in the form of Kreig turning toward the sign and walking over. Gerald stared at his retreating back for a moment before following in a slight half-jog. Kreig never failed in making people follow him. It was scarily effective, really, and the second they both arrived at the sign, Kreig turned to Gerald with an expectant look on his face. Gerald understood the look perfectly.

"Um . . . so, uh, th—the game is called basketball, and the way you play it is . . ." Reluctantly, Gerald started explaining the rules of the game. Kreig listened with the same degree of interest as Gerald had explained it. The whole explanation only took two or three minutes, and by the end of it, Gerald no longer twitched at seeing Kreig's face. Sure, he still seemed about three shades whiter when close to Kreig than any other prisoner, but that would change in due time.

Seeing Gerald up close was the best way for Kreig to understand the contours of his face, since he couldn't very well ask him to model. If he did that, it wouldn't be a surprise gift anymore.

Unlike what Gerald had thought, Kreig did not, in fact, join the game. He merely sat by at a closer distance, his eyes never leaving Gerald's face. To Gerald, this was hell. To Kreig, it was an excellent way to see the boy in motion.

Two hours or so later and it was time for lunch. To the other prisoners, Kreig disappeared without a trace. For Kreig, he was led back down to his cell. Apparently, he would—for the moment—only be allowed on the Upper Level between seven and eleven. During the remainder of the day, he would eat lunch alone in his cell, and in the afternoons, he spent a few hours with the Lower Level prisoners. And then he was alone again.

It was this evening that Kreig took to painting. He thought he knew what Gerald looked like.

Dusty blond hair, dark green eyes and a high forehead. A curious nose and bony, skeletal jawline. In the most physical way possible, he knew what Gerald *looked like.* But he didn't know what Gerald *felt like.* When Kreig drew and painted him, he saw a Gerald lookalike, every detail and structure technically right but not emotionally right. He put the painting to the side and started anew. Another painting. And again, it was wrong. To an outsider, it looked just like Gerald, but Kreig understood that there was something he wasn't getting.

Some aspects of Gerald that he didn't understand well enough to imitate on canvas.

His goal evolved.

The next day, Kreig made a point of sitting right next to Gerald at breakfast in order to observe him as closely as possible. He saw the anxious way he glanced at Kreig between his small, uncertain bites. The uncomfortable shifting. The slight tremble in his shoulders. Kreig absorbed it all, took it in, and applied it to his mental image of Gerald. To Kreig, he was like a little hare. Yes, he felt much like a rabbit. Always ready to run away.

For a week, Kreig studied this angle of Gerald. He saw every little fearful gesture he gave. And each night, he drew this new angle of him with just a little more personal accuracy every time.

His cell, formerly littered with monsters and people from his former life—memorabilia he'd almost forgotten—was now covered in dozens of pictures of Gerald, each more frightful than the next. Toward the end of it, Kreig could paint a picture of Gerald that could successfully evoke terror and fright in anyone who saw it. He painted pictures of Gerald as a soldier, his spear wobbly in his terrified arms, or him lying in the mud, or sitting behind a rock, peering up at Kreig with eyes as large as hollowed burrows.

And it was never right.

It was Gerald as Kreig had known him right before they entered the portal. If he had not met Gerald in the Upper Level, he would consider these anxious paintings to be the true Gerald, as that was the only form of him that Kreig had ever seen. But now, after a week of sticking close to the boy, he knew him to be more than that. Every so often, Gerald would glance away and catch the eye of the other Imperial soldiers. And then he'd give the faintest smile of camaraderie. At other times, while his mind was enamored with anything except Kreig, he'd stare out over the ocean so readily visible from the prison island, and the mildest look of solemn longing would swim in his eyes.

Kreig could not capture these moments. They were rare, and with Kreig at Gerald's side every minute, the boy was more likely to show apprehension and discontent than any other emotion.

He needed a different approach. A way to ensure that he could see Gerald for who he truly was, not just who he was when Kreig was around.

Kreig called this strategy the "Stalk and Observe" method. He did not stay close to Gerald and he did not speak to Gerald. But he watched him.

Gerald himself felt nothing but confusion.

Did he do something wrong? Had he committed some grave sin to deserve this fate?

Not only did War appear out of nowhere as if he were anywhere *near* the same kind of human person as the rest of the prisoners, but he was also acting extremely strangely.

And by *strangely*, Gerald of course meant that he acted *human*.

He ate food, he occasionally spoke, and, most damning of all, he had a face. He wasn't wearing armor that hid his features. Gerald should have been more afraid than he was, but he couldn't help it. Sure, every time he saw War, he wanted to run away, but he understood very well himself that he was no longer acting out of pure fear and terror, unlike how he'd been in the—

. . . the place he was in before he came to this world. That place. Where he met War.

War back then had been less of a man and more of a machine of human destruction. Death incarnate. But the second he took off his helmet and his armor and spoke the language of the Empire . . . all of a sudden, he wasn't just War anymore. He was human. Human and sticking to Gerald like glue, despite how clearly unhappy that made Gerald. But every day Gerald saw War, every day he looked into his eyes, he felt less afraid. He knew it was War, hell, he was the *only* one who knew it was War, but . . .

At some point, he started considering War as less of a natural disaster and more of a person. A human being who followed him around everywhere and didn't say a word but would reluctantly play basketball with him if he asked him to.

So, then, why in the world had War suddenly taken such a distance? One day, he sat mere inches from Gerald at breakfast, and the next, he was sitting at a whole other table. Still staring at him but farther away.

It felt eerie, of course. War was an intimidating man, but even more so, it was only that, all of a sudden, in a way Gerald couldn't entirely understand, he felt lonely.

He'd come there with War. He'd gone to the same interrogation place as War. He'd gone to the same prison as War.

They'd been next to each other all the way, as unhappy as Gerald had been about it, and now that War had simply left him to his own devices, he abruptly felt more alone than ever. Sure, the other soldiers of the Empire were his friends and all, but in that group, there was nobody he considered himself really close to. Nobody he might consider a possible frie—

Of course, not that he would ever consider a bastard murderer such as War to be his friend. That'd be extremely silly.

. . . Still, seeing War sitting over by himself, staring at Gerald from so far away . . . it felt bad.

In a very strange way.

Kreig's observation took a bit of a turn.

Gerald started acting differently almost the first day. He seemed anxious to see Kreig in a different spot. He acted strangely off the entire day, eating less than usual and not playing basketball with the others. Something had happened, and Kreig considered quite seriously that Gerald must think that Kreig was up to something unkind or threatening, or even that he was now free to do what he wanted.

Either way, Kreig was there to observe it. He put every detail to mind.

The times Gerald spent alone, staring off at the sea, grew more frequent as well as longer-lasting. The other soldiers didn't disturb him, believing that everyone had their ways of coping with their battles. Kreig looked on.

Unlike what Kreig had imagined, even by the third day, Gerald did not act any happier than before, merely more isolated. Alone.

At night, Kreig painted pictures of Gerald sitting by the sea, sadness mingling in his eyes. He never drew Gerald happy, only sad and alone. Something was off, but he couldn't tell what. It felt bad. Something there was wrong yet again, and Kreig couldn't tell what. Might it be that Kreig's mere presence at the facility was the cause of Gerald's sadness? Maybe it was what he had done before? He hadn't expected any form of forgiveness, but knowing that his mere presence made his chances of somehow befriending Gerald *this* unlikely felt even worse.

Halfway through the week—halfway through watching Gerald grow more and more distant to the other soldiers—Kreig decided that enough was enough.

He had no plan when he approached Gerald where he sat by the rocks overlooking the sea. All he was thinking about was making things right.

In the mild distance, the sound of seagulls squawking could be heard. There had been no birds on his battlefield, not even the odd oversized vulture or lizardbird. Only the silence of death. Here, he heard much more. The seas roared and hummed with dignified class, crying out to the widowed brides of sailors, singing to the sleepless children, whispering in the ears of soldiers who never made it home. Gerald was one such soldier. The lone survivor of a horrific one-sided battle that nobody had enjoyed fighting.

Gerald looked out over the sea. *"You can sit down if you'd like,"* he said, glancing back at where Kreig stood, large and lumbering and lonesome. *"It's okay."*

Kreig sat down next to him, at an arm's distance. Neither prying nor distant, only close enough to hear Gerald speak his mind and soul.

". . . I never really had time to be a kid. The other guys in my platoon always talked about how they missed home and longed for their childish

days of little care and great love. I hated being a soldier too, but I couldn't miss home. There was nothing for me to miss about it. I was born, I grew up, and that was it. On the battlefield, I was just another soldier. Back home, I was just another kid to raise my younger siblings. And here, I guess . . . I'm just another prisoner.

"There's nothing for you to care about, War. I . . . Back then, I wish you would have taken my life. It was my duty. Not to arrive in this world, not to become some prisoner . . . When my mother and father made me into a soldier, they knew I wouldn't return. So, you see, I can't return. Even now, whatever alliances I make, it's just an overture to my spiritual death. Say, if you were to kill me now, would anybody know? Could you make me disappear?"

At this, Gerald turned to fully face Kreig. There was a certain reluctance in his face and an exhausted tension that Kreig understood all too well. "*. . . Yes.*" That was his answer. An unwilling affirmation.

He had all kinds of skills, several of which could make his enemy simply disappear.

But he didn't want to. No matter what Gerald told him, no matter what he asked for in this regard, he wouldn't do it. It was not because he couldn't, or because he hadn't killed before, or because he feared losing his one chance to meet his family and return to a normal life.

There was something else.

After all, in those young eyes of Gerald, those eyes that begged for death, he saw *himself.*

He'd been older, but he'd been in the same situation. A reluctant soldier forced to kill. After the Unholy War, when the other four of the Five Bodies were killed in battle and executed, he had begged for death as well. He told the Empire's torturers and guards a hundred times a day that he just wanted to join his brothers in the warm soil, and never once did they humor his wishes. The same happened when his party was killed by the Empire. He had turned himself in in hopes that they would kill him and spare his party, but they had been unable to. Without any reliable method to end his life, they forced him into a cell beneath the Empire, again not heeding his wishes for death.

And there he was, refusing the request of a boy in his very situation.

"You'll do it, won't you? Although I can't truly see you as the man who took the life of my platoon, I can understand your place here. You've done this before. You can do this again, can't you?" Gerald said, turning entirely to Kreig. The frailest smile possible tiptoed over his lips.

Kreig did not respond. He *could* not respond. He wanted to break off eye contact, but his eyes were locked in place. He wanted to say something, but his lips were sealed. He wanted to say something soothing, something that made the boy feel all right. Feel better. Only a few words. The words that would have made Kreig feel all right back then when he needed them. But there were no such words. His mouth felt dry. Dry and empty and callous. No words could save this boy.

Only *action*.

What had Kreig needed all those years ago, when he longed only for the embrace of dark death?

"Don't look at me like that. If you'd like, I can turn away. Not that I want to see myself di—"

Kreig hugged him. Although Kreig's arms were big, although they had strangled and crushed and beaten so many into their untimely ends, now, at this moment, they merely held Gerald. He eclipsed him in his raw size. He was a bear, large and imposing, his full body pulling around Gerald, bringing him into a hug that covered the boy entirely. Gerald's thin arms froze in a second, moved spasmodically, and then relaxed. Kreig kept Gerald close, and Gerald was kept close. They did not move.

But when Kreig held him long enough, when time had moved to a standstill and the waves no longer lapped at the stony shores, Kreig could feel the boy crying, little white long-held tears soaking into Kreig's overalls, tiny unwitting hiccups and warm shivers that transferred from Gerald to Kreig like heat and static.

It wasn't one-sided. As Gerald cried, releasing his boyish sadness and the sorrows of too-few too-many years, Kreig listened. He did not cry, as his eyes had long since dried, but as he held Gerald, Gerald held him.

In little clutches, in small movements, as the boy buried his face in Kreig's chest, so too did Kreig bury his head in the boy's back.

They remained there until they released each other, shared a look that said too much, and went their own ways.

When Kreig returned to his cell, he ate neither lunch nor dinner. He slept an hour, slumbering softly, and then, when he woke back up, he took to painting like he never had before. He began by drawing a thin sketch. Two people in an embrace, what had transpired mere hours before. In that time, in that situation, he knew he had seen Gerald for who he was, who he had been.

A young boy who had no business being swept up in all of this. That was who he painted. Alongside an adult man, who had no business being alive either.

Together, they had formed a defiant coexistence. Together, they had watched the sea.

That was what he painted.

Most of his oil painting didn't take more than three hours, but for this one, he went at it for the entire day and the entire night, getting the details right, putting emotion in their faces and in the skies. A true testament to the ever-changing nature of man. As he put the last strokes to the painting—the painting that had left his mind as blank as the canvas—he leaned back. He put his brush in a water-filled cup. And then he used the skill that let him instantly dry oil.

Sand Emperor's Touch (X)

It wasn't a visible skill. To any onlookers, it just seemed as if he touched the painting, but he knew it was more than that.

It was complete, for one. It was complete and beautiful and he felt absolutely no shame when he, at five in the morning, wandered over to the hatch and placed the painting in it. "Please give it to Gerald." No answer. Not that he had ever gotten an answer before when he asked them to do anythi—

"Will do."

The sound startled Kreig, but he didn't show it.

In two hours, he would meet Gerald again. Until then, since he couldn't know how Gerald would react, he spent his hours pacing his cell. Back and forth, glancing around at the walls, each plastered head to toe in paintings of varying degrees of skill.

CHAPTER 7

FACE TO FACE

At first, Gerald was really not in the mood to get up at five, one and a half hours before usual, but when he saw the reason, he had a change of heart. Ever since before lunch when Kreig left him in a stupor, he'd been a sort of zombie. He ate, he walked around, but that was about it. When he got back to his cell by seven, he'd gone straight to bed, something his bunkmate found delightful.

And now he had to wake up at five. Why? Because a guard was at his cell, holding a large packet wrapped in brown, nudging it at him through the bars.

Gerald accepted it not because he was awake enough to but only out of muscle memory.

He looked at the packet, rubbed his eyes sore, and looked back up at the guard, who hadn't left yet. The guard seemed as though he wanted to say something, but instead, he merely grabbed his keyring, unlocked the cell, and stepped inside. Gerald was too tired to react with anything except involuntary paralysis. The guard did not leave, simply remaining where he stood, staring at Gerald and his brown package.

"Is this, um, for me?" Gerald asked, sliding his fingers along the edge of the package. It was large and rectangular, a bit soft to the touch—neither fragile nor robust.

The guard nodded. "¤!&, §½%) ?=+#@/ Kreig." The language the guard spoke was known colloquially by the prisoners as the Language of Mold, though the real name, as a few men had told Gerald, was English. Nobody knew why most guards spoke it, but usually, they refrained from using it.

This was because most of the prisoners reacted harshly to the mere sound of it. Gerald had never heard the language from anyone who wasn't from this world—apart from maybe Kreig—so he held no negative attitudes toward the language itself. But what he did recognize was the name used.

"From War?" Gerald muttered, glancing down at the package in his hands. As far as he knew, prisoners weren't allowed to trade anything. That posed the question: who in the world was War and why in the world had he sent him a present?

Might it have to do with what happened earlier that—no, yesterday?

Maybe so. It had been such a peculiar situation. Gerald couldn't remember ever acting like that before. Sobbing and weeping and wailing his eyes out in the arms of another man. A man who happened to be War himself. It had felt silly afterward, but in the moment, when it happened . . . it felt good. He didn't regret it, and now that he thought about it, he didn't feel like death was his best solution anymore. Sure, it was tempting, but a child didn't necessarily have to return home from war in a casket.

Gerald carefully undid the wrapping on the present.

It was a painting. Gerald hadn't seen many paintings in his days. He knew he could find them in the mansions and castles of grand nobles and kings, he knew the Emperor had a sizable collection, and he knew that no peasant should ever hold one with his bare hands. In shock at what he saw, he almost threw the thing away, believing his commoner's hands were too dirty for it. That was until he took the time to actually behold the painting itself, what it portrayed.

He saw War first, which wasn't unusual, since War had a sizable frame, enough to overshadow Gerald. That was something he knew all too well after what had happened the day before. And yet, War wasn't the only person visible in the painting. There was a sea and a sky and a bundle of rocks overlooking the endless blues merging at the horizon, and there in the very center, cradled tenderly in War's arms . . .

Was none other than himself. Small and young and so entirely *him* that Gerald was frightened for a moment. As if he was staring into a mirror of his soul, the full extent of his pain reflected back in every agonizing detail.

It was beautiful.

A painting so pretty, he felt undeserving to be a part of it.

Gerald placed his arms around the painting and held it close. Where did it come from? Who had created it? It couldn't have been War. A man so talented in death couldn't possibly be a man of the arts. Then again, creating such a fantastic piece of art in a mere night . . . it would've been impossible to commission, especially with such a stunning degree of accuracy. There wasn't a single detail wrong. The gulls, the rocks, and everything unseen. There was something inherently personal in the expression, in how it was made.

"I'd like to meet him," Gerald said, peeking up at the guard, who had yet to leave.

The guard stared at him, said something in English, and unlocked the door to the cell. Gerald made to stand, but the guard pushed him back into the bench, all the while shaking his head. Although Gerald was confused, he understood the sentiment, deciding to remain seated. The guard then proceeded to wander over to the wall, retrieve a hammer and nail from his belt, and hammer the nail into the wall.

Then he held out his hand. Gerald looked at the hand and looked at his painting. The hand made a "give it here" motion, and Gerald relented, placing the noble luxury in the man's hand.

It was mounted on the wall, as though it had always been supposed to be there. Even though it looked much too beautiful for the cold, barren walls of the cell, Gerald couldn't bring himself to object.

The guard made to leave, but Gerald took hold of his arm. Their eyes met, and although Gerald had no idea if his words would go through, he said it again. "I'd like to meet War." It was a weak request; he knew that. Silly, even. In all honesty, he had no real idea why he wanted to do it at all. But, somehow, he knew that it was right. He had to talk to War and find out what their relationship actually was. Doing it in the cafeteria or in the courtyard would be far too public.

The guard stared at him. Gerald repeated himself. "I'd like to—"

"&%¤)/, &&/&(¤# !"##%," the guard said, holding up his hand, a gesture clearly urging Gerald to silence. As instructed, Gerald kept his mouth shut for a moment while the guard removed a rectangular artifact from within his pocket. At his touch, the artifact lit up, and with a few movements of the guard's hand, the screen moved. With a flick, it turned blue and white. "=++(#¤, &/"(." With that said, the guard made a rolling motion with his hand, nonverbally telling Gerald to say it again.

". . . I'd like to see him." The artifact made a few sounds and the guard turned to it, watching as text appeared on the screen. In the upper box, what Gerald had just said was written, and in the bottom box, he could see a line of equal length in what he presumed to be English.

The guard froze in place, turned to look at the painting, looked back at Gerald, and finished the movement with a conflicted expression. Then he stepped out of the cell, fiddled a bit with the rectangular artifact, and brought it to his ear. What followed was one of the strangest things Gerald had ever witnessed, namely a man talking into what seemed to be thin air. It must have been some form of magic, though Gerald had never seen either of the two magicians in his platoon use any such spells.

The air-conversation spanned about five minutes, which the guard spent alternating between submission and defiant pride. In the end, he removed the artifact from his ear, pressed a button on it, sighed deeply, and placed it in his pocket.

Then he turned to Gerald. Apparently, since he reluctantly opened the cell door and gestured for Gerald to exit, the upper echelon must have given the green light.

One prisoner meeting another wasn't anything strange or even prohibited. People met every day, and if they decided to meet in the library or gym, they could even have it a bit more private. Meeting at each other's cells wasn't illegal either, though it did require one prisoner to be escorted there by a guard. At times, the procedure required planning on the part of the guards and staff, but usually, it wasn't a problem.

This shouldn't have been any different, despite the early hour.

At least, that was what Gerald thought while the guard put a pair of handcuffs around his wrists and began guiding him. His mind changed as soon as the guard brought him to a door Gerald had never seen before and used some sort of magic to open it. Once inside, he found the atmosphere to be much different from before. Sterile, white walls, cold light . . . Something was off.

Before they walked any farther, the guard pressed a few buttons on his artifact and held it up to Gerald. A voice resounded from within it, saying "I don't have permission to descend into the deeper levels" in a somewhat female, barely human voice. The guard pressed a few more buttons and the voice spoke again: "Other guards will soon join us to escort you to the inmate."

Gerald wasn't exactly sure what this meant. If War was being treated like a normal prisoner—being allowed to mingle with other prisoners— shouldn't he be in one of the normal cells? Normally, Gerald would have voiced his thoughts, but the guard seemed too annoyed to hear it.

So, he let himself be led through the hallways, and the second he thought that War might be at the end of it, he found himself in front of another staircase going down, and at the end of that staircase, a gradu-ally more heavily armored man would stand. By the time they got to the first elevator, Gerald was escorted by no fewer than five heavily armored guards and Fighters, all tired and mildly disgruntled at having to be awake at such a damn hour.

Another dozen hallways, three more stairs, two more elevators and three more guards, each one tougher and more dangerous-looking than the last.

Gerald had to admit that unless they kept War in the deepest recess of the world, they must be leading him to some execution or something. This couldn't actually be happening.

But, no, it was happening. They just kept going farther down.

By the time that Gerald thought they had surely passed by the under-world, they finally stopped, standing in the middle of a hallway all too like the other ones. In front of the squadron of people, a regular-looking metal door slid open and a well-dressed Black man stepped out. His dark eyes fell upon the group, or, more specifically, on Gerald, and lit up. He didn't smile, but Gerald had seen War enough to know when a man's eyes smiled.

"Ah, inmate Speerhalter! A true pleasure; my name would be Dr. Darius Falk," the man said, stepping up to Gerald without any hesitation, plowing past the guards and Fighters, who willingly parted for him.

Gerald was a bit taken aback, not just by the language the man spoke but also by the sheer weight his presence seemed to hold. "Who are you?"

"I am the head observer of inmate Kreig Wiedermann, and you are, at the moment, a very important figure. Come, follow me inside," Darius said with such perfect confidence that he must have thought that Gerald understood everything he said, which he did not. But, as per what the man asked, he did follow him into the room. This was in spite of the fact that everyone else remained outside, almost as if they had decided on it beforehand.

The room he stepped into wasn't abnormally large, but it wasn't small, either. The wall parallel to the one he entered through was made up of a large, mounted window that showed the inside of another room.

A room containing a person Gerald recognized.

War was sitting by a comically small table atop an equally small chair. His body was hunched over the desk, and in his hand he held a small brush, flowing over a paper with the fluidity of a river and the beauty of a cobra.

The second Gerald stepped into the observation room, the second he saw War, War himself perked up. His body twitched and his face snapped up from where he'd been looking. In one swift movement, he turned to look at Gerald, his nostrils flaring. And in a mere moment, Gerald suddenly felt like a very small rabbit faced by an enormous wolf staring down at him, sniffing his fur and smelling his fear.

"Don't worry; he can't see you. From his side, it's only a mirror," Darius said. "Though he *can* smell you."

Gerald whipped his head around to face Falk, catching the slightest hint of a grin escaping his lips. That did nothing to quell the sudden fear rising in Gerald like a flood. War could smell him? From beyond a *wall*? Not just that; he was being kept this deep underground, constantly observed, even having a head observer keeping a close eye on his every move?

A realization bloomed in Gerald's mind. These people knew. They knew he wasn't just a warrior, that he was War of the North. And still, they had let him up with the other prisoners. What in the world had they been—

"Since he's already aware of your presence, we will soon turn the viewing mirror into a window. I trust you have no objections to this?" Darius said, leaving no room for refusal. And while Gerald stood paralyzed, Darius turned to the half-dozen other people in the room, told them something in English, and waited patiently for them all to leave the room. "Despite inmate Wiedermann's knowledge of their persons, we strive to assure that their faces and names remain anonymous."

"Is—is that so . . ." Gerald muttered in reply. His eyes were glued to War. By this point, War had risen, eyes fixed on where Gerald stood.

Although Gerald hated to take his eyes off of War's face, he felt the need to do so only because he happened to notice that War wasn't wearing his collar. Furthermore, the room itself happened to be a bit interesting. It confirmed the theory that War had, somehow, painted the picture himself. As a matter of fact, the whole room was littered with paintings and drawings and sketches and ink and things that Gerald felt he was too poor to be allowed to so much as view.

And among these hundreds of paintings and drawings, he of course noticed those portraying a young boy, his eyes hollowed out by war, lips thin and skin pale.

Himself. There were at least two dozen paintings of himself in varying situations. Two were mere sketches, three were full paintings—one of which uncomfortably enough portrayed the moment he'd been discovered by War behind the rock from the perspective of War—and all the rest had their own quality and make as well. It was impressive and made Gerald feel somewhat embarrassed. If he hadn't deserved to be a part of *one* painting, how could he possibly justify having a number of portraits usually reserved for nobles?

While Gerald stared at the room, Darius wandered over to a desk, flipped a few switches, twisted a key in a keyhole, and pressed a final button.

A great whirring ensued as something happened to the one-sided mirror mounted in the wall. On their side, the only visible change was the other room becoming slightly clearer, but considering that War's eyes were widening somewhat, the changes on his side must have been grander.

And there they were—Gerald and War, face-to-face.

For a moment, they just sort of stared at each other as if neither had ever expected to see the other in such a situation. And then, all of a sudden, the mildest look of realization and embarrassment passed through War's eyes, and he turned away from the window. Gerald had no idea what he was up to until he grabbed one of the many sketches of Gerald lining the walls, and the moment he did, the piece of paper burst into white flames, disintegrating into flakes of snow at his mere touch.

Gerald, in shock, could only watch on as Falk made a move for the intercom, changed course midway through, and turned to the window, and while speaking with his most intimidating and authoritative voice, said, "Inmate Wiedermann, *please* refrain from using supernatural abilities, or else guards and Fighters will be summoned to apprehend you momentarily."

War stared at Darius through the glass and clenched his fist, making the snow in his hand crackle and melt. ". . . I must destroy them."

As always, War's voice held such calm determination that it simultaneously petrified Gerald and sprang him into action. "War, hold—hold on! You don't have to destroy the paintings!" Going by the way War simply grabbed another piece of art, namely the painting portraying War's perspective of their first meeting, he had no intention of stopping. But he didn't go through with it, either. He held the painting, but he was looking at Gerald. And in a single moment, Gerald understood why. He understood why War had a dozen pictures of him, why he had only now received a painting, and why War was too embarrassed to show him the prototypes. "Are you . . . ashamed?"

War didn't move. His face and eyes turned as frozen and immovable as ice.

"You painted all these, didn't you?" Gerald asked, speaking his words as carefully as he could. War nodded. For a moment, Gerald looked at all those paintings of him, some cruder than others, some less like him than the one he'd gotten. "Have you been trying to paint me for long? Is this all . . . What have you been trying to do?"

It was obvious from the look War gave him that he couldn't say. Something held him back, some silent red-hot form of embarrassment that Gerald had never seen in a fully grown man.

A form of shyness, the kind held in nervousness and uncertainty. "I . . . I only came here to talk. Just to talk." War listened silently. "What happened today, what you did, what I said . . . I really did mean it. But now, I feel like . . . like maybe that isn't the best answer. It isn't what I want anymore, though I'm not actually sure what I *do* want. I never had that choice before. But I think . . . I think, if I talk to you, I can maybe figure it out."

And all of a sudden, Gerald felt just as withdrawn and timid as War was. After all, what he wanted to ask of War was something he had only ever asked once.

"War . . . No, that isn't your name, I'm sorry; do you—do you want me to call you *Kreig*?" Gerald asked, taking a step closer to the window. War hesitated for a moment. He seemed confused by the question but nodded nevertheless. "Okay, then, um. Kreig. Will you be my *friend*?" As soon as the words left Gerald's lips, he felt that embarrassment assault him, making him take a few steps back, his arms waving frantically. "N—not if you don't want to, that is; I'm just a kid and you're some sort of disaster, and even here you're barely human, so I get if you don't—"

"Yes." Gerald hadn't noticed how Kreig stepped this close to the window. "I'd love to." There was a slight thrill in his voice, some little sense of excitement and joy that Gerald hadn't expected.

He was just a kid, after all. A kid and a soldier and someone that shouldn't even have been able to *talk* to Kreig. But the game had changed, and there they were. Face to face. "Then . . . I guess—we're friends now?"

Kreig nodded.

Gerald had only ever had one friend, a kid his age back in his village. He knew the basics of friendship. Loyalty, trust, honesty, those kinds of things. All things considered, Kreig did not seem like the kind of man who could devote himself to those virtues. Though, then again, Gerald didn't know Kreig very well yet.

Gerald nodded. "I'll see you tomorrow, then?"

And at that, Kreig gave the slightest hint of a smile. "Yes."

And that was the end of it.

Darius, for his own part, had been enjoying the show a little more enthusiastically than most should have. After all, Wiedermann was showing genuine interest in another human! Of course, friendship in no way amounted to therapy, but the mere fact that Wiedermann could form such a relationship with anyone—a relationship that could result in the other person willingly descending to these depths just to tell him they wanted to be friends—meant so much.

Of course, Darius knew the reasons behind this. Not just because he knew every given detail of Wiedermann's life both before and after his summoning, but he also knew of Speerhalter's life. The interrogators had gotten those details out of him quite easily.

Even more damning, they had the footage from earlier that day, recorded using Wiedermann's collar, portraying an intimate closeness between the two that transcended reason.

It wouldn't have been out of the question for Speerhalter to utterly despise Wiedermann, or even to attack him on the spot. He had wiped out his platoon, after all. And yet, their friendship had been able to blossom in such a manner. It was delightful for Darius to see, and when he led the young prisoner out of the room with a smile tiptoeing over his lips and a song in his heart, he was already preparing himself to write the report detailing the situation.

More specifically, he looked forward to recommending to all available officers and administrative persons that Wiedermann would be eligible to meet his family in around a week, as long as his situation did not degrade.

It didn't.

During the entire week following Darius's positively worded report, the two prisoners continued sticking close to each other. During this time, although Wiedermann never grew any more talkative, Inmate Speerhalter certainly did. As the days went by, he kept speaking more and more of his mind, his wording becoming personal and emotional and honest in a new sort of way. He spoke his mind, and Wiedermann seemed to delight in simply listening to him speak.

At Darius's request, alongside the assurance that Wiedermann would surely be mentally prepared to meet his family in a week, the people up top made the unanimous decision to allow Wiedermann to mingle with the Upper Level prisoners from daybreak to twilight. Although the quality of his food took a hit, Inmate Wiedermann seemed all too happy regardless.

Apparently, once evening rolled around, the other prisoners abandoned physical sports in order to play cards and other monotonous, thinking-heavy games. It took a while for Speerhalter to teach Wiedermann how these worked, but once he did . . .

The fact that Wiedermann's intellect wasn't his strong suit became readily obvious.

"*Hah! Gotcha, that's a cleared table, buddy! Shouldn't have let me finish my tower!*" one of several Imperials gathered in a circle around a table full of cards said, a crescent-moon grin on display. He gleefully scooped all the cards on the table into his hands to build his pile. Kreig, on his own end, was left with a measly gain of two tens, one of hearts and one of clubs. An absolutely useless yield that no sane man would have gone after.

Gerald gave his thick arm a soft punch. "*I told you, ten of hearts is worthless, ten of diamonds is the big ten! Did you get them mixed up again?*" Gerald's eyebrows were slightly squashed together, lips pouted. They weren't playing as a team, but any downfall on Kreig's part was instantly considered to be Gerald's fault.

"*N—no.*" It was a lie, but Kreig really didn't want to admit it. How was he supposed to know that the three-point super worthwhile card of ten wasn't the heart but the diamonds? Weren't both of them red?

The dealer gave a double rapping on the underside of the table, indicating that it was time for the last round. "*All right, all right, final round.*" He dealt out the cards, four for each player and none on the table since the guy last round cleared the table. Gerald was first and began the round by unwillingly placing a two of spades on the table. A few people chuckled; others grinned calculatedly.

A cleverer man than Kreig would have recognized that if Gerald placed a valuable card on an empty table, aware that it would likely be grabbed by another player during the initial round, it must mean he had a bunch of other, more valuable cards on his hand.

Two people dealt their cards before Kreig, and both of them gave a grumble before placing a worthless card on the table. And when it was Kreig's turn, he took a look at his four cards and placed a two of clubs on the table, right beside Gerald's. The two cards matched and looked very happy together. Kreig smiled in his heart while the players around him argued whether to correct him *yet again* or to just ignore it. Gerald, as

Kreig's "caretaker," decided to speak up. *"Um, Kreig, you have to use the card if you can."*

Kreig looked at the cards. Didn't they look happy? He'd feel guilty if he ruined such an adorable friendship, alongside stealing Gerald's card. So, he shook his head.

Going by the grimace Gerald gave him, it was obvious Gerald knew that Kreig's reasons for not taking the two of spades were neither clever nor wise. He was all too right.

The two friend cards were grabbed by an enthusiastic soldier the very next round, who happily explained that constantly carrying a four had always helped him in tough situations.

The game of cards ended soon after, when a pair of guards approached, urging Kreig to leave. On previous days, when Kreig left, he did so almost unnoticeably. Now almost all prisoners were at least somewhat aware that his situation was a bit different. They just didn't know why or how. Gerald gave Kreig a final wave, wished him a good night, and that was all. Kreig felt pretty good about it all.

It had been a week since he and Gerald became official friends, and he hadn't regretted it for a moment. Gerald, on the other hand, seemed more astonished the more he came to know Kreig, and not in a good way. The first sign was when Gerald realized, at Kreig's second round of cards, that Kreig was just not a very smart man. It all went downhill from there. Not only was Kreig an incurable romantic when it came to friendships, his idea of what a friendship actually meant seemed to be somewhat skewed in comparison to Gerald's.

To Gerald, a friend was someone he could hunt bugs with, someone who gave him a short respite from home, someone who made him laugh and made him happy. To Kreig, a friend was someone he could fight a war with, someone he could be truly honest with in every way, someone he would both kill and die for.

This was a problem, since it had happened more than once that Kreig asked Gerald if there was anyone he didn't like in particular. The first time it happened and Gerald naïvely blurted out that a peculiar seagull with a black dot on its wing kept stealing his bread in the morning, he had to physically step in between Kreig and the gull to keep the man from twisting the neck off of the poor thing.

To Kreig, all life was cheap except for the lives of him and his friends. At this point in time, that meant Gerald and only Gerald. This did not make Gerald happy.

It was an obsession of sorts. All the needs for friendship that Kreig had, all his unused need to protect, all those years' worth of feelings had all been concentrated in a single boy.

But now that would be shared. Now Kreig would meet more people he could care for.

Now he would meet his *family*.

CHAPTER 8

WHERE ARE WE GOING?

About a month or so earlier, Kreig's family had gotten a letter stating in grave, authoritative tones that this was every bit as serious as anything else that had to do with the International Otherworld Combat and Research Organization (IOCRO). In fact, noticing that it was written by IOCRO, in particular, was what alerted them that this might be a bit more serious than what they would have hoped.

To George and Samantha "Sam" Wiedermann, the remaining survivors of the Wiedermann family, knowing that their long-lost brother might still be alive was a promise they had to trust.

When the portals first appeared, many innocent lives were lost. Simply seeing that swirling pool of energy was enough to draw people into it. People wandered inside, and in most cases, they were lost forever, replaced by dangerous monsters and inhuman creatures the world had never seen. Their parents, Angelita and Paul Wiedermann, had both been victims to such an occurrence. They went into a portal, and out came three car-sized blue alligators.

A terrible trade-off, really. And during all these years, the two siblings—George and Sam—were left alone. Their extended family helped with a lot of basic needs such as the bodiless funeral and learning about how to make it work.

But after a few years, they were expected to make do with as little help as possible. They had a pair of grandparents, an uncle, and an aunt, but none of them could spend their entire days—their entire lives—caring for two kids. So, they made do. George resorted to working as much as he possibly could alongside finishing his college degree while Sam focused entirely on school. The stress wasn't exempted from her, either, though.

She turned to a less-sustainable means of dealing with the event. Namely hallucinogens. LSD, shrooms, and, in the end . . . the greatest hallucinogen known in both worlds.

Messiah's Egg.

Back when she took it, people didn't know it awakened people into becoming Fighters. All they knew was that it left the taker with three days of glorious hallucinations varying in strength and subject. That is, unless you didn't have any hallucinations at all. That is, unless a little black fungus sprouted on your palm a week after you ate it.

Which she did. And all of a sudden, she had another way of earning money for her and her brother.

Now her future was no longer in management and leadership but in being a Fighter. It was a hard shift, and she had to give up the drugs and the friendships she had formed because of them, all in order to educate herself into a police officer with main focus in in-portal monster subjugation. She had been fourteen when the portals came, and now she was twenty-four, a fresh recruit in the local station. As of yet, she was only allowed to enter the weakest of portals, but she was happy with that.

In such a way, when she first found the letter in the medium-sized apartment she still shared with her big brother—now 32, then 22, she didn't think anything of it. Or, rather, she imagined it might have been a promotion.

Sure, she knew getting promotions in the mail wasn't exactly the usual way of getting them, but she'd only gotten one so far, and George wasn't home yet. So, when she pulled her blue eyes from the IOCRO logo and let them wander off to the bright-red "*URGENT*" notice, she knew something was off. As the unclever hothead she was, her first instinct was not to call her more-intelligent brother but to tear the letter open, her heart beating quicker and quicker with every word she read.

To the Wiedermann household,

Kreig Wiedermann has been located. He is alive and currently being kept in custody. The matter of his identity is not in question. Furthermore, he wishes to meet you. Please give this letter to Sergeant Jones Krupke to confirm that you wish to meet him.

If you should choose to meet him, there are precautions you must follow in order to avoid an incident. These are as follow:

Do not doubt his identity. Although his identity has been confirmed through all manners known, you may feel uncomfortable believing that he is the same person who went missing ten years ago. If you were to verbally doubt this and question it to his face, an incident may occur and we therefore ask that you refrain from doing so.

Always remain at a distance of five feet from the glass window.

Do not agitate Kreig Wiedermann. Be it through verbal provocation or physical aggression, should any of the members of the Wiedermann household present any threat to the mental wellbeing of Kreig Wiedermann, the entire household—barring Kreig Wiedermann himself—will be removed from the site without question. Were this to happen, please abstain from asking for help from Kreig Wiedermann, as this may cause an incident.

Avoid causing Kreig Wiedermann immense grief. As his mental state remains under question, any cause of grave emotional distress will be removed from the premises.

Finally, every detail of this occurrence is extremely secret, and should any member of the Wiedermann household decide to disclose the information they will be privy to, they will be arrested for Treason. The information includes the location and existence of Kreig Wiedermann.

Further details can be discussed during the visit.

If you wish not to meet Kreig Wiedermann, burn this letter and dispose of it in a suitable manner so as to avoid its disclosure.

Warm regards,

The International Otherworld Combat and Research Organization (IOCRO)

Suffice it to say, although Sam did possess the rationality to wait until her brother George came home before doing anything rash(er), she did so extremely reluctantly. She spent the entire hour before his arrival pacing around the apartment, reading the letter over and over again and closely studying every detail of it to make sure that everything was correct. Truly, it was real.

Not fake.

Her brother was alive. Not George, not some unborn unknown twin, *Kreig*. Kreig was alive and well and—and something here was really, really strange. If they had found Kreig as they said they had, shouldn't he be down at the station right now? Even more alarming, why was IOCRO involved?

Until George was home, she wasn't able to voice these worries. Once he opened the door, everything simply poured out.

"Duuuuude, I got this letter and it was about Kreig but it was also from the otherworld organization and I just—you won't believe it, really, it's written like some sort of super important letter, I don't think I've ever seen something so formal? Except for that formal essay Mrs. Clarke showed the class after she was done pointing out how everything *I* wrote was just horrible, but this is something completely different, this is just—"

George placed his hands on her shoulders firmly, his dark eyes nailing her in place. "What in the world are you on about?" George was a very serious man by occupation, education, and fixation.

Their eyes were locked for a moment, and in a moment of seldom-seen calculation, Sam chose not to speak on and on about what she'd seen and read but instead to point at the letter, still sitting on the table, propped up by a basket of half-brown bananas they never ate. George understood not only the motion but also that if she was shutting up for once, it must be something *truly* shocking.

He paced over to the table, grabbed the letter, and read it from start to end. He examined the sigils as Sam had done before and placed the letter back on the table. "Tomorrow, you will give this letter to the man indicated in the letter. You know who he is, don't you?"

"I mean—yeah, I do, but shouldn't we discuss this? This feels really odd; why would Kreig be involved with all those people? Can't we just meet him? We should—"

"Sam. Do you really think we can refuse this?" George asked, turning to face her fully. She seemed uncertain. He was not.

". . . Yeah. Okay. I'll give him the letter in the morning," she said, for once allowing his authority as eldest to dictate their decisions. With a face full of conflict and uncertainty, she closed the distance to the table and retrieved the letter, placing it back in the envelope. "I guess, if there's anything to say . . . I'm happy Kreig is alive. I think. Say, any chance Mum and Da—"

"No, we shouldn't hope like that. And even with Kreig . . . The wording on that letter isn't giving me any hope, Sam. Something's wrong," George said, once more interrupting her as he only did while stressed.

Sam pouted. "Hmpf. You're always the negative one. Can't you cheer up even a little, you soggy fuck?"

George gave a soft, hesitant laugh. "Heh, no, that's . . . Weren't you the one considering not returning it at all?"

"Sheesh! I was just playing devil's advantage!"

"Advocate."

"Huh?"

"It's devil's— You know what? Forget it. Let's get dinner started."

The next day, as per their agreement, Sam handed the letter to Sergeant Krupke. She made sure to tell him, as formally as she possibly could, that they would love to meet him as soon as possible. He gave a nod in turn and tucked the letter into a locked drawer in his desk.

Two weeks later, after Sam and George had already started considering that it might have been a shared hallucination, they were met with another letter, which stated in formal words how they wouldn't be able to meet Kreig just yet, signed by a Dr. Darius Falk. Again, George concluded that this was not a good sign. When Sam handed the subsequent letter to Sergeant Krupke, she made sure to hammer it in that they would love to meet Kreig as soon as possible. Another week, and another letter. Again, she restated her position.

Two weeks, two letters, until, finally, on the fifth week after receiving the first letter . . .

Dear Samantha and George Wiedermann,

I am delighted to inform you that permission has been granted for an official visit. You will be picked up at Gate 5 of the Guramn Airport this evening at 6 p.m. You will be escorted by armed guards and Fighters. Please do not be alarmed by this; it is merely a formality.

I cannot imagine the joy you must feel at this moment, but I assure you, when Kreig Wiedermann meets you, he will surely be even more delighted.

After all, I should know.

Dr. Darius Falk

They got this letter at 5:21 p.m., and Guramn Airport was forty minutes away by car. Police officer she may be, but that evening, even she did her fair share of speeding. George had never held the car's grab handle so hard before.

Either way, when they got to the bustling crowded airport, they did so with their breaths caught in their throats.

"Shit shit *shit*, we're gonna be late! Do you think they'll take off without us if we're late?" Sam asked as she jogged in place, George only now catching up to her. His forehead glistened with sweat, his eyes hazy and distant. "They won't, right? But even then, we've gotta keep running! These are authority people; we can't know what they're thinking!"

George leaned down, resting his hands on his knees, taking a moment to just breathe. "Haah, haah . . . Sam, I swear, you will be the death of me," he said. "The chances that they would leave without us are extremely low."

Despite all the evidence against her, Sam insisted that they continue running. They got to the gate three or four minutes past six.

"You two must be Kreig's family, huh?" The first thing that met them at gate three was a young man carrying a spear, surrounded by various Fighters and military personnel. He seemed young, bright-eyed, and confident. "Wait, it's only the two of you? Ma and— No, you're really young, so . . . Wait, wait. Hold on. Is— Did . . . Oh. Ohhhh, okay, okay. Now I get why it's taken this long. All right, just follow me, kiddos; I'll take you to the helicopter."

Sam glanced up.

Human, Lv. 344

Not introducing oneself while meeting another person for the first time was something George considered to be very rude, but there was no space to complain, as the man didn't even hesitate to turn around and head out of the gate. Sam and George both followed.

"Hey, miss sis. You a Fighter or something?" he asked.

"Yeah, what about it?"

The Fighter grinned. "Well, well, well. I'm sure you know who I am, then? After all, you've seen my level. My very high, very impressive level that lets me bend steel with my bare hands!"

Sam stared at him for a moment, trying to place his face. "I haven't the slightest clue, dude."

The man froze midway through a pose that oozed pride. "You—um. You really don't know? I'm Craig? Craig the Thunder Spear? One of twenty level 300+ Fighters? Geez, sis, that's— Wow. You're hurtin' my feelings here!"

At that moment, George decided not to disclose the fact that he *did* actually know who this man was. Craig. A prodigy of sorts, one of the youngest high-level Fighters in the world as a pretty direct result of his competitive and risky nature when it came to fighting. He was one of the few people in the world who would gladly hurl themselves at a monster with a level twice as high as theirs. In a way, his accomplishments were admirable.

But in person, Craig really just wasn't the kind of man George wanted to get to know. He seemed like a very loud and arrogant man, just the kind of person George couldn't stand.

As it turned out, the helicopter they would be riding in wasn't any ordinary helicopter. This was a deeply militaristic aircraft, designed not only for high speeds and high altitudes but also long times in the air. For IOCRO, such aircrafts were mainly used for the transportation of high-level Fighters to different parts of the world or for long-distance sniping.

In this way, ranger- or magician-type Fighters would remain in the air-craft while close-range Fighters went on the ground.

This model was a Black Tiger T-6, one of the best long-distance high-speed helicopters out there. George's heart practically jumped out of his chest.

While stepping into the aircraft beside his sister and the Fighters, he had to consciously keep his mouth shut lest he go on a long-winded tangent about why this particular model was superior in all forms as compared to such aircrafts like YOL-P 77 or Halvan Helan A-26. Meanwhile, he could only somewhat understand that Craig, the Fighter, was really trying to pester Sam into admiring him, which wouldn't work in the least. Sam didn't admire anyone. Trying to force her to think highly of him would just make her think less of him than she already did.

Though the presence of Craig *did* present them with a bit of a question. How in the world could Kreig's return require the presence of such a high-level Fighter? Usually, Fighters above level 300 were reserved to fight the strongest monsters and the strongest portals. A few of them even had the distinct (dis)pleasure of being deported inside the portals and into the otherworld, where they would assist the two military bases placed there.

The return of a missing person should not require the presence of such an official. The return of his little brother should not have been this big of a deal.

Unless something was seriously off.

The full trip took two hours. George wished he'd brought a book, and Sam wished that Craig would stop boasting about all the high-level monsters he'd defeated. Although it was against protocol, the two siblings *had* tried to pry information out of Craig several times, specifically about what the need for all this was. Strangely enough, they were always met with uncharacteristic silence.

Things only got stranger when they eventually arrived at their destination. George didn't recognize it at first, and Sam, who didn't have clearance to know much about it—especially not what it looked like—didn't know what she was looking at in the least.

The Other Island. A large island prison containing all intelligent humans and humanoids that had been recovered alive from the portals. Most of these otherworlders were soldiers, army officers, or sorcerers.

The highest-level otherworlder to have been recovered alive had a stunning level of 287. Far from the highest-level Fighter but impressive nonetheless. Especially so considering that he didn't have a system to guide him. As a matter of fact, no recovered otherworlder did.

Except one. Though at this moment, George knew nothing about that, and neither did Sam.

Right now, all they knew was that something was really odd.

The Black Tiger T-6 landed in the empty courtyard outside the prison, and Craig hopped off several seconds before it had even settled down properly. Once Sam and George exited as well, alongside a whole cavalcade of Fighters and guards, they were led into the prison.

"I was asked to ask you if you've read up on the whole things-you-shouldn't-do list that you got in the first letter," Craig said. "Well, uh, didja? This is actually really important, I think. See, I'm not allowed to say a lot on this whole subject 'cause it's top-secret and all, but if you don't follow those rules, something bad's gonna happen. I'm not sure *how* bad, but even with the grand me here, the situation probably wouldn't be resolved too easily. Ya get me?"

George and Sam shared a glance. They had read the guidelines, sure, but in all honesty, they had already forgotten it all.

". . . Okay, uh, yeah. Here," Craig said, retrieving a pair of papers from inside his armor and handing it to them. They each accepted one. "Just read them while we walk. It'll be a while until we get all the way down."

That was somewhat ominous. Though neither Sam nor George were in any place to disagree. Their hearts were already beating at a steady but quick pace, tattling on the fact that this whole situation was getting to them in more ways than one. It wasn't just the high-level Fighter, and it wasn't just the location, and it wasn't *just* how odd everything was. It was also their steadily rising anxiety, their slight fear at what might be wrong.

They descended deeper, down flights of stairs and through locked doors. While standing still in elevators, both Sam and George took the time to read the little slips of paper Craig had given them.

1. Do not doubt his identity.

2. Always remain at a distance of five feet from the glass window.

3. Do not agitate Kreig Wiedermann.

4. Avoid causing Kreig Wiedermann grief.

5. Do not disclose any information in regard to the visit or Kreig Wiedermann's existence to any third party.

Again, ominous in an odd way neither Sam nor George could truly understand. When they shared a glance, a look of silent yet confused stoicism, they both understood that this was not a regular situation. Treating it as such would land them both in big trouble. They had to follow these rules, no matter what. Whatever the reasons, whatever the cause, they would trust in IOCRO, as the world had for these past ten years.

Both of their minds raced with possibilities, but they silently agreed that the only possible response was to simply wait until they arrived. Though as they only continued descending deeper and deeper, as the corridors grew more and more narrow and oppressive, they had to admit that something was wrong. Something was very, very wrong.

The full walk took about half an hour in total, and during the entire trek, Craig barely spoke a word. It was a welcome but suffocating silence.

A silence that was broken at the end of a final long hallway, where two men stood. Sam glanced at both of them before doing a double-take at the second one.

-Human, Lv. 1-

-Human, Lv. ???-

The second man in question was small and squat, the majority of his face shrouded by a hood. This half-hidden face was pale, thin, and ugly in a peculiar, sort of disfigured way, as if someone had taken a frog and placed pliers on either side of its head until it became longer than it was broad. But although his skin was as waxy and pale as a stiff's, his eyes were very much alive. Alive and blue and fascinating to look at. Sam felt her heart skip a beat.

"Samantha, George. A pleasure to finally meet the both of you face to face," the regular human man said, stepping up to the group while the little frog-man shuffled behind him, thumbing at the hem of his dark blue robe.

Both Sam and George pulled a blank. They didn't recognize this man, and by all accounts, he shouldn't have recognized them, either. However, George was ready to take a chance and hazard a guess. "Dr. Darius Falk, I presume?" he asked, walking up close to the Black man to shake his hand, which the good doctor gladly obliged him with.

"The one and only," Darius replied, a shy smile flitting over his thick lips. "Now, before we enter the observation room, I would like to introduce you both to Frank Groda, the highest-level Fighter in the world. Samantha— May I call you Sam? Considering the available records, you see his level as a collection of triple question marks, don't you?" Sam replied in the affirmative to both statements. "Yes, well, Craig, would you be so kind as to inform us of what his level is?"

"Yes, sir. His species is human, and his level is 637," Craig replied, his voice and tone actually somewhat formal for once. As if he actually respected his superiors.

The man spoken of, Frank, retreated further behind Darius, his ears turning a hot pink. Thanks to his minuscule size, he was able to hide behind the larger man with stunning ease.

"If you're wondering why you've never heard of him, we have three distinct reasons," Darius said. "Firstly, allowing his existence to become public knowledge could cause a compromised situation if the world were to be invaded by intelligent monsters or otherworlders. Secondly, due to his appearance, he wouldn't make for as good of a mascot as the current 'Strongest Fighter,' Juha Häkkinen, is. And, thirdly . . . Frank is not a social man. Are you, Franky?"

Frank's eyes seemed to swim in terror.

"And why should we be allowed to meet such a man?" George asked wisely. After all, those three reasons were true, although the second two were rather superficial. He had never heard of this man before, despite his own position.

Darius's eyes narrowed slightly, his pupils darkening in the red light. "Follow me."

They did.

They followed him through a final winding hall, stopped beside a final door, and entered. Craig and the other guards remained outside while Darius, Frank, and the two siblings entered. The room was dark and filled with screens and buttons. Every aspect had the distinct feeling of high tech to it.

But the most eye-catching part of the room, the one half that pulled their gazes like moths to a flame, was the wall facing them as they entered. A large glass screen embedded in the wall.

And inside that fixture they saw something very strange. No, *someone* very strange.

A man larger than any bodybuilder, his eyes white and focused on a piece of paper he was poring over, his ham-like fists flying deftly and painting bold lines in black ink.

Divine Human, Lv. ???

Sam's breath hitched. Somehow, just from a glance, just by comparing the pure sense of power permeating the air around him, she could tell that this man was far beyond Frank. His ??? eclipsed Frank's in a way that Sam simply couldn't fathom. Who the hell was this? What the hell was a Divine Human? Had they—had they captured an *angel*? No, going by the way this man looked—the way his every move and every breath seemed to move the world around him by pure intent—he appeared more like a demon.

That was how Sam regarded the man sitting beyond the glass wall. George's perception was both more and less nuanced, in part because he didn't have her intuitive sense of how strong other people were.

All he knew was that this man, sitting in the deepest recesses of the Other Island, guarded by the strongest Fighter in the world, must have been a fantastically powerful otherworlder. That was all he knew, and although a faint idea seemed to tug at the back of his mind, that this man seemed almost *familiar*, he ignored it fully. It'd be a cold day in hell before he let his thoughts wander in such a direction.

Darius was about to ruin that self-imposed chastity. "Oh, my. He can't recognize your scents at all. Fascinating."

"Is he supposed to?" George asked, his eyes narrowing.

Darius gave a quick nod. "To be absolutely clear, what you're looking at is not just a one-sided mirror. Currently, this is the world's most dangerous subject. Though the fact that he hasn't recognized you yet is a good thing, as it means we have some time to discuss matters before you initiate conversation with him. Unless you would rather that Inmate Wiedermann explained his situation to you himself?"

Any calm that had previously possessed the two siblings now completely escaped them. They both turned to Darius with complete and utter befuddlement, mouths pressed into thin, white lines.

". . . Did I perchance not tell you? Pardon me, I— Frank, would you be so kind as to give me Inmate Wiedermann's black card?" Darius asked, turning to Frank, who was still cowering behind him, though more so out of fear of the man on the other side of the window than of Sam and George. Frank fumbled with his robes for a few seconds before handing Darius a business card–sized piece of black paper. Darius, in turn, handed it to George. "This is his status. Considering your occupation, I'm sure you will find the layout familiar."

Divine Human, Lv. 999+

Guardian of Sacred Walls

War of the North, Survivor, Fugitive

Purge of the Holy (X), Devotion (X), Shine of Divine Light (X), Warrior's Breath (X), Undeath (X), Dragon's Perception (X), Holy Swordsmanship (X), Wings of a Dove (X) (. . .)

Although George had been handed the card, he angled it so that Sam could take a proper look as well. Sam was not a pale woman. She enjoyed outdoor activities in large part due to her occupation, and so her face and body had been rather deeply tanned. In a mere second, this tan was banished, replaced by a corpse-like pallor and a trembling lip that indicated a fear George had never seen in her before. "Wh—what the hell is . . . X-rated skills? Do those even . . . And the level . . . How did— What is . . . Kreig . . . Is this really Kreig?"

"Yes," Darius said before George could raise his voice. "There is no doubt about it. Suffice it to say this is the reason why we couldn't let you meet him immediately. I'll spare you the details, but both his own testimony and all known evidence suggest that Kreig Wiedermann was summoned to the Otherworld ten years ago, the day before the portals started appearing. To us, only ten years have passed. But to him . . ." Here, Darius turned to look at Kreig where he sat, surrounded by paintings and sketches and drawings of people and things. His eyes were solemn. "Too many years have passed. When he returned to us, he was a wreck, to say the least. It's a surprise he didn't cause an incident, considering his mental state."

George tried to follow Darius's gaze to look at the man he was told was his younger brother, but it was hard. He could barely look at the man who sat in there, inside his little cell in his little overalls like some caged animal. "Why is he here?"

"At the moment, Inmate Wiedermann presents an international threat. Through gradual contact with other people and reintegration into small groups, we are aiming to grant him some form of mental stability. Had we introduced you earlier—or, rather, had we introduced the fact that his parents are no longer in this world—an incident would surely have occurred," Darius said. "Now that his mental state is in a better place, it has been decided to introduce you as another facet of his reintegration into society here on Earth. I shouldn't need to say this, but if you do not follow the guidelines we prepared for you, an *international* incident may occur. On the level of what Famine of the East caused."

Famine of the East. A familiar name, one that neither of the two siblings had heard in several years. Calling what that creature had done "an incident" was a grave understatement. However . . .

Even George knew that Famine of the East had been level 800 at most.

Even Sam knew that "War of the North" as a title sounded far too familiar.

Both implications were extremely hard to take.

"We hold no secrets from you. At the moment, you two present part of the only hope we have in successfully rehabilitating Inmate Wiedermann into what can be considered a normal human being. As you speak to him, you may notice that he is very different from how you may remember him. He might not remember your names or faces. He might not respond to what you say. Either way, should anything happen, know that he is not an evil man," Darius said. His voice seemed hopeful, despite the grave words he spoke.

"If he's quiet and dangerous and doesn't even know our faces . . . *is he even Kreig at all?*" Sam asked, a scowl tugging at her lips.

Darius turned away from her. "That's for you to decide. I've only ever known him as he is now. And as he is now, he needs someone to depend on. People who won't betray him." With his piece said, Darius stepped over to a panel of consoles and keyboards. "Are you ready to speak with him? He has awaited this for over a month now."

Sam turned to George. They shared the very same confusions and uncertainties in equal measure. But they had asked for this. They had wanted to meet the brother they thought had died.

As it turns out, maybe he had. Though not in a physical manner.

". . . Yes. We're ready," George said, turning to the window. Kreig was still poring over the paper. His hair was long and unkempt, but it had the same charcoal hue as George's own and their mother's did. Although his eyes weren't visible, somehow, George could tell that they wouldn't be anything pleasant to look at.

When Darius spoke in the affirmative, twisted a key, and pressed a button, the one-way mirror changed into a mere glass window, and Kreig then glanced up, his hollow, far-away eyes settling sweepingly on the two siblings, George's beliefs were reaffirmed. Those eyes were not those of a common man. Those eyes had seen war. War and death and the cause and effect that those two had. He had caused them, too. His eyes were hollowed-out white holes, almost as if someone had scooped holes in a rotten log.

And he didn't speak a word. He looked at Darius, at Frank, at Sam, and, finally, at George. Not a single glint of recognition shone in his eyes. If anything, he seemed more confused.

Darius patted George on the shoulder. "Go on; tell him the good news."

To George, it felt like Darius was way too happy there. Frank was terrified—rightfully so, from what George could tell—Sam was anxious, and George felt no different. Still, he would do as Darius said. So, he took a step forward, established that he was the one who would speak, and cleared his throat. "I—erm. Good evening. K—Kreig. It's . . . It's been a while, huh?"

Kreig didn't even blink. He just sat there, glued to his chair. He'd stopped painting, though, his entire attention focused on George.

"M—My name is George, and this is Sam, and . . . and we're your family. Uh. Brother and sister. And you're our brother. Did—did you know we—"

The pen in Kreig's hand literally exploded. Wooden splinters and sawdust burst from where his hand was, and without so much as glancing at this feat of unbelievable strength, Kreig stood up and walked closer to the window. Good God, he was large. Kreig had always been a bit taller than George, and broader too, but this was ridiculous. George was perfectly dwarfed, finding himself forced to arch his neck just to meet Kreig's eyes.

Then, Kreig spoke. "I've waited long."

His voice was not how George had remembered it. Not that he remembered it well. There were videos of Kreig, of course, but both George and Sam avoided them.

This voice was simply not Kreig's. It was much too deep, much too old, much too unlike what a child should sound like. That was what Kreig had been when they last met. A child, barely even grown. And here was a man who had happened into a situation much different from what he should have been in.

"Is—is that so—"

"Kreig," Sam said, stepping up to stand beside George. "What have you been up to these past years?" Kreig just sort of stared at her, breathing deep, conscious breaths. "Oh, me? Well, I've been here and there, you know, did my time with drugs and all, the whole situation and everything really got to me, heh, um, did you know that the Otherworld organization forgives any drug charges that any Fighters come in with? Yeah, really weird, you know, but they also gave all these other benefits, like all of a sudden you become a citizen of the world and you can travel and settle down wherever you—"

"Sam, keep quiet for a second," George interrupted her. "Can I ask you something, Kreig?"

If he'd been younger, if he'd been the same boy he was when he left, Kreig would have smiled innocently. At this age, at this moment, he merely stared back. "Of course," he said. "Anything."

George pointed a straight finger through the window at a single painting mounted on the wall like the head of a lion. Kreig slowly turned to look at it. The painting was fully finished, only lacking a suitable frame. The man portrayed was white in every sense of the word. White hair, white skin, white lips, white fingertips, white eyes. He was a rare sort of human. Not an albino. There were albinos in that world, yes, but this was another kind of creature, born from drinking an elixir distilled from a sort of mushroom far rarer than the Messiah's Egg. "Who's that?"

Kreig looked into the eyes of the old man pictured. In his heart, only gratitude remained for this man. "The White Pope." Kind eyes, gentle smile, warm hands that touched his heart.

The man who had roused true faith in Kreig, a faith he had never once abandoned.

George sneaked a peek at Darius, who shrugged in turn. Nobody knew who that person was, or who 99 percent of anybody else on Kreig's walls were. It was all unknown people with unknown connections to Kreig. Even if they asked other prisoners who they were, unless the prisoners came to Earth around ten years before, chances are they wouldn't know who anybody was. The only one who knew was Kreig, and his lips were sealed, not that anybody had the gall to try to pry the information out of him.

George pointed at another painting portraying a refined, slender man, wearing beautiful robes and a dazed expression. He seemed like a lord of some sort, especially with his seaweed-like hair. "And who's that?"

"My former lord." A title fitting that sort of man.

George pointed at another painting. "And that?"

"The sub-leader of the Royal Guard."

"And—" George's finger froze mid-point, hovering just in the air. His eyes widened. Weren't those paintings supposed to only portray unknown people? People from the other world that nobody had ever known? Then why was—

"Peter," Kreig said softly. "The Priest." Indeed, although the garb he wore was odd, it was clearly divine in some aspect. And although he was older than George remembered, although his eyes were weary and his smile was strained, it was Peter all right. The boy that sometimes came home with Kreig for a round of some action game they used to be able to afford. One of many such boys. Kreig had been rather popular, after all.

The question was: why was he wearing that, and why was he a painting on Kreig's wall? Kreig answered him before George could so much as ask.

"I didn't go there alone." Simple, to the point, and only devastating in the words that followed. "Though my return was lonesome." Peter's fate went unsaid, but the implication was clear. Looking at all the other paintings, all the dozens and hundreds of portraits and sketches and pictures of people and humans and only that, George came to wonder what kind of life Kreig must have led without them. What people had he met? What sights had he seen?

He almost felt tempted to think that this might be a good thing if it weren't for the fact that he couldn't consider the man in front of him to be Kreig. Forget his size, forget his sheer aura of intimidation, forget that he was locked up on an island for otherworlders. His voice was off. The words he said were unlike what Kreig would say. His body had changed, and in that malformed body, an equally malformed soul resided. George had seen Fighters who had entered portals with humans in them. Fighters with no choice but to kill famine-ridden farmers who had accidentally wandered into portals.

He had also seen killers who had stepped beyond the first horrors of murder, soldiers who had grown so used to the act of death, so used to committing it on others, that the thought of their own death wasn't even soothing. Merely mundane.

Somehow, this Kreig seemed to exist in both of those forms. The young Kreig, the mere child of his youth, could never possibly have grown into such a monster.

And yet there they were, under strict orders not to question his identity.

"I'm sorry," Kreig said. George looked up, meeting the larger man's gaze. "I don't mean to frighten you. Or make you unhappy. I understand that I appear very different from how you may remember me. But if you were to wish me gone, I can disappear. Not just from your lives."

"No, no! Not at all!" George exclaimed, shaking his head. "Of course you shouldn't! We're—we're happy to have you. You're our brother! Even if you've changed, you'll always be our brother. No matter what." It was a lie. Not a complete lie, not an evil lie, just a little white lie. One told to everyone there, including George himself. He didn't want to admit it to himself, but at the moment, his doubts were so deep and heavy that he couldn't possibly admit that this man before him could be related to him by blood.

"... Thank you." Kreig turned away. Somehow, despite the lack of any physical markers for it, he seemed slightly flustered.

It was a human act, one that made Sam only feel a little less nervous. Her brother didn't feel it. Not a lick of it. He couldn't tell from a glance that this person was barely human. If even that. His race wasn't human, his level wasn't human, and to hear her brother talk to him as if he were only made her hair stand on edge. She wanted to point this all out.

But she couldn't. After all, now she knew the use of those guidelines. No human on Earth had a true sense of what 999+ meant, including her. But she knew that if they did something wrong, if they let their amiable masks slip for only a second, God only knew how much damage would be caused, how many lives would be lost. She had to stick to the guidelines, had to make sure she didn't say anything wrong, had to keep Kreig calm—

"Where are Mother and Father?"

His words were softly spoken in mere confusion. There was no underlying intent, no prying need, merely an innocent question. The worst kind.

After all, it was a question they couldn't answer. *Don't cause grief. Don't cause any intense emotions.* Those who had prepared the meeting knew what would happen. Darius knew what would happen. Frank, who silently raised his hands in preparation for a battle of any kind, knew what would happen. Sam and George, who now turned to each other, mouths dry and glued shut, did not know what would happen. They swallowed and tried to smile, but it came out as forced and alarming.

"They—they couldn't make it," Sam lied. "There's so much work to do nowadays; sometimes, we just can't keep up!"

Kreig watched them for a few seconds, long enough for them to wonder if he'd seen through their words, but then he lumbered off to his chair and collapsed into it, a sigh of relief escaping his shut lips. "Thank God. Thank God; I was starting to fear the worst. Tell me, how do they do? I cannot remember their names. Will you tell me how they are? Do they still work or have you taken their need for work? Letting their weary old bones rest?" The slightest hint of a smile hovered around his lips, and his eyes seemed to dance.

There was no way they could tell him he was wrong. There was no way they could tell him that their parents had died in one of the most painful ways possible. "Of course we have," George said, his own smile trembling. "Sam's a police officer. A Fighter, even!"

Kreig nodded sagely.

CHAPTER 9

LIGHT TOUCHED HIM

He knew they were lying about something. He just didn't know *what*. He hadn't recognized them at first, and he still didn't. Their names and faces didn't ring any bells, but he hadn't expected them to. The girl was younger than the boy, her hair a stunning red while the boy had hair as black as Kreig's own. Going merely by facial structure and mannerisms, Kreig could accept that these two were his siblings.

Seeing them set his heart aflight and alight. After all, there they were! In the flesh! His family, alive and well, and they weren't even *trying* to run!

Of course, had they tried to run without giving an appropriate reason why, he might very well have had to run after them. They were all he had. Though if they said they wanted to leave, he would waste no time in opening a hole for them—or any other kind of exit. He knew in his heart that he should have been more cautious. Deciding right off the bat that these people were to be trusted and that he would protect them with his life was foolish. But his faith *did* dictate the importance of family.

Therefore, he happily forgot all possible questions and devoted himself to these two, in body and in soul. The moment they introduced themselves and the moment he heard their voices, he was happy. Happier than he'd been in too many years.

And now something was off. He wasn't using any skills, although he did have lie-detecting ones, but even then, he could tell that something was being withheld from him.

Though since it was his *family*, it was okay! He'd trust their judgement.

"An officer. I was a peacekeeper myself, once," Kreig said in reply. His sister—a police officer. To think she'd walk in his footsteps. He'd almost feel honored if his memories of being an officer weren't so muddled.

Sam perked up at the mention. "Huh? You were? Wait—what? When!?"

"In the Empire. I had a career of thirty-three years." As much as he hated to admit it, his memories were not only fringed at the edges and stained with hatred but also colored in a vague tint of nostalgia. Despite everything, it had felt good working for the Empire. Ordering his soldiers around and fighting in wars for reasons that went no further than the orders from his lord was a simple but luxurious lifestyle.

"Huh? Dude, seriously?" Sam's eyes were as wide as a starstruck kid's. "*Tch.* Guess you've already surpassed m— Wait— Dude, how old *are* you?!"

Unable to muster the ability to answer her, Kreig stared at her, hoping his silence would get her a little quiet, too. It worked. Her lips compressed into a pout while her—their—brother stepped closer to the window, opened his mouth to say something, and was cut off when Darius jerked so hard on his shoulder that he flew back and away from it.

"Keep five feet away from the window at all times," he said, and George seemed so perfectly taken aback by this that he froze in Darius's grasp. All the while, Kreig tried to understand what had just happened.

". . . Yes, sir," George said, which made Darius let go of him. "Erm, what I was going to say was—"

"Five feet away?" What a fantastic reminder of his old days in prison. Of course, beneath the Empire, down in that sealed room, the distance had been five *hundred* feet rather than five. But before that, before he became a soldier of the Empire, people indeed had to stand five feet from his cell.

Both Sam and George seemed deeply uncomfortable with the straight-forward confrontation. "It's just for security. Or something," George said, trying to console Kreig.

But Kreig was curious. "What else?" He could remember the ones he'd had before almost too clearly. *Don't feed the prisoner. Don't give the prisoner anything. Don't tell the prisoner any news of the outside world.* He wasn't malicious in wanting to know this, merely curious.

"I—Kreig, are you— Darius, we're not allowed to . . . Are we? I don't . . ." George seemed deeply conflicted about the whole thing. Despite the pleading looks he gave Darius, the man responded only by shrugging. As long as they didn't outright breach any of the rules, they were allowed to disclose them. "Um. Okay, uh . . . We're not to tell anybody you exist."

Kreig could understand that, to a certain point. Few people inside and outside the Empire knew where he went after his capture. It only made sense that they'd keep that same level of privacy here.

"And—and we shouldn't agitate you. Emotionally." Odder than the last, but Kreig could somewhat understand that as well. Despite what he liked to think at times, he could get emotional pretty quick. "Or cause any . . . any *grief.*"

Kreig furrowed his brows in thought, then glanced up from where he'd been sitting, meeting the wide-eyed gaze of George. "*Grief?*"

And from where Kreig sat, in his little room, looking at those four people on the other side of the glass window, he was given an excellent view of how all four paled significantly. The little frog-like man, who had previously brought his hands down, now raised them again. His hands trembled. Not good for casting magic or using spells. Sam, another Fighter by trade, thumbed for any sort of weapon to use. Her fear was a betrayal, but one that Kreig was ready to forgive at any time.

This was it. The thing they had denied him the displeasure of knowing. He could tell at a glance, and yet he hadn't meant to pry. He really hadn't. But now that the chest was laid open before him, could he really deny his curiosity?

He stood up. Looking down at them, he knew he could get his answers if he just pressed them a little. Grief this and grief that; he hadn't shed a tear since his years of youth. Whatever they told him, he'd keep it together, and in doing so, he'd prove that he was a brother they could trust. A brother who wouldn't require them to follow strict rules just to appease. He'd be calm, he'd be relaxed, and they wouldn't need to fear him as they did now.

Kreig stepped as close to the glass as he could get and bowed his head so that his eyes were still in the frame. The people in there cowered. "*Please tell.*"

George was only barely able to rip his eyes from Kreig, and once he did so, the person he looked at was Darius. His eyes spoke for him. *Is it all right if I tell him?* or *What happens if I do?* So many questions, none of which Darius could answer. For once, he, too, cowered. His silence urged George to speak. "That—that is . . . I was going to tell you, someday. Right now didn't feel like the right time, and I didn't want to upset you, so—" Stalling for time. ". . . You promise you won't get upset? Or—or do something strange?"

Kreig nodded, victory spreading through his mind like a drug. He knew George would crack. "Of course."

". . . Okay. Um. It . . . It happened the day after you disappeared. The same day all the portals first started appearing. The day started out normal. You remember, don't you? Well—that morning, when you and Sam left for school and I left for college . . . Mum and Dad left for work. And . . . and they just didn't return home. I'm sorry. I can't imagine how this must—"

Except he could. Many years ago, George had heard those very same words himself, and he'd taken them in stride. When all was said and done, the one who needed condolence wasn't himself but his sister. So, he'd taken his time to attend to her and made sure she knew he wasn't going anywhere. It relaxed her, made her happy, and let George focus on anything but his own emotions. Right now, he was watching himself from an outsider's perspective.

Kreig stood in there, his eyes white and snowy as he stared at a fixed point on the wall. It was impossible to tell if his breathing was quickening or slowing down.

He just stood there. "That isn't true," he said. "It isn't."

Sam bit her lip. "Look, Kreig, I'm *sorry*, but—"

Kreig took another step toward them, putting him so close to the window between them that his face and chest were pressed up against it. Then he took another, causing the three-inch-thick glass to whine and crack as he merely walked through it, the Dragonheart walls crumbling before his feet. He simply walked through the wall, as if it hadn't even been there at all. George gave a panicked shriek, a perfectly fitting response, while Sam and Frank prepared for some sort of physical confrontation. Darius wondered where'd he'd gone wrong and if he'd ever see his wife again.

A mere second, and the wall that separated the siblings had been torn down fully. A mere second, and Kreig had broken every promise he had made to them.

He stood in front of them, his overalls dusty with glass and metal.

Before even a single person in the room could react, he reached out and grabbed a firm hold of Frank's neck. The frog-man was effortlessly hoisted into the air, and as his mind and heart raced, trying desperately to figure out some sort of spell that could save him, Kreig eliminated the need for it by forcing eye contact with him.

Slumber (X)

Frank slumped over. If it hadn't been for his soft snoring, all members present would have assumed him dead.

"Inmate Wiedermann, what the hell did you do to him?!" Even then, a certain observer did need his answers. He was thoroughly ignored. Instead of answering the scientist, Kreig turned to his brother and sister and took a step toward them. He released his grip on Frank's windpipe, letting the small man clatter to the floor. At this moment, the fire of fight was extinguished in Sam's eyes. Her adrenaline could not override her terror, and any thoughts of trying to fight Kreig were gone.

Kreig stood before them. "It isn't true." The mere act of denial.

It wasn't because he missed his parents. It wasn't because he knew he would grieve them if he did remember them. No, in every sense of the world, it was a childish, selfish deed. When he had returned, when he had found out that his family lived, he assumed the best: that all his family members were safe and sound. After all, hadn't he earned it? It *had* been 130 years. It would've been unfair for him to lose people again when he had already lost everything.

Terribly unfair. So unfair that even a man of 147 would break down into a childish tantrum.

Sam shook like an aspen leaf. She was the strongest of the two, and yet, right now, she was weak. Utterly and completely incapable of whatever needed to be done to stop or quell the force before her.

As much as she hated to admit it, she had never been the adult of the family, always the little sister who cried big and dreamt big.

The one who always seemed to know what to say had been George. "... It's true, and I'm sorry, but there's nothing we can do anymore." But even his words could only move so many hearts. And even then, that was only the hearts that *wanted* to be moved. "You're acting up, and—and I don't know what you're trying to do at all, but it's true. It's true, and I'm sorry."

Kreig just stood there in front of them. So close, they felt suffocated. His large hands clenched and unclenched, and his stony face seemed pained with its own lack of expression.

He fell to his knees. ". . . It isn't true . . ." Now it was only a mumble. A weak, disbelieving mumble like an engine that burned up all its fuel. Pathetic, if it hadn't been him. Even on his knees, Kreig was still much larger than the two of them. Large and imposing and so, so small. He was tiny where he knelt. Tiny and childish and inconsolable.

George placed a hand on Kreig's shoulder. ". . . But at least you've got us, huh?"

Such simple words. Barely even a condolence. It shouldn't have had the effect that it did. It shouldn't have made him feel the way he did.

His mood flipped. Although a sorrow-filled frown was on the cusp of possessing his face, it changed. The sorrows he felt became a sort of joy for what he had. He didn't have his *entire* family, but he had *enough*. Enough to be happy, enough to forgive himself, enough to protect. Unwitting tears, carrying joys and sorrows of years past, pooled in his dark eyes. With the tears, they lit up. "You . . . Yes, I do have you. I . . ." A tear fell and he buckled over, going down on all fours, his long hair falling beside his face, obscuring his siblings from his view.

A pair of warm hands fell on his back. He tilted his face up. Now they were looking down at him. Now they were equal.

He stretched his right hand toward George, saw how the man flinched, and let his hand stall midair. But he didn't give up. ". . . May I touch you, brother?" George glanced at Sam, both of their faces filled with apprehension and uncertainty. Still, he nodded. Still, he approved of Kreig's touch. Kreig merely touched the hand and held it in his own. It was such a small hand, like the hand of a child. Naked and uncallused. He loved this hand. In his heart, he pledged an allegiance. The very same he had given his lord all those years ago. He still remembered the words.

My life is yours; my heart is yours. In my hand I grasp your life. In my soul I grasp your heart. May my sword never betray you. He released George's hand. "Sister?" Sam gave a shaky nod. Hers was more like his own. Muscular, hard, well worn by fighting and working. Not the hand of a girl; the hand of a woman. He repeated his unspoken words and released her hand.

In his heart, a contract had been signed. In his heart, he had accepted these two.

With his hands now freed, with his heart now filled with gratitude so deep and so extensive, he remained on the floor as his hands clasped together. "Thank God, thank God . . ." Tears streamed down his eyes anew. He leaned down, farther and farther, until his forehead tapped the floor, until he was bowed down before the Lord. He hadn't prayed since his escape from the last prison he'd been in. He didn't want to escape; that wasn't why he smiled. He simply knew that now, this very second, was when he needed to break his vow of silence.

"O, enduring Lord whose forgiveness permeates the worlds that believe . . ." The words flowed from his lips like nectar, true and old and never forgotten.

Shine of Divine Light (X)

It was a skill that had evolved from Prayer, a skill that only one man in both words could make use of. The earlier forms of the Prayer skill granted protection to nearby believing allies, and the more who joined in the prayer, the stronger the effect. Not a bad effect, and compared to the effect of the X rated skill Shine of Divine Light, it could be seen as more useful. After all, all that Shine of Divine Light did was allow the sun to shine upon the believer, no matter where they were, no matter what time of day it was. Entirely useless on a sunny day in a field.

But hundreds of feet beneath a prison inside a dark cell, the effects could be rather devastating.

As Kreig's hands remained clasped in prayer and words dropped carefully from his lips, a distant rumble could be heard. Crashing and crunching, and the whole room shook as something seemed to drill its way through the fifty-odd layers of rooms and metal and concrete above them. Somehow, all three conscious people there understood instinctually who the cause was. And still, they had no idea how to stop it, or even if they *should*.

All they knew was that the rumbling was getting closer. Shouts and screams began ringing out above them, too distant to truly make out but close enough to understand that it was coming close.

And then, finally, the room shook as though gripped by an immense earthquake. The framed portrait of Darius on the wall threatened to come loose, and half of the paintings in Kreig's cell fell from the wall and clattered to the floor, a final crash resounding through the whole room. The roof above Kreig gave in, cracking and crashing, dust flying everywhere as what had been a wall insulated with metal and steel framing became a hole.

Until the dust settled, not one person understood what had happened. And when it did, they were presented with the graceful visage of Kreig praying as lazy streams of sunlight tapped down on his broad shoulders.

Light touched him.

"Thank you, Lord. Amen." The prayer ended, and with it, as Kreig stood up, so did the light fade, replaced by silence. Not total silence, of course. Up above, various alarming sounds could be heard, such as dozens of people speaking in hurried tones. Finally, after a few seconds, an alarm went off, signaling that all able people should evacuate. The cause for the incident was unclear at the moment, but what they *did* know was that some manner of ability or skill had been used to plow a hole straight through the entire facility. Nobody had been harmed, but if this had been a conscious attack, there was no telling what could happen in the near future.

But the people in the lowest level knew better. They had seen what happened—they just didn't know how to react yet.

Kreig stood there, arms at his side, his face as stoic and stony as ever.

"Inmate Wiedermann . . . please return to your cell," Darius said, frowning deeply, clearly unsure if his words would actually be respected.

For a moment, they weren't. Kreig stood there, still dwarfing his siblings. He looked down at them, they looked up at him. ". . . May I touch you once more? Only once." They turned to Darius. His face was dark and he was clearly upset. Arms crossed, he tapped his foot. But his rage at *them* was entirely unfounded and he knew it. They hadn't done anything. Their way of handling the situation had been lackluster, and he had expected them to handle it with more tact. It wouldn't have been his place to inform Wiedermann of his parents' passing, but with this . . . Part of the fault lay on him. He waved his hand, giving them the go-ahead.

George and Sam turned to Kreig. "Yeah," George said.

Kreig reached his arms toward the both of them, hesitated, and then carefully pulled them into his arms. A hug, to signal the closing of this act. A hug, to signal the beginning of their relationship. He held them close, he held them as softly and gently as he could, and until they hesitantly returned the embrace, he did not release them.

While in his arms, George spoke a few words. "If you . . . no, *when* you get out of here, know that you can always find a soft bed and a warm meal in our home. Yeah?"

Kreig released them, looked at them both once, gave a smile, thanked them for visiting him, assured them that he would come to visit, and wandered back into his cell. He sat down at his desk and continued drawing.

Before Darius could say anything, the door was thrown open with a bang, revealing Craig and his whole posse of Fighters and guards. "Sir, we need to evacuate! There's been a breach! Is everyone all right here? I've got a—" His words came to a halt as his eyes fell on the tumultuous situation inside. Frank was in the corner, snoring as if everything was all right, and the wall between the observation room and the cell was busted—suspiciously enough in the shape of a man. And the roof was smashed too. Just a small part of it, yes, but when Craig walked inside and looked up, he was given a beautiful cut-through view of the facility, including a fair few heads, some looking up, others looking down. All in a state of shock and disarray.

Interesting additions included a man still sitting in the bathroom despite it all, an old man wearing headphones with his back to the hole (still diggin' it) and a prisoner almost at the very top, clearly considering the idea of jumping into it to escape. Though since the hole was several hundreds of feet deep, jumping really wouldn't do him any favors.

Craig was given a nice view of it all, including how Darius, his frown lines more apparent than ever, shooed the two siblings out of the room.

This was the worst day of Darius's life. This incident wasn't as bad as it could have been, but it was bad enough. The words of his superiors echoed dully in his head: "*If Inmate Kreig Wiedermann causes an incident, it's your neck on the line.*" And there he was. There was a hole in the middle of Other Island, and the wall between the observation room and the cell was completely busted. He'd never hear the end of it, if he wasn't just fired on the spot. The only positive he could think of at the time was that Kreig wasn't showing any intentions of fleeing and his relationship with the Wiedermann siblings had improved.

"The very same helicopter that brought you here will soon see you off. I'll keep in touch with you, assuming I remain on the observation team." Darius sighed as he removed them from the observation room. The alarms were still blaring to high hell, with the red lights flaring against his retinas.

"Dr. Darius, will we—will we be allowed to meet him again? Y'know, as family and stuff?" Sam asked, her eyes awkwardly hopeful.

Darius shrugged. But as he looked at them and saw their childish hope, he remembered something. He reached inside his jacket, recovering two sealed letters. "...I almost forgot. Forgive me. We were unable to mail them, due to the secretive matters of Inmate Wiedermann's existence. Please, once you've read them, destroy them by fire. Make sure that no trace remains. Unless you can promise me this, I will withhold them both."

The siblings shared a glance. "We promise to destroy them."

Darius nodded. "Good. The first was written closely following his initial incarceration, and the second was written a week or so later. Please read them thoroughly." He gave them the letters, they accepted them, and then they left.

The two siblings briefly considered opening them immediately. Curiosity gnawed at them like rabid dogs, but they agreed to save it for when they got home. They hated leaving that whole mess for Darius to clean up, but they had no choice. They really didn't. Neither of them had a rank anywhere high enough to get involved in that. All they could do was sit and stew over what they just experienced. Their brother was back, and boy, was he in a whole mess of trouble.

The implication of his existence to the world as a whole was just not something either of them wanted to think about. And their role in it, to boot? It was too much to think about, and so they decided to not even try it.

That was until they got home. The time was 11:53 p.m. They were dog-tired, but they knew that there would come no better time to read the letters. Knowing Kreig, they couldn't be all that long. Kreig wasn't very talkative back down there, so they doubted he'd be any wordier on paper.

They were wrong, but that wasn't the first thing they noticed.

The first thing they noticed was a childlike doodle of five people. A mother and a father and three kids. All smiling and holding hands. Then the letter.

It would be a lie to say that neither George nor Sam shed a tear that night. The first letter was grave. Every word contained so many unsaid sorrows. It cut them deep and it begged for forgiveness all at the same time. So much was left unsaid. Everything was all right there, everything that nobody had told them. He was a soldier. He was a believer in a religion. He was a human, and he knew that he had done wrong, yet he would not tell them what.

They reluctantly burned it before they read the second one.

The second letter was far briefer, more of a quick update than an explanation of his entire state. And, as the beginning of the letter said, the back of it did include a self-portrait. It was almost completely identical to the man they had met before. The only detail that changed was his eyes. The eyes of the man they had personally met were almost completely empty, void of emotion and thought. These eyes, the ones they saw in the portrait . . . they were honest and showed his character in truth—as it was, not how it looked. He was laid bare before them.

The actual letter was only hard to read in that it detailed his loneliness and exhaustion. As it was, neither Sam nor George could help him with that, although, after all they had seen and felt . . . Suddenly, they really wanted to help him.

Even if it meant allowing his abode in their own home.

CHAPTER 10

RED SKIES AND MUD

nd so, due to breaking not only the wall and large parts of the prison but also a promise not to cause an incident, the board has decided to penalize Inmate Wiedermann with isolation for a week and no longer. Should you choose to verbally or physically oppose this, the penalty will be far harsher than mere isolation." So spoke the voice over the speakers.

Isolation.

Kreig did not fight it, of course. He just sort of sat there all day while a number of confused but silent construction workers fixed his wall and a few Fighters—including that little one that'd been there during his meeting with his family—stood around staring at him, thumbing their weapons. The little one in the robe seemed upset but wouldn't outright say anything.

He had a rather high level, though; Kreig had to admit that. The wall was, by the magic of great hurry, finished in a mere day.

And then his isolation began. It started out okay. Kreig sat and drew, painted portraits of his two new subjects, his brother and sister, and tried to make the most of the situation. But it didn't go well for long. Two days went by. He grew unhappy. After having had the pleasure of human connection for entire days at a time—after tasting such sweet nectar after years of abstinence—he now found himself in withdrawal.

He sat there, genuinely considering the pros and cons of breaking out to speak to Gerald or his siblings, when there was a sudden change in plans. It was the fourth day of his isolation.

The speakers came on. The voice that spoke was neither the head observer nor the usual speaker. This voice was more refined, with a slight accent that Kreig couldn't place. *"Inmate Wiedermann. A situation has occurred. You will soon be escorted to the site of a disaster. Follow the directives of the authorities present, and the terms of your incarceration may change. Prepare yourself."*

Brief, strong-worded, and with no room for any sort of objection, not that Kreig had any. He just sat up straighter. He knew the tinge to those words. Something was going on, and he wasn't about to mess up again. Not when he was so close to the finish line.

Strangely, the sound of the human voice made him feel bubbly. The idea of meeting people again, well, it downright made him happy. And he couldn't tell why.

As per the voice, within mere seconds, the Dragonheart door slid open, revealing three people at the forefront of a train of Fighters and guards. At the front of these stood a sharp-eyed woman wearing a navy suit and matching cap. She exuded authority. As Kreig watched her, slightly dazed, she spoke to others behind her. These people were neither Fighters nor guards but military in uniform and movement. They strode inside the cell with confident movements, surrounding Kreig in an instant.

Human, Lv. 637

Human, Lv. 42

Human, Lv. 345

"Cuff him," the woman said smoothly. The soldiers around Kreig nodded and dressed him in the collar and metal mittens quicker than Craig ever had. Then, with another order from the woman, he was led outside. While walking through the hallway, silent as he usually was, he was generously given some information on what in the world was happening.

"The reports on your silence seem to have been accurate. As this is our first meeting, I will introduce myself. I am General Swansong. Do not fear; you do not need to introduce yourself to me. I know who you are. Regardless, as we do not have much time, I will try to keep this brief. The nearby city of Petuniaria is currently under attack from a wyrm that escaped from a portal within the city limits. There is no one who can handle it but you, and so your brief isolation has been withdrawn for the moment.

"Its level is around seven hundred, according to several Fighters at the scene. We were lucky to receive what little information we have. It has made no attempt to flee the city. Sadly, as there is little we know about wyrms, we can tell you very little about its powers and strength. According to the reports I've seen, you should be able to make do regardless. Ordinarily, even if Frank Groda himself were to enter the battlefield, he would receive backup in some form, but since this wyrm is powerful enough to make mincemeat out of pretty much anyone apart from you, we can only afford to borrow you, Craig, and Frank. We would love to grant you your armor and weapons, but it would cost us far too much in time and lives."

... A wyrm. And level 700, too?

And Kreig was the only person available to defeat it? Kreig was a seasoned monster-killer. He could understand why a wyrm would pose such a problem. Though, of course, he hadn't expected one to come there.

He had no objections, and the general didn't speak any other words of warning, likely since she didn't have any. They continued walking, and not even Craig or Frank said anything. Usually, Kreig welcomed such silence. But now it felt wrong. There were people all around him, and yet their silence was suffocating. Wrong. Still, it wasn't his place to speak. Their silence was his.

The walk through the prison ended sooner than usual, and when they stepped into the courtyard where a helicopter sat, Kreig was met with a familiar face. Someone who was also cuffed. Someone who shouldn't be there.

"Huh? Kreig? Is that you?" Gerald asked, his face lighting up in a smile when he understood that it was, in fact, Kreig. *"It is you! Greetings, my friend. Do you know what is happening?"*

The soldiers at Gerald's side kept him from walking any closer to Kreig. Kreig did, in fact, know what was happening, but he didn't feel like telling Gerald. Instead, he turned to the general, giving her a disbelieving stare. She gave him a placating gesture. "Do not worry; he will not be forced into combat. He has only been brought along for your sake. Dr. Falk expressed a strong belief that despite your immense improvements, you may still need some form of anchor in case something were to happen. Craig had assured me that he would fit well for such a role, but one can never have too many. Of course, once we get there, he will be as well protected as any king."

Craig frowned. "Hey, that guy loves me, I'm sure! I think?"

Kreig suppressed the need to lecture Craig. Either way, he supposed the general was correct. And it *did* feel nice to see Gerald again. As for his protection, if the general couldn't keep him safe, then Kreig sure would.

Kreig would have loved to explain things to the still-confused Gerald, but time was scant and they had to get going. They all entered the helicopter. Frank and Craig sat on either side of him, while the general sat in front of him. Gerald sat farther down, surrounded by soldiers yet again.

This time, the flight was quick. The helicopter reached max speed within seconds, at which point it went too fast for Kreig to be able to understand exactly what was going on outside. Then, sooner than he thought, land came into view. Land, and a city.

Smoke billowed from various parts of it in generous amounts, alongside sirens and broadcasted urgent messages and the screams of people whose lives were about to be lost. Kreig heard it all, but he smelled it even more. As they landed, the smell assaulted his nostrils with fearful claws. Concrete and choking black smoke and gasoline and exposed wires and blood. The smell of slaughter. Even more so, biting acid, slick scales, and the murmuring hiss of a wyrm run amok.

Wyrms usually lived in marshes and swamps, where they ate pretty much anything they came across. Once they got a meal, be it a swamp biter or a dragger, it would attack immediately, taking its time to digest the whole thing. That meal would feed the wyrm for several weeks, if not months. If a wyrm found two meals, it was in luck and it would eat twice. That's the thing about wyrms. It didn't have any internal sign of when it had eaten enough. So, when it found a lot of prey, it kept eating.

If it stumbled across a village, it wouldn't stop eating until it had been killed or its stomach burst from overeating. That is, if it wasn't too big for that.

This wyrm was big enough to eat several villages over and over again. It was dark green, with purple around the eyes. An adult, overfed as an adolescent. An adult, still hungry.

Kreig saw it coming around the side of a building. It crushed a car beneath its bloated, scaly stomach, lighter in color than the scales on its back. A thick, forked tongue flicked out of its closed mouth and hovered in the air for a bit before darting back inside. The wyrm turned toward them where they stood beside the recently parked helicopter. Frank prepared a spell or skill; Craig raised his spear. The general barked an order at a few soldiers, and they moved to surround Gerald, who had now gone from confused to afraid.

It was up to Kreig to react. They had tried to hand him a few weapons in the helicopter, but Kreig knew from a single glance that none of them would be of any help to him. Not with a wyrm like this. And so, he had refused, leaving him both weapon- and armor-less. But that was all right.

He wouldn't need any of it for this battle. A wyrm would prove no more difficult for him than a young dragon. And still, he hesitated.

Something there felt off. As he looked into the eyes of the wyrm, those eyes still frenzied with the blood and flesh of countless humans, he found them somewhat intelligent. Far more intelligent than any reptile he'd ever seen. Reptiles were not intelligent. Dragons were only as intelligent as the stupidest humans available, and drakes weren't even worth mentioning. But this creature felt different. Something was off about it. It didn't attack immediately.

It stood there, half-exposed, staring at Kreig, sizing him up as if it knew his strength. And then, it turned around and slithered off in the other direction, leaving Kreig to stare at its leaving form.

"Quickly, follow it!" the general cried, pointing at the wyrm's tail. Kreig turned to her and silently showed off his metal mittens. "Don't worry about it; we've got plenty. Just be quick, please." She was right, but Kreig didn't want to ruin them. Though fighting without hands was . . . Even to Kreig, that might be a little difficult. Carefully, he pulled out one of his hands, feeling how the metal inside the glove groaned and snapped. With one hand out, he removed the other and handed the mittens to a nearby soldier. Freedom.

He stepped toward where the wyrm was going. "Please try not to destroy it completely, as we may still be able to save those trapped within!" the general appealed. "Frank, Craig, please assist him as best you can."

Frank and Craig nodded and prepared to follow Kreig. He guessed he wouldn't be alone. Not that he minded much. He continued walking.

Wyrms could be very fast, but that was in muddy marshes. On dry land, their numerous flippers and their paddle-like twin tails were just baggage. And yet this one was rather fast. Level 700. An elder wyrm, likely older than even Kreig. But not old enough to gain intelligence. No lizard could do that.

Something was off about this wyrm, and Kreig was interested in knowing *what.*

He found it wrapped around what he could vaguely remember to be a gas station. Slight movements easily caused the walls and windows to crack and creak, but the wyrm only had eyes for Kreig. Kreig, in turn, only had eyes for the wyrm.

Fighting. Again. After all this time. He'd gotten a month or so of rest, and now he was back at it again.

It felt wrong. He didn't want to be there, and he didn't want to save anyone. At the moment, he just wanted to go back to his cell—back to playing cards and painting and that easy life he'd always longed for. When he was first summoned, this wouldn't have been the sort of life he wanted, but at the moment, he couldn't imagine anything better than warm food and a roof over his head.

Neither of which he had at this moment. All he had were two weaklings at his side and a weird-acting wyrm in front of him. If he wasn't curious about what was wrong with the wyrm, if this wasn't his best chance of regaining his socialization privileges, he might not have cared enough to so much as raise a finger.

But that wasn't the case. He took a step toward the wyrm. He wouldn't kill it quickly, and he wouldn't kill it mercifully. It had things to tell him, after all.

Its eyes were locked on to him. They were dazzling, swirling pools of stars. Then its mouth opened wide. It had many small teeth angled toward the throat, made for pulling in prey rather than injecting venom, but Kreig knew very well that it was not about to lunge at them. Several holes, barely visible to the untrained eye, flexed inside its throat, opening up as the wyrm coiled.

Kreig took a deep breath. He wasn't relaxing anymore. No more taking it easy, no more casual chitchat. Emotion drained from his mind like happy, warm sludge. He raised his arms and fell into a posture. The world melted away, the dawn sky replaced with a bloody red, the pavement and concrete buildings crumbling to reveal mud and ash and too many bodies to count. He had no weapons, he had no armor, but he didn't need them.

The wyrm gave an immense hiss as its body convulsed and a stream of black, acidic goo shot out of its mouth, aimed precisely at Kreig. In turn, he took a broad-legged stance and crossed his arms in front of himself.

Protect (X)

The concentrated stream of corrosive liquid splattered in an arch around Kreig, not even touching his skin. Everything went slowly. When the acid hit the area around Kreig, it proved its strength, quickly melting everything it touched into a fizzy black mess. Was he hallucinating, or could he faintly hear voices, distantly behind him? No, he couldn't hear it. He couldn't hear anything at all, except for the sound of battle and the stream letting up. As the wyrm's acid let up for a mere second, Kreig bolted at it.

In terms of his own personal merits, Kreig was not a fast man. His power came from his many skills, his physical strength, and his endurance. Speed and intelligence were not his strong suits, but compared to a regular human?

He moved too fast to see.

The world seemed to bend under his momentous will, and in a mere moment, he stood before the wyrm, his bare hands clenching each side of its enormous head. Then, as easily as a knife slips into a pumpkin, he thrust both hands into the snout of the beast, through the thick scales and the skin and the bone. It tried to jerk away—tried to escape—but he wouldn't let it. He shoved both hands into the dry, empty hole he created, and with a mighty jerk, he cracked it open, revealing all its secrets to the world.

It had no blood. It had no flesh, either. Both of these important things were replaced fully by white wire-like roots, crawling and nesting around its bones like the mycorrhiza of a fungus. As Kreig cracked open the wyrm's skull fully, he found a somewhat similar but equally alarming situation. The light-green squishy brain was still there, but large parts had either been gouged out, absorbed by the white roots or simply shrunk. If Kreig touched the shrunken parts, he found that they had gone hard. White roots spread over and inside it like a spider web, snaking into the furrows and the gyri. The brain was overrun with white roots.

And Kreig had no idea what it meant. Just that it wasn't a good thing.

No, that wasn't entirely true. He had seen something similar in someone much closer than he'd like. In *himself.*

Aetherial Knife (III)

Kreig held out his hand and was rewarded with a semi-translucent but clearly strong knife. He balanced it in his hand for a second before turning the blade to the back of his arm and giving a swipe. For the first time in over thirty years, he was harmed more than skin-deep.

A deep red gash was opened up, blood pooling out of the wound as it should. But inside the wound, a bit hard to see beneath the blood but still clearly visible, a system of white roots coiled. They snaked around his bones and webbed across his muscles. Like an extra system of veins, they were the white roots that his holy order was named after. The white roots that granted him his strength.

The white roots that seemed to have completely overtaken the wyrm, in body and soul. Something was very wrong.

With the flex of Kreig's hand, the Aetherial Knife was crushed, breaking into what seemed like glass shards. Although Kreig was a man of curiosity, at the moment, he found no issue with completely destroying the body, beginning with crushing the skull and brain with a single stomp. Unlike what the general might have wished, there would be neither survivors nor recognizable bodies in there. This would be his mercy.

Then, while the distant and mumbling voices seemed to come closer, he burned the body using Purge of the Holy. In a matter of seconds, the body and the white roots infesting it had transformed into white snow.

And he was still in wonderland. Blood and mud and red skies. His enemy was dead, but he remained.

Breathing. In and out. In and out. The red skies swirled above, but their speed was slowing, and they were turning lighter in color, disappearing, slowly, slowly . . .

When a hand suddenly touched his shoulder and he instinctively attacked it.

There was nothing behind him, nothing for his fist to connect to. Just more mud and blood. His chest heaved. Up and down. In and out. Where the hell was he? Why was he alone? He shouldn't be alone. Not on the battlefield. He had to fight something, *anything*. And *now*. Fight fight fight. He had to fight. Otherwise, he died. Otherwise, every single person that had died so that he could live would have died in vain. Otherwise, he was a failure.

His breathing grew quick. The mud beneath his feet swirled in time with the deep red skies. Clouds and dust and a mist of death. All around him, everywhere, all that existed in that place, all that *could* exist, were enemies. Enemies, and fights, and—

"*Kreig?*"

He was small. Young. Dirty blond hair and a childishness that should never have been placed on the battlefield. Kreig released a hissing breath. "*Gerald.*"

The boy stood there, alone, up to his ankles in mud and corpses. His eyes were bright and confused and—and couldn't he see everything that was going on? Why was he there? He shouldn't be on the battlefield. Allies shouldn't stand before Kreig. If they did, they wouldn't stand for long. It was the wrong place. "*Go away.*" Although Kreig's voice was hoarse, although his every breath seemed to choke on the heavy air around him, he spoke. For Gerald's sake.

"*Huh? Why should—I'm sorry, you don't seem fine. Has the battle been long? Have you—*"

"*LEAVE!*" Kreig bellowed, taking heavy steps toward his only friend. He had to get him out of there. Gerald couldn't be there. What if an army attacked? What if bad people invaded? What if—

And all of a sudden, Gerald wasn't dressed in his overalls and his vaguely hopeful expression. He was wearing light armor. Light armor and the red cloth of the Empire, and his eyes were so big and not like a child's. "*K—Kreig . . .*"

Kreig stumbled back. The Empire? There? Now? Attacking him with a mere single soldier? Hah! They must be assured of their victory! Very well, if they were to ask him for it, if they begged him to show his power, then—in the name of the White Pope—he would! By God, he would! This soldier would—

Something touched him.

Kreig looked down and found a boy, barely of age, wrapped around his midsection. Gerald looked up. Their eyes met.

The mania was banished, the red skies expelled, the mud and blood were gone. Replaced with asphalt and blue skies and a deep, all-consuming sense of dread and shame.

"*You okay, Kreig?*" Gerald asked, disconnecting himself.

Kreig nodded, but he didn't feel okay. Not at all.

Not in the least.

The general seemed mostly happy with the situation, although for some reason, Craig appeared a bit upset. He was off in the corner, clutching at his arm, hissing curses between ragged breaths. Gerald helpfully informed Kreig that when Craig confidently approached him after he defeated the wyrm, Kreig had wasted no time in attacking him, though the punch had missed. Even then, despite missing by several inches, the air from the blow had been enough to completely shatter Craig's arm.

Somehow, Kreig couldn't muster any pity for him.

General sighs of relief could be heard from around as people relaxed. Not everyone had evacuated, and these few civilians could now be heard laughing and crying, hugging in relief. It was a lovely, human scene of joy, and yet Kreig couldn't bring himself to enjoy it. He could remember in his early days as the captain of the royal guard, when defeating a dangerous foe and bringing back its head could rouse equally immense emotions in civilians, and he used to enjoy it as much as the battle itself.

Gratitude. Now he felt none.

The general had been upset at first over the destruction of the wyrm's body, but a quick lesson in wyrm anatomy and eating habits changed her mind. Still, she was quite happy with the resolution, expressing how without his help, they would surely have had to abandon the city.

Kreig couldn't bring himself to care. To him, it was just another job. He was led back to the helicopter without any further ado, where he was strapped in beside Frank, though Craig had mysteriously disappeared.

Things got strange once they returned to the Other Island. For the first time, Kreig saw Darius in the meager light of the sun and not on the other side of the window, either. He stood there, arms folded behind his back, a lab geek on each side. Awaiting Kreig's return. Until he stepped out of the helicopter, he didn't know why.

Darius gave a rare, out-of-character smile. "Kreig! General Swansong. You return as heroes, do you?" Something felt off, but Kreig couldn't understand what. Then Darius's eyes fell on Gerald where he stood, escorted by soldiers in a pair of cuffs. "What in the— General, is there a reason for this innocent child to be in cuffs?"

"Huh?" The general blinked dumbly. "He's— Well, Doctor, by all means, it is only protocol. I didn't write it, so . . ."

Darius grinned mischievously. "I'm only pulling your leg, General. After all, I have quite the news." Turning to Gerald, Darius once more flashed an unusual, fond smile and began to speak in German. "*Inmate Speerhalter, I am happy to inform you that, from here on out, you will no longer be considered a prisoner.*"

Gerald seemed far from happy, more so confused. "*M—me?*"

Darius stepped closer to him. "*Yes, youth. Worry not; your new life here on Earth will be provided to you generously by IOCRO, including housing and education. This is in no way for you alone, as we aim to extend this courtesy to all otherworlders below the age of eighteen. And—who knows? One day, we may just do the same for all of these other otherworlders. But until then, we will limit our attention to youngsters such as you. I trust there will be no problems with this arrangement?*"

Gerald shot a quick glance at Kreig. "*What about—*"

Bringing up a hand, Darius effortlessly quieted the younger boy. "*Do not worry about him. With this great achievement, I do not doubt that his days as a prisoner are numbered.*" His eyes grew warmer. "*Once you are both free, I hope that your friendship will continue to flourish. Now you have many new people to meet. Guards?*"

Gerald couldn't even argue as the cuffs on his hands were removed and he was brought inside, leaving Kreig immensely confused. So confused that he didn't even know how to react.

Not even when Darius turned to him and gave him that very same nothing-smile could he react. "I'm happy to say that depending on the board's reaction to this situation, you too may be released within the week. Please look forward to it."

But he couldn't. It all happened so suddenly, leaving Kreig needlessly dazed and overstimulated. In just a few minutes, he had lost his only friend there.

And nobody would tell him what the hell was going on.

"—That was how the situation played out, sir."

One of the dozen board members sitting at the long desk nodded, a smirk tugging at his wrinkled lips. "Is that so? Well done, General Swansong. You have done us a great service. Dismissed."

"Yes, sir," General Swansong replied, respectfully saluting before leaving the room.

All members present, each and every one of the uppermost rank, turned to one of the three leaders of IOCRO. This man was Sir Reiker. The man who had decided to hold out on putting Kreig in a combat situation until Dr. Falk had completely endorsed it. The man who had only now, in the face of such a disaster, decided to go through with it. This was the man who now spoke. "I sincerely hope that there is not a single person here under the impression that we did not dodge a bullet the size of the moon this very hour. Had Dr. Falk not so wisely suggested that Inmate Speerhalter be brought along as a final resort, we may very well have been as burnt as the coffee around here."

A subdued round of chuckles spread across the table until a single man at the edge of the table interrupted them. "Excuse me, sir," Darius said carefully. "But as his status as a prisoner has been revoked; it would be best to refer to him only as Gerald Speerhalter henceforth."

Really, Darius had no place among these men, but as Wiedermann's head observer and a qualified psychologist, his presence was widely accepted. Reiker looked him up and down before finally nodding. "Quite right, Doctor. Forgive the slip of the tongue."

"Don't worry about it." A short pause passed and Darius decided to speak again. "Then, sir, you agree that it would be best to avoid his usage in any form of fighting? If you will allow me to express my own beliefs, I cannot see a similar encounter playing out any better than this one. In fact, knowing Kreig's mental state, it could very well work to destroy previous progress."

"Of course, there is no doubt about that. Should Kreig Wiedermann's mental state degenerate for any reason, his status may need to be changed from 'Dormant Threat Grade X' to 'Active Threat Grade X'. In fact, should he so much as mention a wish to become a Fighter or do anything of the sort, you will personally shut this down. This is one of the many reasons we have agreed to your proposition of acting as Kreig Wiedermann's psychotherapist during his release and return to society. Is that clear, Dr. Falk?"

"Yes. I'm grateful, sir," Darius replied.

"Furthermore, in accordance with your recommendations, we have decided that Kreig Wiedermann is to be released in two days. His isolation will continue during these days. Covertly find reasons to use the speakers when possible. Tomorrow evening, you will explain his situation and how he is to be treated and what benefits he will be granted. Gain his trust and continue to refer to him by his first name," Reiker said. "You are hereby dismissed."

"Thank you, sir," Darius said as he stood up, leaving the room without any wait. He'd gotten what he wanted, and he was ecstatic. Not only had his petition to release Wiedermann sooner rather than later been accepted, but his idea of having himself act as Wiedermann's psychiatrist had also gone through as well.

The reasons he gave for it had been manipulative and selfish in nature. *"If Wiedermann can open up to me, I will be able to better understand the state of his mind and what missions he is able to fulfill. I can keep an eye on him at all times. He'll trust IOCRO better."*

But his true intentions were far less focused on the good of the world and more so on improving Wiedermann's own psychic health. Sure, his siblings and the Speerhalter boy—who would otherwise find education and housing in the same city Wiedermann would live in—would do plenty and be a great help for his personal improvements. But in the end, they knew next to nothing about how to actually care for him. Darius himself was no wiser, but he at least knew better how to care for a man experiencing PTSD and other trauma- and stressor-related mental disorders.

To him, it was an act of personal kindness to help Wiedermann. To IOCRO, it was an act of international disaster prevention.

It wasn't just about making sure Kreig didn't become an active threat. It was also about preventing any future disasters by possibly using him as a Fighter. If he could become psychologically stable enough to fight monsters without having relapses, then they no longer had anything to fear from the otherworld. It was an incredibly objective and inhuman way of viewing Kreig and his personal life, but they had all the right reasons to do so.

It was a thin line to tread, but they threaded it well.

And now it was time to prepare for Wiedermann's release.

PART II

RETURNING TO NORMALCY

CHAPTER 11

WHERE HE BELONGED

Darius appeared inside Kreig's cell the day after he was told he might get released soon. And even after a whole day of isolation, left with his own thoughts, he still couldn't make sense of the situation, much less find it in himself to get excited about his release. What was he supposed to do, smile? Preposterous.

Somehow, Darius seemed happier than Kreig felt, although he had thankfully wiped that odd smile off of his face. Despite the fact that Kreig hadn't seen Darius's face too often, he knew instinctively that the man was just not supposed to smile. At all. "Is there any good reason for you to lack a smile in times such as these? Your release is imminent!"

Kreig merely stared at him, too suspicious to fully understand what the man was saying.

"Very well. I've come to discuss the matters of your release in detail. If anything is unclear, please tell me. Furthermore, nod to prove that you both hear and understand me." Kreig nodded. "Yes, just like that. Now, first and foremost, on account of your conversation with your family, it is expected that you should live with them. Despite this, IOCRO will not only pay you monthly benefits to cover any unexpected situations, you are also encouraged to attempt to find and sustain a job. We do wish for you to reintegrate into society, after all.

"This job will have to be part-time, however. Since you never did graduate from high school, you will be assigned a tutor to teach you during the daytime until you qualify for a diploma. After earning it, you will be free to seek higher-level education, should you feel the desire to do so. If you need or require anything, you will be able to contact the organization through me. I will act as your psychiatrist. A list of times will be given to you. Should you want to change any of the times we meet, I will be as flexible as possible."

Spoken fully seriously. Kreig nodded. Uh-huh. Made sense. Not that he actually understood any. He'd gladly live with his family. The closer he was to them, the better he could protect them.

Getting a job? It had sure been a while since he had one of those, though he wouldn't hate it. And a psychiatrist? Although he really had no idea what that would mean for him, he was sure it'd be fine.

The only part he dreaded was the tutoring. Unlike what one might expect from a warrior such as him, he *had*, at one point, been expected to learn to read and spell and do algebra. His lord had gotten him a tutor. He had almost slain the scholar in a fit of rage after the scholar told him, in the most pompous words that the German language had to offer, that Kreig would never understand even the most basic forms of calculus. Anybody could understand Kreig's righteous fury, and ever since, Kreig had insisted on not touching books or smart people ever again.

He had almost forgotten that school existed back here. He knew immediately that he wanted nothing to do with it.

"No tutoring." Soft words spoken by a very large man.

". . . Is that so?" Darius asked. His eyes narrowed. "Is there any way I could change your mind?" Kreig didn't answer. "We cannot force you; however, should you choose not to finish your high-school diploma, which will surely take less than a year, you may find yourself unable to keep any job worth having. Through our help you may be able to keep one as a gas-station attendant; however, that is not something you will want to keep at forever." Once again, Kreig didn't answer. ". . . Consider it a favor to me. You may choose to drop the tutoring completely if you'd like, but I won't let you do it before trying it for at least a week or so."

Kreig glanced at him. He thought it over for a second.

Everything else on Earth had been ten times better than anything in the otherworld. He'd been treated better, slept in a better bed, and generally had a better time.

Still, being tutored didn't sit well with him. And yet . . . Kreig glanced over at his observer. All right. It was a favor to Darius. He'd *try* it, but no further.

He gave a nod, and Darius sighed. "Great. All right. We'll have whichever paintings and pictures you'd like to bring packed and mailed to the

Wiedermann household. You'll be provided with a map guiding you to your new place of residence along with a paper containing the phone number, address and email of Gerald Speerhalter." Darius stood up. "And, finally, I recommend you get some sleep before all of this happens. Here, we have some— Fighter Craig! The clothes!"

Who would have guessed? In the doorway, poking his head out cautiously, was none other than Craig. His arm was no longer bandaged, meaning that he had no issues with carrying a bundle of folded clothes. Though that didn't stop him from squinting suspiciously at Kreig, who in turn became even more confused.

"The clothes, please," Darius repeated forcefully.

Craig entered the room, put the clothes on the bed, glared at Kreig, and left. Kreig could only barely catch the way Darius bristled and mumbled, "This guy . . ." Then Darius put one hand on the pile of clothes. "Here. Clothes. We may not be too heavily funded at the moment, but we have enough to provide you with a change of clothes. If you are unhappy with them, you can buy new clothes with your siblings. Think of it as a bonding moment. After tomorrow . . . you'll be free. Free to do as you please, free to buy what you can. Until then, I'm happy to have been your head observer, Kreig. Change whenever you wish to."

And then he left. Kreig could only barely catch Darius scolding Craig out in the hall for acting badly. Kreig waited a few moments before standing up and walking over to his bed.

Tomorrow. That's when they'd release him and give him everything he needed to live a normal life. He'd get a job, and a place to stay, and normal clothes, and . . . And, by God, he was ready to cry all over again. He was thankful, Lord, yes, but he knew that if he clasped his hands in prayer, he'd make a mess again. He was happy, but he couldn't show it. These people . . . Although they acted strangely sometimes and although they had forced him to battle again, they had been kind to him. Kinder than anyone had in many years.

It was late. Kreig decided to heed Darius's wise words and sleep. No dreams. Just a general, ever-present feeling of exhilaration as the concept of freedom washed over him. Like flying without the visuals.

Freedom. What a concept. And soon, he'd grasp it in his hand, and everything would be all right.

. . . Assuming he didn't make a mess or anything. That'd be a great pity.

When he woke up a few hours later, the very first thing he did was undress. There was no shame. He knew people could see him who were just beyond the mirror, but he had long forgotten about such embarrassment.

His only real issue was with the clothes themselves. They all had this bland black-and-gray that Kreig could vaguely remember was supposed to be expensive. Didn't only nobles of some certain lineage wear black? Or was it the royal family of the Tripusten Dynasty? He really couldn't remember. All he knew was that black was not only really expensive but also somewhat of a heathen color. Black mold. Unacceptable under the Holy Order.

Had he been the same man as he was five years before, he would have burned these clothes. Right now, though? Right now, he was touching them, feeling how comfortable they were, accepting that this was his new life. He wouldn't discard his religion, but he would accept a few minor differences. Such as this unusually colored garment.

At first, he tried to wear it as he would pants, but he quickly realized that the third hole was made for his neck, not his . . . Either way, in total, there was a shirt with the words *I <3 IOCRO* emblazoned across the chest, a pair of briefs and pants, socks, and a pair of shoes. That was it.

It was enough. Compared to his overalls, these clothes felt tighter—more compressed. But the fabrics were of higher-quality make and overall more comfortable.

He wore the outfit happily and gratefully.

Then, later that day, he was brought out of his cell, taken upstairs, put in a helicopter, and shipped off. No cuffs. No massive number of guards. Just him, Frank, the pilot, and a single soldier. Simple. Easy. Freeing.

The sky seemed very blue outside the helicopter. Kreig couldn't get enough of it. Breathing it in, drinking it all up. Getting drunk off of his new wings and the endless blue sky they promised. Freedom. No cuffs. No nothing. Just him and the sky and the eternal freeing breeze. He grew happier by the minute, and the cherry on top was his family. He'd get to live with them! Him and them!

He couldn't think of a more perfect situation in all of the world.

The helicopter touched down beside a very large, very oddly shaped building. He was guided through it by Frank, who still seemed a bit salty after last time. While his eyes wandered curiously over the interior, Frank helped him pick up his luggage, which was made up of pretty much only paintings. And then, as a final goodbye, Frank clasped a little metal bracelet around Kreig's hand. Then he left.

Leaving Kreig alone. Alone, and free.

Free and already lost.

The whole city was laid out before him, with the thick river dividing the whole of it, small and big bridges hopping over the river, cars honking and people walking and complex architecture that Kreig barely even recognized. It was beautiful, and he didn't even know where to start.

Or, well, he *did* know where to go, but he had no idea how to get there. Maybe those people expected him to recall his way, since this was the city he'd grown up in?

If that was the case, they were wrong. He couldn't even recognize the signs, much less the buildings and landmarks. All he knew was that everything looked extremely high-tech, save for some singular buildings made of regular brick and glass. These buildings, although rare, reminded him of the buildings he'd seen in the capital of the Empire. Robust, well made. Slightly nostalgic.

But before he so much as took a step into this brave new world laid out before him, he made a little promise to himself not to cause a mess. He wouldn't crack any skulls; he wouldn't burn any houses. He would only get from point A to point B. And he especially wouldn't sprout any wings to get there faster. He would walk like a normal person, talk like a normal person, and act like a normal person. After all, he *was* a normal person.

Not a disaster, not a prisoner, not a captain, not an inquisitor, not a chosen one. Just a normal man.

And that was all he longed to be.

But faced with the seemingly endless city that appeared to go on forever with its hurried humans and noisy cars, he suddenly felt overwhelmed. There were so many paths he could walk, so many places he could go. And somehow, he felt like whichever way he went, he would fail in getting home. It was a dreadful feeling, and the only way he could combat it was to just start walking.

He went straight ahead. Right across a road, through a bush that gave an unhappy *crack* as he passed and into a little park adjacent to the airport and the hotel beside it. It was a very pretty park, filled with trees and bushes and a small flower bed beside a fountain. It would probably have been filled with people and dogs had it been anywhere apart from next to a noisy airport. How terribly designed. Kreig, however, didn't really notice it since he had his hands full veering out of the way of a tree.

And then he took a pause and looked around. God only knew where he was, but if he went straight ahead, he'd get out of the park and into the actual city. This was exactly what he did.

The city wasn't quite bustling by modern standards, but to Kreig, who had never seen a city housing anywhere near that amount of people, it felt crowded. Crowded and tight and he *really wanted to get away from there*. So, as any sensible man would do, he awkwardly shuffled through a slightly disbelieving crowd and entered a small bystreet. There were still people there, but fewer. He had room to breathe.

With the rustle of paper, he came to realize that he was still holding the map pointing him home. Thankfully, he hadn't held it too hard, but he still couldn't really understand what it meant. He was good with maps, downright great—he'd done very well to get his squad home that one time—but he couldn't even fathom how this map worked. It was a map of a city, but he had only ever used maps of forests and plains and mountains. There were no indicators of different kinds of texture, only a generally square shape to everything.

Thankfully, his home was marked with a red X. He knew what that meant, at least. He just had to get there.

Maybe he should try using Voice of the Earth? Just a quick check to know which way to go. Nobody would know what he was doing.

But *he* would. He'd know he was making a mess, and he'd feel even worse than he already did. No powers, nothing like that. He'd get there using his own body and wits, and for once, for just one moment, that would have to be enough. If he couldn't even do such a simple thing as find his way home without his strength, what would he be without it?

And that was how Kreig set out to find home, only finding himself more lost in the process.

Going by the map and the river, he knew he was standing on a bridge. But which bridge? There were many bridges—at least a dozen—and he had already been on two others. Back when he hadn't had to move at all, he didn't have to get lost. The whole situation felt ridiculous, but he slowly came to realize that his chances of finding home on his own would be next to zero.

On his own. Alone. A lightbulb flash in his mind. Who said he couldn't, well, ask someone for help?

Genius. A foolproof idea. Those people walking in wide arcs around him must surely have known the way home. Or at least how to get to the patch of green beside his home.

A simple plan. It was perfect in theory, impossible in practice.

Kreig watched patiently as people walked around him, shooting nervous glances at him, hurrying up to pass him. Tapping one of them on the shoulder would be impossible. He might tap too hard and shatter their bones. Then, speaking up to someone? Not possible either; his voice was much too weak. All he could do was . . .

He maneuvered his body to angle it in front of someone who had been trying to pass him by. The young girl, clutching her handbag, walked straight into his chest, stumbled back, and craned her neck to meet his gaze. She visibly paled. Then she returned her gaze to the pavement and tried to move around him again. He took a single step and was once again in her way.

"Can—um, may I help you?" she asked politely, her voice only shaking a little. She seemed to be young but not below twenty. Young and nervous.

Kreig removed the map from his pocket and held it out to her, pointing at the red X.

She looked at the map, up at his face, and gave one of the most forced smiles Kreig had ever seen. "Is this . . . Um, we're here"—she pointed at one of the bridges—"so, if you just go down there and follow the main road and take a left by Thirteenth and Third and then head straight through the park, you'll probably see it on the right. Right? Now, can I—"

Kreig didn't let her pass. He knew for a fact that everything she just said shot through his ears like a slingshot, in one and out the other. He didn't need directions. He needed a *guide*.

Erica wasn't having a good day. Especially not this very second, when the extremely sketchy man had decided to not only block her path to the college she attended but also force her into becoming his personal guide. She'd be more upset if she wasn't so terrified. She'd seen the PSAs about dangerous men who would whisk girls away or smack them into next week for looking at them wrong.

And, man, this guy was *dangerous*. With a capital D. Silent, yes, but ripped like it wasn't anybody's business, and taller than anybody she had ever seen, save for that one uncle she only saw at family gatherings every other year or so. Man, that guy was tall. But this guy might just be a little taller than even him.

College could wait. Right now, she had to guide this man somewhere.

Somewhere that was the police station.

She wasn't an idiot by a long shot, and she certainly had her sense of justice. Enough to know that X probably marked the spot for something heinous. Like drugs. Or children. Either way, she was about to bring this massive crime-man somewhere he might have to answer for his crimes. If he couldn't find his way to the X himself, he was not about to notice her bringing him to the station. And if he did, she could just scream and run away. The city was packed with people! If he wanted her dead, the middle of Space Circle Avenue would be the wrong place to do it!

She gave a cackle.

The big man gave her an odd look.

"Uh—um, say, you've been awfully quiet. Any chance you could"—she grinned to herself, preparing to form a damning testimony—"tell me what X marks the spot for? You don't have to, unless you wanna."

The man's eyes seemed to light up in a hidden smile. "Family." His voice was subdued. Brass. It was unlike how she would expect a criminal to sound like, but it was okay. They were right by the station, and she was about to bring him in for—for something; she wasn't sure what yet. But the map was *really* suspicious.

The man stopped. He didn't follow her inside. "Huh? Aren't you coming?"

The man pointed at the building they were headed into. It was made of bricks and had a glass fixture at the front. A brass plate above the door said in bold, capital letters, police station. The man shook his head softly, making his long black hair sway like seaweed.

Erica motioned toward the inside of the police station. "It's right in there. I promise. Pinky promise."

The man's face just turned disappointed as he glanced about the proximity. "No green."

Shoot. He got her. ". . . Fine. Follow me." Erica proceeded to actually follow the map despite the good chance that it might lead to a shallow grave. She soon realized that whoever gave it to him really didn't consider him too highly. There were little red arrows marked on many turns and a few tips and tricks on how to survive in the city scribbled in the perimeter with scrawly handwriting. Still, they did get there eventually.

As it turned out, "there" happened to be a small residential area beside an equally small park. It was likely the living quarters of many students and up-and-coming families.

Maybe, just *maybe*, this guy wasn't a criminal but had actually gotten lost and was trying to find his family's home? It was a radical thought, so unthinkable from how the man acted and seemed that the idea took her by surprise. The man in question appeared uncertain even as they had arrived. "It's in there. I'll . . . I'll be going now, so you just . . . you do you. I'll do me. No— Wait, that—" The man fiddled with his thumbs for a few seconds before entering. "I didn't mean it like—shit."

At least he'd gotten where he was going. And she was late for class. Shoot.

Kreig watched her leave with what might almost have been a smile on his lips. What a nice girl, going so far as to show him where the police station was. It was a bit of a detour, but since he got home in the end, he couldn't complain.

That is, if this actually *was* home. The building was large, having several floors and many balconies. It was right beside a park, too, so he knew this was it. But once he went inside, he couldn't help but find himself a fair bit confused. Though now that he took a look around, he found a wall of what seemed to be mailboxes, each headed by a name and number. One of these was titled Samantha and George Wiedermann, 621. Mysterious numbers that likely indicated which part of the complex they lived in.

He was in the right house, but he didn't know which apartment they lived in specifically. Likely the 621st one, whatever that meant.

There was only one way to find out. Kreig started climbing stairs.

By the first floor, when he took a peek at the apartments there, he found that they were all labeled with a 1, followed by two other numbers. This must have meant that they were on the sixth floor. No worries; he'd be there momentarily.

And he was.

The climb took a mere two minutes, ending with him standing outside the door of the Wiedermanns', number 621. Kreig's own body easily dwarfed the door. The upper frame was at the level of his chin if he stood with a straight back. He had to hunch down just to get his eyes in the frame. Even then, he didn't dare knock. What if his knuckles rapping against the door broke it? What if he made a real loud sound and ruined something? What if he—

Oh. There was a doorbell.

Kreig swallowed deeply, tried not to think about breaking it, and carefully pressed the small button. A lovely chime resounded from inside the apartment, followed by hurried footsteps and the door swinging open in his face. Since Kreig was standing quite close to the door, whoever was trying to open it couldn't get it open at all. The person in question peeked out from the small gap. It was Sam. "Kreig? Kreig! You're here! Okay, um, hold on, step back a little."

Kreig took a step back, giving Sam enough space to swing open the door fully. A small smile shyly pulled at her lips. She was wearing an apron, too, and a piece of cloth was tied around her head. A chemical kind of smell seemed to linger around not only her but the apartment as a whole. "Come in! We've— Uh, we were told you'd come, so!" A proud grin spread across her face, and she gestured to the inside of the apartment. "We've been fixing up the place!"

Sam stepped to the side, allowing Kreig to hesitantly enter.

The first thing that hit him was how toxic everything smelled. Every spotless surface was covered in an approximate imitation of actual nice smells like citrus or rose. It made him want to wrinkle his nose and leave. He couldn't even appreciate how there wasn't any garbage anywhere or how he couldn't see any cobwebs around the lamps and how the floor had been swept. None of that stuck with him in the least.

Bad smell. He wanted to leave. But he remained.

"So? How is it? We didn't have time to clean up a lot of parts, but . . . I mean, can you tell? You can't, right?" Sam asked, stepping up to stand beside him.

He could tell a lot of things. For one, he could tell that the bread on the table was collecting a nice assortment of different molds and that their ceiling fan hadn't been cleaned on the other side. But he was a guest, and they were his hosts. He would never show unkind behavior to his host or lord. "No, I cannot."

Sam breathed a sigh. "Phew. Thank fuck. You're a regular mystery, you know that?" He did not, in fact, know that. But it wasn't his place to point that out. "You'll be sleeping in the— George!" George peeked his head out of a door down the hall. He seemed tired. "There, that room. You'll be sleeping in the guest room. Calling it a guest room is . . . Well, what it *used* to be isn't important. Right now, it's got a bed and a nightstand and a desk. Therefore, it's a guest room. Not a . . . Yeah."

George's eyes fell on Kreig. "Uh. Hi. I'm not . . . Sam, I'm not done yet; will you please take the time to present some other part of the apartment while I finish up?"

Sam, who had seemed fully intent on bringing Kreig to the guest room, now stalled in her tracks. "You're not— Wow. Shit, okay, uhhh, this is the living room! We've got a couch, and a TV, and a PS4 and that's about it. Um. And also this lamp? Yeah. Neat lamp, huh?" It . . . It was. It really was. If Kreig's eyes weren't going bad, it seemed like the lamp was not, in fact, connected to anything. He'd learned to accept electricity by now. But cordless electricity was something else entirely. "You have seen lamps before, right? 'Cause if you haven't, I can . . . No, actually, I can't explain batteries to you. Don't throw them into nature. That's about all I know."

Sam seemed kind of upset at being unable to explain things properly, but Kreig didn't mind. While Sam cursed herself, he had quietly moved up to the lamp to absolutely make sure that it didn't have a cord. It did not.

Magic. Must've been an artifact. Or something of that ilk. He had never been much good at how any of that worked.

"Okay, so, this here is the kitchen. Right beside the living room. Very useful to go get snacks quickly. Mm-hm mm-hm." She pulled open the fridge and regarded its contents. "Do you, uh, what do you eat? Krupke never told me what you ate, so we sort of just bought a bunch of things in a hurry . . . like meat and potatoes. And a chocolate cake. Y'know, to . . . to *celebrate*. If you'd like that?" As Kreig leaned over her to peer inside the fridge, he found that it did indeed contain a chocolate cake. It had a *7* on it, alongside the words *Happy Birthday Champ* spelled out in frosting. "Yeah, heh, that's . . . Ignore that; it was all they had—"

"Thank you," Kreig said, his eyes transfixed on the cake. "Tonight will be glorious, indeed."

"Oh? That so?" Sam replied, a smile finding its way back onto her face. Unlike when they'd been down there, she seemed quicker to smile now, though Kreig wasn't sure what had changed.

Though, as his eyes fell on a certain something, he realized there was *one* thing he had to say in regard to things he ate. "No mushrooms."

"Huh? Uh, okay. Sure. No mushrooms . . . I'll be sure to tell George; he's the cook guy here," Sam said, nodding deeply before straightening herself out again. She clapped her hands. "Okay! We've done the kitchen and the living room, which leaves us with the bathroom and the two bedrooms . . . Uh, you know how to use a toilet, right? Don't you?"

"I don't need to."

"You don't— Dude. That's really damn ominous. Okay, um . . . We'll skip the bathroom. Just keep your hands washed so you don't spread any germs around." Kreig decided not to mention the fact that his race didn't allow for such dirty creatures to live on or inside his body. "That leaves our bedrooms . . . Uh. Do you need to see them? I mean, I don't mind showing mine, but George might be a bit more . . . Well, whatever. Let's go!"

Sam proceeded to lead Kreig through the apartment, past the guest room and into a room at the end of the hallway, right next to the room Kreig assumed to be the restroom. Sam's room was rather large, had a nice bed, and was designed in a very similar way to how a baboon might design their cave. The most aesthetically pleasing thing to be found was a string of ball lights hanging over a window. The rest was mostly themed with dragons. A shelf of dragon figurines, a dragon-themed bed-cover, dragon plushies, and everything beyond.

She clearly had a style, but to Kreig, who had lived most of his life in a world where dragons were decidedly not mythical, seeing so many of them was like a Swede coming to Germany to find a man obsessed with moose as if they didn't exist. It was jarring in an odd way he couldn't explain.

"Heh, yeah, um. This is . . . I can explain? Actually, I can't. Dragons are just straight awesome. What more do I need to say?" Sam said. Going by her lazy smirk and crossed arms, Kreig could somehow tell that she, in secret, enjoyed his stunned reaction.

She wouldn't for long. "I've killed four dragons." It was true.

Watching her entire body language drain away into horror and shock told him everything about her mental state. "You—you—you— No. Wait. Hold on." She slapped her cheeks with both hands. "*Get it together, Sam!* Priorities! Does that— If you've— Um. Are there dragons in the otherworld?"

. . . Did they not know that?

Humanity had seen a wyrm and one of the Four Disasters—two, counting himself—and they hadn't even confirmed the existence of dragons? Ah, then again, dragons were rather rare. And strong, as well. Still . . . "Yes?"

"Holy shit. Holy shit! That's— Why'd you kill dragons!? What'd they do to you, Kreig? They deserved to live!"

The first one had been a rather young one that was terrorizing the area around the kingdom. The second had appeared on the battlefield between the Empire and the nation of Bagland, forcing the two armies to work together to kill it. The third one had been in Kreig's way as he and his party tried to escape the Empire. The fourth one had appeared only a few years before on a dare to kill Kreig. "They had to be destroyed."

Sam growled. "Grr. Fine! But only because I'm happy that dragons are real!" With her piece said, Sam proceeded to show Kreig the rest of her room, all while wearing a pout to rival any tantrum-throwing toddler.

The dragon shrine was actually the top shelf of a line of similarly cluttered shelves, none carrying books. This shelf was in turn next to a desk and a chair, upon which a screen was seated. Sam explained that it was a "computer" and that the keyboard flaring in sixteen different colors had cost her more than the screen itself, though nowhere near the webcam perched atop the screen. The use of the webcam eluded Kreig entirely, mostly since he couldn't imagine that a profession such as "streamer" could exist. Aside from that, the entire area around the window was filled with healthy greenery. She had a green thumb.

"I'd show you more, but I've got a sneaking suspicion that you'd try to burn my backup dragon posters," Sam said, shrugging dismissively. And all of a sudden, Kreig almost regretted killing those dragons.

Almost.

A door closed in the hall behind them and George appeared. "Am I to assume you've finished showing him what an obsessive dweeb you are?"

Sam turned red in a mere second. "You— Hey! Shut it! I'm an adult woman; I can decorate my room however I want!" She made a solid point, but the finger-pointing sullied it a little. "If you're all done with the whole guest-room thing, why don't you show it to Kreig? If you think he'll like it, that is. Heh."

A very weak clapback that only made George grin. "Of course. I've been decorating all day. Come, Kreig. Follow me." Apparently, the confidence George held in the guest room trumped any doubts Sam could possibly sow in his mind.

Kreig felt like a very ill-fitting third wheel, but he nonetheless followed George to the guest room.

As George pulled open the door and gestured for Kreig to enter, the first thing that hit Kreig was the scent. The overpowering smell of chemicals seemed concentrated beyond the apartment as a whole, infiltrating his nostrils and making them burn. But beneath that, there seemed to be a somewhat hidden scent, like that of fungi. But not any mushroom he'd ever smelled before, and not in the growing phase, either.

". . . Yeah. This room used to be . . . Sam used to have it for the private use of—of psychedelics. That was long ago; she's off the stuff. Just ignore that smell if you can," George said, stepping inside the room fully.

Kreig tried, but the smell was surprisingly distracting, despite the many flowering plants placed around in the room. It really was a nice room, with a large bed and a desk and a few paintings on the walls. There really wasn't much detail to it, either. There was nothing too personal, nothing too expensive. A perfectly normal room by modern standards.

And now it was his home.

The luggage he'd been dragging around for the past few hours seemed so little. It was just paintings. Paintings of people he'd met, paintings of people he didn't want to forget . . . Oh! He'd almost forgotten. There was one painting unlike the rest, one he'd spent a whole night making. One he'd been questioning whether or not he should even present it at all. But he had to. Now that he was *home*, he had to actually make it *his* home.

He walked inside the guest room, *his room*, placed his luggage on the bed, and popped it open. There were only three paintings inside, all three of them dressed in a thick layer of bubble wrap and tape to keep them safe and sound during the trip.

Three paintings he had chosen specifically for this. The rest would arrive at a later date, but these three were special.

He removed one, and from the small size and general whiteness, he could tell from a glance that it was his picture of the White Pope. Finally, after so many years, he would be allowed to properly portray his personal saint of choice. He would be sure to place it well. The second was smaller, darker, and would probably seem a bit uncouth to any outside viewer. It was the painting of when Kreig first laid eyes on Gerald. A precious memory now, a mundane moment then.

And then, thirdly, the largest out of the three. It had warm colors with green and orange undertones, muted slightly by the bubble wrap. Still, the colors were comforting like a pie of pears.

Kreig took the painting in both hands, still wrapped in bubbles, and handed it to George.

"Huh? Is this—is this a painting or something? Wait, did you . . ." George's eyes lit up and he twiddled with the bubble wrap for a few seconds before peeking out the doorway. "Hey, Sam! We got an— Wait. Despite my curiosity, I must say that we should save this for tonight. After we've had the welcome party."

Sam poked her head out of her room. "The fuck are you on about now?"

George ignored her fully and instead looked back at Kreig. "This is a gift, right? For us?"

Kreig nodded. "May it please you."

George smiled timidly. "I . . . I'm sure it will, Kreig."

That was the only response Kreig needed. He turned back to the bed and removed the bubble wrap from his painting of the White Pope. What a pretty man. He'd been appointed Pope only days after first joining the church. People called it a miracle, and Kreig felt no different. There was something very alluring about the White Pope, something about his eyes that held everything inside them like a soft, warm crib. A beautiful man in every way.

"Would you like to hang it up?" George asked, already brandishing a pair of nails and a hammer. Kreig nodded, and George wasted no time hammering up a pair of nails for Kreig's paintings.

The White Pope on the left, beautiful as ever, and Gerald on the right.

Kreig already felt more home than he had in . . . Lord, too many years to count.

The last time he'd even had a house of his own must have been as Captain of the Royal Guard. It had been a small cottage in the middle of the city, nothing much to look at, but it had been home. He'd even had thoughts of marriage, but once he started being thrown into wars, any such thoughts had been abandoned. There weren't many fair maidens on the battlefield. Just blood, death, and—

"Kreig? You all right?"

Huh? Oh, he'd been in the middle of something. Kreig shook off his thoughts like rainwater. "Yes."

"Mrm. Sure. Say, come along; I'll show you my room. I've got a question." The way George said that last part made Kreig's hair stand on edge. Questions. Hopefully, whatever George wanted to ask him wouldn't be too bad. Kreig followed him out of his room, into the hallway, and into a previously closed room. It smelled nice, probably due to the dozens upon dozens of blooming cacti all around the room.

But that wasn't the main thing about the room.

In the middle of the room, hanging from a thread beneath the lily-pad shaped lamp, right above the bed, was a small porcelain girl with insect wings and long ears. The bedcover had a similar girl on it, with black hair instead of blond and wings of gold. The walls were covered in posters of the same sorts of girls, the mat on the floor had them as well, and a shelf seemed completely overrun with small statuettes of them. "Say, Kreig . . . fairies wouldn't happen to exist in the otherworld, would they?"

Fairies? What the hell were—

"You know. Small girls with wings and maybe even long ears. Pixies. Winged elves." The smile that bloomed on George's face made Kreig feel deeply unhappy in having to admit that he had no idea what the hell he was talking about. Humans couldn't be that small. And even if they *were*, what was with the wings? To *fly*? George made a very bizarre face. "You know. If big lizards with wings exist, what's stopping little girls with wings? It makes no sense that one would exist and not the other."

Kreig didn't answer for a moment, hoping his silence would jog a memory proving that fairies did, in fact, exist. But when the silence just became awkward, he decided that the best way to relieve the situation would be to leave the room.

"Hey, Kreig! That's— Curses."

CHAPTER 12

WELCOME HOME, CHAMP

As Kreig left George's room and went back into his own, he was only briefly given a look at how Sam poked her head out of her own room, grinning teasingly at her brother. George, in turn, coughed and cleared his throat in a vague attempt to regain his cool. It didn't work too well, but at this point, Kreig had already returned to his room, closed the door, and sat down at his desk. The chair creaked helpfully below him.

Now that he looked closer, the blooming flowers in his room weren't *just* regular flowering plants but blooming cacti. Very pretty ones, to boot.

Kreig looked over at the window and the painting of the White Pope beside it. Such a beautiful man.

"You'll be fine one day, Oracle," he'd said, and his face would light up in such assured joy that Kreig could only believe him.

"You tell me that, and yet the Empire's forces only close in. It isn't about me, o White One. I have outgrown my selfish and disobedient nature. You were not there, but you must understand that it is not about the Five Bodies or the Cardinals or the Oracles. It is about our faith." Kreig spoke softly, his head and body bowed before the throne of the White Pope.

He hummed. "Who is to carry on the faith of our God—who is to host the White Roots, should the believers die? Who is to protect the people if the Oracles are defeated? You must trust me, Oracle."

"I do trust you, o White One. With all my heart."

"And I do not doubt your belief. As I do not doubt you, you must not doubt me. The Five Bodies move out tomorrow, and you will bring every Oracle and soldier you can muster. Should you die, the Theocracy will live.

Should you submit and relinquish your faith, so too will I die. Remain strong. Remain faithful."

Kreig stood up. "I will, o White One."

The fate of the Theocracy and its people remained a mystery to Kreig all the way until his release from the Empire, until he had been thoroughly changed.

Would the White Pope approve of him now? He was the only one carrying on the will of God, the one man who had survived the death of the faith.

In all aspects, the Holy Order of White Roots was dead. Dead and buried and burnt to keep it down. It had joined the God Below. But Kreig hadn't.

Kreig stared at the picture of the White Pope, desperately fighting the need to go down on his knees in prayer. Before he knew it, the sun was going down and there was a knock at the door. He turned to look at it. Nobody entered. A muffled voice spoke on the other side. "Uh, hey, Kreig? We'll be having dinner in like a quarter of an hour; do you wanna join us, or— You do eat, right? Considering that comment about the restroom, I just . . . Eating is important. Otherwise, we die, I think."

Kreig stood up and opened the door, finding Sam just outside. She looked up at him, wrinkled her forehead, scratched her chin, and spoke again. "Wait. Is this about your weird race? Divine Human or whatever?" Kreig wasn't sure what to tell her. "Hold—hold on. I'm not a racist for asking that, am I?"

She wasn't. Though she wasn't correct, either.

Being able to go without eating and sleeping was an effect of the Warrior's Breath (X) skill, but being able to eat without creating any useless byproducts *was* a trait of his race. Even so, despite eating being entirely optional, he turned to her and said, "I'd love dinner."

"That doesn't answer my question, but, uh . . . Yeah! Okay, let's go!" Sam answered, giving a grin to threaten the moon.

Both she and Kreig soon entered the hall. Kreig lumbered after her as she walked to the kitchen, always glancing back at him just to make sure he was following along, which he was. But even then, once they emerged into the kitchen to find half of it flooded with black smoke, Kreig wasn't surprised in the least. He'd been able to smell the putrid odor of charred flesh the moment he stepped out of his room.

George stood by the stove and turned around as they entered the kitchen. His apron was covered in soot and he seemed suitably perturbed.

"Dinner isn't finished yet." He spoke with a voice as pleasant as a coughing crow.

"Oh, is that so?" Sam asked. "Well, I'll set the table while you finish up! Kreig, will you help me?" Her eyes were so full of innocence; so ignorant of how terribly burnt the food was. Kreig wasn't sure if the proper response was to take over the food-making part or to help her set the table. In the end, as her eyes turned to that of a puppy, he had no choice but to do the latter.

"I'll help."

Sam smiled and motioned for Kreig to follow her as she moved toward the cupboards. Meanwhile, George was occupied with trying to scrape at the charred remains of whatever he'd been trying to make. Sam removed two plates from the cupboard, reconsidered her decision, and took out a third one. She handed them to Kreig, alongside three sets of flatware she'd grabbed from a sliding drawer.

In turn, Kreig brought them over to the small dining table and set everything out. Fork on the left, knife on the right. Just like it has always been done.

Sam disagreed.

"Uh, Kreig? It's the other way around," she said just as she set the cups in all the right places. Kreig could only watch in silent bafflement as she placed the forks on the right side of the plate and the knives on the left. And yet he couldn't disagree with her. All his life, apart from around seventeen years, it seemed, the fork had always been on the left. Even when he came to Earth in the prison, that had remained true, though it was most likely since almost everyone from the otherworld had their cutlery in that position. He'd accept it for now, but if anything else was too different, he might have a few problems.

A few other details were added to the table and everything was ready. Kreig turned solemn eyes on George.

Whatever was stewing on the stove wasn't even proper food anymore. When George set a pan filled with ashes and charcoal and a pot filled with indescribable white pulp on the table, his mood was right on the cusp of true anger. His face was practically red and his eyes were almost bloodshot. He sat down, and Sam followed suit. She was smiling, and Kreig couldn't for the life of him figure out why.

"Dig in." That was all George would say on the matter. Going by how Sam's eyes were all aglow, she wouldn't hesitate.

Now, all things considered, Kreig would hypothetically be able to eat it. Due to the skill Purity (X), any impurity within him would be cleansed, a passive effect that was also caused by his race as Divine Human. However, that didn't mean his taste buds would take kindly to it, or, especially, his trace morals. It was his first night home. Was he really about to eat charcoal simply because his siblings had made it?

Well, yes, but it was more than that. Could he accept, as their *brother*, that they should eat *this*?

He could accept eating charcoal, but he couldn't accept letting *them* eat it.

He glanced at George, quickly establishing eye contact. For some reason, his brother flinched. Almost as if being watched by Kreig was something terribly uncomfortable. Kreig decided not to force George to be the one to break the silence. "Brother dearest . . . if I may, will you possibly grant me the pleasure of supplementing this meal with a dish of my own creation?"

George squinted and wrinkled his nose as if he'd smelled something rancid. He glanced at the food, noticing bitterly how Sam had already shoveled a large spoon of white goop into her face. Even then, he hardly seemed joyous. "Are you sure, Kreig? I never took you for a cook."

"I know enough to improve upon this." He felt terribly rude for suggesting it, but since George hadn't completely rejected it, he might still have a chance to make amends.

". . . Sure, go ahead. Be quick, though."

In a single moment, Kreig's heart was filled with elation. He stood up, wandered over to the kitchen, and took a deep breath, taking it all in. There was a cupboard filled with spices over there. Another cupboard filled with dry ingredients was next to it. The fridge held many groceries he recognized: pork cutlets, various vegetables he did and didn't recognize, a curious lack of chocolate cake, milk and cheese, a startling lack of mushrooms, considering it had been one of the staple foods back in the otherworld, and everything else he needed to make a proper meal.

Despite what one might think from appearances, Kreig was an expert cook. Despite how long it'd been the last time he cooked. Despite all his time without so much as touching a loaf of bread, he knew how to cook.

He got right to it.

Cooking (V)

He moved faster than most could see, subconsciously using skills to clean every surface as he passed. He cut and diced things with such expertise that one might have thought he was purposefully doing it with a flourish when it was, in fact, merely a by-product of his skill. Meat was cut finely by his hand, vegetables sliced, and every proper spice needed deposited in the exact amount required. All without the slightest conscious effort.

Years of cooking for himself. Years of being on the run, forced to cook using only what the cruel wilderness had to offer. He became an expert at cooking using only exactly what he needed.

Of course, after his party no longer required his culinary services, he stopped. Food didn't taste good anymore, and he was alone. Cooking for no one but oneself was the loneliest pursuit of all.

But that wasn't true anymore. Now, he fried and flambéed with purpose. Now he was cooking *for* someone. And it felt fantastic. This was his true purpose, yes. Not fighting selfishly for himself. Fighting for someone. That was—

No, no! Not at all. That wasn't it. He didn't want to fight *at all*, be it for his family or his friends or any other master that might try to subjugate him. Killing was no longer his purpose; war wasn't his only avenue of life. There was more to him, wasn't there? Being a slave of death was not something he would allow anymore. Of course not. Hadn't he decided that he had enough of killing?

. . . Yes. That was it.

He took the food off the stove. In a single sweeping motion, he removed the charred food from the table and placed the food he'd made there instead. His masters had been served. And now, while they ate, he would wash the dishes. Just like how Priest Lin Mu had taught him all those years earlier. He brought the dishes over to the sink. Now he would clean them. Clean and clean and—

"Kreig? Aren't you going to join us?" Sam asked.

Kreig turned to her. She seemed so distant where she sat, and yet her eyes were close. Too close. He felt like her eyes would swallow him whole, those eyes that welcomed him to sit down and be right next to them, right next to the people he loved as dearly as each of his former masters. Did he deserve to sit there? He hadn't deserved to sit next to the White Pope. He hadn't deserved to sit next to the Emperor.

George seemed peeved. "Just sit down, Kreig. You're acting weird."

A valid point. Kreig sat down, albeit hesitantly, his back hunched as he tried to level his gaze with his siblings'. It didn't work too well, but Sam gave him a little smile, likely to encourage him. Then she turned to the actual food. They'd been waiting for him. Just a short while, but . . .

Now that it was over, they turned on the food like a pair of rabid wolves. Though George seemed more hesitant than Sam. She went at it without pause, scarfing it down as if it was her final meal.

George poked at it a few times, seemed to question if it was edible at all, and took a bite. From there on, he just kept going.

"This is really"—Sam took a bite—"good; I thought you"—she swallowed it—"were just making"—she took another bite—"a show? For no"—swallow—"reason. Like just showing off without any actual skill. But this is really good! Like, I don't think I've ever had anything better! Except for that time I went to a fancy restaurant to celebrate my graduation, but that was ... Actually, this might be a little better. Maybe." So she spoke, all while shoveling more food into her mouth than humanly possible. Kreig might have been flattered if he hadn't been putting so much effort into trying to understand her.

George didn't say a word, merely nodding in agreement. Until, finally, he glanced up and with hard eyes said, "Indeed. Kreig, from now on, you're the cook of the house."

Kreig happily accepted his new duty.

Dinner concluded without any other events. But right as Kreig made to stand in order to wash the dishes or help otherwise, Sam urged him to remain seated. A mischievous spark glistened in her eye. He didn't like the look of that, but he couldn't reject her. So, he remained seated, all while he unhappily watched how George and Sam washed the dishes and whispered into each other's ears about things Kreig chose not to listen in on. It was their own business, after all.

That was why when George left Sam and Kreig in the kitchen and went down the hall and into his room, Kreig didn't have a single clue as to what was happening. Sam gave him an equally mysterious smirk as she excused herself from the room as well.

Leaving Kreig alone. Alone, and very scared.

Something was happening. He could smell it. George was in his room, close to a wooden cupboard. He opened it and removed something from inside. Something old and worn and dusty. Sam had wandered into her own room. It smelled sweet there. Then that sweet smell was replaced with fire. Fire and wax. Candles? Must be. If it wasn't, Kreig wouldn't hesitate to fly from his seat to put it out. She and the fire approached her door. There was excitement in the air. She gave two soft knocks at the door. George replied with three knocks.

Kreig swallowed deeply. What in the hell was—

"*Welcome home!*" Sam and George shouted in unison as they burst from their rooms, Sam holding a chocolate cake lit with candles atop it, George timidly clutching what seemed to be a large book. Kreig froze. Sam and George both shared a glance before walking down the hall, side by side, until they were close enough to place both the cake and the book on the table in front of Kreig. He stared at it, mouth agape, eyes trembling.

It said, *Happy Birthday Champ*. And a *7* beneath.

Sam and George sat down on either side of him. "Come on, blow it out!" Sam said with a crescent smile. A single candle burnt atop the cake. It was beautiful. A pretty little flame dancing just for him, lighting up the dark room and the dark world with its glow. Just beyond the candle he saw the faces of his siblings. His broadly grinning sister, so happy and excited that the air seemed to fuzz with joy around her, and his brother, carrying a more subdued yet equally fond smile.

Both welcoming. As warm as the candle's glow.

The world started to blur. The candle's flame stretched out toward the darkness as the tears pooling in his hollow eyes distorted the world with beautiful, malformed joy. It was everything and nothing. Even as a tear fell, briefly showing the world as it truly was, clear and true, it was quickly replaced by another, equally heavy—equally needed.

Sam and George's features seemed to twist in care and concern. Expressions he hadn't been given in in a long time. In too long. There was no pity to give him under his religion. There was nobody to pity him in the Empire, either—he was a soldier, after all. And after that . . . After that, anybody faced with him could only pity themselves. "Kreig, are you all right?" Their voices were melodic. Caring and pitying in a way that Kreig had sorely needed.

"No," he confessed. "I am not all right. I haven't been for a long time."

George and Sam both shared a look, though Kreig could barely see it. ". . . We know," George said. "We read your letters. I'm afraid we did not quite treat you right when we met. I hope, I *sincerely hope*, that you will accept us as your family with this." He smiled a tender little smile. "As we will accept you."

And for once, the smile Sam gave was neither exaggerated nor large. Merely enough.

And Kreig cried. He sobbed and he wept and he was *home*. Two hands fell on his shoulders, just like before, but now these hands were so warm. Warm like little docile flames, domesticated like candles burning, warm like the loving embrace of home.

He was home. He was finally home.

Not just on Earth, not just among people he liked.

Home.

He blew out the candle. The little smoky wisp trail didn't smell bad. Sam grinned and cut a slice for everyone. There was a fork beside his plate, and he took it in his hand. Thoughtlessly, he barely noticed how the metal whined and twisted in his grip, eventually becoming so disfigured, he couldn't possibly use it for anything. Sam commented on it, suggesting she bring out a new one, but Kreig denied her.

It would be fine if it was for them.

Mend (V)

A warm glow enveloped the twisted fork, making it straighten out and shine as if it was brand-new, which for all intents it was. Neither George nor Sam could pull their gazes from it.

Kreig stabbed the fork into the cake, took a small piece, and brought it to his mouth.

He smiled softly. "It's too sweet." But that didn't stop him from continuing. One bite turned into two and then three. By that point, both George and Sam had accepted the soft, feather-like silence, enjoying their own cake in the process. Kreig didn't like sweet things. Not cookies or cake or pudding or sweet liquor, even after a long day's work.

But he'd eat this cake since it was with his family.

Even though his throat was burning and his eyes were watering, he'd eat it.

Only one slice, though; any more than that and he'd probably pass out.

"Say, Kreig . . ." Sam jerked her fork at Kreig's own. "What's up with that skill? What you did with the fork. I've never seen it before." There was a manic glint in her eye, and George seemed to grow only more tired as he noticed it. At some point, she had pulled a notebook and pencil out of God knows where.

"It's Mend." Going by the way Sam nodded for him to continue, his measly description wasn't enough. "It allows you to repair items and things, though nothing that was once alive. Or is currently alive." A simple skill. He'd learned it when a blacksmith from the Empire was brought to his lord's castle explicitly to teach Kreig and his soldiers how to repair and fix armor and weapons. It was just in case their things were damaged in battle. That granted him the Skill. As a matter of fact, that was the story behind almost each and every one of his skills.

Do a thing many times, get skill. Keep doing the thing, skill ranks up.

Despite how mundane the process was, Sam seemed really interested in scribbling it down. Then, when that was done, she looked back up, a sly smirk crowning her face. "You wouldn't have any other unusual ski—"

George lightly punched her arm. "Hey. Don't interrogate him on his first day. You and your skill-wiki can wait."

"Grr. Okay, fine. But you've gotta give me a list, Kreig! It's for *science!*"

Kreig didn't want to promise her anything strange like that, but he gave her a nod, just to appease her for the moment. His complicit response seemed to slightly upset George, who shook his head.

As Sam pouted and cut herself a third slice, George apparently decided that the time was right. He retrieved the book he'd placed on the far end of the table and slid it over to Kreig. It had a simple title: *Precious Memories.* Kreig let his hand run over the cover. It was almost square with the cover being a red, leathery sort of material. Thick, sturdy. Dusty and old.

"It's a photo album," George said. "Open it up."

Hesitantly, he complied. The first page he saw featured a picture, framed in the very middle. There were five people: two adults and three children. Two boys and one girl. A mother and a father. The sky was almost entirely black save for the flowering bursts of fireworks, each more colorful than the next. Without these fireworks, you wouldn't even have been able to see the smiling faces of the family. Fireworks. Just like the ones they'd had back in the Alumni Kingdom. There, they had been called fire flowers. The mother and father each had a glass of some bright liquid, but that wasn't what Kreig noticed the most about it.

The older brother was the most similar to how he was now. George. And the younger sister, whose cheeks still held those childish dimples that they did now, retained her flaming hair as well. And in between the two of them was a young, broad-shouldered youth. It must have been him.

Then these two people, smiling so brightly . . . The man must have been his father. And the woman; his mother. So young, yet so old. He was much older than them now, but that didn't matter. He glanced up and looked at his siblings, both smiling solemnly. "What were their names?" he asked. But even though his voice was soft and mellow, they heard him perfectly.

"Angelita and Paul Wiedermann."

That was it. Yes, yes, he could recall that—

There was a pang of pain that lit up in the back of his head, and suddenly, any thoughts of their names and faces were murky again. Gone. Not that he could remember them. It had been many years—of course he didn't remember them. Not the warmth of their smiles or the closeness of their hugs. Then why did it feel as if he almost recognized their names? And why—

A flash of white-hot pain blossomed in his head again and he buckled over, grasping at his head. Quick breaths. He was fine. He was okay.

You're fine. You're okay. Don't worry about it.

Yes, he wouldn't worry about it. Instead, he turned the page. It was a small collage of pictures, one page filled with pictures from what seemed to be George's birth, the other side shared between Sam and Kreig himself, each getting a half. He turned the page again. His parents with him and George as children. Another page, and they were a little older, joined by Sam. With every page he turned, another year passed. Pictures taken on holidays he couldn't recall existing, eating food foreign to him, becoming people he had only seen in hindsight.

"That was Christmas '98; I was ten, you were five, and Sam was only two," George would explain as he pointed to a picture. Christmas: an unfamiliar holiday. It seemed to take place around Yuletide.

Then, were even holidays different on Earth? God Below, he would surely get in trouble trying to celebrate the ones he knew. Then again, there was only one holiday from the Theocracy he'd been able to celebrate since its fall, namely Yuletide. Though, again, was it really that important *what* he celebrated, as long as it was with his family?

A little voice in the back of his head told him, *Yes. It's important to praise the right God.*

"And that was when we went to Silver Dollar City in 2009, and—" George paused, his hand shaking as it held the corner of the page. He couldn't turn it. Sam had frozen as well, even though her eyes weren't on the album but instead on Kreig. She seemed afraid. Fearing his reaction even though he hadn't given it yet. He could already tell what he'd find on the next page.

He reached out his hand and gently turned it.

Two obituaries recounting the loss of two beloved restaurant-owners, dated November 6, 2010. A single article telling of the tragedy that befell a high school and five families as five teenage boys all disappeared one day without a trace in 2010, November 5. George spoke quietly about it.

At first, when those five kids disappeared, people just saw it as an isolated incident. Then, the very next day, the portals opened. It had been a Saturday, so both Sam and George had been at home, worrying about Kreig, hoping the police would find any leads. Although it was a Saturday, both Paul and Angelita had been at work, since they owned a boat restaurant that rested on the river. It had to be open on Saturdays and Sundays. That was when the business was booming.

Neither Sam nor George knew what happened after that. In fact, nobody did. They went into a portal and oversized alligators came out—

"Mud Drakes." The way Kreig said it, with such absolute certainty, Sam and George could only accept it.

Mud Drakes came out of it. Those creatures went into the river and weren't completely exterminated for weeks. Back then, there were no Fighters yet. Nobody knew anything about these things. Soldiers and military flooded the city, but in parts of the world where the military was barely used or already in battle, the efforts to slay the monsters fell on the police. Even then, with so many portals and such great confusion, any forces available were stretched thin.

Many lives were lost in the first few months. And then the Fighters started appearing. Slowly, hesitantly, they showed their faces. They created forums online, tried to talk to each other, tried to contact authorities . . .

In the end, what really brought the world back to a sense of normalcy was the appearance of IOCRO. They became protectors of the world, vanquishers of monsters, and researchers of the unknown. Every country that wanted the use of their military and supply of Fighters had to submit to them, give them funding and resources to keep them going. But it was never really enough.

Fighters appeared and grew stronger as they fought. If it hadn't been for that, the militaries of the world would never have been enough.

PSAs on what to do if you found a portal were released, the main point being *Don't go into them*. Websites and guides on what to do if you awoke as a Fighter were made, movies and books on the noble pursuit of fighting were written . . . A lot happened. And in those ten years—those long ten years when Sam and George had thought they would forever only have each other—only five monsters with a level above 500 appeared.

This was most notable, since only creatures below level 300 could reasonably be destroyed without the use of overwhelming nuclear force. Of course, they still required several tanks and bombing of a different kind, but it wouldn't lay complete waste to the surrounding area. Furthermore, once a few Fighters with a similar level appeared, they could destroy the creatures without leveling cities as well.

And then a winged bull with a level of 552 appeared. Most Fighters who saw it first reported seeing a *???* instead of the level, and that was when they knew something was very off.

It seemed mythical, with a golden mane and three crown-like horns and giant wings. Almost divine. Beautiful.

Three Fighters who personally saw it were recovered alive only because they decided to run. For three days and nights, the bull was fought with every measure possible, IOCRO denying the use of nuclear warfare under the belief that if they opened the door to that possibility, it could open the door to widespread destruction beyond just clearing out monsters. It was killed with a single nuke, but most of the city was brought to the ground as well.

The second was Famine of the East. When the Fighters saw its level, saw that horrible giant maggot swallowing and eating like gluttony personified, they knew they were dead. It took two nukes.

And then the third one appeared in 2016. But by then, they had a total of three Fighters with a level of at least 450, so they could handle it. Only barely.

And the fourth one . . .

They both turned troubled eyes on Kreig.

"That is, if they aren't keeping any other weirdly strong guys down in the Other Island . . ." George hypothesized, but Kreig quickly shut it down with a shake of his head.

"I was alone. I would have known."

George shrugged and continued, though the rest was brief. The fifth such creature had attacked only the other day. A wyrm. According to the reports, its level had been somewhere above 500. For some reason, though, IOCRO wouldn't give any official statement on it, apart from that the loss of lives was a tragic one, but the wyrm was defeated soundly. There, Sam poked her nose in, describing in the words of someone who had been there, that people on the internet were discussing if there'd been a cover-up. However, most theories were disregarded as hoaxes, including the one absurdly stating that a prisoner cracked open its skull and set it aflame.

Kreig could feel a sweat coming on. He turned to stare down at the table, hunching his back. "The latter theory is correct." At least his voice, quiet as it was, didn't waver.

Both his siblings turned to him, and all of a sudden, he wanted to retreat into himself like a turtle. "Is that so?" Sam asked, leaning over the table with her eyebrow quirked. "And you would know . . . how? Met any other high-level prisoners down there? Made friends capable of killing that wyrm?" Kreig froze, eyes blankly staring at a certain spot on the wall. His mind went blank. Sam grinned while George's complexion faltered. "Unless, my dear brother . . . you had something to do with it?"

Kreig swallowed. Why was he feeling so nervous about admitting this? It wasn't anything out of the ordinary. "Yes. They asked me to kill it. I followed their orders."

If it was the truth, why did he expect outrage?

Sam turned to George. "Makes sense."

George nodded. "Yes. Though now that we know that the strongest Fighter has a level of around 630, I don't see why he couldn't have fought it, or any other high-level individual . . ."

"It had a level of 700."

That quieted the both of them. ". . . 700? Isn't—isn't that, like, a lot?" Sam said, squinting as she tried to comprehend the number. Kreig just shrugged. Levels weren't too important. The real crux of any foe was intelligence and skill. "Okay. In other words, you fought a strong thing so they didn't have to use a nuke?" Kreig supposed that was what happened—God only knew what a "nuke" was—but he didn't like what happened, either. If Gerald hadn't been there to pull him back out . . . "Good work! Isn't that great?"

Her smile was enough to quiet his worries. ". . . Yes."

Still . . . Although she seemed happy he'd killed the wyrm, and although he could understand that killing it was good, he didn't *feel* good about it. In fact, while trying to tell her that he killed it, he'd felt the same way he did before confessing to some stupid sin that would surely disappoint the priest. He had expected a scolding. Instead, he received praise.

It felt wrong.

And while Kreig devolved into an emotional breakdown fueled by confusion and uncertainty, George stood up. He went entirely unnoticed by both Sam and Kreig and wandered away, through the hall and into his room. When he returned and sat down, he did it with a bubble-wrapped package in hand. Kreig lit up at the sight of it, instantly pulled out of his ever-darkening thoughts.

"The hell is that?" Sam asked, clearly not in the know about it. That was why, when George then handed the package to Kreig, she just got more confused.

Kreig ran his hands over it for a moment. Smiled, and handed it to Sam. "Thank you."

Sam was just about to hand it back to George when he stopped her. "No, no, it's a gift for *us*. Open it, you dingus."

Kreig was too excited to really register the quick banter that flew between his siblings while Sam tore off the bubble wrapping and touched the inside. She stopped mid-curse, turning to look at the painting in her hands. George's tongue stalled equally quickly. Kreig leaned over the table, getting a good look at what he had spent so long to create.

A simple scene, painted with warm colors and friendly smiles. Kreig in the middle, wearing regular peasant clothes and a soft smile, with Sam in a warm pear-green dress on his left and George in orange on his right. Behind them, a warm fireplace crackled, and all three of them held the faintest smiles on their faces. Although Kreig was too shy to touch them in real life as casually as he did in the painting, there he had one arm on each of them. They were together.

A family picture. Kreig could feel a smile creep up his face just looking at it.

He hadn't dared to so much as put it up in his cell. That wasn't where it deserved to live. That wasn't its home. *This*, on the other hand? Here, much like how Kreig himself felt, *here,* it was home.

It only lacked a frame. Sam carefully ran her callused hands over the edge of it, feeling the organic bumps and ridges in the hardened oil, granting their painted counterparts immortal life. "It's . . . it's *beautiful*. Did you paint this, Kreig?" He nodded. "I . . . Thank you. George, let's just—let's put it up now. Right away."

George gave a smile as warm as the painting's glow. He stood up, and within mere minutes, the painting hung on the wall, right there in the living room as though it had always been there. Then he returned to the kitchen table, where only half a cake and a pile of bubble wrap remained. George took the bubble wrap in hand and was just about to throw it out when a hand fell on his. It was Sam. "Dude. You are *not* throwing out unpopped bubble wrap. It's criminal!"

He put it back on the table and sat down. "I hate to admit you're right."

Kreig had no idea what they meant until George took hold of the bubble wrap and gave one part a squeeze.

Pop!

Sam grinned and followed suit. *Pop! Pop!*

This went on for a few seconds until Sam turned to Kreig. "Kreig. Why aren't you popping your bubbles?"

Well, if they invited him so cordially. Though even as he reached out for it and took the odd thing in his hand, he couldn't help but feel afraid. What if he couldn't pop it? What if he was a disappointment to his siblings? He held a bubble between his thumb and forefinger. He just had to squeeze, going by what they did. Just a squeeze. Make it pop.

. . . It wouldn't pop.

"You can crack the skull of a wyrm but you can't pop a bubble?" Sam asked indignantly.

Damn it. He had to prove himself now. Not a lot of strength. If he pressed too hard, something bad might happen. But not too weakly, either. Kreig took a deep breath. Not too strong.

He pressed lightly.

It didn't pop.

It *exploded*.

The scant air inside the bubble between his fingers escaped with such speed and force that the sound it created was nothing if not a small sonic boom. It didn't cause any damage apart from the eardrums of all members present. Kreig blinked at the successfully popped piece of plastic in his hand. He glanced up at his siblings.

George and Sam looked very strange, their hands midway to protect their already damaged ears. Good God Below—

Despite the immense regret he experienced at failing to pop the bubble, he was still able to heal both of them to remove any long-term damage.

Collective Catharsis (X)

A warm, reddish glow enveloped all three of them as what little damage had been inflicted was healed in a matter of seconds. A few seconds passed. Sam was the first to speak up. "Okay, yeah, uh. No bubble wrap. Maybe." And Kreig could only agree. If he just didn't think too hard, he wouldn't use the wrong amount of strength. But he hadn't had to control it for over thirty years before he came to Earth. And now, to suddenly start using the littlest strength possible to do mundane things . . .

It was harder than bisecting a dragon, that was for sure. But he'd do it. He'd make sure of it.

After that, the evening concluded rather simply. Sam and George showed him his birth certificate, which they had apparently kept all these years. They told him they'd introduce him to a computer and phone tomorrow, alongside updating his ID, since he currently didn't have one. His tutor would arrive the day after tomorrow.

Until then, they'd get him a bit more acquainted with the world. Until then, they'd sleep.

As the evening grew into night and as the moon rose over the city, George and Sam both decided that enough was enough. They'd save the rest of the cake for later. They prepared themselves for nighttime; George showed Kreig the pajamas they'd bought specifically for the occasion, though they'd need his help buying other clothes, and told him to sleep. Usually, Kreig wouldn't sleep at night, but since George told him to do so . . .

He put on the pajamas and slipped into his new bed. It creaked. But it was larger and softer than the one he'd had in his cell.

He fell asleep without any further ado, giving a final look of gratitude at his portrait of the White Pope.

But his night wouldn't be as peaceful as he might have wished.

CHAPTER 13

———

BELOW DIM STARS

He hadn't known how many years had gone by. It had felt like a thousand, but he knew it couldn't have been more than fifty. His body remained the same age, but his mind felt sluggish. The only thing he was thankful for was that he hadn't been alone down there. There were other prisoners in the catacombs of the Empire.

A few were even from the Theocracy, though they were very few—very few. More had been recovered at first, but as the years dragged their feet, more and more of these people were taken.

Executed. Killed.

A fate superior to remaining as a prisoner. It was hell. Food was scarce, drinking clean water even more so. Kreig had believed that he had accepted his new, otherworldly life. He had lived there longer than he had lived on Earth, he had found love and purpose in the Theocracy, but here, now, he uselessly found himself longing for the simple pleasures of his teenage years.

They released him only after his will had been shattered a thousand times. Only after he had sworn his loyalty, only after he had spat in their faces, only after he had kissed their boots, only after he had pretended to give up his religion, only after he had been taught the tongue of his captors, only after he grew more silent than not, only after he stopped reacting to their whips and chains, only then did they know that he was truly broken.

He prayed, yes. In his heart, he sang the psalms that Peter had written so many years before. He spoke words of faith and longing.

That wasn't what saved him.

When they pulled him up, when they dragged him out of his cold, damp cell, he expected torture, isolation, or execution. Not release.

He was met with a black sky and a crescent moon grinning down at him. It was so bright that his eyes felt dry and burning. Stars upon stars shone down in full intensity as if he hadn't spent a single year down there. Years before, he might have taken this moment of release, this single moment where the Empire's streets were laid bare and the night wind rustled through his unkempt hair, to escape. To break his chains and throw the soldiers to the side and run, run, run.

He didn't. He stared up, looked at the stars, and lumbered after his new masters.

He couldn't let himself die. If he tried to escape and he was caught, he would be killed. If he tried to escape and he succeeded, he would be hunted forever. The Theocracy had fallen, he was a heretic, and if he didn't submit, the faith would die with him. He had to remain alive.

Such a vow lived on in his heart. He had to live.

And yet, he felt misplaced. The free wind felt wrong, the castle he was shuffled into was cold and foreign, and the lord who presented him in fluid German was a stranger. It was all wrong. Wrong and bad and he was in the wrong place and why wouldn't they take him home yet?

Not home to Earth, not home to the Theocracy and the Holy Order of White Roots. Home to his cell.

Where every day was the same and nothing was off and he was in the right place. This freedom was wrong.

You're in the wrong place. Wrong wrong wrong get out of there.

Go home, home to where every day is the same and nothing is bad. Home where you're expected, home where your faith is safe. Go there, Kreig, go there and—

Kreig awoke in a cold sweat, his head pounding and his chest heaving. He could feel every hot vein in his head. Thumping and bumping like something unknown in the night. His pajamas felt tight and uncomfortable, and his bed was much too soft.

He swung his legs over the side of the bed and stood up. He had to get out of there. He had to go . . . somewhere. But where? Not here.

Elsewhere.

Sneak (V)

He moved through the apartment as silently and quickly as a tiptoeing cat. He merged with the darkness. He hated sneaking, but sometimes, it was what he had to do to survive. Now was not exactly such a moment, but he despised the thought of awakening his siblings more than he did sneaking.

The door was unlike the ones he was used to in many ways, but he figured out how to unlock it quickly enough without having to use a skill he hated even more, namely Lockpick (II).

He went down the stairs, out the door, and into the cool air that blew across the city like a wave of chilled water.

Breathe. In and out. Wander here and wander there. The sky was dark but the city was bright. Too bright. He could barely see the stars. But up there, just beyond the gray and the tempered clouds, he saw stars. Stars of brightest white, hidden in the black. Stars he both recognized and didn't. He used to love watching the stars, seeing them twinkle and shine and light up the world.

They were in different constellations there. Different stars in different positions. But they were still stars, and they were still bright, and he was still—

No, no. This was home. Where he was before wasn't *truly* home. This *was*.

But as he looked at the stars he didn't recognize, in a world he didn't remember, in a city that had forgotten him, he suddenly felt hollow.

He wasn't home. Not yet.

He had to *make it* home.

And that would take work.

He fell to his knees. The sky was empty with nothing above him. He clutched his hands together and let the words fall from his glib tongue. It was one of the first prayers he'd learned before he even understood the beliefs of the Holy Order. Before he accepted it into his heart. But he remembered it. Through all these years, it was one of the prayers he wouldn't hesitate to speak in any situation.

It was one asking for guidance.

"O White Roots, God Below, white snakes of grandest truth. Form into paths, white paths of white gold, and let me walk upon your back. Show me the way, show me the truth." The moon shone upon his back—a single ray of light, like a spotlight for him and him alone. All prayers he knew were in English. He didn't understand it at first, but the mere fact that he and his four classmates spoke English as a first language was seen as a blessing, something fantastic. Only the highest Oracles and Cardinals spoke the language of roots fluently. Sure, the Five Bodies couldn't speak a lick of Mandarin, but they learned quickly enough.

Peter even became a scriber when the opportunity arose, creating lyrics for chants and texts for prayer. He had written many of the prayers Kreig knew by heart.

After Kreig had spoken his prayer, asking for guidance from his God, he stood up.

Unbeknownst to him, he and his display had been seen by a single soul. A single woman saw his prayer and how he lit up the little street. She was a prostitute, a woman in a desperate situation with a desperate need for reason. She wasn't a believer, but now that changed. Now she had seen a chosen one.

Now she had received her *guidance*.

Kreig didn't linger in the streets for long. His God remained silent, but he could tell his place was not in the streets, below dull stars. It was inside. In his *home*. That he knew.

He went home, not knowing how this small display would change his future.

"Huh? . . . Kreig? What're you up for?"

Kreig walked in to find Sam hunched over the fridge, an entire slice of cake in her hand. No, not an entire one. A half-eaten one. It was a complete mess. It honestly disgusted Kreig a bit, but he couldn't bring himself to tell her to stop.

Lacking any reason to cease, Sam took another great bite out of her slice. "Couldn't sleep, huh?" She was entirely right, so Kreig had nothing to reply with. "Guess so. Yeah, I know how it is. First night in a brand-new place . . . Gotta be tough, man. But it's better than being down in that cell, right?" She grinned, giving a fantastic display of her canines. Kreig flinched. "Yup, yup. Maybe even better than what you had before coming here. I mean—we haven't really been told anything. We've seen your status, but that's, like, nothing."

". . . There isn't much to say." In truth, there was a whole lot to say. He just didn't feel like unloading it all upon his sister.

"No, no. No way, dude; you've shown me there's a cat in the bag. Now you gotta let it out," Sam said in all her grand wisdom. As Kreig tried thinking up a proper response, Sam cut herself another slice and went over to sit on the couch. A glance back at Kreig urged him to follow her.

So, there they were. Sam on one end of the couch, Kreig on the other. She was sprawled out, lazily holding two slices of chocolate cake, eyes slowly blinking. Kreig sat upright with his hands resting formally in his lap. He was secretly hoping the couch wouldn't buckle under his weight, but Sam didn't seem bothered in the least. "Say, what's it like?" she asked. "In the otherworld, I mean."

Kreig scratched at his cheek.

What was there to say? It was . . . It was a pretty normal place. There were monsters, he supposed. Not many of them here, now that he thought about it. Not all monsters were born monsters, though; a lot ate unusual mushrooms or Messiah's Eggs to become changed into monsters. But most were born. Dragons were born monsters. It was the same with most drakes.

As far as he could tell, the flora was . . . There were much fewer mushrooms here. Back in the otherworld, mushrooms were not only as large a part of most diets as meat was but also as common and large as most plants. Finding tree-sized fruiting bodies was far from rare, and the uses often extended beyond just eating. Many potions and poisons were concocted from mushrooms. He didn't smell much of anything like that here. Though it might just be the region causing it, and other continents and nations had a larger fungal population.

Then there were also the cultural properties. The architecture here was different. People ate in a different manner—God forbid all the etiquette he'd learned all those years before prove useless—people acted differently . . . Though, again, a lot of it might be regional. And, even more so, a *lot* seemed to have changed since Kreig was last part of any actual society.

". . . Little is different," Kreig said. After all, humans were still the dominant species. The sky was still blue. People still breathed air.

"That's no answer," Sam pouted. "Come on, just a little something. Like, uhhh . . . What kind of pets did people keep? Dogs and cats?"

Pets? Ah, there *was* that, wasn't there? "Last I recall, nobles enjoyed keeping magically awakened humans as pets. In some parts of the world, Magus Humans aren't considered true humans and can be bought and sold as slaves or pets. Disgusting operation. For one man to own another . . . It is a sin."

Sam seemed troubled by it. "Is—is that so?"

"Otherwise, young four-legged drakes are often quite docile. Though once they reach an adolescent stage, they must either be released or slain."

"Drakes . . . Oh, yeah! Aren't two-legged drakes those T. rex–looking things?"

Kreig's mind drew a blank. ". . . What?"

Sam explained with animated movements what dinosaurs and T. rexes were, and when she finally explained that some could fly but they all died out millions of years ago, she was only left with a dazed Kreig. There used to be—what? There was a massive race of drakes with thousands of species . . . and they all just *died out*? Impossible. What killed them? It must have been an amazingly powerful creature. If it was strong enough to kill millions of drakes, it must have an extremely high level. Possibly as high as Kreig's.

He must be wary of it.

"Anyway, tell me more about the otherworld. Something fun, though, nothing scary like that, yeah? Like . . . what part did you like the most?"

A hard question with an easy answer. "The comrades I made." The Five Bodies aside, his squadron had been a fantastically goofy bunch. They barely even respected him as their leader, despite his capabilities. But they had been loyal to a T, and when they won a battle, they could party for days. When the vice-captain died, the party and their mourning had seemingly drowned the whole capital in misery.

He hadn't been too close to the captains of the other squadrons, but he still knew he could rely on them in a battle.

But after all that, the people he had learned to trust the most must have been the party he formed between the wars, when his duties went from guarding the throne to defeating monsters prowling about the Empire. Those people had been as close to him as anyone, and when the Empire turned on him, they were his greatest allies.

"That is really clichéd. But also sweet! So, I'll accept it. Not sure what else to say, so . . . What're you most excited about, coming back home?" Sam smiled, even when Kreig turned to her with a blank stare. "I mean—I get you're happy, and we are too! But what're you the *most* excited about? There's gotta be something." She waited a moment, her eyebrows squishing together in thought. "Hrm . . . How about tacos? I remember tacos were your favorite food. It was even written in your diary! Heh, not that we, um, read it or anything."

. . . If he was excited about anything, it wasn't some Earthly food. It wasn't soft beds, either, or clean clothes. Not a warm home, not unfamiliar stars.

"Meeting my family." As simple as that. As complicated as that. Having family meant having people to love—people to protect. Years before, when he had had so many people to love, so many saints and comrades and soldiers, he hadn't thought that loving someone could be so important. Now he knew different. He couldn't love himself. But he could love his *family*.

Sam smiled. A soft smile stained with chocolate frosting. "Is that so?" Kreig nodded. "I'm . . . glad. Hey. Let's go to bed, yeah?"

"Of course."

CHAPTER 14

FIVE ROSES STANDING ALONE

Morning came around quicker than Kreig expected.

He knew it was morning for two reasons. The first was the knocking on the door, and the second was that the sun was beginning to peek through the blinds. A voice at the door, most likely George's, informed Kreig that if he wanted to continue acting as the cook of the house, he might want to get up and make some sort of breakfast, even though the hour was early. Ordinarily, they wouldn't have any business being up at this hour, but as George explained it, they hadn't taken two days off work to diddle around. Also, he'd better get to it quickly, since Sam would probably throw a fit if she didn't get her morning fix.

Those were two explanations Kreig could understand. Within five minutes, he had peeled off his pajamas and dressed in the clothes he'd arrived in. Still tight, still somehow better than his overalls.

"Oh, you're awake!" George said as Kreig pushed open the door into the hall. "Your hair is . . . We'd better have you take a shower. After we buy you new clothes, that is." George nodded wisely and Kreig mimicked him, mostly since he had no better idea.

And now, breakfast.

Strangely enough, the kingdom he was first summoned to didn't consider breakfast to be anything important, while people of the Empire constantly told him it was the most important meal of the day. Since Kreig had spent fifteen years in the kingdom and later the Theocracy, he didn't consider breakfast anything special. Even though he'd spent a larger part of his life in the company of people of the Empire, he had somehow never lost his belief that breakfast just wasn't that important.

George seemed to lean closer to the Empire's views in this regard. It was all right, though. He'd learned several dozen recipes for Empire- and Reigna-styled breakfast foods.

He just hoped his siblings would enjoy it even though it was hardly modern by their standards. At least, that's what he thought. George and Sam had probably never even tasted otherworldly food. The only reason there was even a possibility for them to was that the food served on the Other Island had mostly been otherworld food to appease the other-worlders. The food he'd been served down in his cell was, however, different. Likely Earth food.

He cracked his knuckles and got to work. By the sound of it, Sam was still asleep. And going by the way he blinked one eye at a time, George was about half-asleep. Kreig himself wasn't tired in the least.

But he knew just the kind of breakfast that would get them on their feet again. From what he could smell, all the necessary ingredients were present, although a few spices seemed a little off. Might have been their manufacture or preservation process.

Either way. As he did last night, he moved through the kitchen like a whirlwind, some paprika there, some non-fungus flour there, eggs there . . . Swept up in his own work, he barely noticed George staring at him, silently enraptured by Kreig's pure expertise. And by the very end, when it was all in the oven and Kreig knew it'd be ready in ten minutes, George tapped him on the shoulder.

Kreig almost jumped out of his skin, but he was able to keep it together enough to turn to glance at George, half-washed bowl and dishcloth in hand.

"Kreig. How did you do that and what in the world have you made? It hardly smells like any sort of breakfast I've ever seen, and why is it in the *oven*?" George asked, pointing one accusatory finger at the oven.

That was three questions in one. If Kreig took a deep breath, he could surely answer it all. "The Reignian of my party taught me this recipe while we were on the run. It is usually meant to be baked over a weak fire, constantly turned. You have no such thing apart from this weird oven. I have always been a very good cook. It relies on intuition, which I have a lot of." There. He said it all. And now, he wouldn't be able to speak for about five hours.

George seemed fully confused. Or maybe overwhelmed? Either way, should he have asked for any further explanation, Kreig would have had none to give. There were the facts, and there was nothing more to it.

"... I'll wake Sam up. There's a long day ahead of us, and I trust that whatever you make will satiate us." If it didn't, there was surely something wrong with their taste buds.

This would wake them up. He was sure of it.

George went and got Sam, and soon the three of them were sitting at the table once again. Each of them was looking down at what seemed to be a pocket of flaky bread before them, alongside a few vegetables that Kreig picked almost at random. As with last night, George showed an inherent distrust of the odd meal while Sam was just about ready to attack it despite her clear exhaustion.

Each of the three took a bite, and their expressions changed in a moment. Kreig felt nostalgia for his old party members. George seemed pleasantly surprised.

Sam breathed fire.

She threw herself at her glass of water, downed it in a single gulp, ran to the fridge to swallow milk directly from the carton like a beast, became upset when it went empty and ended her little spree by swallowing several large mouthfuls of water right from the tap. Her chest was heaving and her face was red, but boy, was she awake.

This was always the best kind of breakfast when the whole party needed to wake up and *fast*. Especially so since there was a mushroom-filled dish that was extremely similar in look and form, meaning that oftentimes party-members would feel groggy, see the flaky pocket, and take a bite before knowing or asking what it was filled with.

Kreig used to get around it by simply never eating that meal, since he couldn't eat the mushrooms. But as he grew used to spicy foods, he found it more nostalgic than anything. Sam didn't seem as enthusiastic.

"WhatthefuckwhatthefuckjesusSHIT my tongue is on *fire*—" she spat out between gulps of water.

George took another bite of his breakfast. "Wuss."

He wasn't wrong. Though, then again, the old which-kind-of-breakfast-is-it trick used to make even the hard-assed pikeman burn his throat. So, it was less so a weakness on her part and more so that George was strange.

Sam growled something horribly immature in return and chose to cautiously eat the bread instead of the entire thing. A sensible approach. The ranger usually threw it in the river after he realized what it was, but by then, it had already served its purpose of waking everyone up before the Empire advanced further on them.

"Okay, all right. I'm done. My tongue is less charred now. Fucking hell. Let's just—let's just go. We've got a time and a place, and the time is nine o'clock, and the place is the police station. If you two aren't ready in *five minutes*, I'll shove a boot down your throats," Sam said as she advanced to the front door. Neither Kreig nor George could refuse her.

Both were ready within the allotted time span and off they went.

Kreig realized pretty quickly that he recognized the path they were walking. Only barely, of course, as much of the city was still unfamiliar to him, but they were walking the same road he had walked to get home. The same he'd been guided through. It felt nice, finally recognizing something about this world, about this city he'd once grown up in.

Sam and George talked a lot. Or, rather, Sam talked a lot and chattered up a storm while George replied with single words and short sentences. Kreig barely said a thing.

And then they arrived at the police station.

He'd been there before, hadn't he?

Yup, he had. The bronze plate with the title written on it was the very same, as well as the white steps and everything. It was less crowded at this time of day, but he still recognized it.

That girl sure had been kind to bring him there. Had she known he'd need it?

Surely not. Then again, the world worked in mysterious ways.

They entered. Kreig noticed the second he stepped inside that no few eyes turned on him. And not in surprise or fear, although the latter was present, but more so in silent, unified acknowledgement. As if they'd been expecting him. It felt tense, but Kreig couldn't possibly act rashly while his family was there. No, he followed them, letting the fact that so many people were watching him so intently remain in the back of his head.

"Hey, Leo, I'm here for the nine o'clock ID thing? Kreig Wiedermann. Look it up. Should be right in the box," Sam said openly to the first man available behind the counter.

The man in question, Leo, seemed more confused than anything. "Uh, ma'am, do I know you?"

Sam pulled a blank. "I, er, uh. Dude, we meet every day!" Leo didn't seem any wiser. "It's me. Sam! Do I look *that* different in normal clothes?" Although Kreig had no idea what she could possibly look like in a formal setting, he could tell by Leo's expression that her hypothesis was at least somewhat correct.

"Sam? Oh, all right. Sorry. Um, Kreig Wiedermann would be . . ." Leo craned his head where he sat, glancing beyond George and up at Kreig. "That's the guy. All right, the photo things are over to your right, which you should know by now, and try to ignore the guys stationed there; it's for the safety of the police station and the place as a whole. I think. Between you and me, I have no idea what's going on."

Sam scratched her cheek. "Yeah, understandable. All right, see you tomorrow, Leo." There would be no explanation from her side.

As per the receptionist's guidance, Sam and George both brought Kreig to the right of the front desk and sat him down on a little stool. All the while, they tried to pretend that the people standing in all corners of the room didn't each have a level above 200. Kreig himself was just lost and confused, hoping the guidance he received from his siblings would be enough.

Sit on this chair. Look at the strange thing in front of the chair. Look happy. No, not like that. Just look natural. Good enough. You can stand up now.

And through it all, Kreig felt more like a tagalong than anything.

Finally, they made him place his inked fingertips on a piece of paper, and that was that. According to the receptionist, although an ID would usually take around six days to be delivered, this was a special situation, and they would be able to hurry it to such an extent that it would arrive later that day. Neither Sam nor George seemed too surprised by this development, simply saying goodbye and leaving it at that.

"You did great, Kreig!" Sam said enthusiastically, although Kreig wasn't sure *what* he did. "Next stop: a clothes store of some sort! I haven't really planned this part, since I'm terrible at clothing and stuff, so, uh, George. You're the suit guy. Where do we go?"

"Sam, if we bring Kreig to my regular tailor, he'll throw a fit. Kreig's built like a log. Let's just go to that mall in the middle of the square."

Sam pulled her lips tight. "I mean—yeah, but . . . Are we *allowed* to do that? Y'know . . ."

"If we weren't allowed to bring Kreig wherever, he wouldn't have been allowed home. Come on; let's go there before rush hour comes along." And since Sam accepted his words, they all started wandering in a certain direction while Kreig felt just a smidge left out. It wasn't as though he couldn't hear them or anything, and still, they talked about him as if he wasn't there at all. It felt odd, but since it wasn't his first time being treated like an object or mindless machine of human suffering, he couldn't find it in himself to complain about it. Especially since it was his siblings doing it.

And all of a sudden, when Sam and George started talking about random things again, he didn't feel like he was just silently listening in, a muted part of a larger conversation. He felt like he wasn't even a part of it.

So far from his family that he was hardly even walking with them.

"Kreig? Are you—" Of course, it wasn't the first time he'd felt a bit left out. Soldiers in the mud at his feet, proclaiming love to people Kreig didn't know and grasping for each other's hands just to have someone to hold on to in their final moments. *"Everything all ri—"* Even while on the run with his party, even though he acted as their leader, he was oftentimes mostly ignored. The bard sang and the ranger joked with him and everyone was talking, and at the time, Kreig had felt perfectly content just being a part of the fellowship. It wasn't—

"Kreig!" Sam was right in his face or, rather, standing on her tiptoes atop an elevated fountain, face-to-face with Kreig. "We've been trying to call out to you for a while. Are you all right?"

Huh? Was he— Of course he was all right. He'd just gotten a bit lost in his thoughts. "Yes." He sincerely hoped she wouldn't need a better explanation, because he really didn't want to give one.

She smiled in relief. "That so? Good, good, you seemed a bit . . . Anyhow! We're here now!"

Saying so, she gestured broadly all around. As it turned out, the fountain she was standing on was just the centerpiece of a very large plaza. It was half-crowded with people, everyone milling in and out of restaurants and stores with nary a care in the world. The sun had almost risen to stand above them and was currently splashing off of the fountain in large droplets.

George made his presence known by stepping into Kreig's view. "Where would you like to go first?"

. . . Where?

"There's like a bazillion stores here! I used to go to that one over there all the time," Sam said, pointing straight at a little store on the edge of a building, with the sign Pam's Candles. "Ah, good times. My favorite were the vanilla ones."

"Yes, yes, of course. Now, Kreig. This mall over there"—George pointed at a building a bit larger than the rest—"has a lot of stores. Some for women, some for children, and a few for men. We'll be going to the men's ones, and if they have nothing in your size, we'll consider finding a specialist tailor. You wouldn't happen to know your sizes, would you?"

. . . Sizes? As in his height?

That was . . . He used to be pretty normal for a man, but as he grew stronger and as his race changed, well . . . "I cannot remember." He genuinely had no idea.

George shrugged. "I figured as much. Let's go to Keaton's; they've got too many yardsticks for their own good."

Kreig wasn't sure what was going on, but he was damn happy they didn't continue asking him for answers or directions on where to go. He didn't know, and admitting that he didn't know would only lower his beliefs about him. Not that they could go much lower, to begin with.

He just followed his siblings as they went into the large building, stepped onto some magical moving stairs, went up two floors without having to walk a single step, and entered a store. It was filled with all kinds of clothes and fabrics, and it was, by all means, a pretty regular store. The kind of place Kreig hadn't been to in around seventy years. Of course, everything imaginable was different. As with the people outside, as with the clothes he himself wore, it was all very weird.

Not that he wasn't used to being confused.

George entered the store confidently, followed by Sam and finally Kreig. Unlike what one might think, since the suits and shirts all seemed to be of high quality, it was almost completely empty, with only three people apart from the siblings inside it. And one of these three had a familiar scent dangling around him. Kreig knew exactly who he was and where he was. He just didn't know if he should approach him. Was it socially acceptable? What would he have done if he was still seventeen and hadn't forgotten his Earthly manners? Would it—

Oh, it seemed the decision was made for him.

The man in question had apparently noticed Kreig's existence as he made a half-hearted attempt to bolt for the exit before finally admitting to himself that since the three siblings were standing exactly there, he had no means of escape.

". . . Don't I know you?" George asked.

"Oh—uh, no you don't . . ." Craig said foolishly.

Both George and Sam could only squint at Craig where he stood, back hunched slightly as if to hide from their gazes. It wasn't as though he was in civilian gear, either, no. Just beneath his floral-patterned shirt and light-brown khakis, one could clearly see the hard, modern armor pressing against the fabric. As if it couldn't be any more obvious, it was also pretty clear that he wasn't lugging around an oversized tennis racket. He was carrying his spear. In broad daylight.

"This is—ha-ha, um." Craig scratched behind his head, clearly flustered. "Look, you're not supposed to see me, so can I just, like, leave?"

Cryptic, but the three siblings stepped to the side. Craig spent no time passing them, and as soon as he was out of the store, he was—by the smell of it—ushered away from the main hallways and into a smaller store by someone. There he met a collection of other people, who all smelled of metal and sweat. Kreig chose not to inform his siblings of this, since they both seemed content with ignoring what had just happened.

Kreig only felt a bit sad that Craig's arm had healed so nicely. No scraping bone shards to be heard.

". . . Okay, so"—George confidently moved to the back of the store—"here. It's a self-measuring station, although you can call for assistance if you require it. Since both I and Sam are at your disposal, that won't be needed. Just step over here and we'll do the rest." Kreig listened intently and moved over to where George had directed him. All things considered, he wouldn't need to do a thing.

And he didn't. While Sam and George bickered over this and that, wrapping measuring tape around his chest and midsection and hips, there was nothing he really had to do.

A familiar experience. It had been many years earlier, but whenever he had armor to be forged or fine clothes to be tailored, he'd get measured in a similar capacity. Though, at that time, the ones doing it were usually either workers or the tailor himself. He wished he could remember what his measurements had been back then, but it had most likely changed by now.

"And as for height . . ." Sam placed the end of her measuring tape at Kreig's feet and tried to pull it to the very top. She was nowhere near tall enough to do this, though, so she handed the end of it to Kreig, who understood the gesture well enough. With an arch of her back and a squint of the eye, she was able to get a good look at his height. "Holy cow! Yeah, we'll definitely need to have a few things specially tailored . . ."

George silently nodded in agreement. Kreig wasn't sure if having things "specially tailored" would be a good or bad thing. Regardless, he hoped his existence wouldn't be too much of a plight for them.

"I think I may know just the place," George said.

Not one person out of the three questioned it. The tapes were put back in place, and they left the store without buying a single thing. It felt like an extremely rude thing to do, but Kreig figured it must be some Earth-culture thing.

But it wasn't that simple.

The second they stepped out of the mall, Sam must have noticed something, because she made a sound like a startled hare and ran off toward the fountain. Kreig could only barely make out how she enthusiastically greeted someone and was greeted in return by one of them saying, "Why, if it isn't the rookie! What're you doing out here? And not dressed in gear, either?"

"Hey, I won't be a rookie for long! And I've got the day off, so there's no need for me to dress up at all. Though aren't you both in the Portal Fighting division? What, have portals started going invisible?" Sam asked jokingly, peering about the square suspiciously.

One of the two officers shrugged. Kreig and George curiously moved toward them. "Nah, nah. We're not here for that. This is more of a . . . *crowd control* kind of—" The officer's eyes fell on Kreig. "Whoa! That's the— Why is—" His eyes flared wide, both of them focusing way too much on Kreig. He felt far too seen. And once one of the officers pointed him out, the other noticed him as well.

"Oh. Oh, sh— Sam, sorry, we gotta go," he said, taking a hold of the other officer's arm and pulling him away. In a matter of seconds, they were gone, lost in the crowd.

"That's kinda weird . . ." Sam said. "Oh, no, wait, I get it. It isn't *that* weird. I think. Uh, let's not talk about it! George, where are we going?"

George was still reeling from what just happened, but he was still able to muster a response. "We—uh. I imagined something like this might happen, so I scouted out a nearby store that takes orders for strange clothes. Just down the street." Sam gave a thumbs-up. They continued walking. And yet, there was a sour taste in Kreig's mouth. If he took the time to look for it, he could smell that those two officers hadn't left at all, merely reclaimed some distance.

Even more so, Craig was also about. He was at a safe distance, of course, together with other people who smelled like stress. If Kreig really looked for them, he could tell that there were about twenty, thirty such people prowling about. And that was just in the vicinity.

There was something off there, but since both George and Sam had decided not to consider it too deeply, they must also know about it. And since Kreig was the only one not in the know, it must be about him. Not an attack, not anything like that. Just a sort of surveillance. Of him. Despite the fact that he'd never hurt his siblings. And he'd thought he'd gained their trust, too. "*You're free,*" Darius had said.

Perhaps so, but not entirely. Then again, he had never been truly free these past 130 years.

"All right, we're here."

Since Kreig had nothing to say on what might look best on him, he fully allowed his brother and sister to decide for him. George seemed to argue for the modest, meaning that he thought Kreig would clearly look best in a fine suit and an ironed shirt. Sam, who had no fashion sense, disagreed, explaining that the more colors, the better. She was wrong. In the end, the sensibly flustered shopkeep could only try to make some sort of peace between them by asking Kreig himself what he wanted to wear.

Since Kreig became silent as a rock at the mere mention of deciding what to wear for himself, the shopkeeper soon assumed that he was either mute or deaf or both. The responsibility quickly returned to Sam and George.

A decision was made. fifty-fifty casual and formal, and Kreig himself would choose what to wear on a daily basis.

And then, with the clothes done and ordered, they left the shop.

After that, they went back to the main square, entered a strange shop filled with strange things, and picked out a "phone." Sam assured Kreig that George would teach him how to properly use it once they got home. But just as Kreig was about to accept that this was it for their daily excursions, George gave a timid proposition.

"Hey, uh, Sam. Couldn't we bring him to . . . you know?"

Now Sam knew *exactly* what he was talking about. The school. Frederick High School, just down the street to the right. Where Kreig had last been seen before his . . . before whatever happened to him took place. To him and four others. It . . . Well, by all means, it wasn't a terrible idea. The school hadn't shut down or anything, though since it was a normal weekday, there might be kids about, but . . .

Sam turned to look at Kreig where he stood in that stupid *I <3 IOCRO* shirt, lumbering like a bear in human form. Those damn kids wouldn't dare approach him like that. No way, no how.

But that wasn't the issue, and it certainly wasn't why she hesitated. She had two reasons.

Firstly, would it be good for Kreig? She was far from psychologically trained. George knew a whole lot more about that, but she was pretty sure that, all things considered, going back to the place where all the trauma that Kreig must have experienced might be . . . bad somehow? *"Don't do or show him anything that might trigger any sort of emotional outburst,"* that doctor had said. Then again, if he hadn't responded as badly as she and George had thought he would to seeing Mother and Father's obituaries . . . it might be fine?

The real defining factor there was that George had suggested it. He probably had his reasons.

Then, the thing that really made her hesitate was the second point. She knew that there were people trailing them. All things considered, she had noticed them pretty quickly. It wasn't just in the here-and-now, either; they'd been hovering around their apartment yesterday, too. But that was fine. She had accepted it.

Even so, these weren't just nameless officers of the law. These were people she *knew*. People who were trained to stand guard outside portals in case something happened, people who were just working in the portal division until they could move to a less monster-heavy division, people who liked their doughnuts with jelly in them, not cream. All these fantastic workers who all collectively agreed that tailing a bunch of siblings out shopping was probably the most boring thing of all, no matter who Kreig was.

Would she really accept that these people would have to go on working even more just for her and George to show Kreig his old school?

"George, I'm not—" And while she'd been thinking about all that stuff, George had already begun walking in that direction, with Kreig sending forlorn gazes at her where she stood on her lonesome. "H—hey! Wait up!"

"Watching you think is like watching a penguin try to fly."

Sam pouted. "No need to be mean about it. Sometimes, things need a good think-through to clear it all up!" For some reason, George didn't seem impressed, scoffing at the mere idea. "Geez. Are you sure this is a good idea? With the—with our friends far back, that is. Won't they be mad we took a detour instead of just doing, like, exactly what we needed to do? We got him a phone, we got him clothes . . . do we really need to give him a look at what he lost, too?"

"Sometimes, you need to see what's left behind to truly move ahead, Sam. Like with the obituaries," George whispered. "What's happening to Kreig isn't anything easy, but we can't coddle him and pretend everything is the same as how he left it. He can't reintegrate into the world of the past; it doesn't *exist.*"

He was right. He was completely right. She knew he was right, and yet— Sam glanced over her shoulder.

Kreig was walking there, towering above them, hulking and huge and silent. Could he seriously not hear them? Not a word they were saying? Or had he just decided to keep quiet for some reason? Whatever the reason was, it must've been a stupid one. She had heard him speak. He had a quiet, rumbling kind of voice that was very unlike how she remembered his voice to be. But the words he spoke were nothing but the truth, *his truth*, and she respected that.

If anything, she wanted to hear him speak more. Have him let it all out. But she'd let him take his time, and if he just wanted to listen to them speaking, that was okay.

They reached Frederick High School. Dreary name, really. It was named after the founder, who thought his first name was unique enough for the school to avoid any copying. Surprise, surprise, it actually was. It didn't make the school any more interesting, though. In Sam's experience, it was almost wholly filled with jocks who tried their best and nerds who were too lazy to do anything with their knowledge. Kreig had, at the time, been a part of the former clique.

Man, he'd been quite something back in the day. Charismatic. Yeah, that was the right word. Big and brassy, and when he talked, everyone listened.

Not as good at joking as one might have expected from such a popular guy, but he made do.

He was really the living proof that you don't need to be an expert at studying to be a success in life. She'd always loved that about him, how he seemed to grab life by the horns and never let go, grinning all the while. As if just the act of living were a competition. He made do. Whatever life threw at him, be it a spin ball or a bad test score, he always bounced back. A true optimist.

He was different now, in almost every way, but . . . she was sure that he still had that golden heart. He had to.

Nobody had told her exactly what he had done in the otherworld yet. She didn't know, and her optimism was choking.

They entered the school.

It should have been crowded with kids. However, since it was barely eleven, there wasn't a soul in the courtyard.

"Do you recognize anything?" George tentatively asked Kreig.

There was no way he would. But, nevertheless, Kreig let his eyes wander. He looked up at the old brick walls, half-built in the early 1800s, half-built ten years back when an attacking monster destroyed much of the school. Luckily, since it had been a Saturday, only one loitering teacher had been harmed, who survived with only minor lasting wounds. Sam couldn't see any dawning recognition in Kreig's eyes, and she understood that.

He turned from the building, away from the students staring mournfully out of the windows, and to the courtyard itself.

It was pretty small, guarded on all sides by the school buildings. In the middle, a large acorn tree stood proud, the upper branches almost touching the tops of the buildings surrounding it. It really was a gorgeous tree, but it had been much smaller a mere ten years earlier. A whole lot smaller, as a matter of fact. But with how the world was nowadays, people didn't really question it when trees grew faster than—

Hold on; by the looks of it, Kreig was about to question the tree.

He just wandered right up to it, all without a care in the world. "Uh, Kreig, what are you—" But Sam couldn't say any more, because now Kreig was hunched over, sniffing the ground like a truffle dog. Was there actually anything down there worth smelling? Sure, he had an amazing sense of smell, beyond that of a common man, but why would there be anything down there to begin with? She shot a confused look at George, who gave her an equally confused glance in turn.

Even so, they didn't stop him.

He sat there for a moment, glanced back at the two of them, and then dug a little in the soft dirt around the tree. Then he proceeded to pull out a small, black, truffle-like ball. It was a little larger than a marble. Despite being covered in dirt, the form was unmistakable.

Was that—

Kreig crushed it between his fingers. A red liquid splattered out on his hand, alongside flaky pieces of white flesh. Yeah, that was definitely a Messiah's Egg. God only knew how many pictures and textbook chapters Sam had read about it. Now, the real question was: why was it growing in a school, how had Kreig smelled it, and why did he destroy it for no reason?

Kreig stared at his messy hand for a moment. ". . . Instinct." Ah. Sure. Right, that explained it.

And then, as if he hadn't just popped a budding Messiah's Egg as if it were nothing, he placed a hand upon the soft earth, closed his eyes, and muttered a few words.

Truth (I)

In a matter of seconds, something changed. From where Kreig held his hand, something akin to white threads seemed to blossom, digging into the dirt and the base of the tree with such speed and vigor that it stunned Sam silent. These white threads snaked their way into and through the tree, climbing inside it, infecting it, turning the whole tree entirely white in mere moments. The bark, the sap, the leaves, and everything else became as white as the whitest snow.

Beautiful, yes, but . . . "Kreig, what the *fuck* did you just do?" Sam asked, torn between arching her back to view the acorn tree fully and glancing down at where Kreig still hunched.

He stood up and turned to her. There was a peculiar glow in his eyes. "After all these years . . . I can still do it." Before Sam could follow up with the obligatory *Do what?*, Kreig continued. "This tree was a host of the white roots. Now it has been awakened to the Truth. The Messiah's Fruits it will bear will be the sweetest of all, and its roots will happily harbor the Messiah's Eggs to awaken us humans. To think I could still do it here. Despite how the Theocracy fell so many years ago . . ."

Again, extremely cryptic in a way that Sam couldn't even begin to fathom. She was just hoping that "awakening" a tree didn't constitute vandalism of private property. He just made it white. That wasn't illegal, was it?

Ah, though, the law never did say anything about using otherworldly powers or skills to do it . . .

Err, it was probably fine! Nobody would know a thing so long as they didn't tell anyone.

"Kreig," George said, catching the attention of both his siblings. "Come over here." He wasn't standing at the very edge of the courtyard, but almost. A monument quietly stood surrounded by chains and two benches, placed out of the way but still in a way to bring attention to it. It was a simple monument, really. A row of five roses, each standing tall and proud and made of now-tarnished bronze. Each of the topmost petals had been touched and caressed until they shone as brightly as they did ten years before.

"There used to be more flowers around it," Sam said, "but it's been a long time. Now they just leave a few flowers every week." Some of the roses were more touched than others; some had fresh flowers even today. Others only held withered chrysanthemums, soon to be removed by an old groundskeeper who wished he hadn't known the kids who represented the little bronze roses.

Kreig stepped closer to the roses, his eyes transfixed. Five. Each had a little name engraved in a nameplate by the stem.

Peter Willowgrove. Jamie Schwartz. Rudy Winter. Charlie Swallowbird. And Kreig Wiedermann. Priest, Cardinal, Monk, Churchrat, and Paladin. Executed, missing in action, killed in combat, missing in action, and fugitive.

He bent down. Five little roses. Five little lives lost in a world all too unlike their own. He reached out and touched Peter's rose.

Peter had been the intellectual among them, always just on the cusp of doing something truly worthwhile with his cunning nature. He was nothing until he found his passion for writing and analyzing scripture. He excelled at researching and understanding the most minor aspects of how faith worked. He figured out how the "system," as he called it, seemed to favor faith-related skills and how even the most mundane of chants, so long as the user believed in them, could have an intense effect, be it healing or otherwise. He was the brains of the bunch, the only one who could understand the time and place they found themselves in.

He was a good man.

Jamie wasn't a very smart man, but for what he was, he was a genius. He knew every aspect of his magical spells and rites, yet he never grew arrogant as so many had before him. Adhering to every rule and virtue the holy order proposed, he relinquished the possible pride he could have found in the great magical strength he carried. He instead let his patience for those below him and his humble nature prosper. He was no healer, but his mere presence was enough to soothe the most anxious minds. When the Five Bodies missed home, he was the one explaining calmly how what they had now wasn't all that bad. And they trusted his words.

He was a good man.

Rudy was, despite his profession, not a patient man. He wasn't a fighter, either. While Kreig took to head-bashing like a fish to water, Rudy clashed with it. He was unable to find any pleasure in punching and kicking and shouting the words of a religion he didn't believe in. He carried his fists for no one but himself. The words of the kindest monks fell on deaf ears, and he didn't hesitate to retaliate. The one thing that calmed him down and brought him to the ground was the gentle camaraderie of the others in his same position. This revealed his anger to be a mere mask covering his grieving nature, and he shed it. He never truly accepted the God Below as his lord and master, but he fought alongside his friends nonetheless.

He was a good man.

Charlie didn't have anyone before coming there. Rejected by everyone in class, he expressed a subdued delight at being somewhere that wasn't Earth. He missed his family, sure, but there wasn't anything else he truly lacked. He gained friends and a belief he used to lack, and that was all he needed. Although he was never openly thankful to anyone, in silent moments beneath the starlit night, he would occasionally express just the slightest hint of longing. A single word of truth, telling far more than any prayer could. There was no doubt that he loved the other four, just as they loved him.

He was a good man.

And Kreig . . . Kreig *survived*.

He was not a good man.

Something seemed to grip at Kreig's heart with invisible claws. It felt strange, all of a sudden. He could remember every aspect of these four people, from their appearance to their personal beliefs. And yet, he couldn't remember a single thing from the day he had been summoned, apart from the moment he woke up in the otherworld. It left a bad taste in his mouth.

Only one thing there felt worse to him.

There was a monument here. For *him*. Something he had never deserved and never would. Not in death, not in life.

He didn't deserve to be placed next to his deceased comrades.

He bent down, eyeing the rose in front of him with its glistening golden petals where people had touched it and the still-shiny nameplate that stated in bold letters like a gravestone when he was born and when he was summoned. No flowers surrounded it, because his siblings had known his fate as of over a month before.

He picked the rose. The metal stem snapped right in half, bringing the rose to his eyes.

His siblings seemed as though they wanted to say something, likely along the lines of "*Please don't destroy public property*," but he had no ear for it at the moment. The rose was a false idol of his lacking death.

It would burn in his hand.

Purge of the Holy (X)

It burned into petals of snow. But he wasn't done. These people, these roses . . .

Nobody had ever told their families what happened, had they? After all, nobody knew any details about it. And maybe it would be cruel to force such a harsh reality upon these grieving families, but he knew right then and there that they needed it. They had to hear that their sons had not died in vain inside a portal to feed some oversized animal. They were soldiers of God, and their families deserved to know that.

"Where do they live?" he asked. His siblings shared a glance.

"Um, you aren't going to, like, extort—"

"No."

"Oh. Okay. Uh . . ." Sam scratched at her neck. "I'll make an assumption and guess that you know what happened to the other four, right?" Kreig nodded. "Right. Then . . . you're going to tell them? How they—how they *died*?" Kreig didn't deny that. "I . . . Yeah, I can understand that. Losing a loved one is— It's the worst thing I've ever experienced, I think, but not even knowing *how* or *why* it happened is just— There's no closure, you know? Never knowing if they went out in a blaze of glory or snuffed out like a dying candle. I don't think we can mail any letters—this whole affair is probably pretty confidential—but I guess you can deliver them personally?"

He could accept that. "I will." Consider it a well-meaning gesture to his former comrades. Even if he had to jump through hoops to get it done, he'd do it.

Sam turned to George. They could accept that, couldn't they? It was needed, after all.

They went home.

CHAPTER 15

LETTERS FOR THE REMAINING

Even though neither George nor Sam ever had the need to buy a printer, they *did* keep paper and envelopes in the house. This was mainly because Sam once had a phase where she enjoyed handwriting letters and stamping them with wax seals to give to crushes, friends, or teachers she actually liked. Thanks to this, they were able to get Kreig paper and pencils faster than they otherwise might.

The only thing separating Kreig from writing four individual letters to four individual households was George's incessant need to first introduce Kreig to a phone.

"It isn't complicated, it's just—" And then he went on to explain in the smallest words possible how this little rectangular thing was, in fact, extremely advanced. In the end, though, his main points were in "This is the button to press to call me, this is the button to press to call Sam, and this is the button to call the authorities in case of an emergency." Everything else was by far too complicated for Kreig to fully understand. Messages? Social media? Internet? Kreig felt a headache coming on.

And when that was done and Kreig had successfully pressed the button to call George twice and George seemed happy with his use of the little artifact, he then went on to threaten Kreig's sparse sanity with teaching him how to use a "computer." In other words, a bigger version of the phone.

At this point, Kreig could not listen. The information went into one ear and out of the other. George noticed this, and although it made him a fair bit irritated, he finally decided to cut his whole explanation short.

With a final grumble and a reminder to keep the phone charged and on hand at all times, George left Kreig's room, leaving him to his own devices. All he had were his desk, his paper, and a pencil. With this and nothing more, Kreig would narrate a tale to people he had only ever heard about. A tale of hardship and woe and truth. He would spare no details, not in how it began, and not in how it ended, either. Only his own identity would remain hidden. He'd write it as though he were an outside force, merely observing.

Each of the four letters would be slightly different, focused on one of the four boys and how their lives played out.

In the otherworld, they had all become adults. As adult as five child-soldiers could become, at least. They had lived full lives, seldom lacking anything, becoming fulfilled as humans. Upon their deaths, all of them were over thirty-five. They had not died as children—they had died as men.

Kreig hoped that knowing their children had not died young would bring them some form of solace. The tale he spun them was almost non-sensical in nature, he knew that, but he hoped that he could earn their trust. If he couldn't earn it through usual means, he always had the skill Change Will (V), though it was not one he liked using. For now, he was prepared to use even underhanded methods to ensure that his comrades remained known and remembered by people other than himself.

It took him two hours to fully write the letters and to completely pour out the memories of his first thirty years in the otherworld. He could only hope that it would be enough.

He placed each letter inside an envelope, addressed them to the families of the deceased, and sealed them shut with wax he had borrowed from Sam. And now he only had to deliver them.

Whether they accepted his letters or not, he would make them understand exactly what happened.

At two, after a hearty lunch served by the new cook of the house, all the letters were finished. Done. Complete.

Ready to be delivered.

Apparently, as Sam explained it, casually sending these letters through the mail might cause some sort of trouble for the authorities. Hence, Sam convinced George to drive Kreig to wherever it was they needed going. Of course, as required by the law, Sam technically *did* have a driver's license. The issue was that George, being a sensible and wise man, would never in a million years let his sister get anywhere close enough to his car in order to drive it.

She could zip around on her scooter as much as she liked, but it would never change George's mind. It was his car, and if she wanted any part in it, she was better prepared to be relegated to the shotgun seat.

Even then, the car in question only had a pair of front seats, lacking any passenger seats in the back. After all, for ten years, he had never needed any more than two seats.

So it was that he sat behind the wheel of his car, glancing somewhat anxiously at his brother where he sat clutching a bundle of four letters. Each of them was written in the most gorgeous handwriting George had ever seen. It was completely different when compared to the letters he had written them. It was melodic, bright, and elegant, the kind you wouldn't expect to see from such a barbaric-looking man. It might have been a bit unkind to call his own brother barbaric, especially after seeing him labor over these kind letters for so long, but Kreig was truly a barbaric man, despite his warm heart.

One who, if he clutched too hard, could make a pencil explode. Who could pluck a metal rose and burn it with a mere thought.

Of course, George felt unsure. He was living in a house with a massive wall of a man and a Fighter sister. This was the kind of situation you saw on late-night soap operas where the twist was that the baby was a Fighter. Absolutely stupid and, to a normal person like him, borderline terrifying.

These were people who could easily crush bones, should they wish to. Sam didn't even have a high level, barely enough to enter the more medium-leveled portals that might appear at times, but even she could lift things several times her own bodyweight.

It wasn't scary, it wasn't terrifying, only worrying.

And somehow, Kreig was a hundred times beyond that or even more. In truth, nobody actually knew the true extent of his strength. Not as far as George knew, and he had deliberately looked for it. But every aspect of Kreig, from what he'd experienced in the otherworld to what his status was, had been locked behind thick walls. There was no way for George to read any of it, leaving him with a hole that he desperately wanted to fill. This was in spite of his own rank, which was only barely enough to know that Kreig existed.

What had Kreig experienced? Why had he changed? Why couldn't he remember anything?

Ten years earlier, before all this happened, before the unknown invaded the known and the world got all topsy-turvy, George had known everything about Kreig. He knew how Kreig always made a big show of following in his father's footsteps but really just wanted to be like his mother. She was a kind, caring woman who gave her everything to her art: the art of cooking. But Kreig was too boyish to let himself look up to her, and George knew that. He knew his brother.

But now, he barely knew his brother at all. The death of his brother had been mourned, and in some way, George couldn't fully connect these two people in order to believe that his brother had been revived. Or even that he hadn't died at all.

The only real way George could think of how to connect these two people, the Kreig he knew and the Kreig that was sitting next to him, was to know what had happened. Who Kreig had become during his years.

"Kreig," George said, peeking at his brother. The man showed no change in expression at being named, merely continuing to stare straight ahead. He fiddled gently with the letters in his hand. "Say, tell me. I'm aware you came to the otherworld, but, if I may ask . . . how did that happen? Did a portal appear beneath your feet? Usually, that's how people find themselves in the otherworld. Even more so, you wouldn't happen to know why you disappeared a day before the portals opened?"

Much like always, Kreig sat in silence for a pretty good while, eyes locked straight ahead. But he wasn't moving his hands about the letters anymore. "The world went black. When I awoke, I was in a coffin."

That was certainly worrying. It almost sounded as if he died right then and there. Though, since he was most definitely *alive*, that wasn't possible.

No portal. "Really? A coffin . . . And then what happened?"

Kreig pressed his lips together, clearly reluctant to speak. But after less than a minute of complete silence between them, the only sound being the whirring of the car motor, Kreig spoke softly. Somehow, the tale he spoke felt muted. Apparently, Kreig had been summoned by a good church in dire need of help, and he had, as a man should, helped it. He had killed monsters and done what had to be done to bring prosperity to a country in a bad place.

It was a heroic tale, but it didn't feel real in the least. There was no mention of any physical pain or death or personal hardship. Almost like it was just a soft-hearted parody of the truth, told to keep George happy.

It felt strange, but just as Kreig explained how the kingdom he resided in had become so believing that they appointed the pope of his religion as the leader of a Theocracy, just as George felt he had worked up the courage to ask Kreig what *really* happened, the GPS gave a beep, signifying that the travel destination was on their right. And yeah. There it was. A large, almost run-down apartment complex modeled after the countless gray blocks of Soviet Russia. The height of brutalist architecture.

This was the kind of place that the Swallowbird family resided in. It was nothing fancy, nothing that cost much.

George stepped out of the car, followed closely by Kreig. The apartment complex was at least fifteen stories high, but the Swallowbirds lived on the first floor. Although Kreig was far from eager, he still trailed after George, a single letter clutched dearly in his hands. He almost gave off the same feeling as an inexperienced teenager on his way to hand a love letter to someone he was sure wouldn't respond in kind. They entered the complex.

They wouldn't talk to them. They'd just go in and out, leaving a letter in their wake. Unseen, un—

"May I help you?" There she was. The girl George had seen on the internet profile. Brown hair tied up behind her head, sunken but still clear green eyes. The young miss of the house, barely fifteen.

Annie Swallowbird, baby sister of Charlie Swallowbird.

George gave an all-too-forced smile. "No, that's all right. We're only passing through."

Annie didn't seem quite happy, but she couldn't refuse them. So, although hesitantly, with a sidelong gaze, she stepped inside her apartment and wasted no time locking the door. George wasn't even surprised. Had he been alone, she likely wouldn't have been as apprehensive, but since Kreig the living mountain was there in person, it made sense for her to be more cautious than usual.

As Kreig took a step toward the door to put his letter through the mail slot, George stopped him by gently placing his hand on his brother's chest. From just that touch, George could tell almost instinctively that if Kreig hadn't stopped, George's arm might have been broken by him simply moving. Now, as unfun as those thoughts were, when Kreig turned to him, eyes bright and confused, George knew he had to explain. "She's cautious. We'll wait until she steps away from the door to give her the letter."

By the looks of it, as hesitant as he was, Kreig accepted it, stopping fully. Then he turned to the door. He took short, quick breaths through his nose. And after just a minute, he said, "She's left the door."

George didn't question it, simply nodding at the door in a gesture that said it all. Kreig gave a nod in turn.

Kreig approached the door, thumbed the letter a few seconds, and pushed it inside the little slot on the door. He gave a sniff and retreated.

And George barely heard the sound of quick, thumping footsteps on the other side and the door being thrown open, before someone grabbed him and the world blurred into a flurry of colors and things and all of a sudden he was back outside, in the arms of his brother. His glasses were lopsided. What the hell had just—

"I brought you outside to evade her discovery." Right. That explained it.

George wobbled out of Kreig's grasp, feeling his guts all squirming and unhappy. He felt bad, really bad. Humans weren't meant to move as fast as they had just moved, and he could feel it. How fast had it been? A wink of the eye and he had moved several dozen meters. "Right, thank you, that was— We don't want to be discovered. For national security reasons. Or something."

It wasn't as though Kreig argued this or was even trying to make an argument of his own, but George still couldn't stick around there. If Annie decided to walk out of her apartment complex to investigate who sent the letter, they'd be in trouble.

So, he made it over to the car, got Kreig to sit in the other seat, and drove off. "One down, three to go." Once George got the GPS all configured to the next spot, he turned to Kreig. "Now continue. About the Theocracy you served."

Kreig froze in his seat. He glanced away.

"It was . . . not a good time."

But in George's silence, Kreig found himself too uncomfortable to withhold the past.

The Theocracy fell. It had been too ambitious, Kreig said. Trying to spread to countries that rejected the belief and everything to do with it. And then . . . war happened. Kreig's voice was so low when he spoke about it that George could barely hear it. Death. Hundreds of thousands of soldiers and civilians were slain. There was no way to soften the truth. He almost died. Painfully, he admitted that he was captured by the enemy— that he was kept in a prison beneath the Empire for almost twenty years.

". . . Are you still a believer?" Maybe it was an insensitive question, but for some reason, George *really* wanted to know if his brother was some sort of zealot for an otherworldly religion.

Kreig didn't answer.

Not until they reached the household of the Winter family. These people lived in the suburbs, so all George and Kreig had to do to deliver the letter was to exit the car and place it in the mailbox. Back into the car, and off they went.

"I am," Kreig said. "Despite it all."

That said more than George wanted to hear. But he didn't know any details, nothing concrete. Nothing about the religion except what little Kreig had told him. Therefore, instead of taking an opinion of sympathy for the hardships his brother had gone through, he saw it in a more modern sense. The religion Kreig held *did* subject him to oppression and hardship, going by the tone of his voice. But wasn't it somewhat earned, considering that they had attempted a *crusade*?

Maybe he should have been more on Kreig's side, but he couldn't help it.

The Schwartz household, or, rather, what remained of it, was in the same suburbs as the Winter one. Same business, same situation. Kreig returned to the car, and even without any prompting from George, he continued. As if to justify himself.

By this point, going by the few markers of time Kreig presented, he was far older than George was. Even older than their parents had ever gotten. But the years kept coming, and Kreig kept explaining, the soft and sweet niceties peeling off to reveal the grim reality behind it. He didn't *just* subjugate humans as a pawn for the Empire. He was a soldier. He did what they told him to do, no matter how morally depraved.

The air seemed to turn heavy between them. Kreig's voice was like lead, pressing down between them, crushing George into stunned silence. Yet he kept speaking.

Details, specific missions, exactly who died where and when. His voice was cold and rough. So many years, but every aspect remained painfully relevant.

"Kreig, it's okay, you don't have to—"

"I do." He continued. He spoke of one time he was sent on a private mission. He wasn't a captain yet, just an abnormally powerful pawn. Obedient. He hadn't known. By then, he still thought there were *some* depths to which he wouldn't be forced to sink, some sort of good in him that had survived it all. That he was still a good man.

That changed quickly.

It was the day before Yuletide. Or, rather, the day everyone in the Empire celebrated Yuletide on. In the Theocracy, it was usually celebrated the day before.

This, alongside several other customs and traditions, were simply things that Kreig had to get used to. His comrades, the other soldiers and officers of the Empire, knew a parody of his life. He'd been captured and tortured by the *Theocracy*, only rescued when the Theocracy fell and the country was destroyed, crushed into a muddy wasteland up north where the sky was always red.

This, too, was something Kreig accepted. As a matter of fact, he was *thankful* for what the Empire did for him. In a certain sense, at least.

Warm food. Whole clothes. Work and comrades. After twenty years in prison, he had to forget his hatred at some point. Forgive, forget. Cherish what you have instead of longing for what was already gone.

It was during this time, before he was fully comfortable with his German, before he was fully integrated into the Empire's walls, that an officer of the crown approached him with a private mission in hand. A rolled-up parchment dripping in the perfume of the Emperor, a telling marker for any subservient. Kreig didn't like perfume, not then, not now. The parchment spoke in long, strung-together words about something he had to retrieve from up north. Something that had been buried with the Theocracy when it should have been brought back to the Empire.

Since he used to be an inhabitant of the Theocracy and a major player in it too, it was for him to go get "it." A simple mission. Travel north alone, retrieve it, and return with the item.

Simple. Mundane.

Suspicious.

Usually, when Kreig felt a knot of uncertainty ball up the pit of his stomach, he had people to turn to. People cleverer than he was. People who could look at a piece of text from all angles and tell him what was unusual and what to do about it. His main comrade in this department had been Peter, who, despite his eccentricities, was a very quick and thorough man when it came to things needing a good think-through. But he was dead. Still, even without him, Kreig did currently know such people.

The man who sat right across from him, scarfing down a stupidly normal-looking sandwich, was one such person. Erwin Strohesser. But secrets were secrets. Kreig could turn to no one with his suspicions for fear of being charged with treason, a crime usually punished by death or two hundred lashes.

He didn't mind the latter, but dying wasn't something he wanted. Not yet. Not before passing on the faith he had learned to love.

That was his reason for living, and right now, that meant not questioning his mission. He'd do it, and he'd see what was up with it when he got to the north.

Traveling there was no easy feat. Usually, no soldier would ever try to brave the wilds on his own, but Kreig had no choice in the matter. He had no squadron and no comrades. Just him and the world. In hindsight, part of the reason he was given the mission at all might have been to test his loyalty. To see if he'd try to run.

He didn't. A stupid choice, but his curiosity really did get the better of him. So, he traveled north.

His strength was only barely enough. Monsters and animals and the temperatures all attacked him, but he took it. These animals were known to him, from the thick-limbed frosty lizards that barely moved to the dune-covered quick-footed drakes. Snowstorms and meters of snow and frozen lakes that housed clawed crawlers all met him.

Home. Dear, detestable home.

Not a place he had ever traversed fully alone, but he made do.

The Empire was a very northern country. Above it, not much could grow at all. It was all cold and frozen and dead. There was only a single country that had been able to survive and prosper up there.

And now, Kreig saw it again, after all these years. Now he saw why it had survived.

It wasn't warm but it wasn't cold, either. A moderate temperature that had let crops grow bountiful and people live in harmony. Every house and every wall and every church that had once been there was torn down and destroyed, replaced with mud. The blue sky was gone, a bleeding red overtaking it like a plague. He could barely stand upon the ground. Now, he only had to find *it*.

He stood there for a full minute. The realization of what he was looking at settled inside his mind and his body like a massive, cold snake. The terrible nature of it. He hadn't seen it like that before. How it was all just gone. The one spot in the frozen wasteland up north, the magical, divine place where the warmth was everywhere, reduced to mud and cinders and—

And he wasn't alone anymore. The mud squirmed and twitched, forming into what seemed like worms, all coalescing and collecting around things, until these rose. Kreig had never seen them before this moment.

Mud-movers. The second he sliced one open, he saw not only ashen mud spraying but the shards and fleshy, rotten remains of a man. It was no secret that the remains of the dead at times arose to become monsters. It was not an uncommon sight to see it in the aftermath of a large battlefield. But this wasn't a battlefield. This was a *slaughter*.

Believers and atheists and mothers and children, killed and reduced to muddy abominations.

Kreig's first instinct had been to run. To turn around, and flee, and *damn this mission and damn the Empire to the soil.*

But behind him was only a hundred more acres of mud. A thousand more mud-movers reached toward him as if he, as their sole survivor, as their Oracle and Body, could save them. As if he could grant them relief.

"Kreig, please, you don't have to say any more, I'm sorry for asking, you don't—"

He tried. He really tried. Days and nights he spent there, and he hadn't developed beyond the need for sleep and food yet, so he could barely stand. Every time he turned around, he saw another mud-mover. Every time he killed one, he was presented with a dirty, tarnished skeleton. Another civilian he hadn't been able to save. Death, death, death. Muddy lands and red skies.

Every time his eyelids fluttered close, every time his mind went blank for just a moment, he fell back and the mud greeted him like an old friend.

"Come," it said. *"We're all down here."*

But he couldn't sleep. He fought and he fought, and when a mountain of mud rose like God Himself emerging from below, and when a cloak formed out of mud and when its hand held a golden, beautiful scepter that he knew had to be *it*, that half-decayed skeleton stared back at him, its flesh blackened and oily, its neck sliced by the blade of a guillotine, and Kreig knew who it was and it knew who Kreig was and he fell on his knees, sword and shield falling at his sides, claimed by the mud, and he stared up at that great figure looming overhead, mud slipping off of its half-exposed form, and Kreig wanted to say *"I'm sorry, Peter"* and *"I'm sorry I couldn't save you,"* but his mouth was stuck and he couldn't breathe and Peter wouldn't leave and he couldn't stand and he didn't want to see *but he had to see* and then when Peter was close enough to touch him, close enough to touch his face and end it all right then and there, Kreig stood up.

He ran. He ran, and he ran, and he ran.

All the way home to the *Empire.*

"Where the sky was blue and I could live in peace and everything was—"

"Kreig, I get it, I'm sorry for asking, so please, will you stop that?"

Kreig hadn't noticed it, but when he looked down, the world bleary and red and muddy, the metal in his hand, the part of the vehicle he was in, the side of it, it was crushed, and he still held it. It was crushed. He had destroyed it. Such a dear thing of his brother's. Gone. Destroyed by his hand.

He—he did it again, he just—he destroyed, and he destroyed. Everything he loved, his brother, his country, his religion, all destroyed, at his hand, destroyed, gone, ruined—

MUDDY.

What Kreig held in his hand at that moment was not the crushed ball of car-metal but the half-destroyed helmet of a man he'd slain. It could have been any man from anywhere, but in Kreig's trembling hand, it was just a helmet.

He brought death everywhere he went. The bleeding sky loomed upon him. He seemed to move, but he felt nothing.

Everything was so quiet. Like the wind wasn't roaring and the bones hiding beneath the mud weren't chattering and creaking and cracking under the weight of a thousand sins. Soldiers and civilians. Believers and faithless.

"Kreig, is everything all right?" George asked.

What was he, that man in the mud, doing there? Who was he? The only living man in a field of eternal massacre, his body half-submerged in the mud, looking up at him with no great malice and no great fear. Not young, not old. Barely a man. Was he an enemy? Soldiers were usually younger. Then a mud-mover? Impossible; the man had a face.

Kreig raised his arm, placing the edge of his sword at the level of the man's throat. "Speak your name."

The man reacted peculiarly, glaring at Kreig's hand rather than the blade. "Kreig, what are you doing?" It was off. It was all off. He was alone, alone and there *and he shouldn't still be there, why was he there?* "I'm trying to drive, Kreig; please put your arm away." Although Kreig thirsted for answers, he had no mind to put up with the mocking words of someone already in the mud. With a flick of the wrist, he forced the blade through the man's throat.

But the man's head didn't slip off. He simply glanced at Kreig, confusion and mild discontent evident. "Your eyes are . . . Are you *here*, Kreig?"

Here? Why, of course he was—

The sky flashed blue but his head flashed white.

His brother wasn't in the mud anymore. He was sitting down in a luxurious white throne, facing to the right, shooting quick glances at Kreig. His skin was so pale. "Look, Kreig, do you want me to stop the car? If you're not feeling well, that is," the White Pope said, his white eyes catching another brief glimpse of Kreig.

Everything in this world was wrong. This place couldn't exist. This man, sitting in front of him like a beautiful specter, could not possibly still be alive.

This was all—

George's hand fell on Kreig's. The world flashed again, surged as if alive and buzzing, and then it was all gone.

The car had come to a stop beneath him, the wind hummed distantly, and right there was George. Concerned. The car stood parked at the side of the road, half of it propped on the sidewalk. A warm hand touched Kreig's own. "Are you okay?" George asked in a low, soothing tone. Kreig would have been a fool not to see the hints of fear in George's eyes, the way they trembled ever so slightly, how his black hair matted against his forehead.

". . . Yes," Kreig lied. He hated lying. He hated untruth and dishonesty so much, but when he couldn't even tell what was real and fake—when even the very reality that surrounded him seemed untrue—he couldn't bear to speak the truth.

George pulled his lips tight. "They didn't leave us aimless. Before we met you, before you came home, we traded letters with a man. Dr. Darius Falk. There wasn't much he could tell us about *you*, but he did tell us a few things to look out for. Some situations to avoid, some signs that you may be experiencing some form of"—George glanced away from Kreig for a moment—"dissociative reactions. Derealization. Like you weren't quite . . . *here*."

"I am here," Kreig said, omitting the *now* that he spoke in his heart.

"Yes, you are. But I can't just . . . I can't tell at a glance. I can't always know, so when you're *not here*, can you try to tell me? If you can, that is. In return, I . . . I promise I'll avoid *taking you there*," George said, still unable to meet Kreig's eyes. The air seemed thick between them, like water. Like they were both calmly drowning, each in their own seat. ". . . I'm sorry. You don't have to talk about that kind of stuff from now on, okay? Not to me, not to Sam, not to anyone. It's okay; you can just keep it to yourself. For now. Until you can have someone comfortable to talk to."

Kreig looked down at his hands. Thick, callused, old. "I hear and obey." Words he had spoken more times than he could remember, words all men above him had demanded.

"Don't say it like— Yeah. Okay, let's go," George said, pulling the car out onto the road, back to their mission. There was only one family left, one letter to deliver. A letter that weighed heavy in Kreig's hands. A terrible tale of a good man. A tragedy to witness, a comedy to experience. Yes, Peter had always laughed about it, never expressing any wish to go home. He didn't hate his family; he just didn't care for them.

The notion of living a new life always appealed more to him than the former life they all rapidly forgot.

By this way of thinking, Kreig couldn't imagine that Peter's family would possibly miss him, since he barely gave them a thought himself. Despite his doubts, Kreig had put his all into the letter. Every detail he could recall, every part of Peter's person. Every flaw and virtue.

But as Kreig's thoughts drifted, he couldn't help but feel how they kept returning to what had happened just minutes before.

There was something wrong with his mind. Something that made him see things that didn't exist and feel like he wasn't even where he was supposed to be, and he didn't know *what* was doing this. But George did. George had been there, and George had looked him in the eye and said he knew a bit about it. But not enough. Something was wrong with his mind, but Kreig didn't know why.

He wasn't dead. Wasn't that good enough? Why did it have to be more than that? He knew healing spells of all kinds, he even used them regularly, so why was his mind damaged?

He was fine. He was okay.

The car stopped. "We're here."

And they were now at the Willowgrove residence.

CHAPTER 16

MRS. WILLOWGROVE MOURNS

Kreig stepped out of the car. The mission was simple, as simple as any he'd ever tried. Easier than going to the north and retrieving a thing he didn't even understand.

The house was small and a bit run-down. It was gray and barely painted, boards and hinges almost falling off in places. Parts of the roof seemed about ready to tumble off, and what little there was of the garden out front was clearly overrun. It was completely filled with weeds that had been allowed to grow as they would, feeding off of the remains of what seemed to be a wilting rosebush. Even the door, white and ordinary, was flaking.

Most worryingly, the house didn't have a mailbox. The only way for him to leave his mail would have to be to leave it on the porch and wait for them to discover it.

But that wasn't a good idea; even Kreig knew that. Leaving it right then and there was basically begging for someone unrelated to come peek, so simply dropping it at their doorstep was out of the question. But there were other things he could do to gain the attention of the people inside. An idea bloomed in Kreig's mind. He pressed the doorbell.

"Kreig, what's keeping you?" George asked, stepping out of the car and going right up to where Kreig stood. Being a polite man, Kreig turned around to face his brother, letter still in hand.

Before Kreig could tell his brother about his fantastic idea to ring the doorbell and leave the letter on the doorstep before the inhabitants could open the door, he was interrupted by a door creaking open behind him.

He turned around and was greeted with an old, bespectacled little woman, peering out from a small slit in the door. Her eyes shifted from cautious curiosity to alarm in about as long as it took for Kreig to fully turn toward her.

"Please," she said, shaking her head timidly. "I haven't got any money left. Leave me be; I have nothing to give you sharks." Her eyes were muddy and dim from years of grief, of holding in what should have been let out.

George stepped closer to the door, giving a salesman-like smile as he tried to excuse both him and Kreig. "No, that's all right, ma'am. We seem to have gotten the wrong house, so we'll leave in a—"

Kreig held the letter out to her. It was small and torn at the edges, but the seal was pressed with as much care as possible. The title on it read, *To the relatives of Peter Willowgrove.* The little lady's eyes widened upon seeing it, her lower lip trembling, torn between a frown and a flood of words. "Here," Kreig said. "Take it." She looked up at him, her gaze flitting between his broad frame and the little letter he held out to her. He pushed it closer to her. "It's about Peter." He hesitated for a moment before speaking the last few words, the words he knew would convince her. "About what happened to him."

And all of a sudden, her dim, gray eyes—the same color as a half-frozen, half-dead lake—brightened up in meek hope. A reaction that Kreig hadn't expected in the least.

"Please, step inside," she said, opening the door for them.

George gave Kreig an unhappy, desperate look as if to tell Kreig to just leave the letter and run, but Kreig couldn't do it. Since Kreig went inside, George had no choice but to follow. What was presented to them was a house that seemed on the border of loved. Urns, lamps, and carpets in warm, friendly colors. Dusty cupboards and corners filled with cobwebs and dead fruit flies. Pictures of smiling people. Framed obituaries.

It was a quaint old home that had forgotten to be loved, left untouched for so long that it had begun to rot.

The woman, Mrs. Willowgrove, led them into a living room, where she left them on the couch for just a minute. Before long, she returned with a pot of tea and a pair of porcelain cups. She sat down in the silken armchair adjacent to the couch. "Tell me," she said in a whispering tone. "What is this about Peter?" Something in the way she said his name, something in her frail voice, seemed fundamentally broken. It was beyond despairing.

Then Kreig saw it. On the only non-dusty shelf, where a little hand-made tablecloth kept things from touching the shelf, there was a bundle of pictures. Pictures of a young man in glasses that Kreig recognized all too well, right next to a smiling man and a woman much younger than the one sitting in front of them. But she still had the same pale-blue eyes.

Peter's mother.

Kreig felt the letter weigh heavy in his hands. He held it out to her. She glanced at it, her forehead creasing in vague uncertainty. Until, finally, she took it.

George, who had not even touched his cup of steaming-hot tea, made to stand. "Well, this has been delightful, but we really must be—" Kreig put his hand on George's shoulder. ". . . Let me go, Kreig. We need to leave." But Kreig was much too strong for George to oppose. And he still wasn't meeting his gaze. "Kreig, seriously, we can't—"

"No, I'd like you both to stay," Mrs. Willowgrove said with such earnestness that George, despite knowing fully well that what they were doing wasn't in accordance with protocol, had no choice but to sit down.

Kreig had no good reason for doing this. There was no reason for him to be opposing his brother and dancing to his own whims. It was childish and unusual and he absolutely *had* to do it.

Of all the Five Bodies, Peter had been the most liberal. He was always the one refusing to be trained to obedience, opposing the will and needs of his superiors. The only one he listened to was the White Pope, but even then, as soon as he left his presence, Peter wasted no time analyzing his orders critically. If he didn't like the work given to him, he usually told Kreig to do it instead. A dog's work, but it was this part of Peter that Kreig truly admired. Not his intelligence, not his wit, not his faith. His *freedom*.

If it was in Peter's name, Kreig was sure he could muster the courage to go through with his own will. And right now, that will of his, so muted it might as well not exist at all, was telling him to stay. If only to explore the strangeness of the situation.

After all, this wasn't how this place should be. This wasn't the kind of woman Peter had described when he explained why he didn't mind coming to another world.

"They won't mind," he'd said. *"All they care about is work and good grades and all those frivolous things that define the rigid structure of that modern, sterile hellscape we escaped. Sure, this place is no paradise, but compared to back there, isn't it Heaven? No nagging mothers or strict fathers. Nobody to tell you that you've gotta stop reading and get back to doing schoolwork. Nobody complains about how nothing gets done. Just you and what you can do. Isn't it fantastic, for once, to be free?"*

An absent father and a negligent mother. That was the home life Peter had painted. And now Kreig was allowed to witness that home life.

A mother whose entire face was much older than it should be, eyes dragged down by unshed tears. Pools of murky water in her eyes. Kreig had to know if the story Peter had told was a mere falsehood or something else. What this woman held.

Her hands trembled, eyes downcast. She focused on the letter. "... If I were to read this, what would I learn?"

"What truly happened."

"God preserve us. Please, have some tea. Forgive my silence as I read," she said. Her trembling fingers slid over the smooth envelope before pulling off the wax seal and removing the four carefully folded pages inside. The handwriting on these was in a bold, clear cursive. Mrs. Willowgrove let her wry eyes slide over the words for a moment before looking up, a vague smile blooming on her lips. Her eyes fell squarely on Kreig. "My, you do have beautiful handwriting for such a large man."

George twitched. It was clear that he understood the conclusion she had reached. And still, Kreig wouldn't leave. He wouldn't even *try* to change her mind on it.

He simply sat there and watched wordlessly as she carefully read each page.

Her demeanor changed ever so slightly after every paragraph she read. The reserved, cold exterior seemed to peel back, and when that softer layer beneath was finally laid bare, when her eyes started to tremble and her lips quivered, yet another layer was revealed as she read more. As she found out another detail of the life her son had lived without her. She learned of every part, from the very moment he rose from the casket to when he decided that being a priest was dumb. All the way to the time, after over five years of strict atheism, he finally accepted his new God.

She was at the halfway point of the third page when she looked up, a trembling smile pulling desperately at her lips, her eyes bleary and wet, and asked, in the most hopeful way possible, "He got *married*?"

"... Yes." In truth, when it happened, even Kreig had been surprised. But she was a fantastic woman who admired Peter for more than his wit, and they had gotten along beautifully.

Mrs. Willowgrove smiled a deep, fond, unhappy smile that seemed only to regret not being there. "I see. I'm glad. I had always thought he'd never find a woman; he was always holed up in his room, never finding any friends. God, I'm glad. Thank God." A single tear dropped from her eye, and she turned back to reading. As she finished the third page, her smile turned mournful and tragic. Her joy turned to bitter sorrow as she read Peter's role in the Holy War and the Unholy War.

War was never pretty, especially not for the soldiers. It had been harsh on Peter, but he never had so much as a chance to recover. As one war ended, it seamlessly transformed into the other. Ten years of war. Ten years of suffering.

She got to the last part of the last page. This was where she broke down.

The dam was broken, the icy lakes in her eyes shattered, and they flooded out onto the page in her trembling hands. She buckled over, clutching the wet papers close, holding them to her heart as if to bring the life her son had lived without her into it. The life he had lived, those thirty years that had made him into something so different, a fully grown man she barely knew. It was a tragic sight to see.

She wept, and she wept, and now Kreig could not honestly accept that this had been a cold, callous mother who felt nothing for her child. Peter had been wrong.

And he never knew it.

And that hurt Kreig far more than Mrs. Willowgrove's mourning did.

After the letter was read and tears had been well and fully shed, she looked back up, her reddened, old eyes meeting Kreig's own.

She seemed far older than she really was. The woman in the pictures seemed to be only around thirty, while this woman seemed almost fifty or sixty despite only ten years having passed. Clearly, these years had taken a toll on her. They weighed down her weary face and body with grief to such a point where she could barely clean—barely even care for herself, if her greasy hair and tattered clothes were anything to go by.

"You're Kreig, aren't you?" she said, a glint before unseen now shining in her clear eyes. With her tears expelled, she now seemed far younger than before. Despite how unhappy George seemed that Kreig had been recognized, neither he nor Kreig made any move to correct her. A smile, genuine and rosy, bloomed on her lips. "Thank you for taking care of my son."

Kreig nodded deeply. "He was a close friend. It was only natural."

Her smile broadened further as she leaned back in her chair, holding the letter to her chest. "Yes, of course . . . . To think he'd make such good friends. Still, it must have been hard on you, all of this. Tell me, what happened after his—his passing? You needn't tell if you'd rather not."

Kreig opened his mouth to speak and mentally prepared himself to retell the tale he told only an hour earlier. But all of a sudden, he found himself struck by a thought. A little detail, a little spurt of his own will. An expression of his freedom that Peter must have given to him. "No," Kreig said softly, "I think I'd rather not."

He had good reason not to. The last time he spoke of such a part of his life, he felt himself pulled back, absorbed into his own memories, body and soul. He couldn't afford to do that in front of her.

Still, refusing her felt like an irredeemable sin, something unacceptable, punishable with fifty lashes and solitary confinement. It was something so fundamentally different from his own personality and will that it almost felt as though Peter had acted through him as an arbiter of freedom. A sense of dread welled up within him as he foolishly expected some sort of punishment for daring to refuse the request of someone.

She merely smiled, eyes and all. Softly. So softly it felt like a bed of feathers, a heavenly cloud of rose petals. "That's all right. This letter is enough in every sense."

George seemed to breathe a sigh of relief, but Kreig still sat tense and immovable.

Huh? That was it? No frown, no words of disappointment, no callous explanation of how selfish he was to refuse the request of another? Nobody telling him that to reject the word of the cardinals and priests and the White One was to reject the word of the Lord Below? That every sin of irresponsibility that Kreig indulged in would merely lead to his body being denied entrance into the caring womb of the White Roots below?

. . . Nothing like that?

". . . You're welcome," Kreig said, yet to fully understand what had just happened. His refusing someone had been accepted. His own feelings had been validated and understood.

She turned to George. "Tell me, young man, how would I contact you again? I'd love to have you and your closest over for dinner sometime. It's been too long since I've had company like this; I fear I may come to miss it too much after you leave."

An hour before, there would have been no doubt in George's mind about refusing her. Sure, by the use of a computer and some basic thinking, she could find out his name and address quite easily, but if that happened, George could still tell the authorities that at least he hadn't willingly given her that information. But an hour before, he hadn't seen the effect Kreig's letter had had on anybody. An hour before, he hadn't seen a grown woman cry.

". . . My name is George Wiedermann, and you can call me at . . ." With all the reluctance of a knowing sinner, George admitted all sorts of information to her, from where he lived to his phone number.

When all was said and done and she lit up like the sun and pulled out a notebook to scribble it down, George strangely felt that he hadn't done anything wrong. *Nothing at all.*

"Thank you," she said after everything. "I'll be sure to call you sometime."

Since the tea had been finished and their numbers had been exchanged, there was nothing left. Although reluctant, Mrs. Willowgrove showed them the door, and with a wave and a smile she hadn't worn in too long, Kreig and George left. Neither spoke to the other, not about what had happened and not about what might happen. They just drove in silence. It was a warm sort of silence, where neither party felt compelled to speak at all. Not because they had nothing to say but rather that there was nothing that had to be said.

It was comfortable, despite the thoughts whirling through George's mind.

Was it the right choice? Had he done the right thing, to let her know their names and faces? How could he possibly believe that such a kindly old woman could be a threat to them? And even if she was, did he have anything left to fear with Kreig around? Just by what he knew so far, couldn't he order Kreig to do anything for him? What did he have to fear when the greatest threat in the world was subservient to him?

. . . What the hell was he thinking? Kreig wasn't some object, nor was he mindless. He had his own life. He was George's brother. This wasn't about him, this was about making Kreig into a real person again, making him whole after all he went through. Abusing a man in such a position would be downright evil.

But he couldn't be soft on Kreig. No, despite what it might seem that Kreig needed, he couldn't treat him like a child. That'd be truly dehumanizing. He would let him recover, but he'd give him a little push when it was needed.

That was what George was thinking.

Kreig's thoughts were pretty much silent. Sure, he was unhappy that George's car still had a chunk of the door gouged out, but other than that?

He was . . . happy? Was that it? Was that the emotion surging through his body like healing magic? But he had done wrong. There was nothing good about saying no to someone who wanted something from him. It was selfish. He'd been selfish, and although *she* seemed forgiving enough about it, Kreig himself certainly wasn't. Never had following orders been a bad choice for him. It had let him survive, and being rebellious certainly hadn't.

There was a reason Kreig was alive and Peter was not.

Peter wouldn't give up his faith. He wouldn't buckle under the heels of the Empire. He could take the torture, but he couldn't take the idea of being subservient to someone he didn't respect. So, in part because the Empire wanted to prove a point to Kreig, he was executed. With his death, so too did they kill a thousand unwritten scriptures and a thousand unsung verses. Freedom plucked the wings of the bird.

Freedom at the cost of life wasn't freedom at all.

That was how Kreig saw it.

When he came out of it, the car had stopped and George was looking at him as though he had something he wanted to say. But he didn't, and Kreig couldn't respond to silence. They went inside the apartment, greeted Sam, told her in light tones what had happened, and that was that. Kreig made dinner, they ate it gladly, and so it went. As evening rolled around, Sam took a seat in front of the television while George took a seat by the table in order to do their taxes.

This left Kreig a bit outside. In the end, with nothing else to do, he found himself a piece of paper and a pencil and sat down to draw. A sketch of Mrs. Willowgrove. Another of Annie Swallowbird. And then, finally, as if in preparation for a future painting, he drew Mrs. Willowgrove and Peter. Both as they were, with Peter at the age of forty-seven and Mrs. Willowgrove as she had been when Kreig saw her. Together, as if nothing had happened at all. Just a sketch.

George leaned over the table, getting a good look at what Kreig had drawn so far. "We should get you some painting supplies." A perfectly objective statement that Kreig couldn't disagree with.

Sam piped in. "Yeah, we'll buy you some tomorrow evening! We'll both be going to work, so one of us can just drop in at some store somewhere. By the way, uh, you've got two things to do tomorrow. First up, you've got that whole tutoring business, and then at like three you've got this appointment with a psychiatrist, I think? The dude we met down when we saw you the first time. I'll write a note with the times when I can remember it."

George agreed with her, and they spent the remainder of the evening collectively existing in the same vicinity. At one point, Sam retrieved a slice of cake from the fridge, but Kreig didn't want any. Later, everyone went off to bed.

Kreig still didn't like the thought or feeling of sleeping, but . . . he still did it. The bed was soft, and after a rather eventful day, his eyelids were heavy too.

He fell asleep pretty immediately.

CHAPTER 17

CRIME MAN AND TUTOR GIRL

Was that all you came here to ask? Dude, you're straight-up weird. Okay, see, a lot of the weird stuff all those Cardinals have been telling us to read was really just a sort of a prelude. Like you know how the Jewish people are still waiting for the Messiah to arrive, right? We're all sitting around on our asses, twiddling our thumbs, and singing pretty songs, hoping that the God Below will do something.

"So far, nobody's told me exactly what *He's* supposed to do, but I don't think it's an apocalypse or anything. More like an egg finally hatching to reveal a phoenix, I think.

"He'll come. We don't know when or anything, but someday, He'll rise from the ground and show us the way. I think. That's what all these books you can't bother to read say, at least."

I read them when I can.

"Huh? That so? Gee, what a surprise! The big dumb jock Paladin actually has the sense to read the scripture he believes in. Wow. Wouldn't expect that from you, Kreig."

I never expected you to start writing chants and prayers.

"Oh, that's, uh . . . just a pastime. You know, you've gotta have something to do when you're not healing random sickos and stuff. Heh. I was planning to author a book, you know? Something of an autobiography about—well, about this. Who else to do it? But, I guess . . . You know, the feeling of hearing your psalms sung in church for the first time is just—it's, heh, it's something else. Not that I'm attached to it!"

Of course you aren't, Peter.

"Don't say it like that, dude. Well, anyway, I answered your question. I'll be going now, yeah? But, uh, Kreig? Before you go?"

Kreig looked up, his vantage point small and unclear where he sat cross-legged in the darkness that seemed to go on forever. What was it?

The massive moving mound of mud and bones heaved up to stand, the very ends of it slowly moving into the edges of the endless darkness. The skull, yellowing and stained with rotted flesh and mud and blood seemed to smile as it stalked down and hunched before Kreig. Face to face.

"Thank you for letting me go."

The smiling skull and the endless squirming mud erupted into shining white flames that licked and fawned over his dying form, flooding the whole of the abyss in blinding light. The fire enveloped the dead man and burned him, purging his existence from the world, bones and mud and soul. All.

Leaving only a golden spire.

Kreig picked it up, watching nostalgically as it melted and re-formed into a large, golden broadsword.

And then Kreig woke up.

With a strange calm, he let his eyes wander over his small living space. The room was bathed in blackness and there was a sheen of sweat on his brow. He'd dreamt something weird again, but he couldn't say that it had been entirely bad. It had only been odd. Like a mash-up of his entire relationship with Peter. Especially the end of it. It hadn't been like that, not really. Barely.

He got out of bed, his bare feet tapping the cold wooden floor. The room was still dark, but he could tell that this would soon change.

Kreig walked over to the window and opened it. Cold air flooded his room, catching his worn hair and the edges of his clothes. It felt good. Refreshing. Like the soft winds would peel off all the sweat and mud and he'd no longer be weary and worn. Sometimes, in the dark nights when he suddenly had a thought after so long doing things without any conscious thought, what brought him back always seemed to be that cool night breeze. He was quickly brought back into that nothingness by a soldier or a mud-mover or just a wandering monster, but those few moments of rest were special to him.

The moon had almost entirely gone down, and from the dying embers of its meager light, the sun rose. Its rays stretched out over the city like desperate, clawing wraiths.

Dousing the dark blue world in endless red light.

And all of a sudden, things were wrong again. His heart dropped and his breathing stopped. Eyes wide, he felt his grip on the window frame tighten, the buildings seemed to slowly sink into a massive, all-encompassing mass of mud, rising toward the red, bloody sky, Kreig's breathing hastened, his heart beat quicker and quicker, a white-hot heat in his head pressing against the back of his eyes seemingly spreading down his spine and into his arms and making them too hot to touch and too cold to keep warm and everything was wrong and his tongue felt too big and the red sky seemed to invade his mind, ripping it open with cold, slick hands, and right as he well and truly felt like this was it, this would be the end of it . . .

He turned around.

The red retreated, the mud slipped from his body, and he could breathe again.

He took a seat at his desk, and until the sun stopped being red, he wouldn't turn to look at the window at all. Once the sun was a mild orange and the sky was a friendly blue, he stood up. The clock in his room told him it was almost six. Going by what his siblings had said, today would be the day they started working after taking two days off to help him. Kreig had no idea *when* they had to leave for work, but since neither of them was awake yet, Kreig had the perfect opportunity to make them some sort of breakfast before they fully woke up.

So, after dressing in his thrice-used clothes once again, he stepped out of his room and went to the kitchen, where he quickly got to cooking.

A hearty, Empire-style breakfast meal. Far from simple, but surely filling enough for his siblings to work well.

And, behold, when his siblings woke up only half an hour later just in time, they actually seemed somewhat delighted for the meal Kreig had made. Sure, despite her general curiosity, Sam seemed unusually cautious about the breakfast, but once she got a taste, she didn't stop. Kreig would be a liar if he said it didn't feel somehow fulfilling to see someone enjoy a part of his usefulness that wasn't combat.

Once they finished their food, both turned to Kreig.

"Okay, uhh, Kreig. Here. I wrote a list with all the things you'll do today!" Sam said, sliding a little paper over to Kreig. It seemed simple enough.

8:00—Meet tutor (become friends!!)
8:30—Do a bunch of school stuff (bleh!)
12:00—Eat lunch (and make some for the tutor, too!)
3:00—School ends (yay!!!)

4:00—Go to the psycho dude (Address: 15c Karl-Oskar Street)
5:30—Come home (pretty please?)

"Excuse what is written in the parentheses; Sam insisted on giving a personal touch to it," George said. Kreig didn't see any issue with it and pocketed the slip of paper. "Oh, also, before I and Sam leave for our stations, we need to get you washed. I'll show you, so just . . . follow me and listen, will you?"

Kreig obliged him. The whole process was really quite simple. George told him how to use every kind of shower liquid, helped brush his hair, and then sent him inside to do it.

By this point, Kreig knew how to shower. But exactly how to use all these different kinds of cleaning liquids had been unknown to him. Fascinating. And after a mere half an hour spent stealthily trying all of the different soaps just to see what they did, he emerged. He was washed and ready to do Normal Things. He had a towel wrapped around his midsection.

After another quarter of an hour where Sam and George both fought over how best to clean Kreig's now-wet hair, Kreig was all ready.

Apparently, his siblings had been able to get some oversized clothing by threat of treason, so he was all clothed, clean, and ready when they left. That left him alone in the apartment. The silence was deafening and he just sort of stood there. He wandered over to look at the painting hanging in the living room. He inspected the battery-powered lamp.

The clock hit eight. Kreig was standing in front of the front door, breathing deeply. They should be there by now.

8:05. Where were they?

8:10. Why weren't they there?

8:15. Whe—

Knock kno— Kreig tore the door open.

"Hi! Glad to meet you! I'll be your tutor from now on; happy to—" Her eyes widened and her hand stalled mid-reach.

Kreig sniffed the air a few times. Ah, it was her.

At this moment, Erica realized that she might have come to the wrong place.

"Ack— *Crime man!*"

Damn it, damn it, *damn it*! She should have known!

Not from the start, of course, but she had stared at that map for half an hour straight when she had to guide that—that *criminal* here! Had she completely forgotten what the house looked like in only two days?!

Well, yeah, but admitting it to herself felt wrong. Instead, she decided to believe that she had thought it couldn't possibly be about the same guy.

Totally, yup. She was not a forgetful woman; otherwise, she wouldn't be a teacher!

Ah, lost in her thoughts, she had completely forgotten where she was. After all, she wasn't just anywhere, no; she was standing outside the door of the crime man she had given directions to, clutching her heavy handbag and trembling like an aspen leaf. Thoughts racing, she stared as the crime man took a step to the side, bidding her entry.

"N—no, that's . . . Hey, see, heh, funny coincidence! But, um, I've got a high school kid to tutor here, and I'm definitely at the wrong door, so," Erica said, "bye!" With a well-trained spin on her heel, she readily turned around, trying to ignore the immense hand that softly landed on her shoulder. She leaned her head a little, a trembling smile on her lips. "Yes, what is it?"

"I've been expecting you." That voice again. Monotone, broad. And, somehow, against all odds, unthreatening. Soft.

Erica swallowed. Damn it, she should just leave! Who knew what kind of hellhole was in there? For some reason though, that old curiosity of hers pulled at her. It was a horrible idea, so uncertain it made no sense. But, still, she had to take the chance. "Say, you, uh, wouldn't happen to be 'Kreig Wiedermann,' would you?"

He nodded. *Fuck.*

It was the right address, she was staring at the right man, and according to the contract she'd signed, if she didn't turn up to one of the tutorings, she'd be charged on the spot. Maybe she should have spotted a few signs there, but, damn. It was a sweet deal. It even had dental! It was far from the normal kind of tutoring, more of a long-term deal, and she'd taken it. It was a good way to pay the rent and quell her growing student debt.

This was just another reason why she hated teaching. She should've never gotten into this hellhole of a profession.

"Is that so?" Erica said, trying and failing to muster a somewhat-genuine smile. This guy, *Kreig,* was just as silent and terrifying as when she'd guided him through the city. High-schooler, her ass. Nevertheless, he waved her inside, and damn if twenty-seven years of learning how to act polite didn't overtake her entire nervous system. She went inside, even giving Kreig a thankful nod as he closed the door behind her.

But it wasn't as though she had entered his lair or anything; no, this place was remarkably normal. A bit rough at some edges, that battery-powered lamp seemed *really* weird, but other parts were just plain mundane.

Even beyond that, in some ways.

The living room, connected to the kitchen, seemed decorated by someone who had only just left their parents' home. A hideous lime-green carpet clashed horridly with the robust leather couches, and although the TV was big, it was barely modern at all, despite the PS4 sitting right next to it. Going by the titles of the games next to it, Kreig at least had pretty good taste. And then, the only detail of the living room that her eyes truly fell on, that she truly stopped to look at, was a painting hung up above the TV.

It was excellently made, really. Erica would know, since she had once planned on becoming an art/music teacher. But this was beyond anything she had ever so much as *tried* to make. It wasn't the scope of it, either. A simple portrait of three people in a warm, firelit room. Who else but Kreig in the middle, with a woman on one side and a man on the other. All three had this serene, unapologetic joy to them. Not happiness, nothing so bombastic, just the gentle joy of loving and being loved.

To portray such a complicated emotion through such a simple picture was awe-inspiring, and at a single glance, Erica knew she had to know who made it.

"Tell me, crimina—err, Kreig. Who did you commission to paint that portrait?" When Erica turned to the man, her eyes were glittering like blazing stars. She had no intention of commissioning the amazing artist herself; she just wanted another painter to add to her to-love list. The many commissioned and ready-bought paintings in her home aside, she was the kind of person who enjoyed looking at art for art's sake. Be it simple or complicated, with enough skill, she found herself loving it all.

Kreig made no changes in facial expression, but Erica knew that something had shifted. "I painted it myself."

. . . Nah.

Nope. No. Nuh-uh. No way.

Erica let her head whip back and forth between the phenomenal painting and the so-called artist. He was a large, bear-like man whose hands were defined by calluses and scars. The painting was made with soft, gentle strokes. Then, too, the artist of the piece must be of a similar nature. Calm. Quiet. Soft-spoken. Mysteri— *Damn it, it fits! Shoot!* No, no way these had anything to do with each other; she *couldn't* accept it!

"It's nice!" she said, making the false assumption that he was either lying to her or pulling her leg. Damn students. Never a kind thought in mind. "Will you show me where we'll be working?"

Kreig stalled for just a moment, as if her offhanded compliment needed time to sink in, Once it did, he briskly turned his back on her, as if to hide some little expression of embarrassment. "Follow me." What an unusual man. And he was a man, too. Sure, his face seemed youthless in a false sort of way, but everything seemed to tell her that he was older than her. *High-schooler*. Bah.

Following his back, Erica was brought down a hallway and through a door on the right. As expected, not a canvas in sig—

Ah, though, on the wall, she *did* see a few paintings. Two, to be exact.

One portrayed a young, mud-stained boy raising his arms in futile defense against his aggressor, namely oneself, the observer. There was a very strange duality to the painting. While Erica felt rightfully horrified to be seeing the situation from the eyes of the one who was causing the fear and pain of the young boy, there was also an odd sense of nostalgia to it. The boy seemed painted with loving, careful strokes to get almost every aspect of him right. Almost. He wasn't quite a full person, the one who painted it didn't know the entirety of him, but . . . enough to make *this*.

The other painting was not as intense. It was just a portrait of a man. The only odd aspect was that the man couldn't possibly be human. His skin was rendered in a non-blooded absolute white, and the same reigned true with his hair and eyes. There was something off about him. But with the loving, heartfelt strokes, it didn't *feel* wrong. Rather than cursed, he felt divine. A beautiful man. For some reason, that phrase seemed to pop out to her. The man himself seemed far from pretty, hardly even average, and still, it felt like the right phrase to describe him.

She didn't comment on the paintings. There were other paintings in the room, but they were drab landscapes of no soul. No emotion.

Kreig showed her a desk with a single chair, and while she sat down to get more comfortable, he excused himself to go get another chair from the kitchen. This gave her ample time to examine the desk itself. Or, rather, what was on it. There were lots of papers, a few envelopes, an ink pen, and, most importantly, a few solid sketches. A few were rougher, some less so. One or two were immensely clear, showing the artist's vast grasp of proper anatomy and shading.

In grim horror, Erica felt the facts of the matter sink in. Kreig was, in spite of his appearance, a fantastic artist. Even better than she was.

Kreig soon returned with a chair in tow. He placed it by the desk and sat down to face her, clearly expecting her to do something.

She just pointed at the sketches. "Did you do this?" He nodded, flustered. She slid a blank paper over to him, curiosity once again killing the cat. "Could you show me?"

. . . Show her what?

She hadn't even told him her name yet. The only reason Kreig knew that this girl, who also happened to be the nice girl who guided him home, was his tutor was that she showed up at the right time and, well, said so. She was really polite about it, too. And then she even went and said—said that his paintings were . . .

Well, she complimented him. She complimented something that wasn't combat prowess. She didn't compliment him because he successfully dispatched an entire enemy battalion or because he took down a strong monster. She complimented him because he *painted well*.

It felt good. With that in mind, he really couldn't figure out what she wanted him to do. Did she want a sketch or something?

He picked up the blank sheet of paper and a plain pencil. Draw something . . . something simple and quick. She was probably only asking as a formality, so he obviously wouldn't put much effort into it. An easy sketch of the first thing he could see. His eyes instinctually fell on his new tutor. *Right.* There she was.

He put his pencil to the paper and got to it.

Artistry (IV)

The pencil moved easily, outlining her face in simple detail. The way her nose shyly dipped upward. The thin layer of makeup and how it flaked at the edges. Her bright eyes and short, almost curly hair. Thin lips, faint smile. A simple portrait, lacking color but making up for it with tiny details and sophisticated shading. All done as per his skill. Really, he had barely done anything himself. It was all just the work of the skill.

With the picture drawn, he handed it over to her, hoping it wouldn't be graded. She looked at it for a few seconds, looked up at him, glanced back at it, and put it on the table.

"I'll give you an A in art, so don't you worry about that," she said, sliding it to the side. It was graded. Now if Kreig could only figure out what *A* meant in terms of grades . . .

Last he'd been graded, that noble tutor had given him an I in all subjects except for combat, where he gave him a reluctant X. A fine man. Kreig should have ripped out his spine while he had the chance. Damn his lord for stopping him. Well, with this person, he might not have to do something as rash and immature as threaten with violence. He'd do this for a week at most, and then he'd ask to have the tutoring stopped. That was the plan.

The tutor leaned down beside the desk and grabbed something from her purse. It was a heap of five or six thick books, each in colorful prints with large fonts spelling out their purpose.

Math 5b, History 2, that kind of stuff. Each of them had pictures on them that seemed to have very little to do with the subject at hand. What did mathematics have to do with surfing?

"Okay!" she said, "Let's get right to it. See, I have no idea where you left off, so we'll just check through these to get a sense of where you're at in terms of knowledge. Let's begin with going through some of what you know just to see where in these books you need to pick up." One of the books, in a pastel red and labeled *Math* was in front of them, and she had no fear to open it pretty much midway, revealing a language much closer to Mandarin than English. Strange texts and strange words. "Do you understand this?"

Kreig slowly shook his head. That was a language beyond him.

She turned back a few chapters. "What about this?" Nothing. Another few chapters. ". . . This?" Not in the least. Another chapter. "Tell me you know this." He didn't. She turned the final chapter back, revealing the very first page of the very first chapter. "So, it has come to this, huh?" Kreig gave a hasty nod. He dreaded the whole book, but he wouldn't dare tell her.

She grabbed another book and repeated the very same thing. He didn't understand a thing. Nothing made any sense, and at one point, Kreig started to wonder if he maybe just couldn't read at all.

That couldn't be the case, though, so he reluctantly dismissed it.

"This? No . . . This? No . . . Thi—"

"I recognize that," Kreig said for the first time in the entire lesson. His finger was pressed squarely into the History textbook, making a little imprint in the chapter titled *Renaissance*. Sure, he couldn't recognize *all* of it, but a lot of it felt somewhat familiar. The architecture, the clothing . . . it was similar. Not quite how he remembered things, but much closer than the current era was.

"Seriously? Hey, that's great! Then we won't have to do all these previous chapters!" she said, flipping back to reveal pages upon pages of information Kreig couldn't fathom in the least. Unable to bear telling her that he didn't know any of that, he kept quiet. "All right! I think that's the last of it, so we pretty much have to do everything from start to finish. But that's fine! I'm all up for a challenge! Probably! Actually, I'm not, but if I don't even make an attempt, I won't get a paycheck, so let's go!"

Kreig appreciated her undue enthusiasm, but just by looking outside the window, he could tell that the time was nigh. It was almost noon.

He slipped the list from his pocket. *Lunch at 12*. It was time.

Kreig rose from his seat. The tutor flinched, dropping the math textbook as her head whipped around to face Kreig. "Uh, um. Everything cool, dude? We don't have to do math if you don't want to. Lots of people don't like math. Really, uh, if you don't wanna do math, we can do tons of other work! Heck, it's our first day! We can just, I dunno, take it easy? The important thing is that you have fun. No, wait, the important thing is that you *learn*! Yeah, yeah, learning is important! And also fun. No need to look at me like that!"

Kreig had no idea why her voice had risen in pitch. Very weird.

He turned around. "Lunch."

"—Huh?" The tutor glanced at a clock hanging in the room. "Oh! Oh, ha-ha, of course! That's—that's what you were on about. Right. Lunch . . ." She slowly stood up from her seat.

Kreig led her back to the kitchen, not even glancing back at her to make sure she was there. He knew she was there because she had the faintest smell of dandelions about her. Not from a perfume, nothing obnoxious like that, just a pure scent of dandelions. As if she was the kind of woman to frolic with the flower most often considered to be a weed. Right off the bat, maybe because of this, maybe because of her generally friendly nature, Kreig liked her.

Erica, on the other hand, had very opposite feelings toward *him*.

Though they would soon mellow.

There she was, five days before the midterm exams, watching as a man she had assumed to be a criminal acted like some sort of magical whiz in the kitchen, using all these knives and spoons and things to cook stuff she could barely comprehend. Before she could even notice that something had been dirtied, it was clean again, swept back into a cupboard as if he'd never used it.

Erica, being the kind of cook that could burn milk and cereal, was left in a silent stupor the entire time. She was only brought out of it when he placed a plate of food in front of her.

With just a whiff and a taste, a surreal realization set in.

Aha . . . So, that's what this was, then.

Kreig must have been some sort of cook/artist genius who dropped out of high school to focus on his art or something. But then when the social security checks stopped rolling in and he realized he needed a high school diploma to become a world-famous artist, he decided to get a tutor. Maybe. Really, she was just making it up on the fly, hoping it'd suit the situation. If this was the case, which it actually wasn't, she would have felt a little enraptured with being allowed into the private abode of such a person.

Then again, the whole art thing was still up in the air, but either way, he was one heck of a cook. She ate happily, if somewhat guardedly, shooting little glances at Kreig.

After all, what if he had poisoned it? She hadn't seen him doing any monkey business, but, then again, he had moved too fast for her to see anything. Her suspicions remained.

In and out. Teach him, get out. Simple.

At the table, she didn't speak a word. Neither did Kreig, for that matter, but it still felt just a little awkward. Before she could so much as offer to clean the plates, Kreig had stood up, cleaned the plates in a matter of seconds, and made to wander back to his room. No room for questions or suggestions. He was a strangely assertive man, that was for sure. In a silent kind of way.

He was completely unlike any of her former students. She followed him.

The rest of their session together was simple, really. They checked through all the books again, made sure he really, really knew next to nothing about anything, and then got to reviewing what he *did* know.

"You're good at cooking and art; what else would you consider your strong points, considering everything we've discussed so far?"

Cooking would mostly qualify him for home economics, though it wasn't a subject that was part of his final grade. Art *was*, but she had no doubts about his grade there. That left her with everything else. There were about a dozen subjects, five of whose textbooks she had brought today. Among those, she was sure Kreig must be knowledgeable in some subject. You couldn't get as old as he was without learning *something*. Anything.

Kreig stared at her for a second. Those empty, vacant eyes of his grew even more distant until he finally leveled his gaze on her. "None."

. . . All right, that was, uh, not very promising.

"What about . . ." She grasped at a straw, hoping he hadn't just had his body ballooned up for looks. "Aren't you good at PE? Physical education?

Such as being strong and fast." Not a reach, considering he was built like a castle. *Good deduction, Erica! That's sure to get him nailed down!*

"... I'd say I'm rather strong."

Nice! Good! This way, Erica wouldn't have to do any of the dreary PE-related stuff she so hated. It was horrible, really. She had no conditioning, and although she had grown to accept her own lack of speed and strength, having to try to teach someone with a better condition than herself was an absolute impossibility. This way, she could just note down an A and be done with it!

Ah, cooperation. What a delight.

"Great, okay! Anything else? Let's say ... Know anything about philosophy? Plato and Sartre or whatever?"

He shook his head. All right, that was a bust.

"Any chance your painting has made you learn anything about, for example, time periods from the view of art and artists?"

His eyes narrowed slightly, but he didn't say anything.

She took that as a no.

"... All right, uh, do you speak any language other than English?" she asked, mostly just to get it out there.

"I speak Mandarin and German as well, alongside a little Afrikaans. Nothing too complicated." Now, *that* had her surprised. Was that so? Not just a second language, but a *third* on top of it? Impressive for someone who seemed entirely disconnected from the regular curriculum. The languages were rather spread out, too. It pretty much gave him linguistic access to most parts of the world. Asia, Europe, the Americas, *and* parts of Africa. A very good language palette if one were, say ...

... secretly a former master artist and chef on the run from the authorities after having toured the entire world, finally finding himself in America, trying to make do by getting a diploma through the help of a private tutor.

Right. That had to be it. That'd explain his quiet confidence and everything else, too! Oh, how clever she was, uncovering this entire ruse through a mere half a day there. Surely, if she were to continue tutoring, obviously not because she actually wanted to, merely for the sake of curiosity, she could uncover the entire mystery behind it. Every aspect of who Kreig Wiedermann was, should his very name not be an alias.

Lost in her wild fantasy, she forgot to ask Kreig if he actually *could* speak three languages. It was the truth of the matter, but for Kreig, watching his tutor spiral into a hunched ball of cackles was, well ... mildly concerning.

"Okay! Any other *hidden talents* I should know about?" she said in such a drawled-out voice that Kreig was at a loss for words.

"None." He said it as starkly as he could, all to make sure she wouldn't poke at him anymore. The idea of having to explain to her that he was especially proficient in out-of-combat physical interrogation didn't quite appeal to him. She seemed to slump a bit at the refusal, but once both she and Kreig got back to the work at hand, they did pretty well.

Sure, no *actual* work had been done. It was only their first day, so his tutor spent their time together by introducing him to how they'd work together; what they'd do and when he should ask for help. The basics of tutoring. Kreig listened intently, trying his best to really understand it. He didn't do too well, but since he knew his tutor was a nice woman, he also knew that she probably wouldn't mind if he asked her to repeat at a later date. All things considered, she seemed like a much better tutor than his former one.

Though . . . that could change, as many things did. Just meeting her changed nothing, and he still planned on dropping the whole situation sometime next week.

Probably. All things could change, after all.

The clock hit 2:50, and that was the time his tutor considered right. She stood up, left the textbooks on the table, said she'd bring more tomorrow, and walked to the door, accompanied by a silent, thoughtful Kreig. Once they were at the door, once it was open and she stepped out, only then did he speak, after long consideration.

"Tell me, tutor . . ." She turned to him, eyes full of cautious wonder. "Do you have any name for me to call you by?"

Her brows shot down, a frown twisting her lips. Then, her face suddenly did a complete 180, eyes and brows flashing up in shock. "Oh! Oh, uh, yeah! Of course I do!" She smiled. "It's Erica. My name is Erica Hildebrand, and I'm happy to be your tutor! Call me Erica, though; a few of my other students felt like it was disrespectful, but tutoring and teaching are different things. I'll see you tomorrow, Kreig."

He nodded. "Well met, Erica."

And that was that.

CHAPTER 18

THE BROKEN MAN

That left Kreig with one hour until he needed to be wherever it was he had to be. There was an address, sure, but he had no idea how to get there.

Thankfully, before he could spiral into some sort of confusion-fueled panic, he got his wits together to take another look at the list. Sure enough, right there on the back was a little map of how to get there. It was even written out with a line to follow to get to the right place. There was no space for getting lost since it was obvious where he was meant to go and how to get there. It even said that the time it should take him to get there by foot was around thirty minutes, and even if Kreig added fifteen minutes in case he got lost, that still left him with a quarter of an hour with nothing to do.

He could draw, of course. Always an option. But for some reason, he didn't feel like it.

As a matter of fact, he didn't know what to do *at all*. Worst of all, there was nobody there to tell him what to do, either. No schedule to refer him to anywhere, no specific activity he could indulge in that he truly enjoyed, no enemy to go kill . . . He was unoccupied.

Empty.

It felt horrible.

He started pacing. Up and down the hallway, into his room, flipping through meaningless pages in the textbooks, up and down the hallway, into the bathroom, goggle at all the weird things, up and down the hall-way, open the fridge for no reason, up and down the hallway . . . stand in front of the screen in the living room. It was a big, fancy, shiny thing that seemed to follow rules beyond Kreig's understanding.

No, well, that wasn't *quite* true. He did know a few things, like that there was a little plastic thing that could turn it on.

He picked up the remote, tracing his finger over the buttons. There were a lot of them. He had no idea what any of them did, so in an effort to keep himself occupied, since only three minutes had passed, he pressed each of them, from bottom to top, one by one, until:

"—Reporting live on the blue-grade portal recently opened in Hong Kong, China. Officials report prolific Violet Team Lilac Panthers entering the portal, their up-and-coming star Fighter—" At that point, Kreig stopped listening. It was just a violent torrent of information about things he couldn't possibly understand. Portals were one thing, he'd gone back in one of them, after all, but these people were talking about famous managers and star Fighters and fans crowding and differently graded portals. Kreig was just left staring at it, like a man staring at a raging fire. No control.

And before he knew it, the time was 2:30 and he really had to get going.

Since he had no jacket—not that he needed it—Kreig donned his shoes and hurried out of the door. His heart rate seemed to spike, but he could barely tell why. He had faced dragons and immense armies and the strongest men for the past thirty years, and *this* was what made him sweat as he hurried down the stairs? It was just a meeting with someone. No more stressful than meeting the Emperor or his lord. Just a man.

Hell, he even *knew* this man. He'd known this man for his entire stay underground. There was no reason to fear meeting him again, and there wasn't even any tangible punishment for not keeping the time.

Apart from disappointing his siblings. The greatest failure of all.

He had to get there on time.

With the map in hand and a stern pace, Kreig walked through the streets, abusing every mental skill he had, his immaculate spatial awareness and his ability to understand maps to get where he had to go. Finally, after what felt like far too long, he found the address. Considering how long it had taken him to get there, despite his best efforts, he was probably late.

The entryway was really just a large door facing the street, much like every other door. It entered an equally normal-looking apartment building in a row of similar ones, each built of red bricks. Kreig wasn't sure what to do, but after testing the door, he found that it was open. He might as well enter. Inside, he found a row of stairs and a short corridor. None of them held the address he was looking for, so he climbed the stairs.

There, on the top of the fourth and final floor, he found a single door. 15c Karl-Oskar Street.

All he could do was knock and hope he wasn't too late and wouldn't be despised for it. And after a minute or so, during which Kreig was bold enough to try to knock *again*, the door opened grandly, revealing Dr. Darius Falk standing right there, a mildly curious look on his face. "My. You're early, Wiedermann."

. . . What? "I didn't mean to be."

"Why, I'd say you're"—Darius raised his arm, pulling up the sleeve of his jacket to reveal a beautiful golden watch—"about twenty-seven minutes early. Come on in." Darius then proceeded to give Kreig the most affable, lighthearted smile he had ever seen, as if this wasn't a mistake at all. Even then, it wasn't as though Kreig could find it in himself to beg for forgiveness for a crime Darius didn't notice. He followed Darius inside the apartment.

It felt, in a word, luxurious. But in a very minimalistic sense.

It was plenty big, with wide halls and inviting rooms. But it was far from empty. Many well-polished little tables and cabinets carrying small, equally shiny trinkets lined the hallway and the rooms. It could be little trays or animals made of crystal and glass. It was all sculpted and made in such a way that when the sun hit them just right, it was refracted into all the colors of the rainbow. Another small drawer carried a silver tray with different kinds of liquor and crystal bottles atop it, alongside small and wide glasses.

It all had this vague air of fancy. The abstract paintings on the wall were all framed in gold-painted wood, and the furniture was a strange blend between nothingness and swirling wood.

Kreig wandered through this cacophony of modern and classic with a somewhat-baffled look on his face, unsure of how to respond to it. Darius didn't seem the least bit interested in introducing Kreig to any part of it, simply guiding him through the apartment with his back to him. After a while, they reached a room Kreig could only describe as what seemed to be a library. Every wall had a line of bookshelves covering it. Hundreds upon hundreds of books, old and new, hardcover and paperbacks. Some thick, others thin.

And in the middle of this library, there was a pair of soft-looking armchairs beside a small table. The armchairs didn't *quite* face each other, both turned at a faint angle.

"Come, take a seat," Darius implored, walking ahead of Kreig to take a seat in the farthest chair, the one with the back to the only window in the room. Following suit, Kreig took a seat at the other chair, finding it oddly comfortable. It fit his size almost perfectly, unlike most other chairs he'd sat at these past months, which had all felt comically small to him. "I had it specially made by a local woodworker. Fantastic man."

Kreig wasn't sure what the right response to such a statement was, so he merely nodded.

Darius picked up a small notebook and lead pencil from the table beside the two chairs. "You don't mind if I write notes, do you?"

"By all means," Kreig said, despite not really understanding why Darius would need to take notes at all. In response, Darius gave a quick nod, wrote something in the notebook, and then looked back up before handing Kreig pen and paper.

"It's only doctor-patient confidentiality. It means I can't disclose what we say to anyone unless you confess to intending to harm yourself or someone else. In such a situation, I'll inform the proper authorities, which includes IOCRO. The part that you personally should focus on, however, is the former. Whatever you say to me, whatever opinions you voice, I will not tell a soul. Not your siblings and not even IOCRO. Signing this protects you."

Kreig didn't hesitate to sign it, going so far as to gloss over the wall of text written. It all seemed terribly complicated, but he was sure Darius had only good things in mind. He felt like a good man.

Darius accepted the signed paper. "Thank you." He then slid it into a yellow envelope and put it to the side. "Now, Wiedermann. How do you like your siblings?"

He got right into it.

". . . They seem nice," Kreig said somewhat offhandedly. Darius scribbled something in his notebook, glanced up at Kreig, and nodded for him to continue. Maybe if Kreig had known them better, he could have had more to say. As it was, he barely knew what they did for work or if they had any friends or even what they thought of him. "George is a bit fussy. Sam seems childish."

"Is that a bad thing?"

Kreig thought for a second, his eyes wandering up above Darius's head, into the grassy green outside. "Not in everyone, no. Children should be childish. Soldiers shouldn't."

"Who told you that?"

"My old lord. A raven-haired man with little regard for any life apart from his own. He was perfectly content to remain in his own castle, looking down at his guards and soldiers like pawns in one of his games. Even then, he was not a bad man, as selfish as he was." Somehow, somewhere, it felt all right, just speaking like this. It was neither forced nor unwanted. And, somehow, Darius seemed genuinely interested. Not afraid, not unhappy, just . . . there. A listening ear.

"Isn't it bad to be selfish?"

Kreig gave a quick scoff. "You'd think that. I did at first. He only saved me from the execution block to use as his own personal guard—to curry favor with the Emperor. But he did it for a good reason. He had a son. Cute kid. Wanted to be a soldier like anybody. That kid was my lord's everything. He had nobody else. He'd kill anyone for that kid."

Darius wrote something down. "Did you know the child yourself?"

Kreig paused for a moment. The reality of the kid's short little life flashed before his eyes, and for a moment, it felt like he was in his arms again. That golden-haired little kid that only wanted to become like him. His smile had the same scent as the flowering lichens crowning his lord's mansion. Young. Tender. Go—

"Your lord. What kind of a man was he to you?"

The sound of Darius's voice snapped him out of it. "My lord was . . . He was my lord. I never knew him outside of bowing before him and lowering my head as he approached. We shared no brews, nor did he ever join me on any mission."

"Who joined you on these missions, then?"

Kreig swallowed. He'd never forgotten their names. Not their faces, either. And so, he spoke of them. From the young recruit who quickly became a veteran, to the veteran who almost recognized Kreig for who he was. He fondly remembered the boy who'd try to elope with any young, fair milkmaid he laid eyes on. Every person he spoke of, he spoke of in the most charitable of voices. Even their sins were painted as triumphs, their deaths laid out as grandiose and beautiful instead of haunting and tragic.

And after all of it, Darius sat there, his eyes boring into Kreig's. "Do you regret outliving them?"

A pike crashed through Kreig's heart, stifling his breathing. Of course he did. They were dead and he was alive. He'd be happier if *they* were blessed with this accursed immortality. Surely, even the least of them had more to give the world than Kreig did. Less destruction to rain upon it. "I regret the things I've done that they wouldn't have."

Darius didn't question it in the least. He didn't even ask *what* he did. He just nodded and turned back to his notepad. "What kind of job are you planning on applying for?"

". . . I haven't thought about it." Until now, he'd pretty much just been going where he was told to go. Though, if he remembered it correctly, Darius had indeed told him to try and get a job. Assuming that *soldier* wasn't on the table, he could probably do pretty good work for that organization that found him. The one that fought the monsters. He'd worked as a monster-killer before, so he could easily do it again. It was just supposed to be a part-time job of some sort, so he should probably do something he already knew he was good at. "I could fight monsters."

Darius frowned. "No. Absolutely not. Considering your reaction when you fought the wyrm, forcing you to fight monsters unnecessarily will only further worsen your mental well-being. No, if anything, the job you attempt should be as opposed to your former occupations as possible." It was an unusually hard line for Darius, but at this moment, he knew it was a stance he had to take. He wrote down Wiedermann's reaction in his notebooks. "Say, do you still paint?" Wiedermann nodded. "I recommend you continue doing so. If you have the chance, picking up an instrument wouldn't be bad either. If you talk to your brother about it, I'm sure he will have plenty to tell you."

There was no doubt about that. After all, Darius had personally told George about a few things he might want to introduce Wiedermann to. All in due time, of course. For now, just getting Wiedermann into the swing of his new life was far and away the best they could do.

So, Darius watched carefully as Wiedermann thought the situation over and finally nodded, accepting it.

"I'm glad," Darius said. "The next time we meet, we'll talk more about the future. Thank you for being truthful today. I'll see you next week."

Wiedermann seemed a bit taken aback by the abrupt end, but as usual, he didn't question Darius's words in the least. He stood up, gave an appreciative look, and wandered away. The height of simplicity. Very like the man, and not something that Darius expected to change anytime soon. And that was fine. This would not go quickly, and even then, it *would* leave scars. Wiedermann could never return to being the Kreig he used to be, but he could still grow into becoming a better *Wiedermann*.

That was what Darius hoped for. If he was allowed to work in peace and if Wiedermann remained cooperative, he could surely get there.

While waiting for his next client, Darius took out his phone and wrote a short email to George Wiedermann, speaking in warm tones about how

Wiedermann had left a mere minute ago and that he had opened up rather easily. Though, in George's case, this might be more of a danger to look out for than anything good. Darius had not missed the look on Kreig's face when he thought about that child. If Darius could get him to such a point with minimal probing, having his own brother ask the simplest questions could likely get Kreig to a similar point or even beyond. If the latter happened, it might cause something terrible to occur.

Darius wrote openly about his worries without great detail and then placed his phone back in the inner pocket of his jacket.

There was a knock at the door, signifying that Darius's next client had already arrived. A few minutes early, just as Wiedermann had been. Darius stood up and confidently strode through his apartment until he reached the door. He gave no thought to hesitation, merely pushing it open to greet someone he knew better than Kreig in some regards.

"Hello, Doctor. Am I late?" Gerald asked, standing in the doorway, dressed from tip to toe in what he clearly considered to be very uncomfortable clothes.

"Not at all. Come on in," Darius invited, stepping aside to let the boy enter.

THE YOUNG MAN

Gerald stood there for a moment, his large eyes blinking slowly. "*Is it—* Sorry, may I come inside?" He seemed hesitant to ask, and Darius fully understood why. He reacted to the whole scene with a mild, relaxing smile to lessen Gerald's fears.

"*Of course. Your English has gotten much better, too. Though, in my house, you need never speak too formally,*" Darius said in his best German. He hadn't learned it for this specific purpose, and he certainly hadn't had to use it in a long while, but it made him happy that he had such good use for it with the young Gerald. As Gerald nodded hastily, Darius turned back inside, making sure to grab a small bowl of assorted nuts and dried fruits for Gerald before entering back into the library. Gerald was right behind him, and after only a little moment, they were each seated in their respective chairs.

Gerald eyed the bowl of assorted nuts and fruits with lusting eyes. Gerald didn't do anything until Darius gave an approving wave of the hand. Once he did, the teen went rabid, throwing himself at the bowl and stuffing the little salted things in his mouth.

After gobbling down about half of it, the boy carefully wiped his mouth on the edge of his long-sleeved shirt and sat up straight. "Thank you, Doctor."

"You're always welcome to anything you'd like in this house, Gerald." Darius removed a blue notebook from beside his chair, a different one from the light-red one he used for Kreig. It already contained notes from their last session, which Darius quickly picked up from. "Did you tell that Annie girl in your class that you'd like to be friends?"

This made Gerald perk up. "Ah! Yes, Doctor, I did! Seeing her sit on her own was— I'm glad I talked to her. My friend Jay agreed too, though she seemed to have some strange idea that Annie deserved not having friends. Very strange. Either way, Annie agreed, and she turned out to be even nicer than I thought!"

Gerald genuinely smiled at the thought of having gained a second friend, and Darius felt a hum of contentment seep through his body. They hadn't been meeting for too long, but even at such an early moment as this, it was still clear that Gerald was making very quick improvements. As he had expressed in their former session, Gerald hadn't truly had more than one friend before coming to this world. And now he had two.

"Is she getting along with Jay?"

A little frown found its way onto Gerald's face. "I'm not sure about that. They are both very different people with very different thoughts and lives. They might become better friends soon, but as of now, they have a long way to go."

"Have you told your adoptive parents yet?" Darius asked, absently writing in his notebook. His attention was fully focused on Gerald.

"Huh? Do you—do you mean Andrew and James?" Gerald asked, leaning closer. "Yes, I informed them only yesterday. They appeared delighted at knowing I had gained yet another friend. Andrew went so far as to suggest he pretend to arrest one of them to see if they had any ulterior motives. I'm not sure what he meant, Doctor. Is this normal behavior for a policeman, or ought I be worried?"

Darius gave a chuckle. "No, no, it's nothing like that. I'm sure he was only joking with you. You know how parents are."

". . . Doctor, I'm not sure I do any longer. I hold no disdain for my former parents, they brought me up right, but now that I know these people, I'm starting to wonder if I truly *was* raised properly." For a second or two, Gerald clearly mulled it over, clasping his hands together. "Tell me, Doctor, were your parents kind?"

An odd question, but as a psychiatrist, Darius had every reason to be honest with Gerald. "I don't believe they were, Gerald. Few are. But my parents, much like yours, did their best. Despite this, you have every right not to thank them for what they did. Even though it might have been the best they could at the time."

"The best they could . . . Yes, I'm sure that's what they did. Despite what you say, Doctor, I will not dislike them. They brought me to this world, and although it has not always been kind to me, I believe, at this time, it is a good thing to have been born."

Darius couldn't help but smile. "That's good to hear, Gerald. Always hold that in you."

The rest of the session progressed rather routinely. Gerald talked about how the school he joined was treating him and issues with the faint language barrier, though he remained immensely thankful for Jay, the only one in his class who spoke German fluently enough to understand him and teach him English. He spoke of subjects he found interesting and anything else on his mind. Apparently, unlike almost all other otherworldly prisoners recovered, Gerald held no hate toward the English language, likely on account of his youth.

The only thing Gerald found unappealing about Jay was that she still hadn't let him go home to her house. This was something Darius had told him was a normal friend activity during an earlier session. In almost all other regards, Gerald was developing well and becoming genuinely happy. He was accepted by his family, welcomed to his class without ridicule, and able to make friends. In a certain way, it was a far more positive development than Darius had ever dared to hope for. Watching a young boy like Gerald overcome such a terrible past was inspiring in an odd way and gave him real hope for Kreig.

As the session neared its end and Gerald grew more talkative, speaking in warm words about how his foster fathers had planned a so-called movie night for the evening—whatever that was—Darius readied himself to pull the plug.

"Always glad to hear it, Gerald. Now, we've almost reached five. Is there anything you'd like to tell me as a final addendum?"

Gerald, just as last time, furrowed his brows and tapped his thumb to his lower lip. "Forgive me! I forgot to ask last time, but has Kreig been released yet? I'm sure they're keeping him for a reason. Truly, I, if anyone, should know; I . . . I'm just curious. When will he contact me? The phone I have is rudimentary, but I've been assured that should I be contacted, I will know." Gerald waited a moment before speaking again. "Do you think he'd like his painting back? It's framed in my room. I'm afraid I'd rather not take it down."

Darius laughed heartily. "No, not at all. I'm sure he'd be delighted to know you've kept it. He spent an entire night on it, not to mention the days he spent studying your face. Furthermore, he *has* been released, although he still hasn't fully grasped the concept of modern technology. Until he does, you may be met with silence. Take it patiently. He'll reach you when he's ready. Keep in mind that he holds you in extremely high regard."

Gerald smiled deeply. "Is that so? Then I'm glad. Thank you for telling me."

"Happy to tell, Gerald."

And so, the session ended peacefully.

CHAPTER 19

IS THERE LIFE IN PAINT?

In another part of the city, not too far away, Kreig had just finished retelling in soft tones how he'd met Erica and how Darius seemed awfully interested in asking odd questions about him. This little run-through occurred at the dinner table, where a fine meal had already been served and eaten. The day was concluding, and happily so. Both George and Sam seemed glad that Kreig was taking so well to his everyday matters, and he agreed fully himself.

The only other thing that made that evening special was that Kreig had finally gotten his hands on more painting supplies. Nothing too grand, just a few canvases, a sketchbook, plenty of brushes, a small palette of oils, and the like. Simple stuff, really.

For some odd reason, Kreig got to work with an almost-feverish passion. It wasn't *just* that he'd been given something so delightful from his siblings. It was also that gripping thrill of finally being able to do something productive again. Away from people, lost in himself, he was merely painting. He moved as if possessed. And he knew just the sketch to transform into art. He'd already painted Peter once, so the only part he had to really put his all into was portraying Mrs. Willowgrove right. Her eyes were no longer frozen lakes.

He got right to it. As George settled down on the couch with a cup of tea and a book and Sam sat next to him, back at it with the television, Kreig painted. He had a song in his heart that he had to put on the canvas.

In his fervor, he lost track of the time. He moved at a brisk pace to complete the painting, to give form to a love he hoped he wasn't just imagining.

He tried to place Peter's personality, as he became and as he was by the end of his life, and not as she remembered him. Maybe it was a hopeless thought, but Kreig believed that if Peter had lived, if he had met his aging and withered mother, he would have changed his mind. He wouldn't have been frowning like a brooding teen. No, as Kreig so delicately painted it, he'd be smiling. Carefully, gently. He had a hand on his mother's shoulder where she sat just in front of him on an old wooden chair. She was wearing a ballgown that might have been even older than her.

Warmth. Emotion. Deep longing for someone already gone.

Maybe it was conceited of him, but he placed his own emotions in there like a little bird's egg. He missed Peter too. In a way, in a strange, wicked way, he'd known Peter and missed him far longer than she had. Of course he missed his best friend. But did he miss him as much as his mother did?

That was not a question he could answer, and, like many, many other questions, he shuffled it to the side. Big questions weren't for him to answer. He wasn't that kind of artist.

He wasn't the kind of artist that reimagined the real as the unreal; he didn't exaggerate features or create anything fully new and original. He saw what there was, and that was what he drew. A face, a human. A moment from his life. He could put these people in new positions and situations all he wanted, but it remained simple. Unremarkable. Though he didn't expect much. After all, had he not gained this skill through the power of the system?

Could he really say that *he* created this art on his own when he had so much help from the system? Practically speaking, it was entirely unremarkable. Dishonest, even. A fraud.

It was the same with his cooking and fighting and everything in between. It was all thanks to the system. All thanks to the white roots within them.

Without them, he would be *nothing*.

Kreig could feel his grip on his brush tightening, and upon remembering what damage that could bring, he instantly released his grip on it fully, letting it clatter to the floor. Sam was lost in her game, but George noticed it the moment it happened, giving a small jolt before perking up. "Everything all right, Kreig?" he asked, closing his book slightly to focus more on Kreig.

Kreig waited a moment before answering. "I'm not sure." Not anymore, at least. Maybe he'd never been all right, and maybe he never would be.

But wasn't he right? Hadn't his thinking from all these years, this immense gratitude to those that had given him everything he was, hadn't it been correct? Somehow, it didn't feel all right, though. Not since George asked about it.

For some reason, it almost seemed like George could tell certain things about Kreig that not even Kreig could. Like when he was all right and when he wasn't. And maybe, just maybe, Kreig should trust this more than himself.

George slipped an old receipt between the pages of his book, stood up, and wandered over to where Kreig was. He looked up, his bespectacled eyes dimmed with uncertainty and doubt. But he didn't say anything. Not a word. No, where Kreig stood, tense and mute, George bowed down and picked the brush off of the floor. Then he rose again and handed it to Kreig without speaking a word. As a final gesture, he gave a nervous smile. "I won't ask; it's okay. You needn't tell me, and I needn't hear. Just stay right there, and I'll go get some tissues to clean up the floor."

And he did. All the while Kreig stood there like a doofus, watching his brother clean up his own mess before excusing himself back to the couch. As if nothing had happened. As if nothing was—

No, not like that. George wouldn't ask anymore. And Kreig wouldn't tell.

And maybe that was better for all of them.

Around ten, the painting was finished. It was everything he had thought of when he sketched it. Peter was in his extravagant cardinal's gown and his mother in white. As if nothing had changed.

Sand Emperor's Touch (X)

There. Now it was dry. Kreig removed it from the stand he'd been given. What to do now? He could watch whatever Sam was doing. That was always an option.

Kreig leaned a bit to the side to catch a glimpse at what she was so into, only to find her seemingly driving a car around a city. But she wasn't driving like George did yesterday; no, she was recklessly driving straight through the streetlights and—and right into people. She just ran someone over. And then she cackled about it. Should he be worried? Being happy about the death of another when they didn't even hold any horrible hedonistic beliefs seemed almost sadistic. Not to mention the flashing lights and loud, irritating noises.

Kreig wrinkled his nose. Yeah, no. He went and grabbed another canvas. What now? Someone. Paint *someone.* Someone new.

How about Erica? He'd met her only that day; drawing her surely wouldn't be odd. Ah, though . . . For some reason, the thought of her seeing his painting of her when they had only met two brief times felt a bit embarrassing for some reason. Darius, then? Now that he'd gotten a fully proper view of him through his eyes and not his nose, he could surely paint him accurately.

So, he got to it. And two hours later, he had a fully fleshed-out painting with Darius sitting in his armchair beneath that green-filled window and the little blooming flower pots. A little painting that would hang well on Kreig's wall.

It was midnight. Sam excused herself to go to bed, while George sunk further into the couch, seemingly joining with it as he gluttonously indulged in the book.

George. Of course!

But just painting him again felt a little odd. No, now that Kreig thought about it, he'd been doing all these portraits very strangely. Right from his head with nobody to look at. Didn't most reputable painters require a model of some sort, especially of the one they were painting? Of course, of course. His paintings weren't lacking, but Kreig was sure that if he were to have George pose for him, even just sitting on a chair, doing as he pleased, Kreig would be able to extract much more of *George* than before.

"Brother," Kreig said. "Would you sit in front of me as I paint your portrait?"

George flinched so hard, Kreig was afraid he might fly off of the couch. "Huh? I— Where— What? Oh, Kreig! I—I'm dreadfully sorry; could you repeat that?" This he said while his head whipped around erratically, his eyes glancing desperately back to the pages he'd been ripped away from.

". . . I'd like to paint your portrait. Will you pose in front of me as I do?"

It took George a full minute to process the request, during which Kreig was allowed to witness him both escape from within his own imagination as well as retreat back into it. Very fascinating. And, at the end of it, George's brows shot up. "Um, sure! What should I— I have a suit in my wardrobe. Should I wear it?"

". . . If you'd like to?"

Five minutes later and George was dressed up in a gaudy, dark blue thing that honestly might not have looked too bad on a handsome man. It really wasn't the kind of clothing that Kreig could appreciate on an aesthetic level. What were the little shiny buttons for? Why did he have a glittery top hat? What tailor would stoop to this level?

"It's not too modern, but I assure you, I was the most popular guy at the prom," George said confidently, pulling out a cloth rose from somewhere. Kreig really wasn't about to question any of this.

Someone else also wasn't about to let his statement go unchallenged. "Really? *Most popular*? George, I've got a photo of you that might prove otherwise," Sam teased, poking her head out of her room. She hadn't gone to bed. How mischievous. "Though, really, I've gotta ask. What'd you bring out your only suit for? Found a prom date after all these years?"

"Hey, shut it! He doesn't need to know that!" George shouted back, crossing his arms sternly. "Besides, I've got nothing better to wear. A man must always present his best side while having his portrait painted."

That got her attention. "Oh? Is that— Is this—" Her face went through about five different expressions, beginning with pleasant surprise and ending with childish upset. "Hey, how come I wasn't invited? I bet I could look fifteen times better on a canvas than he ever could!"

Kreig stared at her strangely. "You may join us if you'd like."

He didn't see why this was even a question. Fitting two people on a single canvas was as easy as fitting one, although it did increase the time it'd take him to complete it. As long as she didn't mind the wait, there was no reason for her not to join. No issue there. In that sense, the only thing keeping him from getting straight to painting was Sam herself. After all, she was just sort of standing there. Eyes slightly wide.

"Is that an invitation?" she asked. Kreig nodded. Of course it was an invitation; what else would it be? "Oho? Really, now?" A competitive grin flashed across her face. "Very well, then! Watch me beat George out of the park before you have time to so much as blink!"

With that declaration of war, she rushed back into her room. Going by her cackle and general demeanor, it was clear that she was trying to out-dress her brother somehow. Going by Kreig's lacking knowledge of these kinds of things, this might take a while. And so, after taking a peek at his brother and getting a sympathetic nod in turn, they went over to the living room. Together, they decided pretty quickly how they'd do this. Namely, George and Sam would sit on the couch while Kreig painted them, making sure not to get any paint on the carpet, even though Kreig assured George that he had skills that could clean any such stains. George didn't trust him on that. A dirty carpet was a dirty carpet.

"The star arrives!" Sam shouted from down the hall.

Both Kreig and George peeked down the hall, getting a glance of just who they were looking at. She was remarkably well dressed. With how unappealing George was clothed, it almost seemed like a miracle. She wore an ankle-length, frilly thing that shouldn't have complimented a hard woman like her in the least. Light yellow and poofy, somehow, despite it all, the color clashed with neither her eyes nor her hair. It fit, somehow.

"Stunned, are you? Heh, I used to be really into dressmaking as a teen, so . . . I've always got one on hand!" she said with a proud grin, just as George let out a deep sigh.

Since Kreig was already standing by his canvas and George was already sitting on the couch, it was just a matter of waving her over. She made a sound like a startled hamster and darted over to the couch, not missing her chance to do a little pirouette to let her dress twirl beautifully. When she finally planted herself on the couch, sporting a gleeful, lopsided grin, Kreig was anxious to get started.

It was time. He had both his siblings sitting in front of him, George on the left and Sam on the right. George in that odd suit, legs crossed and hands resting freely on his lap. Sam in her proud dress, cupping her head in her right hand, still smiling.

He'd better get to it.

Since he didn't want to be a bother and force them to sit awake for too long, he painted quicker than usual, though with no less detail and care. Every brushstroke, every touch of color he added was given care and momentum, placing it where it had to be for the express purpose of it being there. He transplanted reality into fiction, taking what there was, his brother and his sister, and transforming them into art.

And when that was done, when all the bases were covered, he moved on. His siblings were starting to get tired, but he remained quick-fingered. He had to hurry.

With all the care in the world, taking all the time to fully study every piece of his sibling's features, from the faint freckles speckling Sam's tanned face if you looked close enough to the slight hunch to George's back. He saw it, and he painted it. That night, he studied his siblings closer than he ever had. That night, he truly felt like an artist. A poet of the canvas, an author of the real. He placed emotion and life in their lives, animated them into existence, and made them feel like humans.

And then . . . he was done. It seemed. The painting was right there, starring his brother and sister as they were. As they felt in reality.

But something felt missing. Some little part of them, something he hadn't expressed.

. . . Yes, that was it. He had painted them as they *felt*. As they *looked*. Not how they *were*. An old mistake he had learned to fix before. He just had to do it.

Adding this to an already-finished painting felt like an impossible, daunting task.

But he did it. He saw his siblings, where they sat, and he saw their humanity. Something he had thought that he himself had lost. Compassion, patience, loyalty. He believed he only had one of these. But here, in them, he saw all three. He saw it, and he put it on his brush, and he put it on the canvas. He took their virtues and placed them in the painting. He took their humanity and made it visible.

And there . . . There it was.

His greatest work.

Artistry reached Rank V

Artistry (V)

Rank V: Evoke opinion

Rank IV: Evoke emotion

Rank III: Greater anatomy, perspective, shading

Rank II: Greater color and design

Rank I: Stable hands, smoother lines

For a moment, he merely stared at the painting, the reality of the situation slipping between his paint-stained fingers. It was beautiful, and it was them, and somehow, it didn't feel as if he himself had painted it.

Sam seemed to possess the coy beauty of one of the creatures speckling the inside of George's room, her magical beauty no longer fleeting but eternal and dazzling on the canvas. Her eyes possessed life and intelligence that shone as radiant as any star, and somehow, she was more herself than her real version could ever hope to be.

Her brother was the very same, his expressions brought into this other world with a careful hand, and he sat there, his every limb pulsating with the essence of himself. Although his eyes and body were tired by the strains of life, there remained life in him, beating through his heart and body like his lifeblood. Simply looking at him, at every aspect of his body language and face, granted the viewer a striking sense of who he was and, even more so, what they should think about him.

The painting made the viewer love the two subjects. In the very same way a brother would love his siblings.

Something in the way Kreig had let his arm fall limply to his side, something in how he suddenly held his gaze steady and wide on the canvas must have told his siblings that it was done. He had created it. And it had only taken half the night, too.

Enraptured by what he couldn't believe he himself had created, he was only brought out of his stupor when he suddenly noticed that the couch was empty.

"Whoa! Is that really how I look?" Sam said from his left side. "You're sure you painted me, warts and all?"

George, peeking out from Kreig's right side, let his gaze hop from the Sam on the painting and the Sam in real life. His nose crumpled up. "I'd say it's about the same."

Her tanned face grew a shade redder. "I'm not sure how to feel about that."

During the duration of a short moment, Kreig wondered if he should feel insulted at the insinuation that he would be dishonest in his depiction of them. But that moment passed with the recognition that his siblings surely meant him no harm. While these thoughts flitted through his mind unbidden, George leaned in closer to the painting, willingly letting the noxious smell assault his nostrils up close. Kreig had purposefully used as little of the chemical solution as he possibly could, since the smell was absolutely abhorrent, but George didn't seem to mind it as much.

". . . It's really good." George glanced back up at Kreig, meeting his gaze. "How would you feel about displaying one of your paintings?" He must have noticed the faint shudder that trembled through Kreig's left hand, since he quickly capitulated. "Not the ones of your friends or us, but if you ever were to paint a celebrity or something, or maybe just a still life, it would clearly be worthy of exhibition."

Exhibition.

Kreig had seen many paintings exhibited freely in his days. You couldn't wander down the halls of the Emperor's palace without subjecting yourself to the innumerable glares of the hundreds of portraits dotting the halls like fixtures of the past. Nobody in the royal guard knew exactly who the people portrayed were, but many rumors suggested it was the paintings of criminals right before their execution, or of the Emperor's lovers, or the members of a family line spanning a millennium. Kreig hadn't much cared one way or another. He didn't like looking into their soulless, staring eyes in the least. This meant that his gaze was usually drawn to the few featured non-portrait paintings.

He only ever saw them as he stalked down the halls on one official errand or another, but they always brought him a certain sense of calm.

Pictures of nature; paintings of beautiful scenes in forests and plains; animals and creatures he had never seen and likely never would.

Now that he thought back on it, despite how unfeeling those portraits of people had been, they had at least been brought from a painter's hand completely unsullied. The painter had no help from any outside influence, only himself and his effort. He had been taught by a master once, yes, but even that master had cultivated his skills from only himself. It was a pure effort, wholly unlike Kreig's own.

After all, Kreig had been assisted by the system. It was a firm, guiding hand, making sure his lines were smooth and his anatomy on point.

It made his brush do what it had to and it made his sword strike true. It granted him power and age no man should have. Kreig owed everything he was to the system, and therefore, he was tainted. Dishonest. Impure. Only those whose results had come from their pure, unassisted effort should be allowed the honor of hanging their soulless portraits in the halls of the Emperor's palace. To hang a portrait birthed by the system there would be to make a mockery of the Emperor himself.

And that was why Kreig softly shook his head, a defeated refrain bobbing familiarly through his mind: *You are nothing without the system and you have nothing to bear pride in.*

"I would rather not," he said to his brother, watching as a hint of disappointment flashed through his eyes, and Kreig knew he'd said the wrong thing, but it was too late to take it back and make his brother happy again.

George smiled thinly, his eyes softening. "Of course. Take your time."

Kreig couldn't say he liked the way that sounded, but before he could consider the words on any deeper level, Sam pushed her face into his view. "Yeah, that's great, but what about payback?"

Kreig and George stared at her silently.

George narrowed his eyes, keeping his gaze level with hers. "The hell do you mean by *payback*?"

A characteristic sly grin flashed across her face. "For the painting! It's not like we can just have Kreig paint us and then go on our way without doing anything, right?" There was a mad, sleep-deprived glint in her eyes that seemed to suggest imminent tomfoolery.

George was equally as tired as her, a connection Kreig sadly didn't have. In this bond, his brother must have realized something, because all of a sudden, a small smile crossed his face, bearing that same energy as hers did. "Aha. Gotcha. Heh." He straightened his back and twisted the glittering top hat on his head. "Say, Kreig, will you take a seat? Right there on the couch."

Two pairs of raptor eyes turned on Kreig, and all of a sudden, he knew that he was trapped in a web that he could neither escape nor understand.

And, as he always did when he had no idea what was going on, he defaulted to the one thing that usually worked in these situations: he obeyed the orders given to him without question.

Fingers trembling, pausing only to brush over the painting and apply the drying skill, he placed the brush in a small vat of murky water before plodding over and taking a seat on the couch. There he sat rigid as a stone statue while his siblings gingerly moved the painting he'd done of him to the side and then grabbed a new, blank canvas. They placed it on the stand, sharing looks that gossiped in a language Kreig didn't speak. Somehow, the two of them appeared to have a telepathic link, borne of shared mania. It scared Kreig just a little.

George's face peeked out from the side of the canvas. "Do a cool pose."
Oh. Oh, lord.

Sam grumbled about the stand being too high up before also peeking her head around the canvas, her eyes hard and stern. "Yeah. Do a cool pose!"

Even if Kreig knew what a "cool pose" looked like, he wouldn't have been able to take it, what with how his limbs were all paralyzed in confusion. And now both Sam and George were looking at him in the same way. Like two hounds gazing at a piece of meat.

"Come on, just lie down on your side across the couch. Like—like one of our French girls," George said, waving his hand as if to show how it would be.

Spurred by somewhat clear orders, Kreig laid down with his back to the couch, his arms folded across his broad chest.

Sam shook her head. "No, no, like, on your side, facing us."

Kreig twisted his body to face them, his long legs straight and stiff.

A smile began skidding over Sam's features. "Yeah, yeah, and now put your arm under your head. Like, hand on your cheek." Kreig tried to do what she said, watching unhappily as her smile grew into a grin. "And now fold your left leg a little. Heh." Kreig couldn't tell why, but as he moved his body like a puppet to her words, he felt like a consort in the grasp of a nobleman. Despite that, he had to admit, the pose wasn't completely uncomfortable, apart from the fact that a fair portion of his legs was dangling over the edge of the couch, marking the whole thing as just a bit too short for him to lie on comfortably.

Happy with his pose, Sam gave an enthusiastic thumbs-up before ducking back behind the canvas, George following suit. Kreig couldn't say that he was overly hyped about being on the other side of the canvas, but since it was his siblings doing it, he had no qualms.

Their portrait took less than an hour to fully create, but it contained just as much effort as what Kreig had made for them.

Sam wiped at her forehead, smearing a streak of red paint across it. In her eyes, a conflict was taking place, one between the exhaustion brought on by the late night and the sparking, glittering mania of the situation. That feral grin she had had almost an hour before was still plastered across her face even now, but something in the way it broadened just a smidgen informed Kreig that a change had occurred.

George had a similar expression, if somewhat subdued. Although his face showed none of her expressiveness, his eyes were just as bright, dimmed only by the solemn realization that he wouldn't be getting any sleep that night.

George took a step back from the canvas, a paint-stained hand shooting up to rub his chin. "I'd say it's pretty much done."

"Yeah. Pretty much done," Sam echoed approvingly, arms crossed over her chest. A fire seemed to blaze up in her eyes as she grabbed the canvas from off of the stand and held it up for Kreig to see.

Until now, Kreig had been stuck in a middle point between constant, uninterrupted thinking and sliding into his soldier's habit of waking meditation. He just didn't know how to react. The last time he was forced to pose for a portrait, he had at least been sure that he'd be there for a few hours and that his painter wouldn't do anything unusual. But with how his siblings had been looking at him over the past hour, the situation was completely unpredictable. And now it seemed to have come to an end.

Kreig turned his weary gaze to the painting held in her dirty hands.

It was . . . Well, honestly, Kreig wasn't sure what he had expected, but this sure wasn't it.

First of all, that couch was *way* too small. Almost comically so, being the approximate size of a small stool shoved beneath his body, which, in comparison, was massive. For some reason, Kreig was happy to notice he was wearing clothes. A white, paint-stained apron and regular, modern clothing. A mirror of his current clothing. Still, for some reason, his body reminded him of some sort of massive bull, swollen and huge, lying on his side just as she had wanted. His hair was long, his face was pale and his eyes were hazy.

And he was smiling.

Sure, the smile was just a single, unbroken black line, but . . . it was a smile.

Even stranger, for some reason, it felt *right*. Of course he'd be smiling. He was having a good time, wasn't he? Of course he was. And so was George, and so was Sam.

He carefully slid off the couch to stand. He trod over to where Sam stood. Her wild eyes and bright grin followed him all the way until he stood right in front of her. Wordlessly, she handed him the painting. His fingers brushed over it lightly.

Sand Emperor's Touch (X)

The crude oil painting, clearly amateur, was sealed and rendered immortal.

His mind moved back seventy years, to when he had his portrait painted by one of a dozen master painters. He had been forced to stand still for several hours, his hair tied back as if in preparation for war. His body had been encased in uselessly ornate armor made only for looks, broadsword in one hand and shield in the other. When he saw his portrait, he had felt his heart sink. His eyes were soulless and rimmed with dark bags, face stiff and stoic, a harsh frown tugging at his lips. That portrait had then been hung up alongside a million other soulless portraits down the halls of the palace. Immortalized as another one of the Emperor's mysteries.

. . . This was not that.

Although almost childishly drawn, like something two toddlers with unrestricted access to paint might conjure, it was still better than what that master artist had made. This—this had a *soul*. It wasn't a warrior or a machine of murder. This was him, as he was—as they saw him.

Smiling.

Kreig saw his vision growing cloudy, his hands trembling slightly as they held the portrait. He could feel the edges of his lips dipping, threatening to form a frown. In retaliation, in a weird form of mimicry toward the painted version of himself, he forced a smile onto his lips. A trembling, honest smile.

The painting was hung up in the living room while the one he made of his siblings was mounted on the wall in his own room.

CHAPTER 20

LET'S CONSPIRE TOGETHER

The rest of the night passed in the blink of an eye, spent mostly by cleaning up after the childish event. And when the clock hit six, both Sam and George realized that they still had work to get to. It may have been a Thursday, but it was still a workday.

And so, after an hour or so, they left the house yet again, leaving Kreig alone. But he wouldn't be alone for long, and he knew that.

While he waited for his tutor to arrive, he poked around a little. Not much, not too prying, but he did take a look around. Of course, it wasn't as though he'd dare to touch the television or anything nearby it, but he did find a small row of what seemed to be books along the edge of one of the small cupboards. Once he picked one up and flipped it open though, he realized that it wasn't a book. At least, not quite.

It was filled from page to page with small, odd-looking paintings, periodically interrupted by small bubbles filled with text. "*Wait for me!*" one of the bubbles said. "*I'll see you on the other side.*"

Hm. Although Kreig hardly recognized this exact form, it did somewhat remind him of some murals that could be found outside churches or schools, telling stories in a series of pictures. Except these pictures were very small. And they had text.

He turned to the picture next to the first one. "*Please don't go,*" the bubble said gravely. "*I'm not letting you leave me.*" As Kreig continued, panel to panel, he found that time seemed to be going in reverse. Either that or he was reading them in the wrong order.

. . . Yeah, he was reading them in the wrong order. Though that posed the question: why would the panels go from right to left when text was usually meant to be read left to right? Very strange.

A chime resounded through the apartment, and he was forced to leave the book and the question behind. His tutor had arrived.

She was as radiant as the last time he had seen her and just a smidge less obviously terrified.

Unlike yesterday, they actually spent the entire day, well, working. Sort of. The hours before lunch were spent familiarizing Kreig with the study of social sciences and establishing how he could best learn such subjects. Lunch went well and Erica seemed to, once again, thoroughly enjoy what he had to offer. The time after lunch was spent with natural sciences. Unlike what Kreig had expected at first glance, with the help of her tutoring, he found himself unexpectedly understanding most parts, including those he had believed would fully elude him.

Once she put her mind to it, Erica was surprisingly good at explaining things in a simple but thorough manner. And, at the end of it, he found himself completing, with remarkable ease, exercises that at first seemed impossible.

And when he finished a problem like that, and Erica came over to check if he completed it with the proper solution, and she told him he did it just right, he felt a strange surge of pride.

And when Erica left for the night, he had completely forgotten his plans of canceling the tutoring.

The evening rolled around pleasantly. And, for once, Kreig left his canvas for a moment to take a look at what his siblings were doing.

He might not have been much for books, but upon sitting down next to George and asking what his novel was about, Kreig couldn't help but get sucked into the story as well. Stories back in the other world had always either been very simple or all too complex. It was either some simple knight-and-princess story or some sort of convoluted story about politics and betrayal. Kreig had neither time nor mind for either, so he usually ignored them entirely.

George's story was, if George's imaginative motions and expressions were to be trusted, much more interesting. Sure, it was somehow about politics, but it was about *interesting* politics!

As far as Kreig could tell from George's heated recounting of it, the novel was about a secret evil wizard's rise to power alongside his equally evil master. Even though George was far from the end of the novel, he still didn't hesitate to inform Kreig of the fact that the secret evil wizard would, at one point, murder his master. Kreig didn't understand why he'd take the time to spoil the whole story like that, but if it made sense to George, then it was probably a good idea.

Turning to his sister instead, Kreig found her playing a different game from before, though equally absorbed. Unlike before, she was now running around with a sword, stabbing creatures Kreig couldn't recognize and easily destroying the lot of them with a few well-placed swings.

The whole game seemed very complex. Since Sam had remained focused on the game even as he sat down next to her, he decided against talking to her. Bringing her out of the story would probably just upset her. He turned his attention to the game.

Her character was now fighting a *very big* creature. All the other creatures she'd fought before were either smaller than her character or about the same size. This thing, on the other hand, was immense.

If her character was the size of a human, then the massive sword-wielding wolf she encountered was about the size of a regular drake. Absolutely massive.

Over the course of an hour, Kreig was given a nice view of how his sister slowly grew more and more frustrated trying to kill the wolf. Every time her character died and returned to life, she got just a bit closer to defeating the wolf, each time chipping away just another centimeter of health, predicting more and more of its movements before they even happened. It was almost impressive, if the movements of the little character hadn't been so basic.

And after about an hour of this, she gave up.

Huffing, she almost slammed the controller onto the coffee table before standing up and storming over to the sink, where she downed a full glass of water before returning.

Only after this brief interlude of cooling off was she able to defeat the wolf.

That fight was, despite everything, almost tense. If only because Kreig really wanted his seething sister to win. But she did win! And once she did, she leaned back with a deep, contented sigh, sinking into the couch as if being swallowed.

Happy with his observations, Kreig stood back up, noticing briefly how George took a break from his novel to let his eyes follow him as he wandered back to his canvas. For a short moment, Kreig considered what he should draw. That moment passed quickly, though, when he recalled the thing he'd been staring at for an hour now: the sword-wielding wolf. And the character, of course.

So, drawing from his memory, he painted the fight. It was just a single moment from it, with both parties locked in battle, blood and iron slashing the surroundings.

Once he was done and happy, he wasn't actually sure what to do with it. It wasn't as though he could hang it on the wall. The subject of the painting was almost completely irrelevant to everything he held dear, and he didn't much care for either subject. With his own indifference in mind, he decided to give it to his sister, who accepted it with expressive gratitude, only dampened slightly by her mental exhaustion from the fight itself.

Before Kreig could get back to painting, George quickly told him that if he ever wanted to read any of his novels, he was welcome to pick out whichever one he wanted. They would be in his room, a place Kreig shouldn't hesitate to enter unless George was in it. Kreig gladly accepted the offer, though he'd save it for later.

With that, the evening concluded. Everybody was in bed before midnight, which allowed them a full night's sleep to handle the sleepless night of yesterday.

The next day passed in much the same manner.

It was Friday, and before his tutor could arrive, Kreig spent his time carefully picking out a single novel from the bookshelf in George's room. He felt guilty being in there when George wasn't there, but he'd been specifically told to do so, which made the situation a whole lot more acceptable. The novel he picked out was called *The Collector*, and he only had two reasons for choosing it. Firstly, compared to all the other books, it was much more beaten-up, which would suggest that George didn't care for it. Secondly, it had a pretty butterfly on the cover. Kreig liked butterflies. They didn't hurt anybody.

Sadly, he didn't have time to so much as open the cover before the doorbell chimed.

Heart soaring with mild elation, he put the book on the kitchen table before opening the door. There she was, standing small and petite and lacking so much as a hint of fright. In the past days, she had slowly grown more comfortable around him, culminating in this moment where her eyes held only innocent curiosity. Kreig was happy to see it, and even happier to experience it.

She smiled, stepped inside, and immediately let her eyes fall on the battered novel sitting atop the kitchen table. "Isn't that the novel that inspired those two serial killers?"

Kreig bristled. It *what*?

After picking up the novel and reading the backside, she nodded resolutely. "Yup, this is it. Are you reading it?" Kreig felt hot and ashamed under her gaze. "Good choice! I've heard it's really good, though I've never read it myself. Not yet, at least."

For all his age, Kreig could not understand the smirk that lingered on her lips as she placed the book back on the table.

Kreig hadn't thought about it yet, but the realization that there were serial killers in this world as well made him somehow unhappy. Couldn't they have stayed in the otherworld? Though, again, it did make sense, in a horribly terrible way. As long as he didn't have to meet one, Kreig supposed he'd try to not think about it too much.

The day continued at a steady pace, letting Kreig's thoughts of human suffering leave his mind. Instead, he focused on silently and carefully studying the textbooks he'd been presented with.

Social science before lunch, history after.

It was interesting. As much as he had thought he would despise it, he found himself silently enraptured in the textbooks. He might have wanted to believe it was only because they presented a much-needed understanding of the world he'd left behind, but it was more so that he simply enjoyed the act of learning.

He always had.

To practice the sword was to learn. To survive a battle was to learn. To master an art was to learn.

This was just a more honest form of it. True, in a way. Little facts entered his mind—things about the world he enjoyed knowing. Peter had always been the more knowledgeable of them, but at this moment, Kreig could truly understand what made it so enjoyable to simply learn.

Erica helped him, of course. He never asked for it. After 130 years of being told that asking for help would only reward you with betrayal, he had stopped. He was supposed to know these things. Asking for help was to ask for humiliation.

Then how kind it was for her to give it to him anyway.

It was almost as though she could read his mind. At the times when he got stuck rereading the same page over and over again, trying to make sense of words that didn't seem to fit, she'd step up behind him, let her eyes graze over the page, and carefully explain it in just the way he needed her to. Sometimes, she explained parts he already understood, but he didn't stop her. As silly as it was, being helped felt good. It meant she cared, and that was all he wanted.

So, he listened to her talk and talk and explain and explain, and in the end, he'd hesitantly ask her to clarify a single little part. Just to hear her talk a little more.

And she seemed to enjoy it, somehow.

So the day passed. He made her lunch, studied history with a bizarre hunger, and learned about people from days of old.

When she left, he had two hours before his siblings arrived. Or, rather, about one hour before his sister came home, with his brother coming an hour later. Until then, he prepared dinner.

But making dinner isn't something that takes up the entirety of the time it takes to do it. No, there are plenty of moments of leisure where you only need to wait for various things to finish bubbling and boiling. In these small moments, Kreig picked up the novel. It was interesting in a strange way, he supposed.

The part he liked most was that it gave him a true look into the life of a regular person. Or, as regular as Frederick could be. It was a curious read, but he enjoyed every page of it.

Two hours later, his siblings had both returned home, weary and fatigued, and dinner was served.

Once they all sat around the table, they got to eating. Sam wasted no time complaining about her workday, talking about how Mr. So-and-so was an incompetent ass and that Officer Krupke was up her ass about this and that and how she'd had to travel out to the middle of the countryside to remove some portal or another. At the mention of a portal, Kreig's ears perked up.

Apparently, the portal itself was very low-level, but since it wasn't completely out in the countryside beyond human civilization like some, they had to subjugate it or it might harm the civilian populace. Her rant continued for a few more minutes before George scratched his chin and remarked that since Kreig was technically a civilian, speaking about these matters was illegal with him in the room. Sam, in turn, turned a nice shade of white. Arms flailing and sweat beading, she implored Kreig to ignore everything he had just heard. He accepted her words solemnly but decided against using a memory-wipe skill on himself since they probably wouldn't want him doing that at dinner.

A short silence befell the table. That was, until Sam spoke, her brow furrowed and eyes distant as if she'd been mulling the question for a while.

"... Say, Kreig," he said, "what religion do you believe in?"

Kreig's hand stalled, fork almost in his mouth. Lifting his gaze from the table, he met his sister's eyes.

Sam glanced away, but she didn't retract her question. "When we first met you down there, you prayed, right? It wouldn't be so strange to assume you held a belief of some sort." Kreig and George exchanged a knowing look, and George seemed just as apprehensive and unsure as Kreig did.

Carefully, Kreig placed his fork back on his plate, looking his sister in the eye.

Being religious wasn't necessarily a bad thing in the other world. It was simply a matter of *which* belief you held. That was the aspect that could decide whether you got an encouraging pat on the arm or a summary execution. Accusing someone of being of the White Roots was to threaten death, and until now, Kreig had pleaded atheism when faced with such a question.

In this moment, he let his silence speak.

Before Sam could say anything else, George smiled softly and spoke in her stead. "I think she's just curious, if that helps. Neither I nor Sam are much religious—"

"I'm working on it!" Sam interjected.

"—but if you want to exercise your religion somehow, I'd be delighted to make accommodations of some sort. A little shrine, foods specific to your religion ..." George shrugged. "Whatever you need."

Kreig could feel his jaw slowly set.

He was pretty sure he knew what George was saying, but even then, he couldn't believe what he heard. It was simply not something he had considered. Not at all. Much like speaking English, he shied away from any overt expression of his religion. Praying was about the one thing he could do without fear. Holy Scripture, sacred artifacts, blessed foods and drinks—he'd barely even given them thought these past hundred years or so. Only in brief fits of nostalgia did he let his mind linger on the days gone by.

Kreig folded his hands on his lap and looked down at the table, away from his brother's encouraging eyes. The words he spoke were heavily weighted by years of never even considering them: "I'd like a shrine."

George smiled but remained quiet. His silence gave Kreig room to breathe, to speak.

Memories of the way things were supposed to be slowly rose to the surface of Kreig's mind. "A small mat, to place the sacred things upon.

Though I'll need to create them." Kreig placed his hand across his mouth. "Wood, some form of metal, and, if possible"—recollection flitted through his white eyes—"the Blood of Oath." Until now, his brother and sister had listened to him in careful silence. Only now was it broken.

"Blood of what?" Sam asked, her face twisting up in confusion.

Kreig froze as the words echoed back to him, and he struggled to pull himself together. "It is hardly necessary." It was a flimsy excuse, and not one that worked on such a curious woman. Her silence forced him to speak. ". . . The true version is derived from the crushing of the Messiah's Fruit. Most common versions, used in smaller churches, only contain a small percentage of actual Blood of Oath. The rest is made from the distillation of the bloodwort." His voice grew certain. "If we are to do this right, I will settle for no less than pure Blood of Oath."

George made a face. "And where do you suppose we'll get these 'Messiah's *Fruit*'?"

Kreig fell into a brief silence. "By this point in time, I do not doubt that the tree I awakened has started bearing fruit. Whether they are ripe or not remains to be seen."

"You better not be talking about the tree I think you're talking about," Sam said. "But I can't think of any other tree you could be talking about, so . . . Uh, what exactly are we supposed to do? We can pick up stuff for the shrine tomorrow, but I don't think we should try picking any apples from that tree. Seriously, trust me." There was a knowing glint in her eye.

Kreig neither noticed nor understood it. "If you'll let me, I could easily acquire a basketful in the dark of the night. With your permission." Neither of his siblings missed the hint of challenge in his voice.

George was just about to reply in the negative when Sam spoke up. "Y'know, that's *actually* not a terrible idea!" George seemed just about ready to question her statement, but she continued. "Get in there, steal a few magic apples, get out of there. Knowing you, it would be easy-peasy, right?" Kreig gave an uncertain nod, clearly put off by her sudden enthusiasm. "But you're not going alone." Ah. There it was. "I'm coming along. George will stay here at home and do . . . stuff."

A knowing gaze was exchanged between the brother-and-sister pair.

"Of course," George said slowly, much like a conspirator only just now joining in. "I'll prepare anything else that might be needed. More than mere fruit is to be used, correct?"

Kreig gave a curt nod. "Indeed. We'll need a proper bottle, burnt wort will do fine, alongside a cloth and a bowl. The rest will require only the skills I have, though many villages had special distilleries to prepare it."

"It'll be ready when you return," George said, his eyes focused on Sam's. There was an exchange of unspoken words, but Kreig didn't catch it. Instead, he turned back to his food. After all, they *had* been in the middle of dinner.

Acquiring the Messiah's Fruit would just have to wait a little.

CHAPTER 21

HEIST

Yeah, uh, yanno, this might not have been a fantastic idea, now that I think about it," Sam said from where she walked beside Kreig, hands stuffed in her pockets. It wasn't extremely cold or anything despite the dark night, but she had still felt the need to wear a jacket.

Kreig glanced down at her and got an apprehensive look in return. It was likely meant for the situation as a whole, though, not him specifically.

And, everything considered, the situation did deserve a smidgen of trepidation or two. Although the sky was dark, the streets were pretty much bustling, shops and bars and windows lit up so brightly, you could barely see the stars at all. Even though Kreig and Sam were in an area of town not commonly associated with nighttime activity, the two often found themselves passing one citizen or another hurrying by with their own mission. A lot of them carried a cloud of alcoholic stink, but Kreig didn't feel the need to point it out.

Their own mission was, after all, somewhat similar. Acquire the Messiah's Fruit and process it into the Blood of Oath. And to get it, they had to first find the tree that Kreig had awakened a few days before.

Since they knew the way there, they had no reason to say much. And still, Sam spoke every so often to voice either her displeasure or, less commonly, a question.

"The fruits aren't poisonous, are they?"

"No," Kreig answered quickly.

Sam scratched her chin. "Make you high? Or awaken like the Messiah's Egg does?"

"No," Kreig said again. He'd been answering similar questions all night. By now, she likely knew almost as much about them as he did. This information was mostly just that the fruit was harmless in almost every situation. You could eat it. It tasted somewhat sweet but it didn't contain all that much nutrition. Dried, candied, or mashed, it simply couldn't live up to any other sweeter fruit. Even when fermented, it didn't do much in terms of intoxication.

Sam didn't seem to like his answer, but she didn't voice her feelings.

Before she could repeat yet another question regarding how dangerous the fruit was or wasn't, they arrived. Almost.

The school was a fair distance away, but Kreig had stopped her in her tracks, one hand hovering over her chest. Looking up at him, she found his gaze affixed firmly to the school looming just at the end of the road. It was far too bright to be closed. Lights seemed to shoot up and around and over the entirety of the school. Most of these concentrated beams of light focused on the crown of the tree poking up over the school building.

That was the tree, huh? She really should have seen it before. Unlike the last time she saw it, the tree was now a fair bit bigger, though not extremely so. More worryingly, but not altogether unexpectedly, it remained that pure, snowy white. The only other color visible was what seemed to be clusters of red fruits, covered partially by large black leaves. She didn't need to ask Kreig what they were.

What she didn't expect, however, was to be stopped a hundred meters from the school. Kreig answered her silent question before she voiced it.

"There are people in there," he said, a small question behind his words wondering if people were usually on school grounds at night. They weren't.

She knew who they were, but she also knew Kreig didn't. At the same time, she also knew that her answer wouldn't make him give up. "Let's get closer." Maybe leading him right there was a bad idea, but she knew that Kreig was now hypervigilant. He probably wouldn't hurt anybody, but he could easily get them out of trouble if he felt there was danger.

They moved closer to the gates leading into the schoolyard, keeping in mind to both seem inconspicuous and regular but also watch everything with the greatest attention. Once they got close enough, they found exactly what the lights were there for and who was doing it.

The courtyard was practically crawling with cops. Sam counted a dozen and a half just on a quick scan. Around half of these were lab rats and not actual armed cops, but that didn't still her worries. She had heard about this, of course. She'd never been told just how many there were, however. By the looks of it, it seemed like most of the armed police officers were either there to assist the forensics or to stand guard against thieves or curious bystanders.

Why the hell were they there at night, though? Guards or no guards, couldn't they just study the tree during the day?

Sam's eyes fell on the school building. *Ah. Right, they'd probably want to study it for at least a week or two, and an entire school can't exactly afford to just close down during that time.* Even more so, with how manic a few of these forensic technicians looked, there might be some nighttime activity they really wanted to write down and analyze. Who could tell?

Softly shaking her head, she turned to look at her brother. "Yeah, as you see, with those guards, we're not—"

Oh. No, by the way he was looking in there, he wasn't giving up. That was a problem, though, since Sam kind of didn't want him doing anything that might harm anyone. Or cause unexplained phenomena. Or arson.

She'd agreed to come along, but now her anxieties were flaring up again. She had thought her presence might prevent him from doing anything too strange, but that assumption seemed to have been a bit hasty.

"Hey, whoa, Kreig, you're not thinking of doing anything weird, are you?"

He turned to her, the cogs in his head turning slowly before he finally gave her a wave, indicating for her to follow. They moved away from where they'd been standing with a view inside the gate and over to one of the many walls of the school. They were out of view of any guards or civilians. And there, he hunched down, his hand pressed firmly against the ground. She really didn't like where this was going or what he was doing, but for once, for just one moment, she had to trust him.

Something seemed to shift. She couldn't hear it, she couldn't see it, but Kreig did something. His eyes were closed in mild concentration.

And then the small patch of dirt his hand had been pressed against started pressing back, rising into a small mound before bursting open, revealing a small white branch holding a rather large black leaf, which in turn cradled a clutch of red fruit.

Kreig plucked the black leaf and the fruit off of the branch before sending it on its way with a final command.

All right.

The black leaf cradling the fruit almost resembled a blanket around an infant, especially with how carefully Kreig was holding it in his arms, but any such resemblance disappeared once she got a proper look at the fruit themselves. They were all connected to each other by small black stalks, resembling a large clutch of dark red, almost transparent grapes. Each one was about the size of a golf ball. They looked tasty, but she knew by Kreig's description that they weren't all that much to eat.

"Messiah's Fruit," Sam breathed softly, not really sure how to understand it.

Kreig had no such preoccupations and seemed to know very well that it was time to leave. Sam followed his long strides, at times having to half-jog to keep up.

They soon got home, prize in hand.

The semi-large swaddle of fruits lay on the table, surrounded on three sides by the siblings. A few wine-red fruits had spilled out of the black leaf cradling them, drawing the attention of both George and Sam.

"So . . . what now?" Sam asked, turning her eyes to Kreig. George turned to look at him, since he was the only one who knew how this was supposed to go.

Kreig seemed thoughtful for a moment before speaking. "There are three stages to the process of turning Messiah's Fruits into the Blood of Oath. Preparation, fertilization, and purification. Is there a bowl of some sort that can be used for the first part? It must be large enough to contain the whole of the fruits."

George and Sam shared a look. "Yes, we have one," George said, turning toward the cupboards behind him. "I'm pretty sure we kept it after we moved away from home. Most of the other things we didn't require immediately were kept in a storage unit, but . . . Oh, there it is." George pulled out an obscenely large bowl from inside a bottom cupboard. It had a red outside and a white inside, the paint on the outside only peeling a little.

On the table, it somehow looked even larger than when George had held it in both arms.

Thumbing his lower lip, George continued softly. "Now that I think about it, there are many things stored in that unit that are technically yours. Would you like to visit sometime? Next Saturday, maybe?"

Not really listening, Kreig nodded, accepting the offer while he moved closer to the bowl and fruit.

Both George and Sam watched quite intently as Kreig peeled off the large black leaf, exposing all the fruit and then dumping the lot of them unceremoniously into the bowl. For a bundle of fruit with such divine names, one would expect them to be treated with a bit more reverence, but neither George nor Sam had anything to actually say about it.

But then both of them recognized the about-to-crush-them move-ment that Kreig was about to do, and they had to say something about it. "Hey, whoa, Kreig!" Sam said, Kreig's hands stopping when he glanced at her. "You—you're not going to, like, wash your hands or anything?"

Kreig stared at her like she was an idiot. "No."

Her left eye twitched. "Dude, hang on right there. Uh. You *just* touched dirt with that hand, right?" She pointed one big finger at his right hand. He nodded questioningly, as if that had nothing to do with it. "It's dirty. You can't go making food with dirty hands!"

"My hands are not tainted," Kreig explained slowly. "They cannot be, and they never are." This was in reference to his status as a Divine Human, which instantly killed any impure creature that touched him, be it bacteria or imps.

This was not something that Sam understood or, for that matter, even cared about. "Sure. Okay, but wash your hands first. I don't care if you're the Dalai Lama; if you're going to stick your hands in food, wash them first." Her eyes narrowed into slits. "That's an *order.*"

Faced with that, no matter his reasons, Kreig couldn't disagree.

Scratching the back of his head, he slowly lumbered off to the bath-room. Technically speaking, using soap would only make his hands more tainted than before. But since he couldn't deny her, he washed his hands for a good thirty seconds.

When he returned to the kitchen, hands only slightly wet, he found George presenting him with an apron. "I don't feel like doing any laundry today," he said. Kreig accepted the apron, slung the hooked band over his neck, and tied the string behind his back into a bow. Since he was only wearing a T-shirt, he didn't have to roll up any sleeves, but standing there in the kitchen, dressed as he was, he felt remarkably homely.

With Sam happy about his hands and George happy about his dress, Kreig positioned himself back by the bowl. His siblings stood on either side of him, looking intently at the contents of the bowl.

With the final go-ahead given, Kreig began the first part of the process.

Plunging his hands into the bowl, he began by separating the fruit from each other. For a bunch of grapes, there would be a single stem to remove, but the Messiah's Fruits had a total of four, and each had to be removed carefully without destroying any fruit in the process.

Kreig worked nimbly and carefully, recalling how strong he was now compared to the last time he had done this himself. It had been back before the church fell, back before the church so much as declared war at all, and he'd been told that distilling his own bottle of Blood of Oath was a sacred rite. He'd spent several months on the process, forcing himself to learn every in and out, ignoring his numerous failures, only looking back on his mistakes to learn from them. One of these mistakes was to destroy a fruit before removing the stems, or to so much as break a stem before all fruits had been removed.

Just this step had made him fail many times before, but this time he was no longer just a man, and he did not have access to limitless clusters, either. There was only one chance, and just a twitch of his finger could easily ruin it.

But still, for all his carefulness, he was still able to work quickly, spending only as much time on removing every individual fruit as was needed. Moving his massive fingers between a hair-thin stem and pinching only lightly enough to remove the fruit from the stem and not hard enough to burst either stem or fruit was a challenge he had faced many times before.

After only five minutes of careful separation, he was finished, and in one smooth movement, he removed the whole of the stems, allowing the fruit to tumble freely within the bowl. Gingerly, he placed the stems on a small plate before getting back to the work at hand. He'd need the stems for later, but they were unimportant for now.

Once more, he plunged his hands into the bowl, this time doing as expected: crushing them.

Yet another situation, this time dependent not on immediate carefulness but rather on speed. If he was not quick enough, the fruits would rapidly lose their potency.

Good thing, then, that Kreig's speed was inhuman, and in a mere moment, wasting not a single drop on the table or his apron, the fruit were crushed into a mass of flesh, skin, and juice. And at this moment, the first change came over the fruit as they all quickly turned a brilliant white, as though a thick layer of snow had suddenly covered them.

"Is it supposed to do that?" Sam asked carefully, her eyebrow cocked hesitantly.

Kreig slowly nodded. "It indicates we have done well so far. Had it turned black instead, we would have failed."

Sam bristled at the mention of failure but kept silent. George merely nodded, quietly enraptured in the sequence.

With the fruit prepared, Kreig bounded over to the cupboards, removed a sharp knife and a cutting board, and returned to the kitchen table. No explanation was needed as Kreig placed the previously discarded stems on the cutting board and began to gently whittle off the outer parts, his knife moving quickly and carefully, slicing off the smallest patches of bark to finally remove the very core of the stems. The bark was apparently useless, as Kreig uncaringly passed one finger over them, turning them first into white fire and then into snow so fast that both George and Sam thought they must have imagined the whole thing. A shared glance removed such delusions.

The cores of the stems were then chopped up into a bunch of smaller pieces, and by merely using the end of his right thumb, Kreig was able to grind them into a thick paste. A swipe of the knife brought the small glob of paste onto it.

He then put this paste into a very small bowl, put the knife to the side, and turned to look at his siblings. "Neither of you has any issues with blood, do you?"

A pair of concerned eyes met him. He took it as a no.

Aetherial Knife (III)

Their looks of worry only intensified when the shimmering, crystalline knife materialized in his hand. Kreig summarily plunged the edge of the knife into his thumb. Both his siblings jerked where they stood, eyelids flaring at the self-mutilation. Despite their shock, they still knew enough not to stop him when the knife disappeared in a flash and he held his thumb over the small, paste-filled bowl.

Unlike what one would expect, Kreig's body didn't actually hold much blood anymore, as most of his arteries were choked shut by his numerous thick white roots. It was with no little effort that a few drops of blood struggled out of the wound, dropping down into the paste and staining it a deep red. A total of seven drops fell before Kreig finally removed his thumb from above the paste, holding it far away from the bowl.

Years before, he had made the mistake of thinking that the more Oracle's blood was used in the fertilization process, the purer the Blood of Oath became. Not so. Using too much or too little would spoil the batch.

It didn't matter what Oracle the blood came from; all that mattered was the precise quantity. Now that Kreig thought about it, he could just as well have used Sam's blood.

Though, with her being from Earth, he couldn't possibly know how the fruit would react. It was best to stick to what he knew would work.

And now, it was time for a part that was usually either automated using machines and workers or done using an Oracle's skill. Kreig had no machine, but he didn't need one.

He stirred his blood into the paste with one burly finger until it became almost black, at which point he dumped the full of it into the crushed white fruit. He took one step back, spread his arms on either side of the bowl, and told his siblings, "Step away."

Stir (IV)

The crushed fruit and the paste slowly began to move and swirl as though it had a mind of its own, turning around and around, almost like a typhoon. A deep hole began to form in the middle of the swirl, the edges rising until they almost exploded out of the bowl. Then, at that point, the mixture suddenly rose from within the bowl, leaving it fully to hover mid-air, a massive ball of crushed fruit and paste mixing together into a liquid, the nearly black paste staining the white fruit with a deep red, the furious stirring working not only to spread the paste evenly throughout the concoction but also to mince the skin and flesh into a semi-homogenous liquid.

The midair mixing went on for only a little more than a minute, at which point it was fully mixed and Kreig carefully let it return to the bowl, the stirring slowing until the liquid was still and calm.

And that was the worst of it. Turning his gaze from the bowl, Kreig was given a good view of how both of his siblings also stared into the bowl, George's brows furrowed into perplexity, Sam's chest rising and falling softly.

The liquid within the bowl was opaque and muddy and only barely looked drinkable.

". . . Is it done?" Sam asked, her eyes begging for it not to be over already.

Kreig ignored her and turned to George. "Have you prepared a cloth?"

George's eyes widened, but he nodded all the same. Moving quickly, he grabbed a small, thin cloth from off the counter and handed it over to Kreig, who accepted it gratefully. Then he looked at the almost-full bowl, looked around the room, and realized that, no, they didn't have another bowl that could hold that much liquid. He wasn't eager to do so, but that meant his only way of doing this would be to use skills. Maybe it was okay, since this whole situation required skills to begin with?

Either way, he handed either end of the towel to his two bewildered siblings and asked them to hold it above the bowl. Then he began.

Whisper of the Seas (X)

Kreig spoke softly and quietly, no louder than a mumble, the words spoken in a language that couldn't possibly exist. The liquid within the bowl quivered, listened, and obeyed. In a stream of dull red, it lifted into the air, nosing through the kitchen like a serpent, listening to every garbled word Kreig spoke. Tumbling around, the liquid flipped over and twisted through the white cloth, leaving a small residue of shredded skin and other solids behind. At Kreig's whispered command, it repeated this looping process four more times, finally ending when the liquid settled down in the bowl, going back to rest.

Sam and George slowly lowered the cloth.

"And you couldn't just use some skill to hold the cloth—why?" Sam asked, her voice curious more than upset.

Kreig looked her over and decided not to admit that it was more fun to let them help than to summon some spectral creature or magical flying hands. But he didn't say that. The Blood of Oath wasn't completely done yet.

The liquid, although a bit clearer now, remained slightly muddy. Normally, this would in most villages be the time when the liquid was left to stand for several weeks, after which the completed Blood of Oath would be diluted to a concentration of about 3 percent or less depending on the situation, the rest of the liquid being made up of the much cheaper wort-wine. They wouldn't be doing that stage, though, since no self-respecting Oracle would settle for such filth. That was only used in lesser churches of the rural kind.

And, for a lack of time, Kreig would finish it here and now.

It wasn't what was usually done, and it wasn't a viable option in most situations, but in this moment, he could do it. As a Divine Human, he had that capability.

Kreig leaned over the almost-finished mixture, closed his eyes, and let a single tear fall from within. It dropped into the cloudy liquid, and the second it joined the liquid, the liquid turned clear. Every trace of opacity was banished in a single moment, leaving behind a liquid as clear and pure as stained glass. It had a deep, innate glow to it, like a sea of rubies, shimmering and glittering in the soft light. It had no smell, but something about it appetized the soul.

It was done.

"Uh. Did you *have* to cry in it, or was that just for looks?" Sam asked, cautiously leaning over the edge of the table to peer into the bowl. Her reflection peered back up at her with the same amount of curiosity and apprehension, and at noticing this, Sam couldn't help but make a silly face, twisting her eyes to show only their whites and sticking out her tongue.

"Any other bodily liquid apart from my blood would have had similar results," Kreig said, omitting the obvious reason why he chose not to spit into the liquid.

George shuddered. "Understood." Much like his sister, his eyes were glued to the liquid. "What now?"

As far as Kreig explained it, the next part was really the simplest one, namely to bottle it. Since it was pure, age would never degrade it. As a matter of fact, since it had a shelf life of several thousand years at the least, this gave them plenty of time to enhance it through community, as Kreig explained it.

Blood of Oath never degraded or grew finer with age. The only way to enhance its flavor and properties was to add a drop of blood from another Oracle from the one whose blood was used in the initial creation.

It seemed that in most villages equipped with a proper brewery suitable for making Blood of Oath kept a special bottle containing a portion of blood from some Oracle or another. This blood was often harvested from an Oracle of the village itself or some nearby province, meaning that having multiple kinds of blood was forbidden according to tradition. However, if an Oracle was to save the village or otherwise help them, oftentimes a small quantity of blood was drawn in order to enhance the year's harvest, alongside making the oldest and purest Blood of Oath the village kept even better.

Kreig himself could list a dozen villages or more where his blood had been drawn and added to their finer products. His classmates never saw it as very interesting, more of a chore than anything, but Kreig always felt honored to partake in such longstanding tradition.

Of course, after the fall of the church, all those villages were burned to the ground and the Blood of Oath was smashed and spilled and drained so that nobody might try it.

A cloud of melancholy washed over Kreig as he remembered the prized treasures of those villages, bottles of Blood of Oath several hundred years old, opened only to add a single drop of holy blood. A tradition now lost to time, a people now dead, their blood staining the soggy mud of the north.

Sam brought him out of it. "So, theoretically . . . I could just add my own blood to this? And make it—what? Better?"

"More potent," Kreig quietly corrected.

A feral light shone in her eyes. "Well, I don't see why not!" And before either Kreig or George had time to reply, she'd already grabbed a knife, holding it threateningly over her hand.

But as fast as she moved to grab the knife, Kreig moved even faster to stop her.

One hand was an iron vise around her slender wrist; the other clutched the knife. His face was mere inches from Sam's, his breathing slow, eyes white and distant. The metal knife groaned in his hand, whining as if mere moments from being crushed completely. Sam fared no better, the skin around Kreig's viselike grip quickly turning white and then a burning red.

When she spoke, it came out more like a pained groan than the soft whisper she had tried to make. "Hey, hey, relax, I won't— You can release me, okay? I won't do anything. Okay?" A trembling, forced smile played on her lips.

Kreig breathed slowly, eyes slowly regaining focus. He looked at her, then at the knife, and then finally at where he held his sister's wrist.

He let her go.

Then he lumbered around the table and returned to his place. "Sorry," he mumbled.

Sam shook her head, still trying to hold her smile, waving her hands disarmingly, though making sure not to move her red wrist too much. "No, it's fine; I . . . I should have warned you. Sorry."

But when Kreig looked up at her and met her eyes, he saw a twinge of fear where there used to be carefree curiosity. Her wrist, no longer white, now regained color, though a harsh red mark in the shape of his large hand was starting to form, taunting him. It made him furious. In the red Blood of Oath below, he saw himself. A red, crude imitation of his face, looking up at him. Every sin plastered on his face like a scar.

The silence was only broken when George, moving slowly and carefully, spoke up. "Do we bottle it? There seems to be enough to fill around four wine bottles." He turned to Sam. "We've got a bunch of empty wine bottles stashed in the storage closet, right?"

"Huh? Uh . . . Yeah? Do you want me to—" George nodded before she could finish. "Oh. Okay, I guess I'll just—"

"Take your time, Sam," George said, giving her a hard look.

She lingered only for a moment, nodded sharply, and hurried over to the storage closet.

For a moment, neither George nor Kreig said anything. Kreig felt too ashamed and angry to say anything, and George seemed intent on letting the moment drag on. Kreig, for his own part, felt perfectly content gripping the sides of the table and staring down at his own reflection in the vague hope that he could psychically banish it to also rid the world of himself.

"I won't chastise you, Kreig." Kreig couldn't bear to meet his eyes. "You know what you did wrong. That you shouldn't have gripped her like that." Kreig almost mumbled something back, a few self-deprecating words about how there was no excuse for his actions, but George spoke first. "But that isn't why you're feeling like this, is it?" Kreig looked up and finally met his brother's eyes. They were filled with kindness and care. "Has anyone ever told you that you did no wrong, Kreig?"

". . . Of course. Many times."

He shook his head. "Not like that. I mean . . . You've been a commander, right? What happened when you made a strategic failure? Or lost a battle? Or had to forfeit a victory?"

Kreig again looked away. ". . . Depends. The order would . . . Isolation. A few days in a monastery. Away from it all."

George nodded. "And the Empire?"

Kreig's eyes went dark, a tremble gripping his right hand. He clutched it to stop the tremor. "It isn't important. What they did."

And for once, the one averting his gaze was not Kreig but George. "You were punished. Harshly. And—and you're still being punished." Kreig couldn't tear his eyes from his brother. "Aren't you? Maybe not by someone else, maybe not in some cell . . . but you're punishing *yourself.* You're even doing it right now."

Kreig let go of his right hand, ignoring how the white mark slowly faded.

George's gaze softened. "We're not faulting you, Kreig. For *any* of this. You're forgiven. Whatever you've done, whatever you'll do . . . I forgive you. Sam, too. We love you, Kreig. And I trust that you'll learn from your mistakes, punishment or no."

Kreig stood there for a moment. Letting it sink it.

It wasn't like with the order, where you could be forgiven if you asked for it, or if you paid for it, or if you accepted some punishment. Or with the Empire, where any failure was punished with death, torture, or incarceration. Until they needed you again, that was. No, this was less than that. It was more. It was *human.*

During the rest of the evening, Kreig only operated with half a mind to what he was doing. Sam finally returned with the bottles, having found three full ones and one empty. With a lack of anything better to do, they drank the wine in the full bottles, if only to empty them. Kreig did not get drunk, since he could not, and the taste itself was—to him—pretty foul. But his siblings seemed happy to indulge, quickly getting tipsy and then drunk.

With his brother and sister too intoxicated to do anything beyond drink, Kreig was left to do the hard work of filling the bottles. It went well, but then Sam insisted on having a taste. George was against it, but once Sam had a taste ("Whoa, it's *sweet*!"), he just had to try it.

Kreig didn't feel like mentioning that it briefly strengthened the powers of an awakened and did so only when Sam had had her fill.

But by that point, his sister had remembered the part about her blood being able to make the Blood of Oath more potent. Kreig had almost hoped she'd forget it, but she certainly hadn't. It was only with extreme trepidation that Kreig let her prick a finger and add a single droplet of blood to each of the four bottles. And the second it was done, Kreig cast his third-strongest healing spell on her, instantly mending her finger, removing any poison and alcohol from her blood, and healing the tissue shrunk by years of psychedelic use.

She was mostly just upset about losing her tipsiness, though.

CHAPTER 22

PORCUPINE IN A SUIT

The next day, after a quick stop at a nearby hardware store, Kreig had set up his small shrine. It really wasn't much to look at: a wooden chalice standing beside one of the bottles of Blood of Oath, a metal pendant Sam had seen fit to gift him ("I found it on the ground; you can have it if you want!"), and a small silver spoon George found in a cupboard ("We never use it"). All because Kreig had told them small pieces of precious metal were fit for the shrine.

Apparently, to Sam, a "precious metal" was just a piece of metal that was precious to her. The pendant seemed to fill that purpose. Scavenged off the ground or not, the little gleam to it told Kreig that it truly was a precious metal.

He didn't mind. Back in the other world, iron was about as precious as silver was here. It made little difference to him.

The shrine was set up in his room, right on top of his desk. Erica noticed it pretty much that very Monday the moment she entered the room. Being the kind of woman who didn't mind blurting out her inner thoughts, she immediately asked about it.

Kreig was hesitant, at best. Speaking openly of his religion was just not something he did, but after the most general description he could give, she, astonishingly, didn't question it any further. Kreig might have assumed she wasn't thinking about the shrine any longer if it weren't for her fleeting, almost longing glances at his bottle of Blood of Oath.

Now, it wasn't as though normal humans couldn't drink pure Blood of Oath. It was about as intoxicating as wine, and it didn't do much else than that. It could in rare cases give the drinker some energy or, even rarer, make them hallucinate, but it was mostly harmless.

That didn't mean Kreig was about to let Erica drink a drop.

This day was bad as it was. Not because of Erica, of course not, but rather what she brought. Namely, *math*.

After a week of avoiding it, he was finally smacked in the face by necessity.

"If you don't do well in math, you can't graduate! Which is bad!" she had insisted, but even then, Kreig felt no real need to so much as try. The later he dealt with this, the later he had to accept that there was no saving him. As his previous tutor had so kindly said, "*He couldn't put two and two together with a three-week period of preparation.*" The scars that man had carved into Kreig were not easily healed, and Kreig didn't even want to *try*.

But where Kreig was childish in his dismissal, Erica acted like a toddler.

That day, Erica reluctantly let Kreig do his favorite two subjects, namely history and social science.

And then, the next day, she only brought the math textbook.

Only. That was all she brought. She put it on his desk, slapped open the first page, and took a seat. No matter how many pleading looks Kreig sent her, she did nothing else. The only other things on his desk, apart from the shrine, were a bundle of papers and a pencil. That and a little device whose use Kreig could not understand.

He poked it a few times. Erica didn't stop him.

If it meant solace from staring at the first page of the math book, he would accept it. After pressing each button in turn, he found that the one that said On turned it on. How novel! There were a bunch of numbers, ranging from zero to nine, alongside a number of buttons with signs he didn't know. But if he pressed the button for two and then the little cross, and then the button for two again, suddenly the screen blinked to show 4. It put it together automatically.

Kreig glanced at Erica to ascertain whether such a fantastic tool was actually allowed or not, if she would smack it out of his hands without notice. But she didn't seem to mind.

So Kreig continued to fiddle with it. Two and two became four. Two and three became five.

Despite his own perceived value, Kreig was not a complete incompetent when it came to math. Adding platoons, counting victories, subtracting the dead . . . these were all things he had done before, and now he had a funky little device that seemed to do it all for him. One times two is two, nine times eight is seventy-two. He was just making sure it worked—that it did what it promised.

And after a while, he finally turned to look at the book. He turned the page and found a list of little questions.

And they were . . . easy? They almost seemed to be. 10 + 5 ÷ 5. That would be 3, no?

"No," Erica said, suddenly looming over his broad back, peeking over his shoulder. Kreig almost crushed the calculator in his hand but showed no other indication of surprise. "Multiplications and divisions before you do addition. See, you divide the five by five, which is?"

". . . One," Kreig almost whispered, hoping his obviously wrong answer wouldn't grant him a smack on the wrist.

But no such blow came. Instead, he looked up to find her smiling, a perfectly serene, flower-like blossom on her full lips. The kind that said everything was all right. "Exactly! And then, one plus ten?"

For a moment, Kreig couldn't tear his eyes from her face. She was very close to him.

He peeked down at the textbook, seeing the little numbers, and if he looked at them and not at her, he might be able to think straight. "It . . . Eleven. It ought to be eleven." His face felt flushed and hot. What if he got it wrong now? That would almost be even worse, having to watch her radiant smile turn strained, devolving into a disappointed frown. Just the thought made his skin crawl, fresh black shame trickling down his eyes.

But her smile widened. "Right! So, then"—she leaned down, right by his side, and he could see her dainty neck right there, and with a little pen, she wrote *11* on the page—"the answer is eleven! Good work. Now, how about the next one?"

The next one was a similar problem. So was the next one. When divisions started being factored in, all he had to do was ask her, and she helped. Not a single word of humiliation. Only a pure, calm joy in showing him how it all worked. They worked quickly and carefully. It was only a few pages in, when Kreig was solving a somewhat complex equation on his own, that he realized what was happening.

He could *understand it.*

The numbers, the signs, the functions and ideas—they all made sense.

He glanced over at where Erica sat. Since he had been able to work on his own for a while, she hadn't had to add any explanation during that time. She gave a small smile and tilted her head. For just a moment, Kreig wasn't sure what to say. "Thank you," he finally choked out. "For helping me. With this."

Her smile deepened. "Anything to avoid the minimum wage."

Kreig had no idea what that meant, so he just nodded and got back to work. She seemed to really mean it, though.

In reality, she only partially meant it. Sure, she was working hard to pay off her debts and remain alive, but that was no longer her main aspiration. Well, completing her second degree was clearly what she wanted to do—teaching was a horrible job—but there were always things to do outside education, no? Right now, could she really say she hated teaching?

She only had to deal with one student, she was being paid quite a lot above the minimum wage, and—well, in all honesty, Kreig was a good student. He listened, he did his work, and although he was very hesitant to ask questions, he never did anything she could consider uncouth. She'd had many students before, intelligent and noisy and mischievous and deviant. None of which Kreig was. But he was diligent and careful, and a very pleasant man to be around.

If every student she had was more like him, she wouldn't mind returning to teaching.

Though, of course, that would never happen. She'd been burned on that already.

But, maybe, someday . . .

That was for the future to decide.

Days passed in near silence.

It was pleasant, really. Somehow, Kreig found that he was really enjoying the whole matter of being tutored, despite his initial misgivings. It was mainly because of Erica. Her academic skills aside, she seemed to truly understand how to talk to him. How to gently coax him into the right direction.

Even stranger, at times, when she asked for his opinion regarding events and historic people and scientific theories, Kreig found himself with an answer.

If she were to ask what he thought about the existence of colonialism or what his opinion on it was, or how it came to be, he would answer what he thought and what he believed. The weak were conquered and the strong ruled, as it should be. Kings rose to power by measure of their privileged birth; churches held influence beyond the measure of individual men. When looking at history from the perspective of a scholar reading the text of the winners, everything seemed to have gone very smoothly.

Kingdoms rose, gaining power and territory, only to lose it again. The ebb and flow of the world.

It all made a lot of sense, but when Kreig told Erica, she looked at him kind of weirdly. Or maybe he was imagining things. Probably.

But the next time she asked about it, her curiosity shone strongly. They should have gone past the Middle Ages by that point, but she lingered, if only to ask Kreig about the movements and decisions of specific kings and empires. Should they have done this? Would there have been a better choice? Was going into war a last-ditch effort or the first thought?

Kreig, being a man who had learned that being honest was one of the greatest virtues, explained his thoughts, albeit a little reluctantly. It felt a bit out of line to talk about it all, but as a man practically raised in war, he answered. The last time his opinions on war had been this intently considered was during his time with the Empire. It almost felt nice, if the subject hadn't been a bit weird.

To Erica, Kreig just became an even greater conundrum. At first, she'd thought his mostly positive opinions on monarchy and dictatorships and historical atrocities had meant he was some sort of fascist, but as she continued inquiring on the subject, more information came out. Specifically, that he was actually a real history buff. In terms of predicting the cause and effect of war, at least. He couldn't name a single European king or Asian dynasty, but when presented with a few facts, he could reasonably predict what its role in history had been and how nearby countries had reacted.

It was fascinating, kind of like finding a fishing genius who had never visited a body of water before.

Only one little thought stopped her from fully believing him to be a military genius who had spent his years after leaving high school as a secret military advisor for the US government. This was the fact that it all seemed to come from experience. And not the kind of experience that she imagined came from sitting in a room with a dozen other old guys discussing where to strike next. More so from in-person battles.

He didn't *just* predict the actions of a king, after all, but so too the actions and lives of ordinary people. Which prices would sink or balloon, what cause this would have in specific regions, and all with the cold analytical prowess of a man who has seen it all before.

At some point, Erica figured that the time period in which he could analyze things the clearest was between 1500 and 1700, though earlier than that was fine too. At any later ages than that, he could only barely understand it, much less analyze it.

The only obvious mistake he made through it all was his estimate of just how many wars were conducted at any point in time. To him, there should always be a war going on—somewhere, sometime. Always another atrocity, always a genocide taking place, as if the world lived in never-ending starvation and plague.

In the end, even Erica had to admit that she had no idea what any of it meant. All she could imagine was that Kreig might be a secret ultra-professional in some sort of war-strategy game about those ages, but even then, that didn't really explain what seemed like firsthand experience. The way he looked wistfully out of the window as he spoke softly of what the victors had to do to remain victorious, or how he bitterly recounted how quickly victory could turn to loss.

There was poetry in him, but she couldn't read it.

If she had asked Kreig about it straight out, he might have answered her honestly. Might. More than anything, he would have been too stunned by the question to say anything.

His visits to Darius were peaceful as well. For the most part, at least.

The man seemed to have an eerie quality when it came to lulling Kreig into a sense of security. And then, while he was at his most talkative, when he'd been gently taken out of his shell, Darius would ask him little mundane questions, and Kreig would answer. Here was someone who listened to him even when he had little to nothing to say. Here was someone who heard his worries and woes and asked him to speak more.

It was interesting; that was for sure.

His siblings took things easy as well.

They came home from work at slightly separate times, but by the time George was home, dinner was ready and served. Then, after dinner, they would all do their own things. George usually read or wrote last-second reports for his superiors and subordinates on this or that, Sam played video games or watched some sort of moving image, and Kreig . . . well, he did a bit of everything.

Sometimes he quietly painted, sometimes he sat down beside George to read a novel, and sometimes he got Sam's permission to read one of her comic books, as they were called, or to even play one of her "video games." It was all awfully domestic.

All this homeliness was punctuated only by his occasional frustration.

The Saturday after procuring the Blood of Oath, they'd gone to check out the small storage unit they kept. Most of the things were their parents', but some of the various paraphernalia had once belonged to Kreig. He didn't recognize a single thing. Trophies and CDs and barbells that rang no bells.

The only thing he actually—somehow—recognized was a little stuffed animal.

As George told him, he'd been quite the collector at one point. Most of them were from carnival games that he'd won, with his intention being to one day give all of them to some girl he might one day pick up. But the only one George and Sam had kept on account of the limited storage place had been his very first win.

It was a little stuffed fish that he'd won at a ring-toss game at the ripe age of five. The fish was rather large, almost the size of Kreig's oversized fist. As a child, and even as he'd gotten older, he'd apparently brought it everywhere until the other kids at football practice told him it was juvenile. But he had kept it, even though the fish was almost the size of his own body.

And here it was. Green and blue, with big, bulbous eyes and a wide mouth. The outside had clearly once been fluffy and soft, but after years of handling and hugging, it had all been matted down into compressed strands.

Kreig decided to bring it home.

But George insisted on bringing one other thing, namely Kreig's old computer. It had been up to date when Kreig die—erm, *disappeared*, so it was still relevant enough for modern use. They brought it home, put it on Kreig's desk, and there it was. Kreig's last excuse not to go job-hunting.

At least he had little Lennart, the fish.

And so began a couple of weeks of what Kreig could only describe as pure bliss punctuated by deep hell.

First, George helped him make a CV. It was far from impressive, and George went so far as to tell him that the ten-year gap alongside his lack of high school diploma might make this a little hard. Kreig had thought it would be fine. During his years, he had amassed plenty of experience in various subjects. Mostly as a soldier, but he'd had his assignments. Chop wood, help in sermons, eat fifteen helpings of half-rotten rations, those kinds of things.

Getting a job would have been easy if George hadn't barred him from writing down his 130 years of additional experience. "IOCRO would throw an understandable fit," he'd said. Kreig couldn't disagree, but he still felt that his CV might not look quite as full as it could be.

So it began.

Despite seeking every half-time job possible, be it cooking or washing dishes or serving, he didn't get a single reply.

At one point, he at least got to attend an interview.

It did not go well.

Suffice it to say that merely attending one was enough to fry Kreig's nerves to the point of jitters at the mere mention of interviews.

It had been for a job as a cashier at a small convenience store on the outskirts of the city. Nothing fancy, nothing that needed any special merits or anything. All it would need was a friendly disposition and a patient mind. Kreig didn't quite have either. Nonetheless, he was invited for an interview.

At first, he didn't even know what it was supposed to be. Funny as it was, he'd never had to prove his competency in front of anyone during his time in the other world, at least not in the same way as here. With the Order of White Roots, he'd quite literally been summoned/kidnapped, so it was more so that they offered him a job that he couldn't refuse. The Empire did something similar, with the whole interview process being more of a debate among advisors than anything involving Kreig's own volition.

He'd never had to verbally defend his aptitude for a position.

When George slowly and carefully explained the process of an interview, every step and quirk that may occur, Kreig could already feel his heart sink. Then, it wasn't just a matter of walking in and getting the job?

No, not in the least.

With the interview a week away, Kreig at least had some time to prepare.

In the evenings, he and George went through the process and held little faux interviews. The most glaring mistake Kreig made over and over again was that he often lost his train of thought when confronted with a new question. He could pretty easily memorize standard questions ("The gap was caused by a prolonged sickness"), but anytime he was asked to elaborate, he just pulled a blank.

With more time to prepare, they would hypothetically have been able to try to foresee every possible question to formulate a standard answer. But with only a week of time to prepare, it was just not possible.

While not preparing for the interview, Kreig took the time to shyly ask both Erica and Darius if they had ever been interviewed. Funnily enough, as he sat there asking follow-up questions and pressuring on relevant points, he realized he was doing exactly the thing he was so nervous about someone else doing to him.

Either way, he found that Erica had spent more time than she wished to admit doing interviews and searching for part-time jobs. As she explained, it was one of the perks of being a student most of your life. As far as tips and tricks went, she explained that you should always try to stand out. There are a billion guys out there who can be a clerk and stand there beeping groceries. What makes *you* special? If he could answer that with a confident air, he'd probably get the job.

Though, in the end, she did warn him not to get his hopes up. Getting a job was all fine and good, and interviews were nerve-wracking in every context, but preparing yourself for success only to collapse at the finish point was worse than anything.

Her words, although mostly meant to be reassuring, did very little to stave off Kreig's terror.

Darius seemed to have a very different impression. Though, then again, he had, in his own words, "not needed to actively seek work for twenty-five years." As he told it, before graduating with a degree in first psychology and then psychiatry, he'd only had to have one part-time job, and only because his father demanded it. After graduating, he'd gone pretty much straight back to the university he recently graduated from.

Then it was a pretty straight path into where he was right now. He got scouted about half a year after the first portals broke out ten years earlier, and ever since, he'd been there.

His advice for interviews was more so a list of subtle psychological manipulations that should help him. Kreig tried to remember them, he really did, but he was so stunned by the thought of turning someone's mind against themselves without the use of skills that he could barely hear it.

Later on, completely unprompted, Sam recounted her interview for becoming a cop. Really, it was more of a psychological evaluation, but still.

She told him to be honest.

Kreig felt like that might be a bit hard when true honesty would probably warrant a call to her own station. George meant that it was less "withholding the truth" and more "just not telling them all the facts." Kreig didn't see the difference.

And then came the day of the fated interview.

Kreig could scarcely remember ever having felt so nervous. Now that he thought about it, before coming back to his old world, he was usually only ever nervous when facing a battle. Even then, at least, in that nervousness, he had known that the punishment for losing was only death. Here, if he failed, he would receive a punishment far worse: the disappointment of his siblings. That was what he dreaded.

The convenience store was on the outskirts of town, and although George was very open to taking a day off to drive him there, Kreig refused his offer. Instead, he wanted to get there himself. The interview was at 8:30.

Kreig got up at six and walked there.

A long trek was good for him. It got his mind off the facts of the matter.

Something he had no choice but to face once he got there.

To spare the details, it went about as well as one might expect from Kreig. He fumbled over a few lines, accidentally jumbled together two responses, and when they asked him which animal he thought he most closely resembled, he pulled a complete blank. In the end, he said porcupine. They looked at him strangely, and for a hot moment, Kreig had wondered if he should wipe their minds and try to do it over.

They ended the interview before he acted on the thought, telling him they'd contact him if he got the job.

A week later, he got an email telling him he hadn't made it.

To say that Kreig was crestfallen would be a dire understatement. Anytime George or Sam so much as mentioned that he should continue searching for a job, he shut down.

It took a small intervention just to get him on his feet again, but the mere mention of having an interview was enough to make him blanch. Slowly, George was able to coax Kreig into continuing to apply for jobs, although he seemed much less intent on actually getting an interview.

He didn't get any, which almost made him happy, but by that point, it had been over two months since he had moved in. With no job in sight and Darius continuously bringing it up during their sessions in order to express the hopes and wishes of the nation and IOCRO, Kreig finally decided that enough was enough. Applying for jobs on the web would get him nowhere.

So, he went straight to the source and asked Darius if he would be able to help him find something.

Darius was surprised at the heartfelt plea but nonetheless promised to contact his higher-ups and ask if they could find some opening someplace. IOCRO, being an international organization of great wealth and power, should doubtlessly be able to find him something.

Though, what that "something" was would be up to them to decide, not Kreig.

"Any prior experience working within the field?" a man Kreig had come to know as Mr. Oakley asked mildly, removing his eyes from the little CV he held in both hands. Although the man was clearly well dressed, what with the almost completely round glasses and half-buttoned checkered suit, his general demeanor suggested an ill-hidden electricity to him. This was most noticeable in his unruly, zappy hair that never failed to catch Kreig's attention.

"Many strong soldiers have been trained by my hand," Kreig replied. A wave of Mr. Oakley's hand persuaded Kreig to continue.

It was mostly a bastardized version of what really happened, but by the way Kreig explained it, one might reasonably think he'd been training youths for the better part of his life. Maybe as a camp counselor or as a teacher of some sort. In reality, it was more that he'd trained young recruits into soldiers, led them into war atop horseback, and sent them to their deaths. A bit more gruesome, but Mr. Oakley didn't have to know about that.

"And the ages of these . . . recruits?" Mr. Oakley asked, peering over his glasses at Kreig.

A shudder passed unnoticed through Kreig. "From eight years to nineteen and above."

Mr. Oakley whistled. "Impressive range. Should you join us here at Painstone International High School, the age ranges you'll be working with would be from fourteen to eighteen. This will be no issue for you?"

"Not in the least," Kreig answered the principal honestly. To him, the age of a person really didn't matter all that much. Thirty or twenty or fifteen, their mental processes were about the same. All equally useful in a war.

"Is that so?" Mr. Oakley smiled thinly. "Well, by all means, you seem very suitable for a position here as PE teacher. Is there any specific reason you have for applying? Other than the need for money, that is. Heh." From behind his thick glasses, Mr. Oakley's deep brown eyes seemed to sharpen.

For a moment or two, Kreig sat in silence, carefully collecting his thoughts. Inside, he could feel his heart beat like a jackhammer. "It has been ten years since I was last part of society."

"I am . . . aware," Mr. Oakley said, eyes darting to glance at one of the many stock photos on the wall instead of Kreig.

"I wish to rejoin. Call it a tragic irony, if you will, but I would like to join the world the same way I left it." Now Kreig turned away from his interviewer. The room was mostly brown, on the third floor of the middle-aged building. It was filled with seemingly random items, from ceramic owls to piles of erasers, and it had clearly been in use for several decades by various principals, the most recent of which now sat in front of him.

On the other side of the hefty wooden desk, Mr. Oakley shifted. "An admirable reason, by all means. The gap was of course of great weight, but knowing that you have the courage and determination to rejoin us alleviates my worries." A smile that might almost have seemed playful spread across his lips. "Can you start working on Monday, or is it too early?"

"Huh?"

A hand reached across the desk toward him. "Afternoons, from one to four twenty." He wiggled his hand a few times. "Just take my hand, Mr. Wiedermann."

"Oh, yes. Yes, of course," Kreig mumbled, hesitantly shaking the hand offered to him. The hand was small and dry and thin.

Then Kreig stood up, thanked Mr. Oakley, and left the same way he had entered.

Painstone International High School was not a name he recognized, nor was it any school he had ever attended. This school was more on the outskirts of town, and although it had old buildings and was relatively well staffed, somehow it had still gained a reputation of being low-class. This was most likely since it was so far from the luxurious city center. Kreig didn't mind.

He was still in shock even when he came home.

During the one hour it had taken for Sam to get home, he just sat on the couch thinking. It was like he couldn't accept that it had gone so well, that he'd actually succeeded in getting a job. Next Monday. That was in three days. From one to four twenty. According to Mr. Oakley, he'd need to be there an hour or so early to get his schedule. And then—then . . .

The door opened. Sam stepped inside, carrying two bags of groceries, one in each hand. "Hey, how'd the interview go?" Kreig turned to her. "Oh, that doesn't look good. Uh, just so you know, there's always more openings, okay? If you can't find anything, I'm sure you could become, like, a matador or something! Maybe a cowboy? The world is full of possibilities! Just 'cause you didn't get this one doesn't mean—"

Kreig hushed her with a wave of his hand. "No, I got the job."

"You—you *did*?! Whoa! That's great, Kreig! I'm— Would it sound weird if I said I'm proud of you? 'Cause I am. I really am." Dumping the groceries on the kitchen table, she moved over to stand in front of him. His facial expression was of desolation. "Okay. Uh. What's up with that, dude? Did he make you a janitor or something? Damn that Oakley! I could totally get him arrested for money laundering and tax fraud, yanno?"

"There's no need for that," Kreig said. "I'm merely . . . No, it'll be over soon. I need some rest."

Sam frowned. "You want me to make dinner tonight? Sure, I'm not as good as George, but—"

A shiver gripped Kreig and he forced down his nausea. "No, no. Not at all. I'll fix up something easy."

A hand fell on his shoulder and he looked up, eyes meeting his sister's. She smiled sadly. "Take all the time you need, but . . . if you want to talk about it, I'm here, okay? I might not have fought any dragons or anything, but I know what life's like here on Earth."

"Sure," Kreig said without conviction. What he felt right now wasn't something he imagined someone as young as Sam could understand.

The sad look she gave him almost made him think she might prove him wrong.

George came home an hour or so later. At dinner, Kreig recounted how the interview had gone, getting congratulations and pats on the back. If only to avoid making George worry as well, Kreig forced himself to muster a smile of some sort.

Surprisingly, just as they finished eating, Sam presented a tub of ice cream. Apparently, she figured that whether he got the job or not, he could still use some sort of celebration or whatnot, so she'd gotten one with strawberry, pear, and vanilla in it. Kreig avoided telling her that the sweetness was numbing his tongue.

The evening turned to night. George went to bed early, leaving Sam and Kreig to their own devices.

Kreig was trying to paint what the principal looked like, but every time he thought he might get a part right, he remembered another detail. It never felt quite right. Next time he saw the man, he'd need to pay more attention to the way he looked instead of trying to calm his own heart.

Lost in his work, he didn't notice how Sam paused her game and turned to look at him. She seemed thoughtful, arms slung over the couch.

"It's not how you'd think it'd be, is it?" she said. Kreig turned to look at her. "When I finally realized I was sober, it didn't feel like anything at all.

Not when I got into the academy, either, or when I got my job or anything like that. Even when you kill a big monster and save lots of lives, it doesn't feel special. You just go on living afterwards."

Kreig didn't say anything.

"Hey, it's okay! That doesn't mean what you did doesn't matter, or that it isn't impressive or anything. You'll keep going, you know? At first, you'll be super nervous, and you'll make a bunch of stupid mistakes, and I'm sure those kids are going to laugh at you, but that's just how it is." She grinned slyly. "If anybody does anything weird, you know you can always ask me to come get 'em, right?"

"That shouldn't be necessary," Kreig said.

She smiled. "All right. Just call me if you need."

Kreig wouldn't know it until much later, but the next Monday, his future would be irrevocably changed.

Whether for the better or worse would depend on many factors, none of which he held any sway over.

PART III

RETURNING TO NO APPLAUSE

CHAPTER 23

JAY CROOKS

"We're getting a new PE teacher?" Jay Crooks muttered to herself in the dim light of the morning rays.

Her room, small and shabby and filled with a peculiar smell that couldn't be washed out, was mostly only lit by the decade-old laptop sitting on her third-hand desk. At the moment, the screen showed the homepage of the international school she begrudgingly attended. Right there, squeezed in between a plea to stop smoking on school grounds and a list of sick teachers, sat the news of a new PE teacher.

Jay huffed lightly. And she'd just gotten used to not having PE, too. Hrm.

A glance at the clock told her that the time was 6:45 in the morning. PE was in the sixth period. She'd been awake since—what? Three? No, it had to have been earlier than that. Either way, unless she decided to try to power-nap through English, she probably wouldn't be able to gather enough energy for even one lap around the gymnasium.

Jay leaned a bit to the right and peeked down at her exposed shins and calves. Yup. Still twigs. Well, no use in just sitting around. With a final sigh and a longing look at her two million open tabs—half of them being Flash games and the rest articles—Jay stood up. Her chair creaked. The floor creaked. The walls cracked. Not that the creaking of half the apartment would wake her mother or anything. That old hag might as well be in a coma.

Looking around, Jay tried to figure out where she might find a plastic bag, one of those you get at a grocery store. Maybe in the pile of half-okay laundry? Maybe in the old cupboard where she kept her free newspapers?

A crinkling sound brought her attention to the floor. Or maybe it was beneath her foot.

Sighing, she bent down, picked it up, and tried to ignore how her back groaned in pain after half a night of gaming and writing. At least there were no holes or anything in the bag, just an old receipt. Now she only had to fill it with a change of clothes. There should be something in the pile of clothes . . .

She dragged an okay-looking black T-shirt out of the pile. Sniffed it. *Okay, yeah, no.* She put it back and removed another shirt. Same thing there. All right, if this shirt isn't okay, she'd just have to do PE in her regular clothes . . . Sniff. *Uhh. Good enough?*

She shoved it into the plastic bag. A little while more of rummaging and she found a pair of sweatpants. *Those count as gym clothes, right? They're called sweatpants, so . . . Yeah. All right.* Since it wasn't as though she had any sports bra or anything, she'd just use the only one she had. And as for socks . . . Her regular socks would do.

Hopefully, she'd be able to explain to the new PE teacher that she didn't have any sports shoes. Hopefully, he wouldn't have a stick up his ass like the last one did.

Or maybe it was a she? The post didn't specify.

Jay suppressed a shudder. If it was a she, hopefully, unlike the one before the last, she'd use a proper bra while doing jumping jacks. That was all for later, though.

If she wanted to get to school on time, she'd need to leave pretty much . . . She glanced at the clock. *Yup. Now.*

In one movement, she strode over to her desk and shoved both the plastic bag and her old laptop into her school bag. In another swift movement, she slung the bag over her shoulder. *All right. Time to get to school.*

Trying not to look at anything too closely, she stepped out of her room, looked both ways, and then moved down the corridor, evading whatever trash and dirty clothes lay in the way. The door to her mother's bedroom was ajar, but Jay knew from a glance that her mother wasn't in there. Otherwise, she'd be able to hear her snoring. Instead, that characteristic sound came from down the hallway to the right. The living room. *Great. One more obstacle.*

Unconsciously, she began to move with an added touch of silent caution.

The hallway ended and she moved through the living room with subdued, almost tiptoeing steps. She made sure not to let her eyes fall on the couch, where her mother lay in a lazy pile, arms flung haphazardly, her naked body only half-covered by a hastily thrown blanket. A sickly sweet scent clung around her. Jay didn't want to think about what it was. Instead, gluing her eyes to the door, she moved through the room with large strides, a sneer dragging itself across her face. Her hand finally fell on the doorknob.

"Have a good day, sweetie," her mother mumbled from the couch. The sticky-sweet smell intensified.

Jay gritted her teeth. "Yeah," she said, escaping out into the open. The rays of dawn blinded her for a moment and she closed the door behind her. The sickly sweet air lingering inside her lungs was soon replaced by fresh morning air. Once more, she didn't fear breathing deeply.

Then, she descended three flights of stairs, slaughtering her calves in the process, before moving out to the sidewalk. However, she didn't head straight for the international high school she attended, but instead, she took a small detour. Jay herself lived in a large, brutalist apartment complex on the edge of town. Annie Swallowbird lived in a similar building, though it was incrementally better than where Jay lived. That was where she was headed, and after about five minutes, she found herself at her destination.

It was almost a miracle that Jay was able to tell which giant gray cube Annie lived in. Once she was there and waiting outside by a desolate parking lot, it only took a few minutes for Annie herself to emerge, her brown hair and green eyes bobbing as she jogged up to Jay.

Human, Lv. 1

Jay only spent a fraction of a second glancing at the pop-up before greeting Annie.

"Yo," she said.

Annie looked Jay up and down. "We're getting a new PE teacher?"

Jay shrugged. "The easy times are over. You didn't stick to that jogging thing, did you?"

"Uh, no," Annie said hopelessly. The both of them started walking. "But I'm pretty sure he won't be as bad as the last one, right? I mean. It'd be hard to top the kinda guy who calls running laps for fifteen minutes a 'warm-up.'"

"Maybe. Then again, he could be even worse. You never really know," Jay said, indulging gleefully in the horrified expression that washed over

Annie. "Hey, if you don't want to try your luck, you could always call in sick?"

Annie shook her head. "No. No way. Mr. Chutz would flay me."

Since the Painstone International High School was on the outskirts of town, walking there from their apartments didn't take too long. Once there, they met up with Gerald.

Human, Lv. 38

Personally, Jay preferred Gerald over Annie. Had it not been for Gerald, Jay would never have so much as glanced at Annie where she sat alone. But of course, the guy couldn't just let someone sit alone like they wanted and deserved; he just had to go and invite them over. But, Jay supposed, that was exactly why she liked the man. He was interesting!

Even if he hadn't been a rehabilitated otherworldly child soldier with a level befitting a Fighter, she'd still find him pretty interesting. He had an unusual outlook on life, people, and the world.

Even better, he had secrets. Lots of them.

Secrets he was terrible at keeping.

Squeezing them out of him had been as easy as making lemonade. With just the slightest prodding, the man had gotten so flustered, she didn't even need to reveal she knew his level was high. And the more he revealed, the more curious she got. In the end, after she had learned about his childhood and how he became a soldier and why he had come to the school at all, there was only one thing she didn't quite understand. One secret he withheld from her ravenous claws.

How it was all connected.

He had been fighting a battle when he came there, but he never explained who the enemy was. He came there alone, yet she knew there was no way in hell he could have defeated a competent party of Fighters alone. He alone was chosen to come there. What made him so special?

There was something here he wasn't telling her, and that clawed at her insides.

Well inside Painstone, the three of them parted, going to their own classes. During some classes, two or three of them would meet, and at other times, they were alone. At lunch, they all met and ate together. Annie alternated between talking in halting German and eloquent English, Gerald doing the same but in reverse. Jay had no problem with either language, but she was content to just listen to the two misunderstand each other.

Compared to Gerald with all his secrets and mysteries, Annie was pretty boring. The only interesting thing that Jay had been able to wring out of her was that her brother Charlie had gone missing when the portals opened. But that was hardly anything unique. Everybody lost someone to the portals that day.

Oh, wait, right, the slightly interesting thing was that he went missing the day before that. Alongside four other classmates.

Right. All very interesting, but when Jay had tried investigating the incident, she'd hit a brick wall pretty much instantly. Nothing there to uncover. Just five rose statues in a courtyard and a tragedy that was overshadowed and forgotten the very next day. An interesting incident worth trying to uncover with the only answer being a dead end.

Gerald was much more interesting. At least she knew she might be able to get answers *someday*.

Once lunch finished, all three of them headed to the same class: PE.

Jay dreaded it. Forget being thin as a twig; she was more like a dangly wireframe. Bones and skin with pretty much nothing else. If she was lucky, she might have been able to get out of this class if the teacher was strict to the point that he didn't allow people without gym shoes to do anything. Maybe.

Gerald parted from Annie and Jay and headed to the boys' locker room, while Annie and Jay went to theirs. After a brief time there, the two headed into the gymnasium. It was a large, blue-floored arena, made for all kinds of sports, none of which Jay liked. If she was lucky, since it was his first day on the job, the new teacher might be kind to them. Maybe. Hopefully.

The class gathered on the bleachers, some wearing custom shirts with their name and number, others wearing regular, colorful sports clothes, and Jay wearing a T-shirt and sweatpants.

The door on the far side of the hall opened.

God, he was big. Tall and broad, muscles practically bulging out of his shirt and pants. His eyes were pure white, giving off the impression that he might be blind. But since he walked confidently, his back straight and strong, that didn't seem to be the case. His hair was long and black, draping down his massive pecs and over his broad shoulders. Somehow, the air around him seemed to resound and vibrate with power.

To most in the room, he looked like the most ripped bodybuilder they had ever seen. Or like a shredded strongman.

To Jay, he seemed like a lot more. Her blood froze in her veins.

Divine Human, Lv. ???

. . . What?

Huh?

No, what?

She glued her eyes to the pop-up hovering in front of her. Why was it that color? What? Why was the level replaced by question marks? Why was he a . . . *Divine Human*?

What the fuck is this?!

A creak of the floor sent her attention soaring to look at the man—no, creature—himself.

Eyes like eternal white fireballs, forever staring at *her. What? What?* Somehow, in what had seemed like mere moments, the massive creature had moved across the floor. Or maybe she had been so struck with fear that the passage of time had slipped her mind. Either way, he was look-ing at her. A cold, biting tremor gripped her body. The room seemed to drop fifteen degrees, the sheer power of his presence choking her, pressing down on her as if to crush her.

Jay Crooks found that she could no longer breathe.

"Good morning. It is a pleasure to make your acquaintance," the crea-ture said in a baritone voice. He continued staring at her. "My name is Kreig Wiedermann. Henceforth, I will train you in constitution, strength, and athletics." No, maybe he wasn't staring at her. Jay chanced a glance to her right. There sat Gerald, his eyes glued to the creature's frame. He should be able to sense it too, right? He may not have access to the system as she did, but he was a former soldier! He had to know what true death looked like.

Then why did he look pleasantly surprised? Why did it seem like a smile was almost brought to his lips?

Why did it suddenly feel like the creature was looking more at Gerald than at her?

. . . It might have been that the creature also had access to the sys-tem. In that case, he would be able to notice that Gerald's level was far above one. And, thus, he'd set his sights on him. Maybe—maybe he'd try to *defeat* him?

Jay shuddered deeply. It wasn't as though she actually understood how high-level people thought and acted. She was just guessing, hoping to God that she might be right. Well, in this case, she was really hoping Gerald and the creature wouldn't fight. Whatever the *???* meant, whatever a Divine Human was, she was sure it didn't mean he was weak.

She looked back at the creature. As it was, while she considered every way this could all go to hell, he'd been explaining the schedule for the day.

Her class seemed apprehensive, but nobody had the guts to question such a man.

"... Then we will begin with running a number of laps around the room."

Oh, so he was a numbskull as well? Damn it all. She bit her lower lip, spending the long moment of everyone reluctantly leaving the bleachers by considering her options.

He didn't seem directly hostile unless cruel forms of warming up counted. Furthermore, since he was somehow able to apply for this position as a PE teacher, he must have had some sort of sanity. Or maybe nobody did a background check on him. Or he bribed his way in. Who knew? Either way, running was out of the question. Trying to go home sick might have been possible if it wasn't for the fact that she'd just have to return another day. Then she—

Oh, shoot, almost everyone has left, better get—

Huh? Jay's eyes fell on Annie's face. The girl seemed completely dazed, eyes squinting as though she was trying to recognize someone. "Uh, you okay there, Annie?"

Light returned to her eyes. "Huh? Oh, uh ... Yeah, sorry. I just thought I might have recognized Mr. Wiedermann from somewhere."

Stop the presses. "You've seen him before?" Now, *this* was interesting.

As timid realization dawned on Jay's friend, reluctance overtook uncertainty. "No. Uh, no, I was mistaken. I've never seen him in my life. I'd remember that, right?" The meek smile on her face seemed to suggest some humor in her words, but to Jay, it was a glaring red flag. *Right.* In other words, she recognized him, but something about her former meeting with him had been unpleasant or whatever, so she didn't want to tell Jay. *Right.*

But there was one thing Annie underestimated: Jay's tenacity as a reporter in the making. "Yeah, you would. He isn't the kind of guy you'd mistake for anyone else, is he?"

Annie had started sweating even before running a single lap.

A baritone voice made Jay freeze yet again. "You three, join the others."

Jay turned around with the intention of saying something along the lines of *Of course, Mr. Monster, I'll do just that right after I finish interrogating my friend about you,* but it came out as, "Uh, yeah."

When she turned back to Annie, a glance was enough to rouse her from her seat. The both of them left the bleachers and joined the others in running around the court. "So," Jay said. "How come"—she panted—"if he's so—unlike anyone else—how come you—mistook him for someone?"

Annie, running next to her, took quick, easy breaths. "It was just a mistake. Seriously, I didn't mean to—"

"Don't be like that," Jay said. But even as Jay continued pressing her friend for details, her attention kept getting pulled toward Gerald. Or, rather, his absence. Usually, he'd be running easily next to them, almost completely unbothered by the physical strain. But now he was nowhere to be seen. He wasn't running with the two of them at the very back, or in the front, or even in the middle. An idea struck Jay at about the same time as she forced Annie to admit that *Kreig Wiedermann* was not a common name, either. Gerald hadn't gone to meet the creature by himself, had he?

She looked for the massive frame of Wiedermann.

The creature was standing over by the bleachers, holding a sheet of paper. His large stature almost completely overshadowed the small, wiry form of Gerald.

Oh, God. Gerald, what the hell are you—

"Okay, okay, I've seen him before, all right? He was, he . . . I don't know. It isn't important, okay?" Annie said from far away. Jay breathed heavily, her trembling body hot and burning and heavy like she was dragging two sacks of hammers behind her. Her heart seemed to beat faster as she stared at how Gerald spoke to Wiedermann.

They were, he was . . .

Well, to begin with, Wiedermann seemed, strangely enough, on the verge of smiling. Maybe. There was some light in his white eyes that hadn't been there before. Some joy at talking to Gerald that struck her as completely unthinkable. And Gerald, well, Gerald was . . .

Strictly speaking, Jay had only known Gerald for about a month and a half. Even then, she considered herself pretty darn good at noticing subtle changes in his expressions. Lying and the like. It was probably since she'd had her fair share of training, but even then, she couldn't quite understand why Gerald would be feeling subdued happiness at meeting Wiedermann. That and clear, obvious recognition. Unlike Annie, he wasn't even *trying* to hide it.

Going by this, by the fact that Wiedermann was happy to meet Gerald and Gerald was happy to meet Wiedermann, it seemed almost obvious that they were, in some way, friends.

The thoughts brought a bitter taste to her mouth. No, that was wrong. It had to be.

That was impossible. An interesting conclusion, but an impossible one. Despite everything, Gerald was not a good liar. Keeping secrets was just not something he did well, so the idea that he could be friends with this massive creature without ever telling her just—

Just . . . Hm. There was one secret he had been able to keep from her, wasn't there? Yes, there was. One that might have been explained with the existence of this . . . *Wiedermann.*

He might—

"Okay, see, look," Annie said between deep breaths. "He appeared at my door. He and this other four-eyed guy. Inner-city type. I barely got a good look at them before they stuck some handwritten letter in the mail and left. Seriously, I don't know him!"

Ah, Jay had forgotten she'd been interrogating Annie. Well, it hadn't needed much effort on her part, but still. Now, *this* was interesting. He left a letter for—

Hang on; that doesn't make any sense either. Annie was as normal as they came. What the heck could a creature have to do with her? And who was the four-eyed guy?

"What did the letter say?" Jay said in a single breath, trying not to look away from Annie too often and break the intentional tension between them.

"I—I didn't." Annie glanced off and away. "I didn't open the letter. What, would you open any letter some random inner-city bodybuilders give you?" A smile found its way onto her lips. Jay couldn't know for sure if it was brought on by the little joke Annie tried telling or if it was the lie she told. Either way, she could make a pretty fair guess.

"Then you wouldn't," Jay panted, "mind if I had it, right?"

Annie's face turned a shade darker. "That's—"

A pair of claps that sounded a little louder than they should have brought everyone's attention to Wiedermann. "Finish this lap and then return here." The creature's voice was louder than it should have been, but the degree was subtle enough for it to be unnoticeable unless you assumed he wasn't human.

His voice still made Jay's blood run cold.

When she turned back to demand the letter from Annie, she found that the girl had increased her pace, leaving her in the dust. Alone at the very back of the bunch. Well, it wasn't an unusual situation for her. She was used to always jogging last. So, it didn't hurt so bad. Barely at all, actually.

When she finished her lap and joined all the rest in front of Wieder-mann, she found that Gerald had joined the group and was standing beside Annie. *All right.* So, that was how it was, then? Well, what Annie didn't consider was that social courtesy dictated that . . .

Jay elbowed her way through the class and joined both Gerald and Annie.

Annie glared at her, but since Gerald was there, it wasn't as though she could leave. Leaving meant leaving both Jay *and* Gerald, and Annie liked Gerald. Thus, they were all together again. Suppressing a grin, Jay came to realize that the three of them were standing at the very front of the group. Right in front of Wiedermann.

Jay was not a tall girl. In fact, she was short even for a girl. So, when a girl a head shorter than other girls stood before a man well over two meters tall . . . Well, as you can imagine, she had to crane her neck a bit. This close to him, the air itself seemed to surge with power, as though it was perpetually charged with static electricity. At the same time, it was cold. Oh, so cold. Like the silent freeze of a snowless winter.

Maybe it would've been better if Jay had remained at the back of the group.

She glanced at Gerald. She had a lot of information to press out of him. The implications at play there were not pretty but she wasn't about to jump to conclusions. Rookie mistake. No, she was going to take her sweet time squeezing it out of him. Same with robbing Annie of her "unopened" letter.

But first, she had to finish PE.

As Wiedermann slowly explained, he was open to suggestions—that nobody would have the balls to present—but for the day, he had a few activities planned.

So began an hour of what can best be described as spartan training. Pushups, laps, planks, and the like forced the bodies of the lazy youths to their limits. Those who couldn't keep up were swept to the side and given individual training regimes, which, by all appearances, seemed designed on the fly. Still, they were perfectly functional, and those subjected to them soon found themselves doing exercises that didn't completely crip-ple them.

Jay was one of these. She was the smallest girl in class, so no matter how much of an effort she made not to fall behind and be subjected to meeting the creature face-to-face, it was only a matter of time. Eventually, she collapsed. He approached her, looked her over, touched her forehead, and told her to go get herself a drink of water and take it easy. As he told her, "*There is a fine line between building your body and destroying it.*"

Sitting on the bleachers, she found the mystery of who the hell he was only deepening.

The only one who enjoyed the spartan, soldier-like exercise was Gerald, who went through it all with unusual passion.

She had to interrogate him. She just *had to.*

CHAPTER 24

A SKIP IN HIS STEP

The pavement seemed to sway pleasantly beneath his light steps.

Following his first day of work in a long while, Kreig almost felt like singing. Or whistling. Or humming. Of course, he did none of these things. But there was a trace, an almost invisible skip to his step. He had a good reason for this. It had, after all, been a very good day.

Training people in the art of combat and condition was nostalgic, but somehow, the part that gave the labor such joy was the simple reason that it would not end in war. The muscles built at the hands of these youths would not be rendered by a blade, nor would they be used to cause equal destruction to any foe. They were simply made for the sake of having. It was movement for the sake of health, not death. It almost brought a smile to his face.

Of course, not all of his new students were quite so pleased with the situation. This was nothing new. Those Kreig trained usually didn't find his training too pleasant, but now he had some elbow room. He'd been told quite clearly that his students would want and expect more games than simple exercise. Kreig didn't know too many such games. The only ones he could remember were those his fellow soldiers would engage in between battles. Though, in due time, he trusted that his students would eventually give him some suggestions to work with. Once they did, he would be happy to oblige them. But for now, they would work their bodies much like so many soldiers had before.

He looked forward to the games. In the teachers' room in one of the main school buildings, the other teachers had told him a few specifics of the trade. One of these tips was the fact that he was free to join the students at their games at any time.

Kreig had asked if this was entirely wise, since his presence might make the game unfair. The teachers had just laughed at him.

"That's the point, isn't it?" the boisterous math teacher had replied.

At the time, Kreig hadn't been able to answer, but now that he gave it some thought, he understood the point quite well. Battles weren't always fair, after all. There would always be one side with more money, soldiers, and mages. The other side had no choice but to make do. If the soldiers wished to survive, they had to defeat their superior foe through treachery, trickery, and intellect.

Kreig himself had seen many such battles play out, occasionally finding himself on the superior side and at other times on the inferior side. The fact that he was alive today proved his tenacity.

Furthermore, playing games with his students might be fun. It could bring them closer together and such.

For now, most of Kreig's students seemed slightly intimidated, which was as expected. Kreig hoped to change that someday. He didn't want to be their trainer, simply barking orders for them to follow. He was their *teacher.* And if Erica had taught him anything these past weeks, it was that being a teacher meant being more than a walking lexicon full of answers.

It meant being a guide. A friend, at times.

The face of his smiling tutor flashed through his head. He felt dizzy and hot.

. . . Maybe more?

Kreig quickly shook his head. No, no. That was . . . not a thought he was willing to contemplate. There was too much in his head already. So, instead, he looked down at his feet. His shoes were all right. A little tight. He looked straight ahead. People parted before him like waves before a boat. A few who weren't looking ahead experienced a brief moment of panic as they glanced up, froze, and then scurried off to the side.

It wasn't too unusual of a sight for Kreig, but at times, he really did wish there was some alternative. Some way he could get home fast without having people escape his path and sight with panic.

He glanced over at the nearby street, where cars and so-called bikes zoomed past. Hmm. Getting a driver's license didn't appeal to him, but a bike might get him out of the way of most ordinary people. All right. Kreig decided then and there to ask his siblings about it.

But first, he had tutoring to get through.

As he came home, he met up with Erica, who stood leaning against a tree outside. She smiled and joined him as they went upstairs. With Kreig's new schedule, they could no longer have tutoring during the day. Instead, they had a shorter session during the evening, right before dinner. None after dinner, though. One might ask how Kreig could afford effectively cutting his tutoring in half, but there was a good reason for this.

He just didn't need it anymore. He'd passed the required tests for a few parts already and was well on the way with the rest. Even more so, if he felt that his tutoring with Erica didn't cover what he had to know, he simply spent his time studying.

Unlike his prior experiences with studying, he now found it almost enjoyable. Especially the history books, which he studied with an almost-passionate fervor. His interest in math remained low, though.

Despite his independent studying, Kreig continued to find his tutelage under Erica the most fruitful time.

Regardless, when the time rolled around, Erica left, leaving Kreig alone to prepare dinner. He enjoyed his brief time of respite, and when his sister came home, he welcomed her with a look. She griped about her day's worries while Kreig put the finishing touches on the food, and once George arrived home, dinner was served.

From dinner to bedtime was a quick shift.

Even as he slept, Kreig knew nothing of the harsh interrogation taking place between two of his very students.

CHAPTER 25

BREAK

will assure you one last time and no more: I was merely asking about his future plans regarding the course. That's all," Gerald said so dismissively that Jay's conviction only deepened. Really, it was almost obvious that this would be her reaction.

"You didn't talk like a pair of strangers," she replied, suppressing a grin that might have told him how much she enjoyed watching him squirm.

Gerald hardened his gaze where he walked beside her, leading his bike by the handlebars. As far as Jay knew, he'd been given the bike on his first day as an adoptee. Considering the color scheme and odd design elements—such as the bright pink bag hung below the saddle—it seemed clear that the bike was probably from the early nineties or so. In other words, one of his two fathers probably owned it before him.

Andrew and James. A pair of pretty good guys, as far as cops went. Of course, being a future reporter, she couldn't find it in her to like them *too* much. They were probably withholding lots of juicy state secrets, after all.

Anyway, the reason for Gerald having the bike at all was a simple one. His house was in the middle of the inner city, not on the outskirts like Jay and Annie. Thus, since the road there was rather long, he needed a bike. Simple mathematics. Then, why was he walking beside his bike and not riding it?

That would be due to the presence of Jay herself. She was currently forcing herself onto him. Right after school, after telling Annie to bring the "unopened" letter the following day, she proceeded to follow Gerald. Hence, since Gerald was an impeccably polite and courteous boy, he couldn't find it in him to simply bike away from her. He had to walk beside her, bringing her to his house even though she never once asked if that would be all right with him. This was all part of her calculations. If she had asked whether she could come over for the evening or not, he would have had a chance to say no, which was a highly likely outcome since he already knew what she wanted to ask about.

But since she never even asked him about whether or not it was all right for her to come along, he never had a chance to refuse her. He was simply too polite and nervous to stop in his tracks and ask, "Isn't your house the other way?"

A little smirk found its way onto Jay's lips. Indeed, she knew how to skin a goat.

Gerald sighed. "I don't suppose you'll drop the subject once we get home, will you?"

Jay made a show of pondering it deeply, furrowing her brows and thumbing her lip. "Nnnope!"

Though, despite her valiant effort, even when they arrived at his house, she hadn't been able to relieve him of a single drop of truth.

Gerald and his adoptive parents lived in a small but charming house just to the side of all the inner-city hustle and bustle. The brick-walled house sat nestled in between similar yet slightly different though equally charming houses, all peering out toward a small park in the city. It was an immensely pleasant little thing, with a garden full of yet-to-bloom flowers and the walls covered with creeping vines. Every time Jay looked at it, she felt a pang of jealousy.

But she knew Gerald deserved it. Far more than she ever would, that was for sure. Indeed, if there was anyone who deserved a pair of loving parents and a cozy house, it was Gerald. Ah, but he *did* deserve getting ruthlessly interrogated by Jay. If only as a punishment for withholding his secrets.

As they came up to the fence outside the house, Gerald turned to look at her. They had walked for the better part of an hour. "You're not turning around, are you?"

"After coming all this way? Certainly not."

Gerald couldn't refuse her. After sighing and unlocking the small gate, he let her inside first. After sticking his bike in a small garage off to the side, he returned, quickly unlocking the door and inviting her inside. Once she entered, he smoothly closed the door behind her, sealing his fate.

The inside of the house was much like the outside. A striped, woven rug that stretched the full extent of the wooden hallway. Along the sides of said hallway hung several landscape pictures and a few mirrors, each framed by what looked like an antique frame. Honestly, it looked like the kind of house a grandma would live in—stuffed top to bottom with things and trinkets from a long life. Jay could remember Gerald telling her sometime that the house had actually been left by one of his fathers' mothers after she passed, leaving it for them to take refuge in. Very little had changed, apart from even more trinkets being added to the mix.

"Don't forget to remove your shoes," Gerald said warily, clearly a bit on edge. Well, she had made her intentions as clear as they could be, so it wasn't as though his reaction was weird. It just made her objective of pulling his secrets out of him a fair bit harder. Though not impossible.

"Yes, sir, will do, sir," she joked, slipping off her shoes and placing them in the shoe rack among fifteen pairs of loafers and oxfords. Gerald had already done the same.

Taking a peek at his watch, he tightened his lips into a line. "Would you rather have a snack or wait and join us for dinner?"

Jay considered the question for a moment. If she stayed at Gerald's house for dinner, she'd likely be served a fresh, hot meal and a possible dessert on account of her presence as a guest. If she went home and her mother came home before two in the morning, she might not have to eat four-day-old leftovers from when her mother *did* come home before two in the morning. That is, a really old pizza.

"I'll stay over," she said. A real no-brainer there.

Gerald frowned slightly without telling her she couldn't stay for dinner. "Okay, um, James recently bought me a new video game for the white box, so if you want to—"

"No, I just want to talk."

"It's in the living room. You can play multipla—"

"Let's go up to your room and talk."

Gerald gave off a strong impression of wanting to crawl out of his own skin. "I don't think it's a good idea. My room is very unkempt, as I haven't had anyone over in a—"

"Annie was over at your house three days ago. Knowing you, I doubt you could dirty it that much in such a short time. Somehow, you're one of the cleanest people I know," Jay retorted, taking a secret joy in watching him flinch. Though his reluctance to bring her to his room was a bit suspicious. He knew that she could interrogate him even while playing a game. "Or . . . is there something up there you don't want me to see?"

Gerald twitched. Ah. Right on the money. "It's a matter of . . . privacy."

Aha, but privacy is nothing in the face of deductive journalism! With a firm hand, Jay shouldered past Gerald and took to the stairs, all the while ignoring the pleas of her friend telling her he wasn't hiding anything at all and that he really just didn't have time to clean. Once upstairs, she took the first turn to the left, which led straight into Gerald's room. She burst through the door.

"Aha!" Jay shouted into the room. The room was, as always, impeccably clean. A simple bed, a simple closet, a simple desk, and barely a single personal item. The only decorative thing to be seen was a painting on the wall. Other than that, there wasn't a single thing out of place. "Uhh . . ."

Gerald sidled up behind her, glancing into the room furtively. "As I said. Nothing of importance."

Jay swiveled to look at him, trying to get over her shock at bursting in dramatically and then unveiling exactly nothing. "Uh—um, if, if there's nothing strange in here, how come you said it was dirty? Huh?" Maybe that'd make him forget her embarrassing entrance just now.

Gerald stared at her blankly. "I remembered wrongly."

"Hey, you were here this morning! How do you forget your room is clean?!" Jay yelled at him, all while he just sort of entered his room all casually as if they hadn't just mind-battled over the contents of his content-less room. He sat down at his desk and turned the chair to face the bed, and Jay sat down on the bed, gnawing at her lip.

"So? What did you want to talk about?" Gerald asked coolly.

Damn it. Maybe Jay had underestimated him. He was, after all, a man who had faced death on the daily for several years. Assuming he wouldn't hold a candle to her in a battle of wits might have been naive of her. She hooked her fingers above her knees, focusing intensely on her victim.

Even though he might still seem a bit shaken, that could just be a cover. Like an onion, his first layer was a facade of coolness, with the second layer being a false premise of nervousness. Jay couldn't imagine how many shrouds hid beneath these two. This might be the most decisive moment in her life. If she could get the truth out of Gerald, she could rest easy. That all depended on the answer.

An answer she may or may not be given.

"I don't know him," Gerald said evasively. "He's not a man I have ever met before."

"Come on, we both know that isn't true. You barely talk to the other teachers, not to speak of the students. Why would you start a conversation with him if you didn't already know him? He looked terrifying, to boot! Why, I'd bet most kids wouldn't approach a criminal like that for any reason." Her reasoning was solid, and yet Gerald wouldn't humor her in the least. As a matter of fact, he would barely even meet her gaze.

"Scared like you were?" Gerald asked carefully.

Jay sputtered. "I—I wasn't scared or anything! Just because he was huge and big and large doesn't mean I'd just get all scared of him or anything! It's just a matter of—"

"Of trying to hide from people bigger than you? It's very like you."

A fierce flush of shame overtook Jay's face. "It— That's not . . ." But before she could drag herself into a tirade about how she wasn't a scaredy-cat or how it was more that she feared bold people who withheld no secrets, she realized his ploy. He was just trying to get her to talk, even at the cost of his own standing in her mind. A mild insult to get her blabbering, trying to protect herself. "Th—though isn't it weird how he let you skip almost the entire warm-up exercise just to talk to you? If he didn't know you, why would he show you any favoritism?"

"I . . . How should I know what a teacher is thinking?" Gerald said, crossing his arms. "I barely know anything about this world, least of all the emotions and thoughts of its inhabitants. As a matter of fact, I didn't even know it was unusual to speak to your PE teacher before now. In the other world, I had no teachers . . ." At this point, Gerald began explaining his conditions of life in the other world, about how he'd only ever been raised by his siblings and that sort of thing. Jay would've been interested if she hadn't already dragged this out of him by force. So, she promptly zoned out while Gerald described, in minute detail, how his every day went.

He got up when the sun got up, helped his father in the fields, played with his only friend . . . While Gerald made a point of deeply explaining every single detail, Jay fully lost track of her arguments. Once Gerald got to the point in his life story where he was drafted to fight enemies, Jay had already let her eyes wander as well. Any attempt she made to stop Gerald from talking was feeble and quickly defeated by his sheer intent. So, she looked around his room. Wooden walls with wallpaper of ducks and little helping elves sleeping beneath a lily pad. An old wooden desk carved with smooth swirls and flower-like details. Wooden cupboard. There was a lamp on his desk.

She turned to look out the only window, which showed the park outside. The curtains weren't drawn, but if Gerald needed to, he could draw them, she supposed. His words were beginning to meld together. She just wanted to sleep.

Finally, she turned her bleary gaze to the single point of interest in Gerald's room: the painting. It seemed to mostly be a landscape piece, with much of the painting being taken up by swirling waves and a luscious sky. The rest was taken up by a person. No, wait, two people; the second was just—

Jay squinted, furrowing her brows. Was that her fucking PE teacher?

Why the hell did Gerald have a picture of Wiedermann in his room? No, wait, on closer inspection, the other person in the painting was . . . Well, assuming she hadn't gone blind or something—a quick rub of the eyes answered that—it was Gerald himself. Being held by Wiedermann. It was a very tender picture. Quaint. Bizarre in every way possible.

For one thing, they were both dressed like prisoners. Wiedermann had an orange jumpsuit, complete with some weird neck brace or maybe even a collar, and Gerald had a red jumpsuit. The difference in color was really slight but Jay was sure they were different. Then, one might ask, why the hell were Gerald and Wiedermann in prisoner jumpsuits? And why were they hugging?

". . . And then I got to my second battle, where I was stabbed in the leg and almost died . . ." Gerald was still going on and on about his life.

Jay inched closer to the painting, ignoring how Gerald's voice rose in pitch. Yup, it was definitely Wiedermann and Gerald. The likeness was staggeringly close. Who had painted this? She knew for a fact that Gerald was trash at all artistic things, so there wasn't a chance in hell that he had painted it. *Hm.* Either way, the painting was clearly based on a real event. Nobody but Wiedermann and Gerald was visible in the picture. Did . . . Did Wiedermann paint it *himself*?

It was an unlikely situation, but one that made sense, all things considered. *Right.*

To summarize, they knew each other before, namely when they were in prison. *Huh? Wait . . . Hm.* Well, Gerald *had* said that he'd been in a prison for otherworlders before this. So, while in prison, he knew Wiedermann. Right. In other words, Wiedermann was an otherworlder.

Jay drew a sharp breath. "Why was Wiedermann released from the otherworlders' prison?"

Gerald choked on his words. "I . . . I'm sorry?"

"You knew Wiedermann while you were both in prison. In fact, you were rather close. Lov—"

"H—hold your tongue!" Gerald stammered, his face red as a tomato.

Jay grinned slyly, knowing she had him off-balance. "I'm just joking, Gerald. I know you don't swing that way. Ah, but you still didn't answer my question. Why did they release him?"

Gerald gritted his teeth, his face dark. "He . . . He deserved it. He deserved to be a normal person."

A smile easily found its way onto Jay's face. After all, she'd finally gotten her opening. A confession of everything. "Was he not a normal person before arriving in this world?" Privately, Jay wondered how the arrival of such a high-level person could have evaded the public eye.

Gerald clenched his fists tightly. "The kind of person he was could never be normal." In his voice Jay could hear the faintest tremble of a deep-seated fear. The kind that could never wash out. "But . . . But that doesn't mean he can't be normal. Really, that's what he needs. So . . . Please. I beg of you, Jay, don't pursue this further. What he was before this doesn't matter. What he is *now* is what he will remain."

Calmly, Jay set her face into a mask of neutrality, pretending his words had no effect on her. "The world deserves to know, Gerald. A man like that can't just be a footnote in the history of the world."

With eyes as hard and sharp as the edge of a sword, Gerald stared at her. "I know that. But you . . . you don't know anything. Not about him, not about the world." Between the two youngsters, tension flared through the air. "You . . . You won't let this go, will you?"

Jay averted her gaze. "I can't." As though it were possible for her to stop at this point. "Could you?"

"I already have."

Gerald heaved a deep sigh, as though finally coming to terms with what he had to do, what he had to say. At the very same time, Jay felt a rush of joy and victory surge through her, her every instinct telling her that this was the end of the line. Her victory obviously contrasted with the defeat of her target, but she didn't mind that. Finally, she'd get the truth out of him. He'd no longer have any secrets to keep—anything to hide from her keen gaze.

She had won. Simple as that. And now, she would reap the bloody rewards of that victory.

Gerald's voice came out like a strangled whisper. "*Leave.*"

"Huh?" Jay said in reply. What? What did he say? Why would he—

Gerald stood up, their eyes finally meeting once more. His gaze was firm and cold, slight reluctance tugging at the corners of his eyes. "Go. You're not welcome here any longer."

Jay scrambled to her feet, her heart beating frantic and hare-like in her throat. "H—hey, wait! That's wrong, I won! I beat you, so tell me who he is and what he did!" Her plea came out as little more than the squawk of a deranged bird. With the finish line so suddenly removed, her mind scurried to pick up the line of the conversation, to throw every single card and question she had at his stone-walled face. "Who is Kreig Wiedermann? Why is he working at our school? Why was he released from prison? Why—"

"Stop it." He had moved so quietly and she had been focused on so many other things that now that Gerald stood right above her, she was almost startled by his proximity. "I'm not saying anything else and you're not asking anything else. I want you to leave."

Nervousness twisted Jay's panicked expression into a trembling smile. "You can't do that. We're having a conversation. I didn't do anything wrong!" Jay's eyes held Gerald's gaze, trying to force him to look her in the eye. He did, but there was nothing comfortable in that. "It's not polite to make me leave. I was just asking questions. Isn't that okay?"

Finally, Gerald turned away from her, reluctance once more gripping the features of his face. "Not about him. I don't . . ." Just as Jay began feeling the slight hope that he might calm down and let her continue his interrogation, a firm shake of the head dispelled any such possibilities. "I'm not going to ask again. Leave. We can talk at school once you've calmed down."

"I'm calm! I'm calm! See? I'm very calm," Jay cried futilely, trying her best to make her smile and her eyes stop trembling. Gerald frowned in disgust.

"If you don't leave on your own, I'm carrying you out."

Jay made a sound that might have been a scoff but sounded more like a toad's death-croak. "Heh. You wouldn't do that. W—would you?" The look in his eyes affirmed it. Her knowledge of his actual strength assured it. Gerald might not be too much compared to most Fighters, but to a normal human, he was next to inhuman. He took a decisive step toward her. She jumped toward the door like a spooked cat. "H—hey! I'm leaving! Look, I'll go, so just . . . I'll go."

He nodded, while staring daggers into her. Slowly, carefully, she took a few steps toward the door. He followed her.

She took one last glance at the painting before leaving fully.

At the front door, she turned back to look at him. "We'll talk tomorrow, okay? I'll be calmer then, so you can tell me—" The door was slammed in her face. For a second or so, she just stood there. Dark clouds swirled overhead. Dark thoughts swirled in her head. How dare he? She had accepted him into the class when no one else had. And now he just threw her out of his house?

Swiveling on her heel, she stormed off toward her home. Getting there would easily take over half an hour, but she knew her mind would be occupied.

Kreig Wiedermann.

A man as mysterious as the portals themselves, according to Jay. At the moment, she only knew a few select things about him. The most obvious one was that he was strong. Immensely strong. Jay had seen her share of Fighters and monsters, and as far as she could see on the internet, there were extremely few Fighters above the level of 300, not to mention the 501+ levels that Wiedermann likely had. Heck, for all she knew, his level might as well be 999 or something. It was a ridiculous number, easily rivaling the strongest monsters ever recorded.

And he was free. That was the oddest part. And it wasn't as though he was hiding from the government or anything; no, he *had* been imprisoned at one point. And they had released him.

At about the same time that raindrops started falling, a stray thought hit Jay in the face. Maybe it wasn't that they willingly released him, but instead that they knew they couldn't keep him? It was possible. Defeating an otherworldly foe and keeping it imprisoned were two very different things, so it was quite possible that said otherworldly foe—see: *Kreig Wiedermann*—might have been able to threaten the facility until released.

That was possible. Whether or not it was plausible was another matter entirely.

Maybe Jay shouldn't have felt that way, but something told her Wiedermann wasn't the kind of man who threatened people. Everything else aside, Jay considered herself to be a rather proficient judge of character, a skill that had been to a great benefit to her during her years. This was the instinct that told her that Wiedermann didn't threaten people; he just hurt them.

She wasn't sure if that was any better. Still, all of that was just window dressing for the facts present. Wiedermann had been released, given a new life, and somehow, he had gotten a job around kids.

It was, frankly, a ridiculous turn. Especially if one considered who Wiedermann really was.

In order for a monster or otherworlder to arrive on Earth, they first needed to pass through a portal. Assuming the portal was found and assigned to a competent police force, a party of Fighters would be sent into the portal. A party of Fighters could be anywhere between three and twelve people, using any manner of weapons and magic. The only way for an otherworldly foe to then arrive on Earth was to defeat and kill this party.

Hence, Kreig Wiedermann, at the very least, had the blood of three on his hands. Considering that the typical party is usually five to six people, according to the IOCRO homepage, he should at least have the blood of around half a dozen on his hands.

And yet, he was allowed to go free.

Of course, there were a lot of ifs and maybes to the story. It was possible that he merely acted in self-defense before arriving in this world, or that he actually arrived many years before and spent about as much time as a man charged with six counts of manslaughter might be. It was possible that the event itself was what caused Wiedermann's eyes to become so white and lifeless. It was even possible that nobody found the portal he entered through, leaving his possible kill count at a sharp zero.

It was all possible. But it wasn't plausible.

She could tell he had killed many. She could just tell. That look in his eye was not one of piety and righteousness.

The solitary drops falling from above slowly turned into a constant pelting of rain, soaking into her clothes and skin, freezing her to the bone.

Yes, Wiedermann was a danger. That much was sure. Even a Fighter with a level of 100 could be seen as a massive liability, despite his allegiance to humanity. A wildcard from the other world with a level of 501+ must be more like a walking calamity, able to crack at any moment. And if he did . . . the death toll could be innumerable.

A shiver clawed through Jay. She couldn't tell if it was from the rain or from the sheer terror claiming her heart.

Yes, Wiedermann was a man who could kill. And the world didn't know. Nobody knew, in fact, apart from the most privileged and hidden elite. The members of IOCRO knew. The Fighters surely knew. But what about the common man, who would be the most hurt if Wiedermann were to do something? They didn't know anything. Nothing at all. They were left in the dark, probably "for their own good," as much good as that would do them when the catastrophe came raining down on their heads.

The cold fear in her heart was overtaken by a savage, burning conviction.

Yes, it was up to her to save the common man, to reveal this man for what he was. If he could even be considered a man any longer. He wasn't even human. Who knew what a *Divine Human* could do?

It was up to her. Yes, it was all up to her. But she had to bide her time. Whatever she said now would only fall on deaf ears. And before she could convince a single person of the validity of her claims, IOCRO and any other hidden entity would censor her into nothingness, or even do something worse. She'd need hard, solid evidence, combined with enough facts to stagger the world.

That she would do. Yes, that she would indeed do.

She would reveal him. At any cost.

For the sake of the world.

CHAPTER 26

WHERE SHOULD WE GO?

Things had been going well for Kreig.

Especially so in his private studies, where his progress had been staggering to watch, in all likelihood due to his immense drive to learn. Of course, this did vary from subject to subject, but as a whole, he viewed his studies more or less as an extension of his free time, even though he personally had no real concept of work-life balance. To him, work *was* life.

As such, he held no distaste for working even at a time when he would usually read or paint.

In other words, he did very well while studying, even without Erica present. Though, as might be expected, with her present, he worked as hard as he possibly could. It was rare that he asked her things nowadays. This was not only out of an irrational desire to show her that he knew what he was doing but also because he had learned how to find his answers on his own, even when it seemed a bit unclear.

It was on one such afternoon, during a break that Erica had almost demanded they take or Kreig would simply burn himself out on work, that the two of them found themselves on the couch, each cradling a mug of coffee with differing amounts of sugar and cream. Unlike their common arrangement, Erica had made it herself since Kreig had never had coffee in the otherworld.

The pastries lying somewhat haphazardly on the coffee table, however, were all made by Kreig. Stretching her arm over the open pages of her book, Erica grabbed one such pastry before stuffing it into her mouth.

Even if Kreig had turned out to be a horrible kid, this tutoring job would totally have been worth taking if only for the food.

She glanced over at Kreig. Of course, his presence was also very worth it. If he'd been some spoiled little government-raised brat, she might just have thrown the books in his face the second he tried something. Luckily, Kreig wasn't like that. He was just a guy. A supremely strange and mysterious guy, but a guy to be sure. Although he'd been growing more talkative than when she first met him, he'd been quiet again as of late, but that was only because he was more focused on his work. He really was doing exceptionally well.

Anytime she gave him a test or anything, he just flew through it. Well, sometimes he got so nervous, he couldn't even put the pen to paper, but she learned pretty quickly that if she just talked to him a little first about the subject, he'd loosen right up.

What a strange guy.

Her hypothesis on his condition remained shrouded in mystery, though she had accepted the idea that he was some sort of secret painter or something. In all honesty, even though she was the curious type in every regard, as of right now, she couldn't think of any possible answer that would make her leave. Well, maybe if he was a secret terrorist or something, but she didn't think so. Kreig was nice. He was also a good student.

Yes, a very good student. That was the most important thing, wasn't it? No matter how good of a person he was, the fact that he was a good student was what kept her there. Yup, that's how it was. Definitely.

Erica sipped her black coffee and glanced at Kreig. The man could barely take a sip of the coffee without frowning deeply, even though the coffee was like 90 percent cream and sugar. Well, more like 89.99 percent cream and a single molecule of sugar, but anyway. On that note, it seemed Kreig had a certain dislike for sweets, since he avoided most of the pastries. Oh, well. More for her! Erica shoved a few more pastries down her gullet. She should probably cut back, but she definitely wouldn't.

This silence was a little concerning, though. She knew Kreig didn't speak much, and she obviously didn't mind sitting in silence with him, but it did feel a little too quiet. And it wasn't as though she didn't have any questions for him, like *How the hell do you have time to work out?* or *Why would you go into teaching?* and *How have I not dissuaded you from such a treacherous path?*

In the end, though, she could only bring herself to ask one question. "Uh, you got into teaching, right? How's that working out for you?"

Kreig tried to stall for time by taking a sip of coffee, only to instantly furrow his brows and scrunch his nose. Next time, Erica would try to make tea or something. This wasn't working. "I enjoy it. It reminds me of my time training soldiers."

. . . Training soldiers?

Erica quickly rewrote her entire backstory for Kreig. Okay, so he wasn't *just* a painter; no, he was some sort of sergeant, too. Maybe he rose in the ranks of the military or secret service or whatever by using his painting skills to sway the hearts of commoners and terrorists alike, becoming a secret weapon or something? It was possible. No, knowing his paintings, it was almost obvious.

"The students haven't been giving you a hard time?" Erica asked carefully, trying not to recall her own time as a teacher. "If they say anything mean, report it to the headmaster. He probably won't do anything, but then you can write in your evaluation that he willingly ignored your warnings. Gives you the upper hand."

Kreig stared at her for a moment, and for some reason, he seemed speechless. "I have had no need to report anything to anyone. The students are most kind to me."

Erica wasn't sure if he was just saying that to calm her down or if that really was the case. Or, possibly, he might just not understand that what the students were doing to him was harassment. Knowing Kreig, that was equally plausible. "Mm, okay, but if anyone says anything you're not sure about, make sure to make a harassment report, okay? Doesn't matter if it was a joke; you can still squeeze money outta them."

"I see . . ." Kreig scratched his head and almost made to sip his coffee before realizing his mistake and putting the cup down on the coaster. "No, the students are not like that. They treat me very well, despite my obvious inexperience. Furthermore, these past days, they have begun growing braver, suggesting various games for us to play. It is most refreshing."

Erica thumbed her lip. "Hmmm, well, yeah, I guess you could call them *brave* . . ." Noticing that Kreig was staring at her, she quickly waved her hands dismissively. "No, no, I just . . . Well, I worked there for a short period of time when I just finished college. Painstone, right? Yeah, I'd recommend you try to get into some other school. I know this city needs an international school or two, but working willingly at one of them is . . . It's admirable, I guess?"

Kreig was still staring at her. "I—I just . . . Look, I'm gonna be honest.

When I worked there, every single kid I met was a dick. Straight as that. I know it's different from year to year, but literally every kid I met was just a total dick. And then I switched to another school, and it was the same thing there! Dicks to me, dicks to each other, dicks to their family . . . I couldn't stand it. Just—just look out for it, okay?"

"I don't think they're . . . *that way* anymore." Kreig seemed to be genuinely trying to search his memories for any evidence of them acting like the dicks Erica knew they were. "Forgive me; I can't seem to remember any such occurrence. Even more so, I am rather close with one of the students, who I can say for sure is not . . . like that."

Yeah, sure. Like Erica could believe that. *That school couldn't change if you hit it with a mortar shell.*

While Erica mentally thought about bombing a school, Kreig seemed to have thought of something. "In what mental state were you when you began teaching?"

"Huh?" What sorta question was that? Of course, she was absolutely exhausted. She could remember wanting a five-year break but only being able to spend a few days in relaxation before having to go to work again. In fact, just three days after her graduation, she had sought a job as a teacher for a few summer courses. Few attended the courses she held, but each and every one of the students would much rather have been anywhere else. Of course, during this time, she also had two part-time jobs that drained her of time and energy.

Then she began working full-time at Painstone. Calling her *tired* would be a grave understatement. No, she'd felt like a zombie who just crawled out of the grave and was forced to work customer service at a DMV.

She'd wanted to die. That's for sure.

Kreig, who had only been watching her until now, piped up. "Were you in any state to comprehend the personalities of students?"

"Of course—" She wasn't. It was only now that she had a semi-stable job and could think about it in this clear state of mind that she could even consider it. She'd been distressingly overworked, working full-time as a teacher and part-time at whatever was open. Why, if she'd met Kreig as she was then, she'd probably think he was a dick, too: barely talking, making her job harder by hardly asking questions, not understanding things as quickly as she would have liked . . .

Anyone can be a dick if you're tired enough.

Kreig watched carefully as Erica sank into a tight-lipped silence. Had he said something wrong? Somehow, she seemed unhappy.

But just as he began readying himself to apologize, she turned to him instead, her eyes shining with an odd luster. "You're right," she said. "You're exactly right. I could barely even read myself and how *I* was feeling, and still, I thought I could at least tell what *they* were thinking. You're exactly right."

Kreig stared at her dumbly. He was right? He said the right words? He swallowed dryly. "Then, you'll return to teaching?"

Her expression of enlightenment collapsed in on itself. "No, that's . . . Well, I probably could, but . . . Or, I can't . . . I mean, dicks or not, the problem was just that I didn't like teaching, right?" Kreig shifted where he sat, trying not to think about what such a statement might mean for their current relationship as teacher and student. "Besides, I don't see how it's important that I'd go back to teaching."

Kreig tried to rack his brains for an answer that might be more substantial than *I enjoy teaching and you're a good teacher so I think you'd like teaching again.* So, in the end, he tried to circumnavigate her entire argument by answering only the smallest of the three questions she asked. "If I talked to the principal, I'm assured my recommendation could secure a position."

She knitted her brows. "What, just like that?" Kreig nodded resolutely, trying to hide his uncertainty. It wasn't as though he could force the principal to do anything. Well, he *could*, but if he did that, his siblings would get upset. Regardless, since she had already been working there for some time, and knowing her obvious skill at teaching, Kreig couldn't imagine a scenario where she wasn't given a job. "Still . . . it's not like I don't have any other job than this one, right? Not to even *speak* of college. It's not like I can just quit."

"If you . . . If you were to work as a teacher instead of your other job, would it make too much of a difference?"

"Right now, I'm working as a cashier," Erica said thoughtfully. "If I worked as a teacher, I'd be working more and longer hours, giving me less time for college . . ."

Listening to her speak, Kreig tried to piece together what her daily life looked like, how long each part took, how much money it gave, and everything else. Of course, even knowing that, he was ignorant on many critical aspects such as how much she needed for expenses. However, it seemed that at the moment, her largest worry wasn't money but time. Kreig may not have had many solutions, but for this issue, in particular, he could offer at least one. "If we were to reduce our hours together, you would have more time to work on college, no?"

Her mouth dropped open. "E—eh? Seriously? Hrm, well, if we only went at it for two hours or so . . ." She seemed to be making a few calculations in her head, the kind that Kreig couldn't even begin to fathom. ". . . it would be possible. I guess? I mean—you won't fall behind, will you? You're already doing great, so if I fail and the Japanese yakuza begins hunting me down, I'm blaming *you*!"

The Japanese what now? Before Kreig could so much as try to understand who those were or how she came to that conclusion, he said reassuringly, "Don't worry. I'll take a few more hours to study every night."

She hummed thoughtfully while squinting at him. "Well, okay!"

Though Erica seemed a bit more open to the prospect now, it was still clear that she held some reservations, probably toward becoming a teacher again. Kreig himself didn't see any real reason to fear being a teacher. Most kids were quiet and did as he asked them. Simple stuff.

Hm. Ah, in the buzz of convincing Erica, he'd forgotten that he actually had a question for her. She biked everywhere she went and she seemed happy to do so; hence, she must know about bikes.

He turned to her meaningfully. She caught his eyes on hers, her cheeks lighting up in a thin blush. "Wh—what is it?" Kreig ran his eyes down her body to her legs, which were exposed beneath a flora, summertime skirt. Her legs were well developed with defined thighs and calves. She may have had a small stature and thin body, but where it counted, she certainly knew her stuff. "E—everything okay?"

Kreig nodded to himself. "Would you happen to know where I could purchase a bike?" In turn, Erica visibly deflated, though her face only grew redder. "The distance to Painstone has been a bit of an issue to me."

"Ah—aha! Okay, yes! So, that's what it was . . . Well, fear not! I actually know a really good store just on the other side of town. I can take you there sometime! If—if it's no issue to you, I mean. But a man and a woman being seen together in public . . ." Somehow, against all odds, her face grew yet another shade redder. "W—well, if you'd rather I recommend you an online shop or something, I can do that instead. No lizard people, guaranteed."

There were lizard girls on Earth? No, considering her use of *people* instead of *females* or *girls*, it seemed they were both males and females, unlike the lizard girls of the other world. Curious. Either way, the lack of lizard people in the shop was probably a good thing.

"Very well, then," Kreig said. "Sadly, I am unable to operate the internet. I hope you will allow me to impose on your knowledge and presence."

Surprise painted her face, and Kreig tried to hide his shame. "Huh? So, we're going to Poirot? Hey, neat! I'll make you buy the fastest bike I know of!"

"Ah, I don't need anything fast, as long as it gets me where I need to go." If he wanted speed, he could just run.

Erica mumbled something conspiratorial about how Kreig must be a time-traveling caveman or something.

Kreig decided not to think too hard about what she thought, since it was mostly incomprehensible. In the end, they decided that they would meet up at Space Circle Avenue a little before lunchtime next Saturday. Kreig thought it sounded good, but at every step of their little plan, Erica lit up a little more. By the end, her cheeks were almost as red as Messiah's Fruits.

Kreig thought she looked pretty cute like that, but the second he thought it, he felt himself grow just a little red himself.

CHAPTER 27

THE THIRD FORM OF LOVE

A week or so passed, allowing Kreig the requisite time to pick up his very first paycheck. Getting it hadn't required a full month of work, since Kreig had started about a week following the last payday, though it did mean his paycheck wasn't quite full. Still, he accepted it happily.

Now to figure out what to do with it.

He had already planned to use a bit of it to buy a bike with Erica, but he didn't actually know how much such a contraption would cost. According to his siblings, it would hardly require the entire paycheck. Which meant that he would have plenty of money left over.

But when he wanted to give this money to his siblings for everything they'd done for him, they wouldn't accept it. How odd. As a matter of fact, they tried their best to emphasize that he use his newfound capital to buy himself something nice. The problem was that Kreig couldn't think of anything better to use it for than to give to his siblings. It was a bit of a conundrum, but for now, he would stow it away until later.

And now, the time had come. Kreig's heart beat a little faster at the thought, though he couldn't quite figure out why.

The time was now 11:15, a quarter of an hour before they had decided to meet. Kreig sat perched on the side of the fountain in the middle of Space Circle Avenue. The little wallet in his pocket seemed to weigh heavily. This was almost a given, since it contained nothing but hard cash. There wasn't a single card to speak of in there. His siblings had considered getting him a bank card or credit card, but after a short discussion, they had decided against it. Even having a bank account was almost too much for him to properly understand.

Kreig was also entirely on board with his siblings holding total control of his bank account. Maybe one day he would want to take control of it by himself, but for now, he felt much safer with that in their capable hands.

Cash, on the other hand, was the safest with him. Who would try to steal from a man who put bodybuilders to shame?

Kreig breathed a deep sigh. Still, he did feel a bit nervous carrying around all this money. Not that he actually had any concept of how much it was worth. Sure, Sam had told him what kinds of food could be bought with this and that amount of money, but it all just seemed to conflict with what he thought he knew. For one, sugar was extremely cheap here. Most vegetables were somewhat expensive. Even the most exotic foods from far-off countries could be bought relatively cheaply at the right store. He didn't really get it.

Just as Kreig felt the need to sink into a little ball of confusion and uncertainty, he felt a hand fall on his shoulder. He perked up and instantly found himself face-to-face with a pretty girl. No, wait, it was just Erica.

"Just" and "just," she really was worthy of being called *pretty*. Kreig wasn't sure how she'd done it, but somehow, she seemed even more radiant than usual, her whole face bright and cheerful. Her curly hair seemed to bounce as she smiled at him, small dimples in her full cheeks. He let his eyes wander down. As usual, she was wearing a flowery dress, one that billowed slightly in the moderate wind. It was pink with yellow flowers printed on it. The fabric seemed to be made of linen or some other simple material.

Kreig had seen many dresses in his days, whether they were worn by aristocrats or peasant folk. The highest of noblewomen often wore dresses made of the finest materials, woven with fibers worth more than many human lives. Such dresses had always struck Kreig as tacky and noisy. Especially the ones with the gaudy colors and the crude floral motifs.

But here, now that he saw Erica in such a dress—in a dress that such noblewomen would scoff at—he couldn't help but feel that such a dress only worked to accentuate her beauty. "You're . . . really pretty." The words dropped from his lips before he had time to rein in his awe.

Her cheeks grew red in a matter of seconds. "Th—that's— I—" She stammered wildly for a few seconds, her eyes darting to and fro before finally settling down on Kreig once more. She smiled bashfully. "Th—thanks."

And all of a sudden, Kreig felt very inadequate. The only thing he'd done in preparation for this outing was to take a shower and wear clean clothes. That was it. In comparison to the way Erica seemed to have grown twice as beautiful, his appearance was almost insulting.

Red-hot shame washed over him. If Erica was prettier than a noblewoman, then what did that make Kreig, who was plainer than a peasant? How could she possibly be seen in public with someone such as him?

"Y—you also look pretty," Erica said, shyly looking away. Kreig stared at her. "Pretty handsome, I mean! Handsome. Not pretty. Well, maybe a little pretty." Kreig's jaw fell open. Somehow, Erica grew redder. Whatever illness that was afflicting her must have been infectious, since Kreig soon felt his own face growing hot. How should he even respond to that? Now that he thought about it, had anyone ever called him that? Well, he was sure that *someone* had, probably before he came to the otherworld. But he couldn't remember that.

Mind flailing for something to say, some explanation of what he felt, he reached for the one thing he knew would work. After all, it had worked on him.

What had Erica said?

"Thanks." He really hoped that such a small word could possibly express the gentle surge of joy energizing him from the inside out. She smiled back.

. . . Even if it didn't express his emotions fully, just seeing Erica smile like that made it worthwhile.

All of a sudden, Erica shook her head wildly, making her fluffy curls shake back and forth before slapping her cheeks twice. "Okay! Bike. Bike to bike on. Yes."

Kreig nodded carefully. "Yes?"

She grinned. "Poirot will stay open until like four, so we've got plenty of time to just walk around and do stuff." Kreig scratched his chin. Do stuff. He tried to rack his brain. No, he couldn't think of a single thing to do in the city apart from what he already did. "B—but first, since it's lunchtime, how about we go eat? There's a café nearby. They've got really tasty salad. Kinda expensive, but hey! We're out doing stuff; that means we can afford to be a little lavish, right?"

Kreig nodded without actually understanding what she meant. "Certainly."

She smiled brightly. "Great! Okay! Let's go; I'm really hungry!"

Kreig agreed. Standing up, he was again struck by how short Erica was. It was almost a little jarring, but at the same time, it made it feel like he was out walking with a little field mouse. Yes, she was like a cute little mouse. Kreig almost wished he had some cheese to give her.

They walked together for a bit, with Kreig following Erica's lead closely. Strangely enough, they didn't just walk straight to the café in silence. Instead, at any time, Erica could stop to show Kreig something, or to explain some little part about a house or a place, or explain how she had once been in one of the many houses for whatever reason. At one point, she even stopped him just to show him a fat little caterpillar on the ground. He didn't really see any need to care too much for it, but at seeing how Erica gently lifted it off the sidewalk and into a nearby bush, he couldn't help but feel a newfound appreciation for the little insect. It *had* let him see a more caring side of Erica, after all.

Eventually, they appeared at the café. Getting there had taken a bit more time than expected, since Erica had stopped every minute or so, but Kreig saw nothing wrong with that. It had been far more pleasant than how just running straight there would have been.

The café itself was called the Hole and was, all things considered, a fair bit out of the way. The name was very fitting, but since Erica made a show of growing ever hungrier just at seeing the sign out front, Kreig found himself with surprisingly high expectations. He trusted Erica's assessment.

They entered. A little bell above the door chimed pleasantly, making a few of the sparse patrons glance up. Then, upon seeing Kreig—who had to duck a fair bit to get in through the door—they quickly returned their wide-eyed stares to their food. A common reaction, and not one Kreig found too strange anymore. Hell, to him, it'd almost be weird if people *didn't* react like that.

Erica turned to him. He looked back at her. Not a trace of fear in her eyes. It felt nice. She smiled wryly.

Then she stepped up to the front counter, where a man soon turned to face her. He lit up at seeing her. "Erica! How pleasa—" His mouth snapped shut upon seeing Kreig. He gulped audibly. "—ant. W—well, uh, what would you like today?"

"I'd like a Caesar salad, and—" She turned around to face Kreig. Her lips were pulled tight, eyebrows pinched together oddly. "What would you like, Kreig?"

Kreig turned his eyes to the menu above where the clerk stood. There were many kinds of salads, alongside various pasta bowls and other dishes. The sheer number of different types of foods made Kreig quake where he stood. "I'll have the same as you." That was the simplest option. If she had decided that this Caesar salad was the tastiest, then so be it.

She smiled thinly. "All right. Then a Caesar salad for him as well."

The clerk nodded, his eyes carefully avoiding Kreig's gaze.

Before Kreig could ask *What happens now?* Erica had pulled him away from the front desk and over to a small table by a window. They soon sat face-to-face. Kreig didn't like to find that she had a conflicted expression. She almost seemed thoughtful. But the worst part was that she seemed to view Kreig with some amount of pity.

". . . How can you stand it?" she asked, finally looking him right in the eye. "You're not a bad guy, so . . . how can you stand everyone looking at you like you're some evil monster or something?"

Kreig resisted the urge to say *Because I am one.* Instead, he said, "It's not something I have control over." It wasn't as though he could force people to think differently of him.

"Well, yeah, but . . . Out on the street, even though you weren't doing anything, people just—they just parted before you. Like they were afraid you were gonna strangle them if they got too close. How can you stand that?"

It was just the way his life was. That was how it had been for many, many years. And people had good reason to react that way. It was not an unfounded fear. In fact, Erica was the strange one for *not* reacting like that. But, of course, Kreig couldn't say any of that. If he did, she might begin to think that there was a reason to fear him. He couldn't allow that. He couldn't bear to lose her. "There is nothing I can do."

She frowned slightly. "Why, if it was me, I'd wanna strangle 'em! I'd just—"

A bowl of salad was put down in front of her, making her whole expression do a complete 180 into pure delight. An identical bowl found its place in front of Kreig. The man who had put them down, the same man who had taken their orders, seemed a bit unhappy with what Erica just said. She didn't seem to notice it. "Thanks, Eustice!"

"You're welcome, Erica."

Erica attacked the bowl without continuing the rather grim conversation of before. Following suit, Kreig took a bite, trying to get a piece of every part in one bite.

Yup, tasty. It was right to trust Erica.

Kreig had tasted plenty of salads in his life but none with this exact composition. He decided to store the recipe in the back of his head, if only because Erica seemed to enjoy it so much. Maybe a little too much. She downright wolfed it down.

On the other hand, she *did* have a tendency to do the same to almost anything Kreig put in front of her. Maybe she was just a glutton? Though her slender and healthy frame would suggest otherwise. Kreig took a bite, staring at her as best as he could, trying to decipher her life. Maybe she just didn't eat? It was an odd line of thought, but if she didn't have any food at home, then it wouldn't be too odd if she practically attacked any food placed in front of her.

Hopefully, that wasn't the case. Kreig would hate for Erica to go hungry in his absence. But if it was the case, then Kreig would definitely offer her permanent abode in his house. The house he shared with his siblings. *Hm.*

No, if he wanted to house her, he'd probably have to first move out himself.

Kreig had, of course, entertained the idea of living on his own, but he already knew that such a plan was many, many years in the future. He just didn't know enough about the world to do so. Unless if he were to move in with Erica, who seemed quite proficient with the world. Of course, such a plan would only be possible if she lived alone. Something Kreig wasn't entirely sure of.

He caught Erica's eye right as she was about to take another massive bite despite her mouth being full. "Whadd is id?"

"Do you happen to live alone?"

She stared at him for a few seconds; chewed, swallowed, and smiled. "Yeah! Unless you count my cat. Name's Sourdough. Really thick boy."

So, she lived mostly alone. With a cat. Cats should be the same in this world as in the other one, right? Kreig could somewhat remember seeing cat-shaped creatures on the streets out of the corner of his eye, although none would approach him. Though this did answer his question. "Do you have food at home?"

She squinted for a moment, her whole face scrunching up cutely. "Is that a compliment or— I've got food at home, I swear! I just— Well, I'm not much of a cook, so most of what I make isn't too tasty, heh. Heh . . ." Was Kreig hallucinating or was that a tear in the edge of her eye? "B—but that isn't important, right? Right. Uh, well, um." She absently pierced way too many pieces of pasta on her fork. "Have you ever been on, like, a date before?" Her cheeks grew a blossoming shade of pink.

Kreig blinked. "What is a 'date'?" He felt a little silly asking, but he did have a good reason. He had actually heard the word on a few occasions.

For example, last night when he told his siblings over the dinner table about his plans with Erica, his sister had teased him, using that very same word. She never explained what it meant. Kreig would like to know.

She looked off to the side, her face growing red as a rose. She began fiddling with a strand of her hair, making it bounce up and down. "W—well, that's . . . When two people who like each other go and do stuff, it's a date!"

Ah. So, that's it. "Then, yes, I have been on many dates before."

Her expression collapsed. "Y—you have?! Hmm, this is my first one . . . With whom?"

Kreig nodded in a businesslike fashion. "With my brother and my sister. At times, both at once."

She froze in the middle of tugging at a piece of hair. "Eh? You—you're—Incest!? No, wait, I don't think that's very . . . Uh, a date is more like—like when you're with someone who you like, but—but more in a . . . not in a familial way? Or—or a platonic way, either. Other than that."

Kreig resisted the urge to scratch his head. Liking someone in a way that wasn't friendship or family? *Hm.* Somehow, Kreig could sense that there was a term for this other-like, a term that he had heard many times before . . .

Erica frowned shyly, breaking Kreig out of his thoughts in an instant. Had he done something to make her upset? He must have thought for too long, insulting her with his uncertainty.

"You're really making me say it, huh?" Kreig gulped. "Th—the other form of love apart from familial and platonic . . ."

Her face turned beet-red at about the same moment that Kreig realized it. Changing the term from *like* to *love* had done it.

His face grew hot. "A—ah, in, in that case, then . . ." He averted his gaze, suddenly feeling very hesitant and timid. "No, I have never been on a—a *date*." He glanced at her. Then he looked away. "Not before this."

Likewise, Erica blushed shyly, quietly poking her fingers together. "M—me neither . . ."

A small lull in the conversation allowed Kreig to pull himself together again to try to still his beating heart. A date. He certainly hadn't thought of it like that, not before, but now that he sat in front of her like this, it truly did feel right. Yes. They were on a *date*. He swallowed hard.

. . . Then again, going by that definition, this was probably not the first date Kreig Wiedermann had ever gone on. From what Kreig knew, 130 years ago, he had been quite the playboy. He had probably gone on quite a few dates and broken his fair share of hearts. This had, of course, changed the instant he was summoned. The Bodies of the Holy Order were seen as pure and divine, unfit to be tainted by the spectrum of human emotion. Especially the bodily parts.

By the time he found himself in a position where romantic relationships would have been acceptable, it had already been too late. He just didn't feel comfortable with it. He only wanted to work. Having a personal life would have been too painful.

Kreig took a sip of his drink. But now . . . now he was freed from that, leaving him to form his own personal relationships. This included friendships and family. And, perhaps, romance.

All of a sudden, Kreig's throat felt very dry and his tongue very large.

They continued eating in silence.

When Kreig put his fork to his bowl, he found it stabbing emptiness. Looking up, he found Erica staring at him. Her bowl was empty, both pieces of cutlery placed across it. When had she finished? Shamefully, Kreig couldn't say. In fact, he couldn't figure out for how long Erica had been staring at him. Neither could he quite understand why she was looking at him like *that*. Not that he disliked it. He had probably given her just the same eyes while she wasn't looking.

But having them stare back at him felt a bit surreal.

She blinked twice. "Oh! I was just— Well, you eat really daintily, you know?"

". . . Daintily?" Now, that was a new word.

Her hands made bizarre movements as though attempting to perform a silent dance routine. "Y—yeah! Ladylike. I guess your etiquette will make up for the both of us?"

"Maybe so." Mutely, Kreig mimicked the way Erica had placed her cutlery across her bowl.

As if in response, Erica stood up. Kreig followed suit. "Eustice will handle the dishes, so . . . wanna go look at bikes? Poirot is pretty close."

Kreig nodded at her. He wanted to say something, but suddenly he felt very, very nervous. Almost paralyzed.

Surely, all those years before, he'd had some sort of confidence. He must have. The kind of confidence that let him win games and defeat opponents and charm the ladies until they swooned. But now, he didn't have that. Now, all he had was a freezing fear that he might do something wrong; that he might make such a mistake that she would never look at him like *that* again.

Eyes stuck to the ground, he barely even knew where he was going at all. Only that he was hopefully following the edge of Erica's dress.

Then he felt something small and soft grab his hand.

He froze solid. Hesitantly, his gaze left the ground. He found Erica looking at him with those big, fawn-like eyes. She smiled wryly at him. "You keep walking the wrong way, so . . . You don't mind me holding your hand? To get you to go in the right direction, that is."

Kreig gaped at her. Wordlessly, he nodded. She beamed back at him, her small grip on his much larger hand gaining some form of confidence. In his heart, Kreig thanked the lord below that he hadn't jerked his hand back or struck her out of instinct. The best-case scenario in such a situation would be that she lost her hand or arm. In the worst case . . .

Kreig shuddered.

Her hand gripped him a little tighter. He glanced up at her. She smiled warmly.

He wanted to hold her hand a little tighter too, but in his shaken state, he wasn't sure if he could do it without hurting her. But with her holding him so closely, she was surely holding on for the both of them.

The bike shop Poirot was placed on the outskirts of the city, near the small villages that naturally formed in the city's vicinity. Kreig wasn't sure how they got there so quickly, but according to Erica, time moved fast when you were having fun.

The shop itself, although small, clearly prided itself on the skill of its owner. It wasn't actually clear whether it was a bike mechanic or a bike shop foremost. It seemed to be a bit of both, and with so many bikes littering the outside of the entrance, it was clear the owner had far more traffic than might be expected for such an out-of-town place.

Had Kreig been alone, he probably wouldn't have been able to enter out of nervousness. The shop really seemed to be of the small, local sort, which would bar him entry if he didn't have a guide such as Erica.

Kreig sighed and turned toward her. She was gone. Huh?

Head whipping around frantically, Kreig found her standing by the door of the shop, examining a bike standing right beside it. It felt like an awfully unsafe place to keep a bike, but the shop owner probably knew what he was doing. Probably.

As Kreig approached, Erica smiled and straightened her back. "Since you'll only be biking between your home and Painstone, I think a casual bike would be best. Unless you want to get into biking as, like, a sport?"

"No, I'd rather not," Kreig said dismissively. His entering sports would be terribly unfair to every other sportsman.

She looked him up and down. "Well, okay! With your body type, you'd be much better suited for powerlifting, anyhow. Or swine-tossing."

Kreig felt his eyebrows knit. Swine-tossing?

Before he could ask her to explain what in the world she was talking about, she'd already gone into the shop, causing a little bell over the door to chime pleasantly. Kreig steeled his spirits and followed suit.

The inside of the shop, much like the outside, was somehow both charming and chaotic. Somehow larger on the inside than the outside, Kreig found himself completely unsurprised by the pile of bikes in a corner, each either rusted past the point of no return or otherwise ruined. Why wouldn't the owner keep these outside? Or, better yet, at some garbage dump. Though, ignoring those, the actual bikes on display were certainly promising. Not that Kreig knew enough about bikes to make any real judgments about them. But, since Erica seemed happy enough, he couldn't exactly say they were bad by any means.

The shopkeep did not appear. Even after waiting for a few minutes, the man gave no hints of meeting them.

Erica seemed to have expected this, since she absently went around poking at bikes, each shinier than the last. Kreig would really have liked to fully leave the bike-shopping to her, but she kept dragging him over to look at the bikes with her. Yes, green was a nice color. So was blue. No, the marks weren't too gaudy.

At around the fifteen-minute mark, the man finally appeared from behind a desk. Lo and behold, the man was a woman.

She seemed to be about thirty years old, face wrinkled enough to suggest a higher age. However, her body and form made it clear that she was still rather young. Especially her musculature told of many hours spent toiling, probably on bikes. Looking at the confounded apparatuses, Kreig couldn't tell what could possibly be done to fix one, but the shopkeep probably knew that better herself.

Clothing-wise, she wore a dirty apron stained with oil, a pair of gloves, some protective eyewear and the like. She looked much more like a mechanic than a shopkeeper.

"Erica! Did someone steal your bike again?" Her voice was somehow both hard and melodic, deep down in her chest, rumbling and strong. Almost male. Her brown eyes turned to Kreig. Not a trace of fear in them. Only mischievous curiosity. "And this is?"

"Kreig, he's my— Well, we're here to buy a bike. For him. S—so don't get any funny ideas!"

"Oh?" A catlike grin spread across her tanned face. "Really? Well, with how many bikes you've lost, I don't suppose you'll have any trouble finding a bike for Mr. Tall-and-handsome, will you?"

"Hey! Stop having funny ideas; they're not funny! We're just—just two pals, out on the town!"

The shopkeeper shrugged exaggeratedly. "Of course. I bet you even took him to your favorite café before this, didn't you?"

Erica's face tightened and she swallowed hard. "Did you follow us?"

"Indeed I did, on my newly developed invisible bike. I saw *everything*!"

Erica gasped, arms flailing up in the air. "Argh, an *invisible bike*! I can't believe this! Has the government contacted you yet to put atomic bombs on them?! Or was it lizard people who tried to convince you to create this abomination of a two-wheeled vehicle?"

The shopkeeper stared at her. Hard. "Yes."

Erica almost fainted.

Meanwhile, Kreig was wondering how in the world an invisible bike might work. Did it also make the rider invisible, or did it just look like the rider was floating above the air? Furthermore, why would lizard people want such a strange vehicle?

"All right, enough about that. I'm sorry to say that I won't be able to sell you any invisible bikes, but I can definitely get you something to take you where you need to go," the shopkeeper said, striding over the floor and over to the bikes. "So? You a professional ox-tosser or something?"

"No, I simply want an easy way of commuting."

She nodded sharply. "Right. With your weight, being a professional biker would probably be pretty bad. Muscle or not, if you're too heavy, you'll just hold yourself back. So, a simple, normal bike, then?"

"If possible," Kreig affirmed.

She frowned. "'Fraid I can't give you that. You look, what? Three hundred, four hundred pounds? Most bikes would buckle under that, mister. But, lucky for you, I *do* have this new ultra-thick bike I made for shits and giggles. I have no idea if it'll actually be able to hold you—it really depends on how much of you is muscle and what's fat—but if it doesn't hold, you'll at least make for a nice experiment." She placed her fists on her hips. "Well, what say you? Ready to take Pigsty out for a run?"

Blinking, Kreig tried to decipher what she just told him. There was apparently a bike called Pigsty, and she wanted him to ride it for science.

Normally, if Kreig felt this confused about something, he'd decline out of pure apprehension. However, after hearing this woman talk about the bike for so long, how could he possibly refuse?

"Of course."

"I—I'm coming along!" Erica said, appearing out of nowhere. She didn't seem as dazed as she was before, though some parts of that state of mind still lingered. "I need to see it. Pigsty. And—and also the invisible bike. It is *imperative* that I see the truth, even if it may hurt!"

The shop owner stared at Erica for a few seconds before grinning and giving a thumbs-up. "Sure thing."

As promised, the shop owner led them farther into the back of the shop, where a number of unusual and unfinished bikes made a massive maze. Pigsty, the bike, was hanging on a blue bike stand, and as she alluded to, the bike was truly thick. Kreig wasn't confident in comparing it to anything, but if he just looked at the difference between Pigsty and a normal bike standing beside it, it seemed to be about twice as beefy.

This in itself seemed like a modern marvel, but it also appeared to be outfitted with other things and gadgets as well, such as a pair of massive springs beneath the saddle and extended handlebars.

Erica would surely have been very interested in it if she hadn't been occupied with looking for the invisible bike.

The shopkeeper seemed entertained by this, which Kreig didn't quite understand, since she *had* promised the existence of an invisible bike. As a matter of fact, Kreig might also have been looking for it if he hadn't been occupied with Pigsty.

Using strength Kreig hadn't expected from her, the shopkeep hefted Pigsty off the rack and placed it on the ground. Then, with Kreig and Erica following, she led it outside.

"All right, here he is. Have a go, buddy."

She handed him the handlebars. With Kreig only holding onto the handle, the bike buckled over. Realizing this probably wasn't what it was supposed to do, Kreig lifted it up by the saddle. There. Now it was standing properly.

Both Erica and the shopkeeper were staring at him. "Yeah. Just hop on."

. . . Hop on.

According to what Kreig had seen, when biking, you'd usually sit on the saddle and have your hands on the handlebars. *Yeah. Right. Now to actually do it.*

Thankfully, the saddle was quite low for his height, so Kreig could sit on it while still keeping his feet on the ground. Although Kreig knew that this wasn't the usual state for biking, he liked to keep his feet on the ground. It felt good. It kept him connected to his God. Though he still wasn't sure what the second step was.

Erica pointed at the pedals. Kreig glanced down at them. Oh, yeah. His feet were supposed to go there, right?

He put his feet on the pedals and promptly fell over.

He looked up from where he lay tangled up with Pigsty. Erica and the shopkeeper looked down at him. "Kreig . . . have you ever ridden a bike?"

Kreig gulped.

New theory: Kreig really must be some sort of time-traveling caveman. That can be the only explanation as to how he's able to go until his late twenties, possibly early thirties, without ever learning how to ride a bike. Either that or he just grew up in a region so poor that he never had access to a bike. Assuming such a place still exists.

Erica racked her brains for an explanation while Kreig fumbled around with the bike, trying his best to get back on it despite his legs trembling.

In other words . . . Kreig grew up in a poor, rural village in some random country—maybe Russia? He *was* very pale, after all—where everybody knew everybody and that kinda stuff. There, he only did two things: physical labor, obviously, and art. Then, one day, some guy, probably a government official or undercover agent or something, came around on some mission or whatnot and stumbled across Kreig, who was clearly a modern master of arts.

Whether he then kidnapped Kreig or not was uncertain, but what *was* clear was that Kreig went on to become some highly valued secret artist for only the highest echelons of society. To the rest, he was a total unknown.

Well, it was *this* theory or that Kreig was a time-traveling caveman. Either one was equally likely.

After falling one more time from the bike, Kreig finally just put it to the side, turning to Erica with a desolate look on his face. "Forgive me, but I doubt I could ever tame such a contraption."

"Huh?" Those words roused Erica from her mindless pondering. "Oh, no, you're not! I can't let you join civilized society without knowing how to ride a bike. Come, come, I'll teach you, fair disciple . . ."

Somehow, her words didn't seem to comfort Kreig in the least.

"Okay, look, you almost got it right, so it won't be any trouble learning, okay? First, you sit on the saddle—yeah just like that, and then you hold on to the handlebar. Easy. But any old sod could do that." In a protective measure, she put her hands on the handlebar, right on top of Kreig's hands. "So, the thing about riding bikes is that you're pretty much surviving on momentum and balance. You really can't hold it upright if you're standing still, so what you need to do is . . ."

At this, Erica tried to create some momentum by pushing the bike forward. However, with Pigsty being an immensely heavy bike and Kreig being somehow even heavier, she wasn't able to do more than puff and grunt.

"Y—you need to move the bike. Get it rolling and stuff." She turned her head to look Kreig in the eye. "Got it?"

"I believe I might."

Erica wasn't sure if her eyes were playing tricks on her, but his face seemed a little flushed. Wonder why that might be?

"Well, just kick yourself going and I'll be right behind you, okay?"

He nodded sharply. A small kick to the ground brought Pigsty to a gentle roll. One more and it was moving at an easy gait.

"A little faster, Kreig! And then put up your feet!"

With a final kick and the bike at an easy roll, Kreig folded his feet, placing them on the pedals. In a matter of seconds the bike, formerly stable and sure, began to tremble and jerk, and the handlebar wobbled back and forth in Kreig's white-knuckled grip. He was able to keep the bike rolling for around five seconds before it buckled out under him, the handlebar giving a final twist to the right to end the trial.

Kreig huffed, pulling his long black hair out of his face.

"Hey, that was great!" Erica cheered. "A few more times and I'm sure you'll get it right!"

He looked over to her, his face briefly flushed with shame and reluctance. Then, upon seeing her excited face, it seemed to simply wash away. "Yeah, all right."

Teaching Kreig to ride a bike took an hour or two, and this was solely due to Erica's excitement. Had she not been as supportive as she was, Kreig would surely have given up the second he realized he couldn't instinctually ride a bike. But that was not the case. No, instead, he made good progress, often with leaps and bounds, until he was finally able to ride the bike for several minutes at a time, his abilities only hampered by his mild fear of falling.

The rest, about where to keep his gaze and how the traffic rules worked, could surely be taught on the way home.

"You'll buy Pigsty, then?" the shopkeeper—Anna—asked, her eyes glimmering. Erica wasn't sure if she had been excited by greed or something else, but seeing an acquaintance happy made her happy as well.

"Of course! You will, won't you?"

"Yes. Assuming I have enough to purchase it."

A fair assumption that worked out well. The clock said 3:26, and it had only taken him like four hours to get a bike. A very reasonable amount of time. And so, they headed home. Had Kreig been a bit more proficient with the bike, Erica might have requested that he pedal while she sat on the carrier behind him. However, since she wasn't much interested in breaking an arm this particular day, she decided to ignore that idea and just spend time walking with Kreig.

During this time, Erica tried her best to teach Kreig the various rules that came with riding a bike. Sure, lots of guys liked to just follow their own rules and ignore everything else, always assuming that the cars would simply swerve out of their way, but this was not something Erica could accept. The day Kreig became such a miscreant was the day she gave up trying to figure him out.

This didn't go all that well, however, since Kreig had pretty much nothing to stick it to. He could understand the words she said, but placing them in a context was impossible.

And so, Erica hatched a plot. A simple, easy plot. She led Kreig to her house.

Her home was really just a small apartment she rented cheaply. It had a good placement and was pretty high off the ground, so she liked it even though it was nowhere near as big and nice as Kreig's.

She left Kreig below the apartment complex to keep an eye on his bike. Bike thieves were a bit of a problem in this particular city, but with Kreig holding down the fort, not a single soul could possibly try to steal it. Meanwhile, Erica fetched her own bike.

Her bike was of the simple sort, with its only real marking being that it was entirely yellow. Other than that, it was a normal lady's bike.

"Up for a ride around town?" Erica asked with a glint in her eye.

Kreig fiddled with a stray strand of hair. "I suppose so."

She slapped him on the back two times. "Hey, no worries; you'll do great! And if you don't, I'll protect you. Promise." A sly grin found its way onto her face while Kreig flushed.

"If you say so, then . . . I will trust you."

And so, they biked.

CHAPTER 28

PAPARAZZI

Ah. That's a bit troublesome.

As the two lovebirds left the apartment complex behind, Jay ducked in behind a bend. She crossed her arms, trying to withhold a grimace. God. Who would've thought that the monster had a girl? Or that they could be so gross together without even kissing? Yuck.

Even worse, this hardly let her learn anything. Taking a few sneaky pictures had been a good way to bolster her growing folder of evidence, but it still wasn't enough by any means. In her very well-thought-out planning on how best to become a pseudo-paparazzi, she had never considered the fact that Wiedermann might actually get a bike. Maybe he sensed her following him? Either that or he had already planned on getting a bike and was just too distracted by his mate to even consider that someone might be behind him.

Either that or he was already used to being followed, but Jay heavily doubted that. If the government had no way to contain him, why would the useless bastards even care about what he was doing now?

Though, of course, there was always the possibility that he sensed her presence and chose to get a bike specifically to leave her in the dust. If he was on a bike, Jay wouldn't have as many opportunities to take notes on his behavior or take pictures of whatever he was doing.

Jay gulped where she stood with her back to the building. Absently, she paged through the pictures she had already taken and the notes she'd written.

Somewhere in her heart, she almost wanted to alert that poor lady who thought she could be the beauty to his beast. However, any such notion was easily dispelled by the thought that if someone was stupid enough to get close to that obvious baddie, they probably deserved the just deserts of such a man's actions. No, it was much better to just keep her eyes on the prize. If she went out of her way to warn the woman—or, rather Erica, according to the rudimentary lip-reading she did from a distance—it may have adverse effects on her plans in general.

It was best to leave that woman to her fate in favor of the world as a whole.

Jay stopped at a specific image. She broke out into a grin.

It showed the massive man lying on his ass beside an almost equally massive bike. Jay giggled to herself. She was damn lucky her target was the kind of man who couldn't even bike properly.

Even more so, from what she had seen from previous stakeouts outside his room with a pair of binoculars, he seemed to have some form of morals, which was a good thing: if he ever came across her or realized she was following him, he'd probably just forgive her. *Heh.* Though she really didn't want to stay around there for too long into the night, since this was part of the route her mother took when stumbling home from "work."

Jay shook her head, bringing herself back to reality. *Right.*

Now that she thought about it, she really ought to follow Wiedermann's siblings (?) as well, just to make sure they wouldn't pose a problem for her future plans. She already knew the woman worked as a police officer of some sort, since she always came out wearing a uniform in the morning, but the man was a bit of a mystery. One of these days, she'd do well to follow him, too.

Though, before that, she really needed to get ahold of a bike. Otherwise, she wouldn't have a snowball's chance in hell of continuing to follow him. And there was only one person she could ask for that.

Jay groaned. If she headed home right now, she might be able to catch her mother before she headed out for her night shift.

Putting away her things into her backpack, she left the apartment complex behind. With Wiedermann occupied with his mistress, Jay was pretty confident that he wouldn't try to burn the country to the ground anytime soon. Probably. Assuming that the poor woman didn't decide to flip her lid at the last minute and slap him or something. It would be a peculiar end for such a date, but Jay was sure the man deserved it.

After a few minutes of walking, she found herself outside her front door. She tried the handle. The door slid open with a single creaking whistle, proving her mother was indeed home. Jay took a steadying breath. She stepped inside.

There were sounds coming from the kitchen. Jay put her backpack beside the couch and entered. She found her mother humming some small melody while gently frying vegetables, rice, and what seemed to be some sort of fish all in one pan. Jay scrunched her nose at the smell. She hated fish. Her mother turned to her with a small, apologetic smile.

"I'm sorry, dear; I know you're not much for fish, but it's important for your body," she said sweetly, her eyebrows pinching together. "You'll eat it, won't you?"

Jay suppressed a sneer in the face of what she knew to be an opportunity. "What vegetables did you put in there?" If that thing had onions, not even Jay could put on a brave face and eat it.

Her mother tried to smile soothingly, giving a wink. "No onions, guaranteed!" She turned back to the frying pan, thumbing her lip. "Onions are also good for you. Especially young girls like you."

"It makes my breath smell," Jay said dryly. She eyed her mother. Wasn't there something stupid and vaguely religious her mother should be saying right about now?

"God prefers His subjects to be strong, you know?" Ah. There it was. Her mother nodded deeply to herself, her eyes taking on a wistful glow as she looked out the window. "After all, if even His angels are praying . . ."

"—Then he must be in a real pickle, yeah, I get it." Jay huffed. Hearing her mother talk about her "'angel'" was almost worse than just talking to her normally.

Her mother pouted. "Now you're making fun of me! I know you don't think I saw anything, or that I'm delusional, but I really *did* see him!"

Noticing an opening in her defenses, Jay shot out her demand. "You know, I'd probably believe you if you bought me a bike."

Her mother stared at her. "What?"

Ah. Oops. Yeah, that was a bit too clumsy. Even her slave of a mother needed a little bit more finesse than *that* pathetic attempt. "I, well . . . I'm just saying that if I had a bike, I could get to school much faster. Then I'd have more time left over for studying, and I could get better grades." *And not end up like you.*

Her mother frowned to herself, looking away. "A bike . . ." Her eyes turned to the kitchen around them. Every surface dirty and scrappy, every pot and pan secondhand. Food made from leftovers and dumpster-diving.

Grease-infused wallpaper left from the seventies. Then she looked back at her daughter, standing in front of her with dark eyes full of ill-hidden contempt. She smiled lightly. "Yeah, we can get you a bike. But you promise to study hard, okay? You've been out really late these past days . . . You won't fall back in school, will you?"

Jay grinned, hoping she seemed appreciative when she in reality felt only joy at successfully conning her mother. Maybe she would have felt bad about it if the world wasn't at stake. Or if her mother wouldn't use that money to buy drugs and alcohol if she didn't use it for a bike.

"Thanks. I'd like it by tomorrow." Jay swiveled on her heel to leave the kitchen.

"W—wait!"

Turning to glance over her shoulder, Jay found her mother looking unusually desperate.

"You won't eat together with me?" her mother said. "Like we used to?"

Jay turned back to the hallway. "I'll eat in my room."

Sitting down in front of her computer, Jay breathed a sigh of relief. *Damn. That had been a close one.* She was lucky her mother was a bit dull; otherwise, she might have rejected Jay. If she did, Jay knew many ways of forcing her to bend to her will, but this was the simplest one.

She booted up her computer and headed online. She had a few notifications of upvotes, comments, and replies, so she clicked her way onto her last post. It was a relatively short text post, an update on a post she made a few days back when she first realized the extent of Wiedermann's power. This update was pretty much just an explanation of how she'd be working to dig further into the mystery of Wiedermann, though she obviously omitted his name and location. Wouldn't want any other up-and-coming journalists getting any ideas. Even more importantly, when she would finally release her full and actual article, she didn't want the internet already knowing everything.

This was just a way for her to get advice and reactions and internet points while she worked.

Most of the comments on her update were encouraging her to continue seeking the truth at any cost and to obviously share any updates with them. Which she would obviously do. A select few were telling her to let sleeping tigers lie, or that assuming she knew better than IOCRO might be a bit narcissistic of her. Of course, these sorts of people were both downvoted into oblivion and told to have some faith. And so, Jay felt completely confident in ignoring them.

She checked the traction of her very first post. It seemed it had hit a thousand upvotes overnight. She grinned to herself and prepared to write another post.

She glanced over at her camera. It was a pretty rudimentary thing, bought secondhand at a garage sale.

Should she share a picture or two of him? If she did, then the people doubting her story would surely realize the stupidity of their reluctance. Though saving all of that for the article she was already making an outline of would work much better. By that point, she might even find some way of really documenting his level and race. News of system-tapping technology was always a big thing, and she could vaguely remember hearing that there were talks of some kind of camera able to take pictures including someone's level and race. Though, of course, these pictures were all really blurry, and—even worse—completely in black and white.

There might have been other ways, but IOCRO was pretty secretive about these things. For most of these things, you had to ask an actual Fighter, but even they were under contract.

She cracked her fingers. *All right, let's stop dilly-dallying.* After replying to a few stupid comments with the obvious answers anybody should know, she got to writing her daily report. Hopefully, nobody would try to convince her to "'rescue" that poor woman.

Meanwhile, across the city, a last-minute dinner had been served to a pair of most interested siblings. Kreig sat down at the dinner table, his gaze blank and his cheeks slightly flushed. Sam and George gave each other a pair of sly, knowing grins.

"So?" Sam asked. "How'd it go?"

Kreig absently moved his hand to touch a spot on his cheek. "It was . . . pleasant. Yes."

George nodded at hearing it, smiling almost nostalgically in recognition of the feelings Kreig must have been experiencing. "I know how that is. It feels like you've got butterflies in your stomach, right? Or that you're walking on clouds, or the world seems to shine like you've had too much wine . . ."

"It feels like someone's watching me," Kreig said numbly.

George made a face. "Well . . . of course you do; plenty of people are following you."

Raising her hand excitedly, Sam blurted out, "Yesterday I got to follow you!" She grinned broadly. "It was pretty boring. You should be sterner with your students!"

Kreig shook his head, wringing his hands atop the table. "Not like that. I'm well aware many of your best men ensure my safety at any time. I am most grateful for such attentions. But it feels as though it is someone else."

Frowning, George tried to rack his brains. "Well, that's . . . Does it feel *more* attentive than the typical escort, or is it something else?"

"I'm not sure," Kreig said, shrugging. "All I can tell is that whoever it is, they certainly don't like me."

"That opens the door to many possibilities. It could be that a new recruit simply has it out for you. If that's the case, you really shouldn't worry too much, since you're immune to almost anything such a man can do." He took a slow sip of water, collecting his thoughts. "If it's something else, like a stalker or something, then I'm sure they can't follow you forever. After all, the guys we've got following you are trained to keep their eyes on the crowd as much as on you. If they see someone suspicious, I'm sure they'll make a report on it." He smiled wryly. "Whatever it is, I certainly don't think you should deal with it yourself."

Sam nodded, making a similar expression. "Yeah, uh, leave it to us professionals! We'll break their bones ten times over; I swear it!"

"No need for anything like that," Kreig said placatingly. "It's not even sure it's anything like that. For all I know, it may very well be a student who's got their eye on me."

George nodded at the suggestion. "If that's the situation, it's a whole lot more complicated. We'll want to deter them from following you, but we also don't want them to know the extent of our reach or your importance . . ." He shook his head. "If it comes down to such a situation, we'll try to deal with it as best as we can. But there's no reason to assume something like that. For now, let's just stick to the idea that one of our rookies is being overzealous, all right?"

Although Kreig hardly felt any better, he agreed with it. Ever since he left Erica's apartment, he hadn't felt the presence, so whoever it was was clearly human in some regard. Then, it should be fine, right? He had no reason to fear any human.

Falling to the pacifying words of his siblings, he put the thought of the malicious gaze out of his mind.

CHAPTER 29

COURAGE

The wind rushed past her face with newfound vigor, bringing her past Space Circle Avenue and the police station she had tried to bring Kreig to when they first met. Smiling to herself, Erica gently recalled the first impression she'd had all those months back. *"Crime man,"* sure. Now that Erica thought about it, of all the people she'd ever known, Kreig might just be the *least* disposed to crime. Or even violence, for that matter.

If having to learn to ride a bike at his age didn't make him resort to violence, she was pretty sure he never would. On the matter of his bike, it really was a cool thing. Pigsty. A bike that could carry a whole pigsty's worth of swine.

Not that Kreig was a pig or anything. No, he was more of an ox. Or a stallion. Or a human male.

Very large and very, very handsome.

Flying through the city on her own bike, Erica felt her cheeks heat up just a little. Then she passed the bend they had decided on, and there he stood. His pale eyes fell on her. She smiled and waved from her bike, trying not to fall over.

"Good morning!" Erica said to her former student, now colleague.

"Good morning," he replied in that always-solemn, constantly stoic way. Maybe she should tell him to smile somehow? No, he'd smile when he pleased. Otherwise, it wouldn't be a real smile.

They both got back on their bikes, and Erica let her eyes linger on Kreig's bike for just a second. *Hm.* She hadn't noticed it before, but it almost seemed like the handlebars came with molded handles! Shaped just like Kreig's own hands. Maybe they were custom-bought? Maybe his Russian mafia boss bought them for him? Cool.

As they biked along the path leading out to the edges of the city, she couldn't help but notice Kreig glancing at her every now and then. But whenever she tried to catch his gaze, he always returned it to the path in front of them.

Maybe he had something to say? Kreig could be pretty shy when it came to initiating conversation, so if she just said something mildly conversational, then—

"Do you feel nervous?"

"Huh?" Erica whipped her head to the side to face Kreig, only barely getting control over her bike. "What do you mean?"

He looked down at his handlebars, not even looking ahead as he deftly dodged a pedestrian. "When I first began teaching at Painstone, I can admit I felt rather nervous myself. Uncertain. I hadn't had a formal position in many years. I was afraid that the students might dislike me, or that I may not be up to par with the expectations of my employer." He lifted his gaze once more, meeting hers. "I can only assume that you may be feeling something similar, if not more severely."

"Huh? Me, nervous? No way! I'd never—"

"To the right," Kreig said softly, prompting Erica to glance back to the road that now took a pretty sharp turn to the right.

Once the road straightened out again, she tried again to collect her thoughts, only to find them jumbled. "I mean . . . I've been teaching for years, Kreig. Why should I be nervous?" Realization hit her. "Unless sewer snakes put chemicals in my water . . . Or I'm scared that the students will be just the same as they were all those years ago and nothing has changed . . . Or I've been brainwashed by ultra-intelligent cutlery trying to get me to become their queen!"

Kreig stared at her for a few seconds. "—It could be any one of them."

She nodded back. "Could be any one of them. I can't be sure." She felt her brows pinching together. No, it couldn't be either one. Sure, one or two were likelier than another, but . . . But if she looked deep inside herself and really thought about it, there was only really one option. "I won't become their queen," she whispered to herself. "I won't."

Oh, and now Kreig was looking at her oddly again.

"I'll protect you," he said, only barely loud enough for her to hear.

Erica glanced back at him, trying to still her beating heart. "—From the cutlery?"

He smiled, one of those genuine, slight smiles that you could tell he truly felt it. "Sure. If they ever try anything, or if they make you feel bad, or if they make you think you are incapable of living up to their expectations, I swear to you that I will protect you."

"From the cutlery?"

His smile grew wider. "You will have nothing to fear but their insubordination."

Erica grinned and did a thumbs-up. "Well, if you say so!"

But for how excited she might have seemed externally, internally, she was even more so. Though it did take a slightly different form. She felt giddy and thrilled, filled from the bottom of her toes to the tip of her head with an exhilarating joy. He'd protect her. Sure, sure, but, more than that, he *cared for her*. Whatever he was, whatever his background, whatever his present, he cared for her. Maybe even as much as she cared for him.

During the next fifteen minutes, she rode on a high, feeling as though she were biking on clouds.

Then Painstone reared on the horizon, and all of a sudden, all those bad feelings hit her again.

She hadn't been there in several years. At first, it had just been that she wanted to avoid anyone recognizing her and asking why she left, but then it became a habit, one that she would actively continue. She'd take long detours just to avoid an unwanted glance at its walls, often being late for appointments and meetings. So, upon seeing that dreaded building once more, she couldn't help but feel as though her lungs were filled with swamp water.

She couldn't tell if her heart was going faster or slower than usual—if she felt infernally hot or freezing cold.

A warm fist gently gripped her hand so softly that it felt like an angel's wings brushing past. She looked up.

They were standing outside the gates of Painstone. He stood close to her, as though guarding her against the intrusive gazes of students passing by. His hand tenderly held hers, easily eclipsing it in his own. His other hand fell on her cheek. "It's all right," he said. "I'll protect you."

A warmth seemed to spread from his hand through her cheek, heating up her head and face, then traveling down through her neck and into her chest, purging her drowning lungs of the sewage and bile, leaving her breath easy and light. Then it seemed to warm every edge of her body, before going out through her mouth, where it became a little laughter. She smiled at him.

"Thanks. I'll depend on you."

And then, in the blink of an eye, she was no longer outside the gates but instead inside the school, standing in a little office she would share with the math and physics teacher and the German teacher. For her own part, she would do both English and French. English was especially important for this school since it was, after all, an international school, meaning that many students spoke rudimentary English at best.

She placed her bag on her desk and unloaded a few things as she turned her thoughts over in her mind.

She'd be able to handle it. She would, right? She'd done this once before; she could do it again. In fact, she already had a first assignment all designed and ready. And she'd give them plenty of time to do it, too. It'd be a good way to check their collective capabilities while also giving her ample time to scope out the exceptional and the struggling. That way, she could pick and choose which students needed more or less help, as well as the ones that might want a little more than she had to give.

She drew a deep breath into her light lungs. Yeah. She could do this.

At eight o'clock, she found herself standing outside a classroom. Even where she stood, the loudness of the class inside was all too clear.

Was it too late to back out?

She could just tell Kreig that *Hey, they told me mean things, so I'll go back to college, thanks!*

. . . But then he might try something silly, like telling them not to say mean things. Or something.

Slowly, she balled her hands into fists. She clenched her teeth. No, she could do this. This was a way to start over, to become the teacher she always wanted to be! She couldn't turn back now, at the very last step!

Drawing herself up, she opened the door and stepped inside.

Thirty pairs of owlish eyes turned to her.

Her body froze.

One of these thirty was thinking something different from the rest. After all, one of them recognized her quite well.

Jay sat up a little straighter in her chair. His new flame, was it? Well, well, well . . . Wasn't this quite the turnaround? Not that she actually cared all that much. Even if this woman had something to do with Kreig beyond the obvious, her level was only 1, so she clearly wasn't anything to be scared of.

She also wasn't doing anything. No, while the class slowly collected itself—sitting down, shutting up and staring straight ahead—she just kind of stood there.

Until, finally, she apparently pulled herself together. "G—good morning!"

Yeah, her voice was about as expected. A few different voices replied, "Good morning," but it was scattered and uncertain.

"My name is Erica, and I'll be your English teacher from here on out! From what I've heard, your last teacher was Mrs. Frently, right?" A few people nodded to her alongside a general series of murmurs, one of which Annie directed at Jay herself.

"Hopefully, this one won't be as bad as Mrs. Frently. Or that last substitute."

"Sure," Jay replied curtly.

"I thought today we might get to know each other better, so I was thinking that you all would each write a little story of your own!" Complete silence. "It doesn't have to be long. It can be half a page, so long as you think that it accurately reflects your skill level. Since most students like having a theme, the theme for this story will be *subverted expectations*! So, just make sure something surprising happens, or a situation isn't what it seems, or the lies of a character are brought out. Though do remember that the most important thing is that you have fun writing it!"

Jay tried in vain to suppress a groan. *Oh, god.* A creative writing assignment right off the bat? Was she a sadist or something?

While the rest of the class fished out their computers, Jay tried to think of some way to bypass the whole situation. Maybe she could feign a fainting spell? Or she could say that she was mentally ill so she couldn't handle any assignments? Either way, looking at Annie, the rest of the people in here actually seemed pretty excited to get to work.

Annie, according to what Jay could tell, was someone who enjoyed the creation of stories. When people started writing lots of stories about the portals and Fighters, Jay could remember Annie reading quite a few of them, as though she were preparing to write some biography following them or whatever.

As Annie got to work writing, Jay reluctantly brought out her own computer. The empty document gaped before her.

Even after ten minutes, she hadn't been able to write a single good line. A lot of possible beginnings but nothing concrete. Nothing worth actually pursuing.

But just as she was about to close the document to write something harsh for her followers she heard the faint tick-tock of the woman's heels step up behind her. Then she passed by to lean behind Annie. "Whoa, interesting!" she said in what appeared to be genuine excitement. "You wrote this? You didn't steal it off a dead man's corpse? Whoa . . ."

Then the two of them began trading banter, with the woman telling Annie many tips and tricks, alongside hinting at possible endings and turnarounds. Well, less hinting and more that she just suggested them straight out. Either way, Annie seemed very excited to continue, so the woman soon left her, quickly turning her attention to Jay and her empty paper.

"Having trouble getting started?" she asked in the most sickly sweet voice Jay had ever heard.

"What do you care?" she sneered. "No, seriously. You don't *actually* care, do you? Look, if you just leave me alone, I'll turn in some pretentious dadaistic poem by the end of this class and we won't talk again all semester, okay?"

The woman seemed completely taken aback, freezing for a second. Jay grinned to herself, feeling a sense of victory over the tawny woman.

But then, as though pulling herself together and drawing some strength from deep within, the woman let her eyes rise again. They were as hard as diamonds. "What is your dream, Jay?"

Jay drew her arms across her chest. Something was off. But for now, she didn't have enough ammunition to do anything that'd really get her off Jay's ass. "I want to be a journalist," she answered honestly.

The woman—Erica—made no sign of backing down. "Why do you want to be a journalist?"

That was a pretty private question, Mrs. Wiedermann. "I don't see how that's important."

Then the woman smiled softly. "I became a teacher because I wanted to make sure kids had at least one good teacher growing up. Bad teachers can do a lot of bad, but . . . To a kid, a really good teacher can mean everything."

"I wouldn't know," Jay said dismissively. A lull in the conversation made the silence stretch between them. Jay looked back at her screen. ". . . I just want to expose the truth."

"The truth?"

"Yeah. There's plenty of secrets in the world. Lots of people with secrets who'd do anything to keep them hidden. I hate that. I want to drag them out into the light, to expose their evil to the justice of public opinion. I want—" Jay paused, realizing what the teacher was doing. Her head whipped around furiously, fully expecting the woman to look at her with those dead, uncaring eyes that all teachers had whenever she tried to tell them anything about herself.

Instead, she found a pair of shining, curious eyes looking back at her. "You want?" the woman asked innocently, like a kid asking their parents to continue the bedtime story.

"I—I want . . ." In her head, the answer echoed dully. "It isn't important. It isn't."

The woman smiled sympathetically. "It's okay. You can tell me when you feel more comfortable, all right?" Her words made Jay nod mechanically. "But since you're much more interested in journalism, how about you just write an article instead?"

"An article?" Jay echoed quietly.

"Yeah! I mean, as long as it shows your abilities, I'm really fine with whatever. You promise you'll put your all into it, right?" The woman smiled mischievously and winked.

"Uh, sure," Jay answered dully. Then, after giving a little wave and a wish of good luck, the woman left to go fawn on another student, leaving Jay confused and uncertain. She turned back to the empty document.

"Do whatever you want," huh? Plenty of teachers had told her that in the past when she didn't want to do the normal assignment. But then, just as she turned it in, there was always that one moment of realization where their eyes turned black as coal and they looked like they regretted ever becoming a teacher. And then they would tell her that this wasn't exactly what they meant and only barely let her pass. That was how it was. That was the game.

Jay frowned to herself. *Yeah.* This time it would surely be the same.

"What is your dream?"

Surely . . .

Jay shook her head. She placed her fingers on the keyboard. Though, maybe this time, she could do something a little more lasting. Something that was sure to hurt.

In the document, she wrote, *Some men aren't quite what they seem to be.*

CHAPTER 30

A WARM WELCOME

Throughout his life, Kreig had never been one to ignore his instincts. In times of dire battle and uncertainty, it was often only his instincts that kept him alive.

But now he found himself actively ignoring the little voice in the back of his head that told him that whoever watched him at night, peeping through his blinds and observing with animosity, was someone to be wary of. That he had to act. That he was a sitting duck, waiting for the end of the world to come to him.

The voice that told him not to relax too quickly.

Kreig stood up and shook his groggy head free of his morning thoughts. Parting the curtains, he found the sun rising slowly among the many buildings of the city, seemingly climbing between them like a big red octopus. For a few seconds, he simply let himself bask in the red dawn sky. If he looked down at the usual spots outside his window, he found a few presences with their attention trained on him.

However, not *that one.*

That particular presence seemed to have an unusual habit of never following him completely around the clock or at school. Sometimes, he could even leave Painstone only to find the presence watching him once he got home. At other times, the presence would leave him for entire days at a time, making him feel as though it was finally over. But then it'd just come back, more passionate than ever.

An enemy he could neither see nor fight. The fact of the matter was that should he ever try to actively hunt down the presence, the organization that imprisoned him when he first returned would surely capture him once again. And for good reason.

His only way to deal with the presence was through the help of others.

After a few seconds of staring at the rising dawn, Kreig got dressed and left his room. He prepared a simple but homely breakfast for himself and his siblings. It was, surprisingly, not in any otherworldly style. His siblings were obviously very interested in the cuisine of the other world, but by this point, Kreig no longer wanted that to be all that he knew. So, he'd been spending his time learning about Earth food. Just simple stuff, things almost everyone knew.

Like bacon and eggs, or pancakes. The only issue Kreig had been able to note so far was that there was no one definition of any dish, especially not the breakfast types.

He should have considered this before, since it was the same with the otherworldly dishes, but when he faced with the fact that there were thick pancakes, thin pancakes, small pancakes, big pancakes, and everything in between, he couldn't help but feel overwhelmed. It made the matter of learning these new dishes slightly harder, but he was an avid learner.

Nowadays, most of the food he served at home was Earth dishes. Some from his home country, others from countries whose existence he had forgotten. Most of the time, he simply picked dishes that seemed nice.

As of yet, not a single person who ate his food had ever complained. Maybe they were just being nice, but knowing that he could experiment with foods without forcing them into fasting felt good.

Just as Kreig flipped a little egg into a so-called over easy, Sam entered the kitchen. She took a big sniff of the aromatic atmosphere. "Heyyy, is that eggs and bacon?" Grinning, she strode over to peek at the frying pan. "You know I like mine sunny, right? Fried on the bottom, none on top?"

"Yes," Kreig answered simply. He deftly cracked another egg into the pan. In all honesty, he couldn't really understand why one kind of fried egg was different from another. It was still a fried egg, right? The only way to make the egg different would be to fry it to the point where the yolk hardened, which just so happened to be how George wanted his egg. Kreig didn't know why, but Sam seemed positively disgusted by this. Same with how George wanted his meat fully cooked through-and-through. Was there something wrong with being cautious?

Right as Sam took a seat by the table, George entered, almost as though he had heard Kreig's thoughts. He gave a quick wave to his siblings before heading over to the cupboards to put plates and cutlery on the table.

Within a few minutes, breakfast was served, with all three of them sitting and eating. Kreig's eggs were scrambled, since it allowed for more varied seasoning combinations.

And for a second, they just ate in silence.

"Kreig," George said a little strangely. Their eyes met. "Are you aware that your six-month anniversary is coming up?"

"My what?" Kreig echoed hesitantly.

A smile found its way onto George's lips. "Of coming home, I mean. To Earth."

Kreig swallowed. Had it been that long already? Six months . . . Half a year. Back in the otherworld, six months would barely be a drop in the sea. Especially not if he spent that time fighting. All those years he spent back there felt like some thick, muddy soup he could barely even perceive. But this short time that he had spent on Earth was completely different. It felt clear, honest, and, most of all, pleasant.

His time in the prison had been pleasant. His time studying was pleasant. His time with his siblings even more so.

It felt like two completely different yet equally long lives. And still, it had only been six months.

That meant he had dozens upon dozens of lifetimes left to spend with his family and friends.

"Is that so?" he answered, feeling a warm emotion spread through his mind.

Sam banged the table and stood up. "What?! Seriously? Dude, we *have* to do something, like a—like a party! Or just a dinner? I dunno, but . . . we gotta do *something*, right? Like, I'll admit I don't even know who we'd invite, but we've gotta do this. Or something. Unless you don't want to, which is totally fine, but if we do that, then I still want us to at least watch a movie together. Maybe."

George nodded while wearing an expression that seemed to suggest he had been planning on suggesting something similar before she grabbed the limelight. "Well . . . Kreig? How do you feel about having a dinner party of some sort? You can invite anyone you'd like."

A dinner party. Just him, his family, and anyone else. Maybe he could invite the presence?

Kreig chuckled to himself. "I believe it sounds lovely."

"All right!" Sam shouted, pumping a fist. "Wait, who are we gonna invite?"

George took a bite of his hard-fried egg, chewed, and swallowed. "We'll leave it to Kreig. The anniversary is in three days, this Friday, so you should have all the time in the world to get ahold of whoever you want visiting. If you'd rather we send invites, we can do that instead."

"No, I'd gladly tell them in person."

And so, breakfast concluded, leaving Kreig to figure out who he might want to invite. Of course, there were Sam and George. Not bringing them would be a crime. Other than that . . .

Kreig left his thoughts to stew as he biked toward Painstone, joining up with Erica along the way.

"A dinner party? Like, a ball or something?"

"I couldn't tell you. I'm no clearer on the subject than you are," Kreig replied, increasing his speed to bike in front of Erica as another bike passed on the other side. "Whatever it is, I seem expected to invite people I know. Not that I know too many."

Erica absently tapped her bike bell. "Hmm . . . Well, you know me, right?"

He looked her up and down. "Would you like to come to the dinner party?"

"Sure!" she said sweetly.

"Then you are invited. This Friday at six, I believe," Kreig said, hoping that this date had been decided on amongst his siblings and not just pulled out of nowhere. That was one guest done and accounted for. By all means, this encounter did give him a measuring stick to judge everyone else he might invite by. If it was okay for him to invite his tutor, then he should also be able to invite Darius, with whom he actually had a session later this evening.

"I'll be there," she said in an odd, wistful voice. "Though, uh, one question?" She furrowed her brows. "What's the dinner party for? Is it like a birthday or an anniversary, or is it to celebrate the upcoming resurrection of the snake king?"

"The snake king is returning?" Kreig asked in genuine surprise. "I was certain I had slain him . . ." But when he looked at Erica again to ask her to elaborate, he instead found her face a perfect blank slate, kind of like a sheep that had no idea where the rest of the herd went. "Ah," he muttered. She was just saying something strange again; she wasn't *actually* talking about the snake king. Though one never knew with her . . . "It is the anniversary of my return."

"Oh, cool!" she said, seemingly completely oblivious of Kreig's mutterings. "What'd you return from? War or something?"

Kreig felt his body go cold. "S—something like that," he mumbled, hoping she wouldn't ask any more about it.

"Hmm. Okay, gotcha," she said, and by the way she was looking, if she'd had a pen and paper, she would surely be jotting something down. For a few minutes, she seemed deeply enraptured in whatever she was thinking about, which really could be anything, until, finally, she perked up again. "You know, you were right."

"About what?" Kreig asked, hoping she wouldn't say something incomprehensible again.

She made a movement in the air with her hand. "The students and stuff. It's only been a few weeks, but . . . it feels good, you know? They aren't too loud, they do their work, they listen pretty well, and they aren't too mean. Well, most of them, I guess."

"Who's being mean to you?" Kreig asked a bit more forcefully than originally intended. For some reason, when he imagined the event of a student being mean to her, he couldn't help but feel an intense need to protect her from that student, to do *something* to help her. He'd already given her a small blessing of bravery on her first day, so maybe one of intimidation might scare away the mean student. Either that or he'd have to get involved himself.

"Hm? Oh! Uh, no, it isn't . . ." Erica's words turned into mumbles as she looked away. When she looked back at Kreig, he found her eyes unusually uncertain. "You promise you won't do something, right?" He nodded at her. "Well, it's this girl—Jay, I think she's called. She was a little mean the first day, and even now she kinda avoids me, I think. But I think I'm getting through to her, so no worries there! Whenever I see her working on her article, she seems really into it, so if I can just cultivate that, I think she can turn into a real model student."

"Jay . . ." Kreig turned the name over in his head and found that it actually hit a bell. "Yes, I have her as well. Scrawny little girl. Despite that, she seems intent on trying to keep up with the rest. A surprisingly hard worker. I believe I saw her hanging around Gerald on my first day, but ever since then, they have seemed almost hostile to each other."

"Gerald is that German kid, right?" Erica piped in. "I don't speak German, but he's been making really good strides in English lately. He's almost fluent!"

Gerald . . . He counted as a friend, didn't he?

As the two of them rolled onto the school's grounds, Kreig found his eyes drawn to where Gerald sat talking with a girl he could swear he recognized somehow. She was around his age, with brown hair tied up behind her head and clear green eyes. And where the two of them sat, they seemed so perfectly ordinary. Just two teenagers, making the most of their young lives.

They were friends, yes, but Gerald was still only a kid. He had a future there, one he could live completely unrelated to the otherworld.

Kreig and Gerald had barely talked ever since the first day, and the reason for that was simple. Although they would always be friends, their lives were too separate. The life Gerald led would be better off if it weren't connected to Kreig's. Maybe in ten years or so, they might connect once more, but until then, Gerald would be better off on his own.

He was part of Kreig's life just as how Kreig was part of his, but the lives they led from now on would be separate. Kreig was a man and Gerald remained a boy.

That was what they had decided upon, and that was an agreement Kreig intended to keep, no matter his sentiments.

The day that followed moved rather quickly, with Kreig now so used to his work that he could do it without giving it much thought. He couldn't really tell what his students thought of him, but compared to his first few lessons, they seemed much more relaxed now, often laughing and talking amongst themselves even while he addressed them all. He didn't mind it.

They were kids, not soldiers. They could afford to have fun and goof off, even to the point of laziness. At one point, Kreig might have looked upon this with a grown-up's ire, but now he just saw it as charming. They had something he had only had in a time before time, but he felt no jealousy. They had their lives, as he had his.

After school concluded, he had a quick session with Erica before heading over to Darius.

"I would be happy to attend," Darius answered coolly. It was 5:55, and the session had only just ended. "I'd love to bring the wife, though she has always told me not to get her involved in my work. You understand, don't you?"

"Of course," Kreig replied, removing his jacket from the coat hangers in Darius's hall. "You may choose to bring or exclude whomever you please."

Darius smiled. "Good. Will you be making the dinner?"

"As always." He couldn't imagine leaving anybody else to it.

"Then I will have nothing to complain about. I can't say I've received too many reports from the surveillance team, but from what I hear, you've got a real knack for cooking. You haven't thought about becoming a professional cook?"

"It's all in the skill. I couldn't imagine lying to someone like that."

Darius's smile faltered slightly as Kreig realized his mistake. "Kreig, we've talked about it, haven't we? Just having a system isn't enough to become a master at anything. All it does is allow Fighters to overcome the natural limits of human ability. But to get to that point, you need tenacity, hard work, creativity . . . anything becoming a master typically requires." He paused briefly. "But I've told you all that before."

"I know," Kreig replied sadly. "It's hard to . . . to change one's mind, I suppose."

Slowly, Darius's face softened into a smile once more. "Don't worry too much about it. You'll get there in due time."

Kreig rubbed the back of his neck. "Thank you. For . . . for everything."

"You say it as though I'm about to die," Darius said with a chuckle. "Well, you'd better be off. Wouldn't want your siblings to wait too long. We all have our schedules to keep."

"Of course. See you next wee— On Friday. See you on Friday."

"I'll see you there. And don't forget I'm lactose-intolerant!"

Kreig waved as he left, slowly closing the door behind him.

For a few seconds, he just stood there outside the door. He brought one of his hands to his chest. There, his heart beat slowly and softly, just beneath the skin and flesh and bone and white roots. Kreig could remember dismantling creatures that had been heavily influenced by the roots. Creatures who had their heart hidden in twining roots thicker than the largest arteries.

Roots weren't edible or even tasty, for that matter. According to his beliefs, the only thing Kreig could do upon finding roots in an animal he had killed was to set that body aflame. If he intended to eat it, he first had to remove the roots—every single one of them—and burn them separately. That was the only way to purify the body and to return the roots to the earth.

His breath grew heavy and quick. Kreig shook his head, hoping to rid it of his intrusive thoughts.

But as he stood there, unwillingly reliving his past, he remembered that there was someone more. A person he had promised dinner to. He had almost forgotten her in the hubbub of his exciting but mundane life. Even better, he had something for her.

He deftly fished his phone out of his pocket. It was an interesting little thing that worked not through magic but instead through technology.

Now, if he could only get it to work.

He turned it on by pressing a button on the side. That much he knew. Then, with uncertainty rivaled only by children and people of his own age range, he navigated to the "phone" part, just like how his siblings had shown him. There, a small list of names shone up at him. He pressed *George*.

The phone in his hand beeped a few times until, finally, it blipped and the screen changed. A voice rang out from the phone.

"*Hello? Kreig, is everything all right?*" George said from inside the phone.

Kreig turned the phone in his hand a few times, looking at it with no little amount of trepidation. "George, I will be coming home late. I aim to—"

"*I can't really hear you, are you—Kreig, try holding the phone up to your ear.*"

Kreig blinked a few times. Then, slowly, he brought the phone to his ear.

"*Can you hear me? Try saying something,*" the phone blasted in his ear.

Kreig held it at a small distance from his ear. "George, I will be coming home late. I aim to invite yet another friend to the party."

"*Is that so? Great!*" There was a short pause where Kreig could faintly hear George talking to someone else away from the phone. "*One question, though: when will you be home? Should we eat without you?*"

"I shouldn't be gone too long."

"*Well . . . all right. We'll wait for you, then. Goodbye.*"

"Goodbye." Kreig stared at the phone for a few seconds. Then, abruptly, the phone blipped and the screen shut down. Kreig shrugged to himself and placed the phone in his pocket again. *Now, then.* He'd better get going.

Biking there was a bit different from when Kreig usually biked. It was dark and cars streaked past, anxious to get home on time, people stumbled about, mostly just interested in getting wherever they were going, and hopefully a little faster than those who weren't going anywhere. Kreig, by comparison, was neither in a hurry nor lackadaisical. He simply went where he was going, remembering the streets only barely.

And then he was there. Standing in front of that old run-down little home housing only a lone woman who looked so much older than she really was.

Mrs. Willowgrove. The poor widowed mother of Peter Willowgrove.

Kreig stepped up to the door, noting curiously how the garden seemed to have been given a new life even in this late autumn. The weeds that had previously overgrown every edge of the garden seemed banished, replaced with friendly vines and blooming seasonal flowers. He turned back to the door and gave it a few knocks.

A couple of seconds passed before the door finally opened, showing the face of a woman Kreig only barely recognized. Her eyes were bright and blue like a cloudless sky, with her warm face only showing the slightest hints that she had ever had wrinkles. She looked young. And as her eyes fell on him, they lit up like stars and she beamed. "Kreig! How pleasant. Do step inside and get out of the cold, won't you?"

She opened the door for him. "Thank you," he said, still feeling a bit numb. It felt as though it had been less than a month since he'd met her last, although he rationally knew it had been at least three.

But looking at her, it was as though she was a completely new woman. The inside of her home told the same tale.

Previously decrepit and run-down, bearing more cobwebs than care, the house now seemed to hold a shine and a luster to it. Every visible surface was polished and clean, every nook and cranny cleared of spiderwebs. It was, in a word, clean.

"I can tell you're surprised," Mrs. Willowgrove said with a sly smile. "But you really shouldn't be. It's been so long since I could just breathe out, and . . . Oh, Lieutenant! There you are," she said, and just as Kreig was about to feel strangely duped, she leaned down and picked up a little thing off the ground. When she then turned around, Kreig found her arms occupied with carrying a very large and very fluffy white cat. "This here is Lieutenant Claws. When I got him from the pound, he looked like a scraggly ball of webbing, but now he's really quite handsome. Here— would you care to hold him?"

Kreig gaped at the feline thing. "No, that's all right. I've never been much good with animals."

She held the cat toward him. Its large, blue eyes blinked at him curiously. Kreig gulped. Silently, he brought out his hands and took a weak hold of the cat. Mrs. Willowgrove released her hold of it, leaving Kreig alone to hold it. Noticing that it seemed a bit unhappy, he tried to hold it against his chest. It dug its paws into him. Slowly, he caressed its back. He hoped to God he was doing it right.

"Mm, I'd say you're quite the natural," Mrs. Willowgrove teased. "It's almost dinnertime, so I would feel guilty bringing you tea . . . Would you join me for dinner, perhaps?"

Kreig shook his head, still unsure whether to let the cat down or not. "No, I told my siblings I would return for dinner."

"Is that so?" she said. "Well, that's quite the shame. Is there nothing else I can do for you? I'd feel rather silly as a hostess if I couldn't entertain you with anything but my cat . . ."

Kreig shook his head, stopping once he noticed how the cat had started batting at his hair. "I came to invite you to a dinner party. If you have time, that is."

Her face lit up. "A dinner party? Well, why didn't you say so? I'd be delighted to attend! When is it?"

"This Friday at six."

"This Friday . . ." She hummed for a second. "I'll be sure to attend! I don't suppose I'll be the only guest? No, of course not. Though I'll have to leave the Lieutenant at home . . . Well, it'll all work out in the end, won't it?" She smiled broadly. "Now, then, you shouldn't keep your siblings waiting, and neither should I keep my dinner waiting. The Lieutenant can get quite fussy if he isn't fed at the proper time."

"Of course," Kreig answered, wondering to himself why the cat seemed so intent on locking eyes with him. It was starting to get creepy. "Then I'll bid you farewell," he said, carefully putting the cat on the floor. It scampered off only after giving a final, longing look at him.

"I'll see you there, love. And don't forget to say hello to your dear siblings from me," she said.

"I won't forget," Kreig replied.

As promised, once Kreig got home, he told his siblings about who would be attending and their preferences. The dinner was largely spent considering possible foods for the event including starters, main course, and dessert. In the end, since Erica would be present, it would be a bad idea to dish out the best foods the otherworld had to offer. Instead, they would simply make do with regular Earth food. Sam wasn't quite happy with this, since she had acquired an affinity for the odd portal foods, but after ensuring that one of her favorite dishes would be on the menu, she was satisfied.

Three days later, the dinner party finally loomed before them.

CHAPTER 31

DINNER, TOGETHER

Long forgotten were his days of battle, of rising at dawn, getting so lost in his fight for survival that the concept of eating at certain times was completely forgotten. Falling and falling and falling into his own void of a mind, acting but not thinking.

Now he remembered those days.

He had been cooking since the crack of dawn, when he had put a large piece of meat in a cold-water bath. Then he had spent an hour or so baking a few sponge cakes, which he left to cool on a rack. During the few minutes he had before he had to get to work, he whipped up a couple of sauces that could stand in the fridge for a few hours.

His siblings, equally stressed, hurried to clean up the apartment at least somewhat and had likewise forgotten to eat breakfast. To their credit, most of the mess in the apartment was contained within their fantasy-themed bedrooms, so a vast swath of the cleaning was purely on the surface. Regardless, the number of hidden dust-bunnies was both surprising and barbaric.

And then they all had to go to work, since it was a Friday and taking a day off so suddenly was out of the question.

When they returned again in the evening, Kreig did so with Erica in tow. She was dressed in a sweet little thing that wouldn't look out of place among other teachers at a school, but there in the setting of an apartment, she looked positively formal. And positively pretty, if Kreig was to give his own opinion.

As Kreig prepared to cook as he had never cooked before, Erica joined him in the small kitchen. He wasn't sure what to tell her. He would love some help, especially from her, but at the same time, he couldn't afford to have the whole operation hampered by her inability to keep up with him. She soothed his worries. "Don't worry; I'll just be washing the dishes while you do your magic!"

He couldn't have asked for a better arrangement.

Really, Erica didn't need to be there so early at all—she was a guest, not a hostess—but she had insisted. Somehow, she considered this to be her fight as well, and Kreig couldn't find it in him to deny her. He did enjoy her company quite a bit.

So, he turned his attention back to cooking. There was a lot to be done, and the first was to cut up the meat. He did so in a matter of seconds. Then he placed the meat in a bowl before creating a small, stout-beer marinade, seasoned well, and poured it in. After stirring this combination until all of the meat was covered in the marinade, he set it in the fridge to marinate for two hours or so. It would have been better had it been allowed to marinate for a bit longer, but he didn't have that sort of time. Not without using abilities he didn't want Erica to see, at least.

As Kreig began to wash potatoes next to Erica, who was washing the knife he'd used moments prior, he couldn't help but glance over at her. He could still remember how scared she had been the first time they had met. How he'd intimidated her. And yet she had persisted. In that sense, she was an incredibly brave woman.

But even such bravery could be broken.

Although Kreig valued honesty incredibly highly, although he truly cherished Erica and hated to deceive her, he couldn't bear to consider the possibility that she might learn who he was, what he had done. Knowing her—knowing how open-minded she could be—she would certainly believe it. She might even act on it.

Kreig gritted his teeth, and in a moment of thoughtlessness, the potato in his grip exploded. He blinked at it for a few seconds, his now-empty palm gaping up at him.

"Holy shit," Erica breathed. Kreig turned to look at her and found the side of her face covered in potato bits. His heart sank. In his mind, heavy, sharp-footed thoughts scattered about like bustling centipedes, running to and fro, chastising him for his mistake, whispering that this was the end, that he could no longer control his strength, that he couldn't even keep himself calm when everything was fine and okay and all right, that if he was not all right after all this time, he never would be. That the next time something like this happened, he would hurt someone he loved—if he hadn't already.

His heart thundered in his ears. His mouth felt dry. All he wanted to do was apologize to Erica, but he found his throat filled with thick, slimy sewage that just wouldn't go away. "I—"

"Wow! That's so cool, how did you— Is there magic involved? Like, was this a trick? No, wait, don't tell me; you had like a spring installed or something? Or—or maybe you hollowed out the potato beforehand! Or you're just really, really strong," she chirped excitedly, her eyes glittering like jewels. "You should try becoming a strongman! Like, a guy who lifts big rocks? Very impressive. Sometimes, there are documentaries on TV about strongmen, and they could lift lots! What's the heaviest thing you've ever lifted?"

Kreig blinked. He smiled and chuckled to himself. "A suit of armor."

"Armor? Armor . . ." She thumbed her lip for a few seconds. "Don't those weigh, like, a lot?"

Kreig felt his smile deepen. He grabbed a towel and wiped the edge of her face, removing the potato debris. Her cheeks reddened slightly. "Of course. Much more than you."

For a second or so, she didn't reply, just looking at him with those same, glittering eyes. Then she glanced away, her cheeks turning even redder. "Heh, yeah, that's . . . Not that I'm all that heavy, so . . . So, it doesn't mean much! I think." Her brows furrowed and she seemed thoughtful. "So, if you can lift an armor, and I weigh less, then you should theoretically be able to lift me?"

Kreig gulped. "That would be the logical line of thought."

She lit up. "Then—"

"However, I would loathe to hurt you." The image of an exploding potato shot through his mind, and he winced.

She stared at him blankly, as though his words were pure nonsense. "You won't hurt me," she said with the conviction of a kid assured that Santa would come for Christmas. "You *can't* hurt me." She grinned. "I'm protected by the gods, y'see? Nobody can ever hurt me, not even a super strongman!"

Somehow, when looking at her tender frame and thin neck, Kreig couldn't help but doubt that. "I would rather not take the chance."

She pouted adorably. "Aw, come on! The last time anybody ever lifted me was my momma! The faster you do this, the faster we can get back to work, you know?"

Kreig glanced down at the potatoes in the sink. He still had quite a few to do. He heaved a deep sigh. "Very well, then." He looked down at his hands, rough and firm with calluses. Still covered in potato gunk. Not wanting to dirty her dress, he washed and dried his hands before turning back to her. She smiled up at him, hands on her hips. The image of a confident winner.

He clenched and unclenched his hands a few times. He took a deep breath and placed both of his hands on her sides as though he was going to dance with her. She jerked a little, but before he could pull his hands back, she gave him a thumbs-up. Trying his best to be as gentle as one could possibly be, he lifted her up like a cat, hands under her armpits. And for a few seconds, she just hung in the air, staring blankly at Kreig's face. ". . . Cool," she choked out.

Realizing that being held underneath your arms like a cat was painful for most humans, Kreig tossed her into a regular, non-painful bridal carry. Her arms and legs folded. "Okay, this is really weird," she admitted.

"Would you like to be let down?" Kreig asked, hoping to God he wasn't about to make a mistake of some sort. Still, holding her like this was, well, nice. She felt warm, and she didn't seem to be in any pain.

She shook her head. "No, no, this is . . . Just a little while longer." She smiled strangely. "This perspective is *really* weird, though."

He had to agree with her on that one. Bending his neck just to get a look at her face felt very odd. For around a minute or so, Kreig just sort of held her. Looking into her adoring eyes, feeling how soft she was. Their heavy breaths seemed to merge. His eyes slowly fell on her plump lips.

Then the front door flew open and George stepped inside. "I'll get to work on the toilet immediatel—" His eyes fell on the two of them. "Uh."

In less than a second, Erica was back on her feet and Kreig had turned back to the potatoes.

George smirked slyly. "So, that's how it is, huh? Well, don't mind me, then."

Kreig swallowed. Once George had left, he sneaked a peek at Erica again, who was just as red in the face as Kreig felt. They worked in silence. Once he'd washed but not peeled the potatoes, he put them in a pot to boil. While that simmered, he got back to the cakes. He'd never been much for sweets, neither eating nor making, but if pressed, he was easily as good as any professional pastry-maker. His only chains were his ignorance of the exact processes.

He got about halfway done with the cakes before the potatoes were fin-ished. Turning his attention back to them, he quickly removed them from the stove, cooled them down, and cut a series of semi-deep ridges along the side of the potatoes. After seasoning and brushing them with butter, he put them all on a tray and set them in the oven.

And now, back to the cakes.

But right as he began decorating them, he felt as though someone was watching him. For a brief, panic-filled second, he worried that the pres-ence would impose itself even on his most private moments. But then he realized that whoever was looking at him was doing so with the most positive intentions possible. He glanced over his shoulder and found Erica looking back at him.

"Cake," she breathed wistfully.

He nodded back at her. *Right.*

Glancing at the sink, he found all the dishes done and put away. Lord, she was quick. In that case, he could easily understand her line of thought. She had nothing else to do, after all. And so, while she watched intently with grand focus, he put the finishing touches on the cakes. A glance at the clock. 5:45. The potatoes had been in for about a quarter of an hour. In another quarter hour, people would begin to arrive. He should probably change out of his current clothes, but he should start frying the meat before that point.

So, he removed the marinated meat from the fridge, placed a knob of butter and some fresh rosemary in a pan, and added the meat once the butter had started bubbling. That should be able to hold its own for the minute or two that Kreig needed to change. So, after telling Erica to keep an eye on it, he left for his room.

When he returned, changed and ready, he found Erica looking very panicked, all while staring at the sizzling meat. She turned to him, seem-ingly on the verge of tears.

Kreig wasn't sure how to respond, so he just took over the meat and asked her to set the table. In reality, Sam was supposed to do that, but she hadn't gotten home yet. Which was weird, since she usually came home *before* George. Maybe something had happened? Then again, she was much stronger than most humans, so only a few regular situations could possibly hinder her to any real extent.

In that case, what if it wasn't a normal situation? What if a portal had appeared, sucking her in? Or maybe a monster appeared, or there was a hostage situation, or the Empire had caught wind of his escape to Earth and invaded in an attempt to finally get him?

Kreig's eyes fell on Erica. All of a sudden, he felt very much like her. He shook his head.

Sam would be fine. And even if she wasn't, he would help her. Whatever happened to her . . . if he couldn't save her, he would at least avenge her.

But for now, he just had to finish frying the meat.

George didn't seem too worried either. At the moment, he was helping Erica set the dinner table. Nothing to worry about there.

Right as the clock hit six, there was a knock on the door. Kreig felt somewhat obliged to greet whoever had arrived, but George was faster.

"Darius, what a pleasure to see you again," George greeted him warmly. Kreig leaned over the counter to catch a quick glimpse of the dark-skinned man. He was wearing a stylish suit, carrying a wrapped bottle of what seemed to be champagne.

"Indeed, George. I'm glad our current meeting can be on better terms than the last." He smiled politely. "Not that you made a bad impression, of course."

"Glad to hear it. By all means, come inside. You can hang your coat on the hangers here."

By that point, the conversation shifted into easy, routine small talk that Kreig couldn't really bother to listen to. He was glad Darius had found his way into conversation quickly enough, though, as he'd hate for any of his guests to be left without company. Since almost every other aspect of the event had been finished or was almost finished, George didn't mind sitting down on the couch, inviting Darius to join him as they discussed subjects that went right over Kreig's head.

After a few more minutes, there was another knock on the door. This time, Kreig was able to open the door himself, greeting Mrs. Willowgrove. She wore a luxurious fur coat, her face lit up with extravagant makeup and plenty of jewelry of every sort and make. "Well, don't you look dashing?"

"Uh, thank you," Kreig replied, suddenly very aware of how simple his shirt-pants combo was, especially when compared to her grand outfit. She smiled at him expectantly. For a few seconds, he wasn't sure what she wanted him to say, but then it came to him all at once. "Oh, uh, you too. You look very . . . glamorous."

She grinned heartily. "Why, thank you! The last time I wore an outfit as beautiful as this one, I easily made all the boys swoon. Oh, you should've seen me."

Shifting into etiquette, Kreig politely took her coat and hung it among the other coats. Sensing where the conversation was the most active, Mrs.

Willowgrove quickly bid adieu to Kreig before smoothly joining George and Darius on the couch.

Kreig took a deep breath. He felt tired already, even though the party hadn't fully gotten started yet. Once again, he found himself gently worrying about Sam.

He wanted to ask George about it, but he was currently keeping both of the guests company. Sure, he did have a few skills he could use to contact George without having to walk up to him and interrupt the whole conversation, but doing so with Erica in the room would be a bit . . .

However, right as Kreig was considering what possible steps he might take, he found George excusing himself from the conversation and walking up to him. "Kreig, could you take Erica on a small walk or something?"

He blinked at his brother. "Why?"

"I need to tell our guests that she . . . well, *doesn't know*. We can't have either of them blurt out something telling, can we?"

Kreig pulled his lips tight. "Of course. I'll gladly distract her." George nodded in response and prepared to leave. "Although I must ask . . . how come Sam has yet to arrive? Has she told you what she is doing?"

George thought for a second before shaking his head. "All she told me was that she'd be a little late tonight, which is pretty thoughtless, but I'm sure she has her reasons. Don't worry about it, and just enjoy yourself, all right?"

Despite this, Kreig couldn't help but feel a little worried. "All right."

He took Erica on a walk.

"It's kinda cold, isn't it?" Erica said, wrapping her arms around her chest. Looking at her, Kreig could understand very well why she might feel cold—she wasn't wearing a jacket. Or anything other than a knee-length dress.

"It *is* October, after all," Kreig replied.

She shrugged, a self-deprecating smile having found its way onto her plump lips. "Yeah, but . . . this morning, it wasn't chilly. It was actually kind of warm!"

She was right about that one. It had actually been both warm and clear, but now that evening had rolled about, big, dark clouds blotting out the rising moon, it was hard to think it was any season except for autumn. Looking at her, Kreig couldn't help but curse himself for not bringing a jacket of his own. Due to his . . . anomalous physiology, he was able to keep warm without the need for clothes, though he still wore them for the sake of decency.

At the moment, that meant he had nothing to help Erica keep warm.

He wasn't sure how long they were supposed to be walking, either. For the moment, they were just wandering around a nearby park, mostly deserted around this particular hour. Although many of the trees framed by the light of dim street lamps were growing orange and red, quite a few retained their summer colors, giving the park that strange feeling you have in between two different seasons, like snow on budding flowers. Still, predictably, many leaves decorated the ground, huddling up against buildings and walls in great piles one could easily imagine a child jumping into.

And still, it was dark. A few months before, at this hour, it would not nearly have been dark. But there and then, it was almost black. And cold.

Erica tightened her arms. Kreig watched her sympathetically.

But as he watched her exposed, pale shoulders, he had a bit of an idea. A little thought. Nobody would know if he used a little healing magic in the dark of the night. She wouldn't know and he wouldn't tell. All he needed was a little bodily contact.

He spotted a bench standing desolate and perfect.

Unthinkingly, he took her hand and led her toward it. In one swift movement, he removed the dry leaves from atop it and sat down. Following his movements, she took a seat next to him. A gust of wind rattled through the overhead trees. A cluster of leaves wafted down like feathers left from a massive bird flying by.

For a few seconds, they sat there, next to each other, watching the natural spectacle of autumn taking hold of the city. His heart was beating fast and hard. For some reason, he couldn't relax. He just sat there, hands on his thighs, trying to work himself up to do it. *Just do it. She's right there.* His face felt scalding.

He glanced at her and caught her looking at him. She quickly turned back to look at the falling leaves. He gulped.

Internally, he chastised himself for being unable to do such a simple thing as touch a woman. Something hundreds of soldiers under his command had been able to do as easily as he could kill a man. Could he really not bring himself to do the most mundane thing in the world?

From the corner of his eye, he saw how she craned her neck to look at the dark, swirling clouds above.

"I like fall," she said wistfully. "I think I always did. There's just something very pretty about life dying only to revive again. Don'tcha think?" Her eyes seemed to hold the whole of the night sky.

He looked at her. He nodded mechanically. And in his mind, he had never been surer of how he felt about her.

When she turned again and they both grew silent, he finally lifted his arm and quietly slid it around her shoulders. He was so afraid. He was scared she might slip out of his hold, or stand up and tell him he was wrong, or push him off of her in disgust.

But she just leaned closer to him, her little body pressing against his side. And she was cold, all right. Her small form shivered gently in his grip. His hand was on her bare shoulder, and he could feel just how cold she was. Instinctually, he chose to press her closer to him. Because he was warm. And if she was just a little closer, he could give some of that warmth to her.

In this moment, where their two bodies were pressed together so close, you could only barely tell them apart, Kreig forgot all about magic and systems and religion. He didn't hold her in order to use some hokey magic on her—he just held her to keep her warm.

With her hand on his chest and her cheek pressed against him, she released a long, relaxed breath and closed her eyes.

He placed his other hand across her upper back. It might almost have been a hug.

Slowly, she grew warmer until their two body heats were the same. If they hadn't had anywhere to go, if this was their final pit stop of the night, the both of them would surely have fallen asleep right there, tangled in each other's arms. But that didn't happen.

Instead, once they were both warm and cozy, she opened her eyes again. Her cheeks were bright and red, and Kreig felt sure that his were the same. Their eyes met.

He hadn't thought about it before, but their faces were quite close now. Their breaths intermingled, and without really thinking, he felt himself leaning closer to her. There wasn't a shadow of fear or doubt in his head. Likewise, he saw how she, too, leaned in—her eyes closed and her lips parted.

Right there on the bench, on a chilly autumn evening, they shared their first kiss, and everything felt right.

When they returned home—both red as beets, Erica smiling strangely and Kreig almost statue-like—they found that not much had changed. The appetizers Kreig had prepared yesterday had been presented to the two guests, and the three were sharing the bottle that Darius had brought, chattering pleasantly among themselves. The time was half past six. It felt much later.

And still, Sam was nowhere to be seen. Now Kreig began to feel truly worried.

"Oh, welcome back!" George said warmly from where he sat on the couch. "Sam sent me a message; she'll be home a bit later, so—"

"—Psych, I'll be home now!"

Kreig turned, finding Sam in the doorway, still dressed in uniform. Looking at her, he couldn't help but feel confused. She knew today would be a special day, so how come she was so late?

"And I brought someone with me!" she declared joyfully, turning toward the dark hall as though expecting for someone to burst out of the shadows. A few seconds passed silently. Sam's grin faltered slightly. "I didn't drag you all the way here for you to stand out here blushing! Come on, get"—she grabbed someone and dragged them into the apartment— "in here!"

A young woman, maybe around 25 or 30, stumbled inside, her face somehow even redder than Erica's. She was wearing a woman's suit with a matching skirt and stockings. With her hair tied up in a tight bun and her glasses almost falling off her face, she had a modest, professional appearance. Seemingly embarrassed, she attempted to straighten herself out, pushing her glasses farther up her plump face. Her lips were drawn tight.

Kreig had never seen her before in his life.

George flew from the couch, curiosity being overtaken by surprise. A faint blush painted his cheeks. "Miss Aardwyre! Why would you— How . . . Sam?"

Sam smirked triumphantly. "A messenger of love always has her ways!"

Miss Aardwyre averted her gaze, appearing quite shamed.

Nevertheless, George approached her, taking her hand in his. "Did she put you up to this? If she did, then I am very"—The woman hastily shook her head. "You . . . came here of your own free will? Well, that's . . ." Seemingly worried, he now turned to glance around at the other guests—especially Darius. "It doesn't look good, a secretary coming to her boss's party. It's not . . ."

Miss Aardwyre's bespectacled gaze fell on Kreig. Her eyes widened considerably, but she made no comment.

George glanced at Kreig, smiled softly, and turned back to Miss Aardwyre. Quietly, far too quietly for any normal human to hear, he said, "Yeah, that's him. But you knew that already, so . . . You don't need to be afraid. If you want to go home, then . . ." She shook her head. "You really don't have to." But her eyes were hard and resolute and George couldn't force her. Sighing, he smiled. "Well, all right. Let's hope we made enough for you, too, shall we?"

That hypothesis was tested not long after.

Indeed, they did have enough for even her, despite the fact that Sam seemed intent on eating for three. Although there were only seven people in total, Kreig felt that it was just enough. Just the fact that these six people had cared enough to come to celebrate with him was enough for him to feel warm and giddy inside.

And, of course, the food was good. There was little question of that.

During the dinner, as might be customary, they talked a lot about Kreig. George and Sam told stories of his younger days, Erica talked about things he had done at school, which at one point branched into a weird discussion on whether or not school lunches should be free. Mrs. Willowgrove talked about how good friends Kreig and Peter had been, which in turn became a long spiel about how silly her poor husband had been.

Kreig, for the most part, listened silently. Nobody expected him to talk, and that was enough for him. Just listening to them talk was enough for him.

The other silent person at the table—Aardwyre—glanced at him from time to time, always somewhat cautiously. Kreig wasn't too sure about her reason for being there or what her relationship with George was, but it certainly wasn't purely professional. As long as she didn't make a fuss, he couldn't see any reason for her not to be there. She seemed nice enough, too.

As the evening progressed and the plates were emptied, Kreig took the role of host and began to clear the table in preparation for dessert. Apparently feeling obligated to help him, Erica stood up as well. And so, while Kreig washed dishes at the speed of light, Erica placed smaller plates and small spoons on the table, alongside coffee cups.

The cake Kreig placed on the table was, all things considered, much more grandiose than the one Sam and George had bought him for when he first returned home. And still, there was no question in Kreig's mind that the two cakes were equally good.

"Come on, Kreig. Take a huge piece," Erica whispered from her seat.

Kreig cut himself an extremely slim piece. If he could choose, he would rather have skipped it entirely, but it was customary that he take a piece first, so that was what he did. Erica pouted, but Kreig was able to convince her that the less he took, the more was left over for her.

The cake passed around quite quickly and soon everyone had a piece, again returning to the previous conversational topic of whether or not civilians should be allowed to own alligators without a license of some sort. Much like with the dinner and appetizers, people enjoyed the cake greatly, and for once—just this once—Kreig let himself feel a bit good about it.

Once Kreig had finished his paper-thin slice, he stood up and left the table.

Hoping nobody was paying too much attention to him, he grabbed a cake-cutter from the drawers and placed it on the counter. Then he slid the second cake out of the fridge and set it beside the cake cutter. Finally, he grabbed both of them, moved carefully through the kitchen so as to remain unnoticed, and silently slipped out the door. Considering that nobody had stopped him, he must have succeeded in remaining unnoticed.

As carefully as one only walks while carrying a cake that took approximately six hours to make, he descended the stairs. He was actually able to walk out the door without touching the door handle, since an old lady and her dog just so happened to be entering. They looked at him strangely but still held the door for him. He gave her a grateful nod and moved outside.

Now came the slightly difficult part. He didn't want to alert them, but he also had to approach them fast enough for them to not escape.

Breathing slowly, steadying himself, he cast a protective blessing on the cake. Just in case.

Then, in a burst of speed, he appeared before a trio of men dressed fully in black. They were crouching within a squad of bushes, wearing protective armor and visored helmets and carrying guns and weapons not really meant to hurt him but more to distract him, if things came to that.

He couldn't see their faces behind their protective masks, but by the way they scrambled back in instinctual fear, he could tell they certainly hadn't expected him to appear so suddenly. The air grew thick with the unmistakable scent of terror.

But when that single moment of primordial fear had passed over, now replaced by hardwired training, they instead shifted their guns and weapons to face him. Several other black-dressed men appeared swiftly from various unnoticeable hiding places. They were ready for an altercation—one Kreig certainly wasn't there to give them.

The moment when their collective gaze fell on the cake—enough for ten grown men—was obvious. The aura of fear and adrenaline that had permeated the autumn air was suddenly replaced by pure confusion, and Kreig took that moment to silently set the cake on the ground in front of one of the men.

Then, in another burst of speed, he was gone, leaving a squad of very confused, silently horrified men and a single cake behind.

Kreig didn't stop moving until he was back inside the apartment. He released a deep breath.

"Welcome back, Kreig!" Sam greeted cheerfully. "Where'd ya go?"

She'd probably find out in the morning, but Kreig still felt obligated to give her some form of response, if only for politeness' sake. "Outside."

She blinked at him. "Well, okay!"

The rest of the evening continued peacefully. In the later evening, they brought out cookies Kreig had baked as an experiment. The discussion on the unlicensed keeping of predatory animals seemed to have continued with the argument that a cat could probably kill a human under the right circumstances, but people were still allowed to keep them.

The guests began leaving at around ten, at which point Kreig felt tired enough to sleep a century. But before Mrs. Willowgrove could find it in her to finally leave, Kreig silently handed her a brown package the size of a painting. She made to open it immediately, but he told her to wait until she got home. She would understand who was on it, regardless of whether he told her or not.

But by that point, he only wanted to sleep.

CHAPTER 32

TEACHER

School again. As usual, the only thing that made school even slightly interesting to Jay was the presence of Wiedermann and his flame. In all other regards, she would much rather have been at home.

Entering English class, she again found her eyes drawn to the woman sitting in front next to the whiteboard. Erica was wearing a knee-length yellow dress decorated with pink and orange flowers. Perfectly normal. Among the other teachers, her only real standout feature was that she seemed to have an actual passion for teaching.

Jay put her things on her desk. As with the last lesson, this one would surely also be spent with a short lecture followed by time to work alone. The only way Jay could imagine a better lesson would be if it were spent entirely by working alone. She had quite a bit left to go on her article, after all.

"Hey." Startled, Jay turned to the left, where she found Annie staring at her oddly. "What's going on between you and Gerald?"

Jay blinked at her. "Between me and— No. Nothing is going on."

Annie frowned deeply and turned away from Jay, looking at the blank whiteboard. "I don't think I've seen you two talk for like . . . almost a month now?" She glanced back at Jay, giving her a blank, quizzical stare. "Seriously. What is going—"

Two claps rang out and the class quieted. "All right, class, good morning again! Before we get back to writing, I would like to discuss a few narrative devices . . ."

With Annie being such an honorable girl, Jay knew she wouldn't talk again as long as Erica continued her lecture. But once that was over, she'd get on Jay's ass again. This would be a problem, since Jay still needed Annie to be on her good side. See, Annie liked Gerald. They were good friends, no question about it. Hence, if Annie found out that Gerald had pushed Jay away, she might make the false conclusion that he had a good reason for doing so. If she followed suit, Jay would have to do an illegal activity or two in order to get ahold of Annie's letter.

At least she was lucky that Gerald hadn't gone out of his way to tell Annie what had happened. That would've messed up quite a lot for her.

"—Of course, you guys don't have to use any of these, but if you feel that they might make your story better, by all means!" Erica said, finishing the lecture.

Understanding that the time had come, the other students began bringing up their computers and whatever else they used to write with. In the meantime, Erica began walking around, talking with a few students about their stories and what they might do with them. The only surprise was that Erica had somehow been able to remember all of their ideas and concepts.

Jay scoffed at the sight but immediately regretted it when she found Annie giving her the stink-eye. Somehow, it seemed Annie had already picked a side in the matter. And, as always, it sure wasn't the right one. Did nobody ever think things through?

Silently gnashing her teeth, Jay brought up her article. She hadn't gotten too far with it, but the really important thing was that she had more information now than she did before. Not enough to write a truly comprehensive report, but enough to get started.

"How's it going?"

Jay jumped almost a foot before finally turning her head to find Erica leaning over her shoulder, smiling innocently. Jay suppressed the urge to either slap her laptop closed or punch Erica. "Yeah, it's, uh . . . going good. Yeah."

Somehow, Erica smiled in what seemed to be genuine interest. "That's great! I'm actually really— Well, I mean, you're writing something totally different, but . . . Did you know you can use narrative devices and such even while writing an article? Maybe not a scientific one, though . . ."

"Huh?" Jay could feel herself grimace in confusion. She pointed at the article still visible on her screen. "How in the—"

"Yeah!" Erica smiled brightly, her eyes shining in excitement as she began to ramble about how journalism also had a purpose to entertain, and that strong use of language can help bring a story to life. Even though

she was speaking fast and strangely, Jay found herself somewhat capti-
vated by it. As ashamed as she was to admit it, she hadn't really considered
trying to make the article feel like a story. Weren't journalists supposed to
report on the truth alone?

Listening intently, Jay actually felt a smidge sad when Erica finished
her small lesson by saying, "Well, do you think that might help?"

"Uh?" Jay said stupidly. "Oh, yeah, of course! I'll . . ." She turned back
to the article, mainly composed of objective statements and blank descrip-
tions. "Yeah. I'll make good use of it."

Genuine relief and enthusiasm showed on Erica's face. "In that case—"

"No, wait!" Jay said more forcefully than intended. Erica looked at her
owlishly. "Just . . . Could I ask a few questions?"

Erica blinked at her for a few seconds. "Sure! Are you writing an article on teachers? I'd love to feature in it!" Hearing a teacher squeal about
something so stupid felt bizarre, but in the end, Jay could only experience
it as somewhat charming.

"Yeah, uh . . ." She glanced off, suddenly unsure of how to ask. "Do
you— Is . . . What do you know about Kreig Wiedermann?"

Erica's expression froze. "He— I—" Her eyes darted to the left and
right frantically. "The PE teacher?" Jay nodded stiffly. "Well . . ." A faint
blush spread across her face. "I think he's nice!"

Ah. Yeah. She didn't know. Looking back at her article, Jay suddenly
couldn't bring herself to ask any more questions. "Thanks. That was . . . That
was all I needed to hear, so . . ." Looking back at Erica, she found the woman
staring at her with a strange luster in her bright eyes. "Wh—what is it?"

Erica clasped her hands behind her back and smiled. "I think you'll
make for a great journalist."

Jay's mouth flopped open and she stared wide-eyed at her teacher. Giving a grin, Erica patted her on the shoulder and left to talk to other students, leaving Jay to simmer in confusion and uncertainty.

"Do you know what it takes to be a journalist?" Teachers.

"I'm sorry, Jay, but we can't afford something like that." Her mother.

"Can't you think of something else? Something . . . Useful?" The counselor.

Jay clenched her hands into fists. She tried to focus her attention on the
article, but before her eyes, the purpose of it seemed to shift somewhat.
Looking at it, she couldn't honestly say that she wanted it to hurt Erica.
After all, *she* didn't want to hurt Erica. Erica was just a normal girl. She
didn't deserve any of this, and this man, this *monster*, had just inserted
himself into her life without ever letting her know the truth.

But Jay could change that, couldn't she? She could make Erica understand.

All in all, a single human life didn't mean much in this world. But maybe it would be enough? If Jay was lucky, if the *world* was lucky, then maybe Wiedermann would leave once Erica split with him. Or he'd just show his true colors. She couldn't know and she wasn't about to pretend she ever would.

Either way, if she couldn't get information out of Gerald or Erica, then there was only one obvious avenue left to try. It would be dangerous, but she had already prepared herself for this situation.

She was going to meet with Wiedermann personally.

On the other side of the school, Kreig easily moved toward the cafeteria. It was regrettable, but on this day in particular, he and Erica could not eat lunch at the same time, leaving him a little lonely. Sure, some of the other teachers had begun speaking with him and letting him into conversations, but he still missed Erica. He wasn't sure why the other teachers were teasing him about it. Was there something weird about missing another teacher?

At least he was able to meet her in the hallway on his way back to the gymnasium. She smiled at him and he looked at her and they both gave a nod. He wanted to hug her and to lift her up and twirl her around the hallway, but by now he had come to understand that this was not appropriate behavior for a school. Still, seeing her certainly made his mood improve, not that it had been low before.

To think that he was finally following in Peter's footsteps . . .

He returned to class. As of late, he had started incorporating quite a few games into the classes, which was met with great enthusiasm from the students. Furthermore, he had also added games he could remember seeing his soldiers playing between battles. These, too, had been met with excitement. Though, as might be expected, a few elements of these games had to be changed or flat-out removed.

Either way, Kreig enjoyed his role. The students seemed to have grown to like his presence, though most still considered him a threat whenever he joined in a game himself. Such situations were exceedingly rare, but whenever they happened, Kreig made sure not to be too dominating. But even with his physical abilities suppressed to the maximum, his mere presence was enough to make the other teams or players frightened into ineptitude.

Kreig found it fun. It was as simple as that.

But during this lesson, something felt a little strange. It was Gerald's class that stood before him, which usually meant that it would be very fun. But Gerald wasn't there. Now that Kreig thought about it, he hadn't seen Gerald all that often lately. It felt odd, but it was probably just a sickness of some sort. Even though Gerald should have been protected from such bugs.

But there was something else as well. Someone was looking at him with malice.

The intensity and the feeling of the gaze actually reminded him of the presence, but somehow, this gaze was even more furious. The presence always seemed somewhat distant and cold, but this one was almost burning. Apart from those surface differences, there was the obvious fact that the presence couldn't possibly be some student, especially in a class that he taught himself, too.

Hoping it was just someone holding a grudge over some small, past infraction, he initiated the games of the day.

Around halfway through the second game, Jay tripped and hurt her elbow. Surprisingly, she actually approached him on her own, which she was usually too shy to do. But in this case, he was happy she had done so, since the injury was actually a little more than normal. She had a small scratch, sure, but she had somehow actually succeeded in gaining a hairline fracture as well. Kreig was somewhat surprised that she had gotten such an injury from a seemingly innocuous fall. Of course, it might have been there all along, but for Jay herself to have never noticed it? A bit unusual.

Knowing that the injury could easily worsen, Kreig led her over to the bleachers. If he was sneaky enough about it, he could heal her in a matter of seconds without her ever having to go to a doctor.

With his goal set, Kreig brought out a small first-aid kit. Looking back at her, he found her eyes intense and hateful.

Confused, he looked at her for a few seconds, unsure of what could rouse such immense loathing. Scowling, she turned away from him. Well . . . that was certainly strange. He tried to take an easy hold of her arm to apply a band-aid, but instead he found that she recoiled from his touch. Now he was just even more confused.

She hissed in pain. Kreig really wasn't sure what to tell her, but after a few seconds of her looking at her lightly scratched arm, she returned it to him. He took it gratefully. Now, if he could just distract her for a few seconds so he could heal her . . .

"Hey," Jay said reproachfully, and he glanced up from her arm to look her in the eye. "What's your relationship with Erica?"

His mouth fell open. "That's . . ." He gulped and pulled himself together. Glancing out over the students bustling, he felt his cheeks grow a little hot. "She is . . . nice. I like her quite a lot." Though, by all means, he couldn't really understand why she might ask such a thing. Was there already a rumor?

For a few minutes, Jay continued asking him unusual questions. Unsure how to answer most of them, he spoke as dismissively as he could. During the whole of it, he slowly came to understand that she had all the makings of a fantastic interrogations officer. Her only downfall was that Kreig had been quite good at it himself once upon a time. The strangest moment would have been when she grew upset over the possibility that Kreig might want to get even closer to Erica. It was all very peculiar. So, once he saw her clicking her tongue and turning away, he quickly applied a little band-aid to the scratch before silently casting a spell.

White Hand (X)

He felt carefully how her bones easily mended themselves without leaving a single trace of injury behind. However, as it always was with these types of spells, it also served to heal various other bodily damages, such as hormonal imbalances, gut health, and serotonin scarcity.

As might be expected, Jay's head turned to face him, her eyes wide and surprised. But, for a few seconds, she was completely unable to react to what had just happened to her. Taking the opportunity in hand, Kreig told her she'd feel better now and that if she wanted to, she could just remain on the bleachers for the rest of the lesson. In a daze, she did not respond. All the better for Kreig, who was able to leave her.

During the rest of the lesson, her gaze held only a fraction of the overt animosity exuded earlier.

He didn't mind, but it did make him question why she would seem so hateful to begin with.

CHAPTER 33

WITTING PAWN

When Jay entered the classroom the next morning, she found a little letter lying on her desk.

Eyes drawn to it, she sat down and began turning it over. For one, it was clearly already opened. The little wax seal that had shut it so tightly was loose in parts, though it still clung to the upper flap of the letter. Not that it was addressed to her or anything. Feeling her brows furrow, Jay made to open the letter fully, only to be startled when she realized Annie was sitting next to her.

"So?" Annie said tiredly. "Will you make up with Gerald now?"

Jay couldn't honestly answer that. Well, sure, there *was* an answer, but that answer might make Annie take the letter back. For that matter, this was *that* letter, wasn't it? The one. The *specific* letter written from a certain someone to a certain someone. Her grip on the letter tightened. "This letter will have uses beyond childish friendsh—"

"Will you stop that?" Annie snapped. "Look, I'm not . . . You're not a bad person, that's not what I'm trying to say, but it's like you don't actually care. If all of this was only because you're on some weird crusade against Mr. Wiedermann, then this is just not something I want to be a part of. Sure, maybe some greater goods are worth sacrificing everything for, but this is— He's just a *guy*." A scowl played across her lips and she pointed at the letter in Jay's hands.

"With this, it's over. If you're willing to break off with Gerald just because you think it might get you closer to some stupid horrible truth that *isn't there*, then here. Just take it. With this, you don't need to hound me anymore, do you? Knowing you, you might even try some underhanded, half-criminal scheme just to get it."

Jay sat there, frozen in place. Was she seriously doing this? There, in the middle of class? Jay's eyes darted about, but nobody was paying attention. Her fingers trembled and her mouth felt dry. "I wouldn't . . ." But it was true.

"I'm not saying that you're evil or anything like that. I—I know you're just trying to do good here and all that, and in a different time I might have felt the need to help you, but this isn't that. What you're doing here is . . ." Annie turned away. "You really hurt Gerald. And if you try going through with this, you'll hurt a lot more people." Annie's eyes met Jay's again, and Jay felt small and strange. The girl glanced down at the letter with a curious fondness. "But that should change your mind."

For the rest of the lesson, Annie wouldn't say anything to Jay, no matter what she tried. The lesson passed quietly and so did the next one. The day simply flew by. At lunch, Jay found herself sitting alone. But she was used to that, wasn't she? She'd sat alone for years before she picked up Gerald and Annie. This was really just a return to form for her.

She could do without them! As a matter of fact, she might even be better off if they stayed safe and sound in their little wallow-holes.

Then she alone might be targeted.

Yes, that was right. This was her burden to bear. A lonesome heroine trying to show the truth to the ignorant world. Her cross to bear.

She waited to open the letter until school had ended, at which point she took a seat outside of the entrance atop one of the many leaf-covered benches. All the trees of the school had now turned bright red and yellow, showering the school buildings and the streets with leaves. It was almost chilly, so Jay was clad in a little secondhand jacket and a pair of gloves.

There, outside the school, she finally got a peek inside what she thought would be the truth she had so longed for.

Instead, she found something of a eulogy for a man she had never heard about. Some Charlie Swallowbird fellow. Though, going by the context, it was probably Annie's brother. The one she wouldn't talk about. The one Jay had tried and failed to discover the truth of.

The eulogy presented a very strange tale of a man who, alongside four other classmates, was brought to another world. There, he was conscripted into some wacky religion following some wacko underground God. In other words, he got brainwashed into some stupid cult. From there on, he apparently lived a pretty typical heroic life by fighting monsters and doing stuff like that.

. . . And this was supposed to be some sort of final truth? What a scam.

Though it should be noted that there were quite a few strange things about the letter. For one, it was written by someone who had gone on that same journey with him, though not named as the other three. Since there were only four people other than Charlie who were taken, one of these must still be alive.

No name was signed, but going by the context, Jay could only think of a single person who could have written the letter.

Kreig Wiedermann.

If this story applied to him as well, then it would mean that he was summoned to the otherworld alongside the four others and converted to that religion. From there on, he apparently survived. All four others died, but he lived on through some unknown means.

Putting the letter back in her backpack, she got back on her feet, letting her mind run in circles while she wandered aimlessly.

He had been summoned ten years earlier. Jay could recall reading in some "Top Ten Interesting Otherworld Facts" article that one year in the otherworld was thirteen on Earth. That would mean he had lived 130 years in the other world. Combined with the age of seventeen when he was summoned, he had to have been at least 147 years old. Wow. What a grandpa.

His race must have given him some sort of longevity skill or whatnot. That was the only thing she could think of.

Still . . . He didn't seem like a hundred-plus-year-old at all. As a matter of fact, he barely seemed fifty! Though that was all very ambiguous. Now that she thought about it, Jay could even remember hearing some people discussing how old he must be. They placed him somewhere around his late thirties. About a hundred years off or so.

Jay snickered to herself.

One hundred thirty years in a world widely regarded as a monster paradise. That would explain his levels. Being a part of some kooky religion explained his race. With this letter, she might actually have some foothold. She could explain where he came from. Who he was before all of this.

Googling his name on her phone brought no results apart from a few celebrities with similar names or fictional characters. Asking around certainly didn't help. But this . . . There should be something about this, right? *Someone* had to have written an article or two about five kids mysteriously disappearing. Sure, it was literally the day before the portals opened, but that was all the time in the world for a hungry journalist.

Walking while lost in her thoughts, Jay eventually bumped into someone around her own age. "Oh, sorry," they said and went on their way. Jay glanced up.

This school . . . This was the school mentioned in the letter, wasn't it?

It was a pretty normal school, all in all, although it had recently been the focus of a lot of attention due to the massive white tree growing in the middle of it. The tree was large enough to peek out over the tops of the buildings, giving the impression that it was absolutely massive, which it certainly was. Tree scientists and botanists from the whole world over had come to gaze at it and take samples of whatever they could think of, including the peculiar red fruit that had grown on it earlier that summer. Since it was now autumn, the fruit had stopped growing.

Jay had heard many rumors of students climbing the tree just to pick a few fruit to eat. They were neither poisonous nor hallucinogenic, and since they were rather sweet and filling, people apparently liked eating them as a snack.

At this time of the year, though, the tree proved its status as a tree by changing colors and dropping its leaves. It would probably have been less scary if the leaves didn't turn completely black before falling.

Since it was pretty late in the afternoon, Jay could clearly see kids her own age leaving the school in small, friendly clusters. She elbowed her way inside.

The tree was even larger, this close to it. The black leaves on the ground were a bit eerie, but the contrast between the snow-white bark and the black leaves was worth watching for a while.

As she stood there looking at the tree, the final students milled out of school grounds, leaving her alone with her thoughts.

This was where Wiedermann had gone to school. It was surprisingly normal, all things considered. Except for a little monument off to the side. She felt herself drawn to it.

The monument seemed to have been made of bronze or some other such metal. It portrayed a row of four roses, each blooming on its lonesome. Each of the four had a little nameplate below, listing their names. She recognized all of them from the letter, though one more than the rest.

Kreig Wiedermann.

His name was on a nameplate, among the others, as might be expected. But he had no rose.

. . . No, on closer inspection, the stalk of a rose could be seen sticking out of the ground, though it almost seemed as though the rose itself had been plucked. Who could have done this? It must have been Wiedermann somehow, but at the same time, someone could just have come by and stolen it for some stupid reason.

. . . nah, it must've been Wiedermann.

Mentally, Jay added *Mutilation of a Monument* to her growing list of Wiedermann's crimes, alongside illegal immigration.

"Hey, kid, no touching the roses!" someone shouted, and Jay whirled around to find herself face-to-face with a raking groundskeeper.

"Uh, sorry," she replied stupidly. "I was just . . ."

He squinted at her for a moment, as though he was trying to recognize her. "Hang on, give me a second," he said in an unplaceable accent. Jay watched mutely how he removed a pair of glasses from within his overalls and placed them on his nose. Then he approached her, still holding his rake. He blinked at her a few times and burst into a smile. "Hey! Well, I'll be— I was starting to think you'd never come!"

"I'm sorry?"

His smile turned strange and thin. "I'm here to help you." He quickly peeled off the glove on his right hand and held out his hand. Jay hesitantly shook it. "Pleasure meetin' you, I'm Rasmus Jung. Agent Jung."

Jay retreated her hand, feeling a strong sense of trepidation come over her. She was talking to a looney, wasn't she? "Uh. Hi. I'm—"

"No need for that; I already know who you are. We all do, so there's no . . . Well, I just want to say I'm a big fan, Jay."

Jay frowned. "You . . . are?"

"Of course! In my honest-to-God opinion, you write much better than all those guys we've got on payroll. I'm not much read up on their thoughts or anything, but I'd say that's why the guys up top wanted us to help you and such."

She felt her head start spinning. She should probably leave. Maybe even call the police. This man—whoever he was—was obviously psychologically ill. "Help me . . . how?"

He smiled strangely again and Jay regretted coming there at all. "Yeah, that's the thing, I . . . Give me a second, I'm pretty sure I . . . Oh, nope, not in there, okay, so . . ." He rummaged through his pockets for a good few minutes. Taking the opportunity, Jay took a few steps away from him. "—There we are!" He pulled a little key out of some weird pocket on the inside of his thigh. "This baby opens up a little locker out in the— You know how to get to the outskirts of the city, right? There's this place called Undulat Park, and if you go there and you find this one tree . . . It's easy to spot since it's not like the other trees, but at the root of that tree you should find a little hole. In there, you'll find all that you need."

He held the key out to her, and in the faint hope that it might make him back off, she accepted it. "Th—thank you . . ."

With that, the groundskeeper smiled, tipped his hat, and got back to raking.

Jay turned around and ran home. Once there, she collapsed into the empty couch, where she lay breathing heavily. Usually, she hated this couch, since her mother used it for work, but right now, she couldn't consider collapsing anywhere else. The key hung heavy in her hand. She held it up before her eyes, letting it dangle from side to side.

It was just a key. A modern one, to be sure, but just a key. Maybe it went to a school locker? Or it was for his lunch box? Or the bathrooms?

She clutched it in her hand.

. . . Or it went into the root system of a tree.

She glanced over at the clock. It wasn't all that late. Biking to Undulat Park and back again would leave her with ample time before her mother got home. It would set her mind at ease. Maybe the groundskeeper had left some stupid gift there, or a dead body, or . . .

Jay shook her head.

It wouldn't be anything. It would be empty, and she would go home empty-handed, and in the evening she could tell her readers all about the strange groundskeeper who called himself Agent Jung and wanted her to go chase rainbows in a park.

That was what would happen, Jay decided.

But that wasn't what happened. Not exactly.

The cold air of autumn rushed past her as she biked without thinking about much of anything. Normally, in a situation as unusual and incomprehensible as this one, her mind would be bustling with thoughts and ideas and possible explanations of what was happening. But not there. Not now. She had already considered all the possibilities.

Thinking any more about it would make her feel dizzy.

She was well outside the city now, cycling on a little path lined with red and yellow leaves.

Undulat Park was a rather large park on the outskirts of the city, usually seen as more of a contained forest than anything you would actually walk your dog in. Jay had only been there as a kid when her mother would take her there to jump in the leaf piles and climb the trees.

A tree unlike all the other trees . . . Jay could only think of one such tree.

Most of the park was made up of birches, standing white and tall and pretty. But there was one tree of a different kind.

Jay could see it even from this great distance.

An oak.

It was massive and stood above all the other trees, easily dwarfing them in raw might. Since its lower trunk was bereft of branches, only the most stalwart and determined of kids could climb it. Jay had never climbed it herself, so she was happy knowing that the "prize" was supposedly among the roots.

A little hole . . . Jay couldn't remember ever seeing anything like that.

The small path she was on quickly broadened into a larger one, and she entered the park. The setting sun, now hidden behind red leaves, only flitted in intermittently, blinding Jay every now and then. The path led straight to the oak, so she felt no need to think much about it.

The path began to twist and wind, but Jay had played this game before. She barely had to think at all as she flew through the bends, swiftly dodging stray roots and stones.

Before she knew it, she stood before that massive, looming oak. The entire forest floor was covered in a layer of red and yellow, giving the impression that the whole forest, including the treetops and even the sky, was on fire.

She parked her bike a few paces off and approached the oak, both of her hands in her pockets. She could feel the key coldly touch her fingers. She gripped it tightly.

This was so stupid. She was being a total idiot, just going ahead and following whatever directions some lunatic groundskeeper wanted to give her. At least this would make for a good post.

Cursing in her mind, she went down on her knees and began fumbling and groping around the thick roots of the tree. This would never work. The ground and the roots were completely covered in leaves. After only a few minutes of shoveling wet leaves, her gloves had turned totally wet and her fingers felt stiff and cold. She'd be lucky if she didn't wake up with a cold or something.

Roots, roots, and more roots. No matter how many rounds she took around the tree, she neither felt nor saw anything.

Yeah, a complete waste of time.

Jay stood up and shook her hands, shaking the water from her gloves. She looked down at her gloved hands.

. . . Maybe if she did one round without her gloves, she might actually feel something? Either that or she wouldn't have to go to school tomorrow.

"Fuck it," she mumbled to herself, and removed the completely soaked gloves. Back to her knees.

She touched every root as carefully as she could, feeling them with her hands without relying on her eyes in the least. But even after going halfway around, there was nothing. Not a single thing. No hole.

But right as she was about to give up and just head home for the night before the sun set completely, she felt something. A little groove. Something completely invisible and strange. If she looked at the groove, it seemed like a bump at most. But her fingers felt a little more. Carefully, still holding one hand on the groove, she removed the key from her pocket.

It slid inside the groove perfectly.

There was a click.

At first, Jay thought she was hallucinating when a fingerprint-sized piece of the bark on the root slid away to reveal a small, metallic surface. She stared at it with wild eyes before shaking her head. It was still there. Hunching down, she swung her head about, scanning for anybody else. There was nobody. She turned back to the metallic thing.

Without knowing exactly what to do, she placed her right finger over the flap. There was a prick and her hand jerked back. A little droplet of blood formed at the tip of her finger.

Turning back to the root, she found that the flap had closed again.

A hallucination? No, she could still feel the sting in her finger. Then . . . There was another click.

Jay whipped her head around and bore witness to how a hatch opened in the ground. She crawled over to it on her hands and knees. The hatch apparently opened into a small compartment, where she saw files upon files and tapes and letters. She felt numb as she carefully removed them.

Some were dated from six months before, detailing the appearance of a powerful otherworlder. Others described the detainment of that same otherworlder. A few were more recent, going over the mundane experiences of his everyday life or describing the life of a seemingly unrelated young otherworlder. The letters were dated a little less than five months ago, inviting someone to meet their brother.

Somehow, Jay felt strange. Wrong.

Who had done this? Who would have the resources needed to do this? It couldn't have been a single person. There was too much. The words of the groundskeeper echoed hollowly in her head.

This had to be the work of some sort of faction. It might be a single government, or a group of truth-seekers, or . . . or something. But why in the world would they give this to *her*, of all people?

She didn't have all that many readers on the internet, which would leave her with the simple possibility that she couldn't be traced back to them. Or maybe that she had a direct connection with Wiedermann. Or maybe they just wanted someone disposable to handle this. Maybe having a young girl doing all this was somehow more believable than if they were to make a move.

. . . It didn't make any sense. This whole situation felt unreal and odd, but wasn't this what she had always wanted?

She had the proof now. She had this, and she had Annie's letter. Did she really need anything else?

Who cares if she was being used as the witting pawn of some corporation? That didn't matter.

The only thing that truly mattered was that the truth was brought to light.

That was all.

For hours, she just sat there in the middle of the clearing, reading the files and documents until it got dark. Then she had to use her phone as a flashlight, but when its battery ran out, she was left in the dark. By that point, the moon stood high above the half-bare treetops, but she didn't want to leave.

She could no longer read them, but she had to continue. She couldn't stop there.

Her hands trembled in fear as she bundled the files. She had to continue reading. What if she went home and he was there? She had to know how to counter him. Among the files, there was a record of his status. It contained a few of his skills and his level and his race and his jobs. It was enough to tell her that he was beyond anything this world had seen before. For one, she got her answer to what his level actually was.

999+.

Higher than any recorded level. According to the reports, it was unsure whether it had capped out at 999 or if there was a higher number hidden behind it. The skills were similar. *Unknown* was a word passed around ad nauseum.

There were even reports on an event where Kreig actually showed his power and effortlessly slew a creature that threatened to destroy an entire city. Jay could even remember seeing such an event unfold on the television. She had assumed they would go in with a nuke or something, but it "sorted itself out." If he could kill such a creature as easily as one kills a fly, then what kind of destruction could *he* bring?

Worst of all was that it was entirely possible. The man was in therapy and constantly under surveillance.

He clearly had psychological problems, and yet they let him roam freely.

Jay gritted her teeth and placed the files back inside the compartment. Then, fumbling with her fingers over the nooks and crannies of the roots, she locked it again, leaving the files—both read and unread—behind. She had to come back. She couldn't bring them with her.

If she did, and someone else found out she had them . . .

A shiver scuttled across her shoulders and she shook her head.

But nobody knew. Yet. One day, they would know. She was sure of it. The people who had given her this information—whoever they were— must have known that she would be ready to sacrifice herself for this. Outside of journalism, her life didn't mean much of anything. It wasn't as though anybody would miss her. She was prepared to die if it meant that the truth came out.

The only problem was Erica.

During the following two weeks, whenever she had time, Jay immersed herself in the files, trying to put every scrap of information to mind just in case she had a confrontation of some sort. The more she knew, the more dangerous she was. If she could describe in immense detail the line of events that lead to Falk in particular taking over treatment of "inmate" Kreig Wiedermann, then even if she was apprehended, she would still have many cards to play.

But that wasn't the only thing that she did.

Somewhere in the back of her mind, she wanted Erica to deserve what was coming to her. Jay wanted it to be that Erica was the kind of person who deserved having their lover be a cold-hearted murderous beast, because otherwise, she could hardly be justified in bringing all this on her.

But she couldn't. Every day, she would talk to Erica and ask her things and make conversation and try her very best to find some flaw or mistake worthy of the pain she would have to endure. But there was nothing.

Erica was a young adult who had grown to enjoy teaching as of late. In her spare time, she liked drawing, bicycling, and collecting action figures. She preferred grading essays to straight answers, which was why she enjoyed teaching English.

And, worst of all, she liked Jay. It was a weird realization to have for Jay, but Erica seemed to genuinely enjoy talking to her. A little before and after and even during class. In the hallways between classes. Jay wouldn't even have considered it if Erica didn't state straight out, "I love talking to you; you always have some funny question to ask!" which was of course followed by another encouragement for her to pursue a career as a journalist.

It was wrong. Why couldn't she just be a bad person like Wiedermann?

So, she shifted her perspective. Erica was a good woman. She didn't deserve the pain, but it was necessary in order for her to realize the truth.

Then she might leave Wiedermann, and . . . Well, whatever happened past that point was useless, since Jay would most likely be dead by that point. Whether IOCRO or Wiedermann himself did it was irrelevant. The important thing was that it was an unavoidable truth, just like the fact that Wiedermann was a danger to the world.

According to the files, according to the letter, according to *everything* . . .

He could destroy the entire country, should he wish to. Not to mention the world as a whole.

The deadline for the article was growing near, yet Jay only felt more and more nervous over turning it in. But she had steeled her heart. On that same day that she turned it in, she would also send it in to as many major publications and news outlets as she could find over the world. Ordinarily, this would probably have no effect, but if that strange organization was truly intent on using her as a pawn, then they might as well try to actually help her.

There were three days left.

Some people were already turning their stories in, but Jay had decided to leave it for the very deadline. Not because she had anything left to write. No, she had documented everything she knew in detail, going so far as to contain little anecdotes of her personal experiences. Things she knew Erica would approve of.

No, the reason she was waiting to turn it in was just that, well . . . it gave her a few more days to be on good terms with Erica.

But as always happens, the day eventually arrived.

* * *

It was a Friday, but Erica felt no great relief because the workweek was over. She enjoyed her work, whether it was with the school or with Kreig, and she had many reasons to do so. The main one was her students.

Her classes could be a little loud at times, but she could usually quiet them pretty easily. Some students were quicker to understand than others, a few questioned her with genuinely good insights, and others simply needed a little guidance to grow better with each week. She enjoyed each of their contributions, and after only a few weeks of this arrangement, she had already grown to love a few students in particular.

Of these, she quite liked the moody contrarian, Jay. Kreig seemed to think she was a bit peculiar, but the both of them had come to agree that her strength was in her tenacity despite the difficulties she faced. For Kreig, that meant she would always try to compete with the rest of the class, regardless of her physical weakness. For Erica, that meant she worked hard, even though her assignment had been radically changed to fit her needs. It was impressive, and Erica had no doubt in mind that Jay could become a fantastic journalist one day, even if it meant that she might have to put her grudges aside.

Yes, as much as Erica enjoyed Jay's presence, it was clear that she had a lot of issues. The other teachers shared the same belief, with one even mentioning that Jay had an immensely troubled home life.

That was why Erica was so delighted to see Jay interested in socializing with her. Hadn't she become a teacher specifically to be the person she had needed when she was young like Jay?

A good teacher can do so much to help, and Erica was convinced that she could be that help. And for a while, it did help. Jay slowly became more and more soft-spoken, eventually even ceasing to ask strange, vaguely condescending questions. They talked about things unrelated to school and all that. Apparently, Jay had once had a cat, though she had to let it go once her mother admitted that they couldn't afford to keep it.

It was a bit sad, and Jay had tried to make a point about how she wouldn't miss it, but when Erica gently pushed her, Jay just broke down and admitted that she still wished she'd kept it, even if it meant giving up her computer or phone. To console her, Erica suggested that once Jay was an adult and was making big bucks off her journalism, she could keep as many cats as she might want. In response, Jay had smiled and turned away.

Such conversations had happened a few times, giving Erica a little glimpse into the person Jay actually was beneath all the anger and presumption.

They were so alike.

The lesson was about to end. About half of the class had yet to turn in their stories, Jay being one of them. Patiently, Erica moved about the classroom, giving final advice and suggestions and making sure that people were happy with the stories that had taken so much time and effort. She moved to stand behind Jay, getting only a quick glimpse at the words on the computer screen before the laptop was slammed shut and Jay whirled around to face her.

Erica smiled and Jay visibly relaxed. Not once had Jay let Erica read what she had written, but that was all right. Jay as a person was quite secretive, which included her notes and written work. But, by the looks of it, Jay had quite a few pages to turn in. Reading them all would be a daunting task, but Erica was excited to do so.

Breaking the silence, Jay said, "I'm done."

Erica's smile grew slightly broader. "All done? Completely done? Nothing to change or fix or anything?"

Jay turned away, unusually solemn. "Yeah, it's done. I'll give it to you once the lesson ends."

Erica's face faltered slightly. Something was amiss. Was the article Jay had spent so long writing not up to her expectations? Had something happened? Did she reach an unusual conclusion? Concerned, Erica bent down next to Jay, going down to her level. She looked Jay straight in the eye. Jay turned away, her face tight. "Is everything all right?"

"Yeah," Jay croaked. "Of course. With this . . . Everything is all right."

Erica scratched her head, but she didn't say anything. She just kept looking at Jay until she was forced to turn back to Erica. Their eyes met, and Jay wasn't able to keep the pain out of her eyes. Again, Erica said nothing. "It . . ." Jay began, but turned away. Erica kept quiet. Jay's lips tightened into a thin line and her face darkened. "After you read this . . ." Her eyes returned to face Erica. There was ill-hidden fear in them. "You won't resent me, will you?"

With this, Erica smiled again. "Nope!" She grinned broadly even though Jay seemed far from comforted. "No matter what, as long as you're happy and proud of this, I'll support it." Jay stared at her blankly. "You put your heart into this, didn't you?"

Jay nodded stiffly. "Yeah."

Erica stood back up and placed a hand on Jay's head. "Then you've got nothing to be afraid of! I'll have your back for sure, even if you publish government secrets and stuff!"

Jay looked down at her lap and curled her hands into fists. When she then lifted her head again, bearing a face brimming with determination, she had a smile on her lips. "Yeah!"

Erica couldn't possibly know it, but she had just sealed her own fate.

CHAPTER 34

LAUGHTER

Another lesson gone off without a hitch. As the bell rang, the students began milling out of the classroom, the last few papers being handed in as they went. Erica cheerfully said goodbye to each of them.

A collection of papers a good bit thicker than the rest of them was placed in her hands, and she met Jay's grim eyes. It seemed as though she had something left to say. "What is it, Jay?"

Jay frowned, probably at herself, and said, "When you get home, make sure you read this one first. And not tomorrow, or even tonight. Before seven this evening . . . You have to have read it."

The seriousness of Jay's words startled Erica, but then again, Jay could be rather serious when she wanted to. Erica smiled reassuringly. "Of course. I'll make sure of it."

Looking off, Jay seemed on the edge of saying something else, but as other students began trying to turn in their own papers, she apparently decided against it. "Thanks. Goodbye."

As Jay began leaving with the rest, Erica let out a cheerful "See you soon!"

Jay glanced back at her but didn't reply.

The whole encounter seemed a little strange, but Erica was quickly distracted by all of the other students. In only a few minutes, she was alone in the classroom. Other classes would soon arrive, so she had better get ready. But before that, she wanted to check something.

She stuck her head out of the classroom door like a meerkat and found Kreig in an instant. He was standing right outside, wearing his usual PE clothes and carrying a little clipboard. With his immense build, the whole outfit seemed pretty tacky, but Erica only found it cute. Their eyes met and Erica could tell that he was happy to see her, just as she was happy to see him.

The time between classes was brief, but it was enough time.

Kreig silently entered the classroom. For a few seconds, he just looked around and fiddled with his fingers. Then, he looked back at Erica. "Would you like to join me for dinner tonight?"

Erica lit up at the thought of Kreig's cooking. "Well, of course, I—" But then she remembered her promise to Jay. An article of that length would take at least half an hour to read, so she really couldn't stay as long as a shared dinner would require. Heart slumping, she dejectedly shook her head. "I'm sorry; I made a promise to Jay that I'd read her article by seven tonight."

He seemed perplexed. "A weird promise. Nonetheless, upholding a vow certainly goes before any dinner. However . . ." He turned away to regard the whiteboard. "If you only stay for the afternoon, I have something I would like to show you."

"I suppose as long as I leave before it gets too late, I should have time, right?"

Kreig turned back to her with the tiniest smile. "Of course. I'll be quick."

Then, before he left for his own class, she gave him a little peck on the cheek, just for luck.

The rest of the day passed quickly, with Kreig coming to visit her classroom every few hours. At lunch, they ate together, and when the bell rang for the final time, they biked home to Kreig's apartment side by side.

The papers cradled in her bag didn't weigh as heavy as they should have.

"So?" Erica asked excitedly. "What did you want to show me?"

Kreig remained silent as he removed a jacket he had begun wearing as of late and hung it in the hall. She watched in impatient interest as he moved toward the middle of the living room, where she found a canvas standing blank and ready. Moving quickly, he retrieved a chair and placed it in front of the canvas.

Erica blinked and burst out into a massive grin. "You're going to paint me!" With a laugh playing on her lips, she skipped over toward the chair, beaming a smile almost only ever found on schoolgirls. Kreig stared at her. She looked back at him. "Or are we doing some sort of role reversal? I'll have you know I got a strong B in art!"

He shook his head. "No, I'm sorry. I was only transfixed by your beauty."

Erica grinned slyly. "Charmer. Very well! As you've been so courteous until now, I shall allow you to paint me. Then again, technically, I guess you've painted me before?"

"Well, yes," he said hesitantly. "But actually no. I never truly painted you a portrait."

"Huh. I guess so!" In one grand move, Erica sat in the chair, trying to get into a suitably preposterous posture without breaking her spine. But right as she got herself comfortable, Kreig handed her a little flower. She looked at it strangely. It was weird. The flower was white with red spots. It wasn't a particularly odd flower, it was actually quite normal, but something about its weight and size felt off. As though it hadn't been grown but rather created. Maybe in a lab or something.

Erica carefully examined the stem. Nothing odd there. Had Kreig's Russian mobster caretakers gifted him a lab-grown sample of a new breed of flower?

Or he'd bred it himself. With Kreig, either one was likely enough.

"It means *Love*," Kreig said absently as he prepared his palette.

"It does?" Erica took a whiff of the flower. Sweet and flowery, a little lighter than a rose but no heavier than an orchid. "Makes sense to me."

After a few seconds of studying the flower, Erica came to realize that Kreig was looking at her. And so, with a flurry of movement, she took a relaxed pose, holding the flower to her nose. From the corner of her eye, she watched as Kreig began to work.

It was hard work, painting someone you loved.

The trouble was to represent them accurately. To show them as they were, to make sure that when you turned the canvas and showed it to them, they were not horrified by your need to please them.

But you can only paint them as you see them, and through your loving eyes, they hold no flaws. They are perfect, and so that is what you paint. But painting perfection is no simple matter either. How can you put emotion into dead pigments and wet materials? Is it truly possible to give luster to eyes whose radiance is a lie?

This was the problem before Kreig. Nevertheless, he was no amateur artist by now. Despite what he himself might say, he had all the skills necessary to give life to the corpse of a canvas.

But he wanted to do more. Simply portraying her as she was wasn't enough. He had no sight to paint but his own, and so, in order for him to make this sight of beauty beyond measure believable, he had no choice but to put not only what he saw upon the canvas but also what he *felt*.

And that he did.

All the feelings in his heart, although they felt overflowing, he put on the canvas alongside his paints. The painting that took form mirrored reality in many ways, but there was something soft about it. Some form and color and motion that put a feeling into it that made just the sight of it feel lovable.

"What do you think about Jay?"

Kreig looked up at Erica, briefly brought out of his reverie. When he now looked at her, he felt her form muted and changed, as though she were a painting. "How do you mean?"

Erica grimaced in thought. "Well, you know, she's . . . I think she has some real trouble at home." Kreig nodded, trying his very best to split his attention between listening to her and drawing her. "But she can get better. That's what I think, at least. You haven't seen anything she's done, but . . ."

"No, she tried to interview me once. She had all the makings of a proper interrogations officer."

Erica visibly lit up. "You think so too?"

"Yes," he said. "Though she will need a bit more training."

"Well, yeah, that's a given." Erica quickly sank back into thoughtful silence. "It's really up to adults like us to make sure people like that don't go off the deep end. Teenagers are . . . Heh, you know. Us meeting her was surely not a coincidence." Erica sighed wistfully. "I bet some higher power is looking after her. Like the lizard king, hoping to make her his bride . . ."

Kreig could feel his brows knit together. Didn't the lizard king already have plenty of brides? Why would he need a human one? Worse yet, how come Erica would know about any of that?

Unsure how to answer, he let her return to her contemplative silence. She was prettiest that way, anyways. Looking off forlornly, eyes glittering with thoughts of whatever strange things her mind conjured.

It only took an hour or two, but he finished the portrait.

And in the corner of his eye, he saw a little message from a system he no longer had all that much care for.

Artistry reached Rank X

He blinked at it, unsure how that had happened. This painting . . .

He tried to evaluate his painting objectively but found that he could not suppress his feelings of adoration. Was it a good painting because he made it, or was it a good painting because it portrayed Erica? He couldn't tell, but while he sat in a silent stupor from the painting, he let the description of the final skill's rank float to the top of his mind.

Artistry (X)
Rank X: Evoke love
Rank V: Evoke opinion
Rank IV: Evoke emotion
Rank III: Greater anatomy, perspective, shading
Rank II: Greater color and design
Rank I: Stable hands, smoother lines

Evoke . . . love?

Shouldn't something like that be contained in Rank IV? Or maybe this was . . .

He stared at the painting, feeling a sigh rise to his lips. It was gorgeous. It was, without a doubt, the greatest piece of art he had ever created. Although his other paintings likewise contained soul and life, this one seemed to hold some other element, some singular emotion above sorrow or joy. Something that described not just humanity but life itself.

Erica, lost in thought, had clearly not realized Kreig had finished.

And yet he hesitated to call out to her. For when his eyes left the painting, he found it still sitting there in that chair, just as lovable as before.

"Erica," he said softly. When she didn't respond, he said it again, just a little louder, "Erica."

"Huh?" She turned away from the flower in her hand. "What is— Oh! Are you done? Is it finished?"

Kreig hesitated for a moment before nodding.

Grinning like a child, she hopped off the chair, still holding the little flower. Kreig remained by the canvas, feeling like a student about to be graded by their teacher. It didn't help that Erica was not only an actual teacher but also *his* teacher. But when she finally moved to his side and let her eyes fall on the painting, she didn't say a thing. Not a word of comment or praise or critique. She simply froze.

Kreig turned to regard her face. It was petrified in a mask of sheer shock.

Then, slowly, she approached the painting, putting her eyes at the level of her counterpart's.

"Careful; it remains wet," Kreig warned quietly.

Not a hair touched the painting. Her eyes slowly moved from her counterpart's face and over to the flower she held. Moving stiffly, she brought up the flower in her own hand and regarded it silently. She smiled thinly. "How'd you do that?" she asked in a small voice. "How'd you make the flower in the painting look so much more alive than the real one?"

In a shrunken little corner of his heart, Kreig wanted to say it was all due to the system, that without its help he could never have done this, that he would be nothing without it and that everything he was and everything he wasn't was because of it. But then the words of Darius rose to his mind, and the gentle praise of his siblings shone through, and he simply smiled at her. "Thank you," he said. "It was only because it was you."

She blushed. Smiled. And began to laugh. It was a strange laugh, not like the peal of silver bells or the chime of a clock, but rather like the dying croaks of a strangled seagull.

And yet, as he heard it, Kreig couldn't help but smile as well, his lips parting into a burst of laughter. He couldn't remember the last time he had laughed. He had almost forgotten how to. But there, now, with Erica throwing her arms around him, he laughed with such mirth that he couldn't remember anything else but this immense joy. He decided right there and right then that should anything happen to her, should anything threaten to remove her from his life, he would fight it tooth and nail. He valued her like a king valued his kingdom, like an artist adored their art.

After a minute or so, their laughter slowly died down, but she still held him.

"I don't think I've ever heard you laugh before," Erica said, breathless. Kreig smiled at her. "It's a good laugh! You should laugh more, I think."

"If you say so," Kreig agreed.

Erica smiled back at him, her eyes filled with shining.

But she couldn't stay all night, and with a parting kiss that Kreig really had to bend down low for, she left for home, leaving Kreig to make dinner for his siblings.

They came home at the normal time, with Sam arriving before George. Since Kreig wasn't entirely done with the dinner, Sam spent a little while helping him finish up.

And there they were, eating dinner just like so many times before.

"Was Erica here?" George asked sensibly. The portrait still standing in the living room had probably clued him in.

"Yes, though she had to leave early."

"Pity. You know, since Mother and Father have already moved on, it's up to me and Sam to decide whether or not she's worthy of you," George said with a straight face.

Kreig gaped at him. What? Why would they decide something like that? Perplexed, Kreig turned to Sam in the hopes that she might clear up this strange misconception. Instead, he found her nodding gravely. "Indeed, indeed. We can't let anyone dirty take our Kreig's hand in marriage!"

"Th—that is preposterous," Kreig stammered. "I'm hardly worthy of *her*! How can you possibly make such a decision? Furthermore, marriage is a bit . . ."

Unexpectedly, George grinned slyly. "All in due time, brother dearest. It all starts with a portrait, don't you know?"

Sam nodded in tandem with his words. "Indeed. I can't tell you how many stories I've seen where a poor artist charms the rich duke's daughter by painting her in all sorts of situations . . ." Grinning as widely as her brother, Sam brought a spoonful of soup to her lips. "Truly, you are a most avaricious charmer."

George stared at her, his expression falling a little. "Do you even know what that word means?"

Sam did not answer, but Kreig was too busy feeling flustered to really notice. He, marry Erica? Why, that would be . . . Well, it would certainly be *something*. If the God Below was willing, then anything was possible. Though, of course, that all remained for Erica to decide on. Kreig could hardly force her into anything. Not that he wanted to, either.

Though the situation did mean that, one day, he would have to be honest with her. Otherwise, there might come a day when she was old and gray and he remained young and strong. Such a situation, as heartbreaking as it was to consider, was inevitable and just. The fate of all living things was to die.

But before that, he had to be honest. About who he was. About *what* he was. About the things he had done.

. . . But that day remained far off and distant. As a matter of fact, the longer Kreig could live without having to go through with it, the better. Her reaction could be quite unpredictable, and if worse came to worst, she might even attempt to share the truth with others. In that situation, Kreig might find himself unable to live the life he had so enjoyed until now. The school, Erica, his siblings . . . There was no end to the things he might lose.

Surely, though, Erica wouldn't do such a thing, would she? Of course, she certainly enjoyed deliberating on whatever odd ideas she cooked up, but she seemed far from intent on sharing these truths with the world as a whole.

That was why Kreig felt quite comfortable in his plans for the future.

Silently, without any need for verbal communication, Kreig handed a wet plate over to George, who dried it off and put it in the cupboards. Since Sam had helped with setting the table, George would now help with the dishes. It was as simple as that, and Kreig found the process enjoyable. He didn't really have to think a whole bunch; he could just let his hands move while his mind cleared itself from clutter and cobwebs.

Absently, he glanced at a clock hanging on the wall. 7:07. Hopefully, Erica had been able to finish reading the article by now, though he remained unsure why that would be needed at all.

On the couch, Sam absently hopped between various channels on the television.

Everything was all right.

Brip-brip.

There was a strange chime Kreig had never heard before. Turning toward it, he watched in quiet confusion as George fumbled through his pockets, finally removing a peculiar little phone Kreig had never seen him use before. George answered the call. "George Wiedermann, 24th Region Director." His left eye twitched. "There has been a— What the hell are you talking about? Who?" He fell silent for a few seconds. "We don't even know who they are?! Well, figure it—"

Sam leaned over the couch and turned to the both of them. "George? What's going on?"

He held up a hand, hushing her. Kreig felt a silent panic creep into the back of his mind. "We need to silence this. This isn't something that can—" George's face grew paler by the second. His eyes flew wide. "It's already across the world? How is that even—" George threw his hands into the air, face flushed. He took a rattling breath and seemed to try to compose himself. He shot one hasty glance at Kreig. "Yeah, he's here. No, we won't . . ."

Something on the television made Kreig turn toward it. The news had come on.

"We're hearing about a— Yes, there seems to be . . . There are reports of a previously unmentioned otherworldly creature that seems to have arrived no less than six months ago . . ."

Kreig could feel the plate in his hand crack and finally explode into little sharp fragments that all fell to the floor with a clatter. George placed one hand on the phone and turned to him, locking eyes. "Kreig, please, don't— Just relax. We'll have this done with, so please don't—"

"Erica," Kreig breathed. A heavy stone settled in his gut. "*I have to get to Erica.*"

Sam jumped out of the couch and placed herself in front of Kreig. "Hey, look, Kreig, take it easy! She'll be fine, she's— She probably isn't even watching the news, right? And if she is, then, I mean . . . They won't mention you by name, right? They wouldn't—"

"The creature, according to the reports, supposedly goes under the name Kreig Wiedermann . . ."

Sam gestured wildly. "That's honestly just—"

Kreig pushed her aside. His mind was a whirlwind of conflicting thoughts and emotions, each centering on the eye of the storm that was Erica. He had to get to Erica. He had to tell her that all this was just some sort of slander and that it wasn't true, and even if it *was*, it was nowhere near as bad as they made it out to be. He just had to tell her that. That was all.

Sam tumbled to the floor, her eyes wide and staring.

A hand fell on Kreig's chest. He looked down to find George looking up at him, still holding the phone to his ear. Slowly, carefully, George removed his hand from his chest. "I can't stop you, Kreig. This situation is . . . I can't tell you what to do or what not to do, but I will ask you to be careful. No matter what happens, IOCRO will protect you and those you love. You have my word. But if you do something to arouse the wrath of the public, we cannot defend your image. So, please. Be careful."

Kreig nodded stiffly and walked over to the kitchen window. He opened it wide. The gazes of his siblings burned holes in his back.

Ruefully, he whispered an old incantation, one he had learned many years before while still trying to understand his place in the world.

Wings of a Dove (X)

His back grew hot and a pair of wings sprouted from it. They were white as snow and large enough to carry him. At his command, they folded themselves across his back, allowing him to step out of the window.

And then, as his siblings watched, he took flight.

Higher, higher, until he couldn't make out the ground anymore, until all that remained below him was a great expanse of black and stars. He felt breathless and weak. His hands trembled. What was happening? How did this happen? Why?

Did someone despise him so much that they would do this to him? Was there someone after his life? Did he have enemies in this world, too?

Behind him, his wings flapped mightily, bringing him higher and higher until the world below couldn't be described as anything but an endless black sea, punctuated by glittering lights.

He had to get to Erica. He had to explain the truth.

But if he truly was being attacked by some malevolent force, some organization bent on his demise, then he could hardly appear at her side empty-handed. Yes, he would need some protection. There was nothing in this world he truly feared from a combat standpoint, but if some immense being from the otherworld had appeared to bring about his end, then he would indeed need everything he could find.

With all the strength and speed he had to give, Kreig flew toward his goal. With the kind of speed he was able to build up, he was there within seconds, crashing through the roof of the police station. A bewildered guard stared at him as he easily destroyed the protective barrier that guarded his weapons and armor. Silently, without answering the guards' hysterical questions, Kreig donned the blood-red armor, placing the sword and shield on his back. His wings emerged from two specific incisions made along his back.

Being back in the armor felt at once homely and disturbing. The scent of blood within the helmet was overwhelming, as were the dried, rusty flakes of blood inside the joints. But he couldn't afford to be picky.

Other officers began rushing into the station, pointing guns and shouting things Kreig didn't care to hear. Without a word, he hunched down and leapt off the ground, bringing himself into the air.

Now.

Erica.

CHAPTER 35

IS IT TRUE?

At the door to her apartment, Erica was enthusiastically met by her cat, Sourdough. Smiling, Erica bent down and picked him up, letting the blond cat lie across her shoulders while she prepared a simple dinner for the both of them. Since she wanted to read Jay's article as soon as possible, she settled on a simple sandwich, of course not before giving some kibble to Sourdough.

Then, removing a small stack of stories, she settled down on her couch. It was 6:27, and she sincerely hoped it would be enough. Jay had never exactly specified that she had to read the whole thing, but Erica would certainly shoot for it.

There was always the chance that if Erica failed to read it, Jay's trust in her might fall critically. The trust of a student such as her was not easily gained, and Erica was adamant in retaining it.

With that determination in mind, Erica quickly sifted through the stories until she found Jay's article. It was an impressive fifteen pages, with the title being bold and striking: "The World Ought To Cower." *Points for being just as clickbaity as a real article*, Erica thought. Cozying up as best as she could, she read the first line on the first page.

Some men aren't quite what they seem to be.

It took Erica around half an hour to read the entire article, during which time her emotional state quickly took a dive for the worse.

The article was simple enough. It began with an anecdote following the author's first run-in with the main focus of the article, Kreig Wiedermann. The very second his name had been mentioned, Erica felt something within her lurch. Then the author explained her home life in great detail, going so far as to explain exactly how she received a system, namely by stealing it from her mother. The article went on to describe how the author came to slowly understand exactly what Kreig Wiedermann was, alongside various pieces of evidence and explanations for his situation.

Of course, it was only the work of an amateur. The wording could be clunky at times, and the thread of the story was often lost. The conclusion, as compared to the introduction, was nothing much.

But throughout all of it, it retained some peculiar honesty.

Erica felt like laughing. It had to be a joke, right? Some strange little fantasy tale, or an article taken from an odd alternative universe where Kreig Wiedermann—*her* Kreig—was somehow a monstrous nonhuman from the otherworld.

That had to be the answer, no?

It couldn't be true.

Kreig was many things, but he was still *human*. This article—this strange little article that she had encouraged Jay to write—was calling him a mass murderer on a national scale. She might have believed it if it wasn't for that part. If someone told her that Kreig was from the otherworld, she might have considered it. But not this. What Jay suggested was simply not feasible. Kreig was many things—clumsy, naive, silly, even—but he was not what Jay was trying to paint him as.

She was trying to make him out to be a monster. Even worse, a monster that the entire world would have to work together to take out. It was absolutely absurd.

... But if she were to grade it as a piece of speculative fiction, then—

Knock-knock.

There was a subdued knock on the door. Erica put down the article and stood up. A glance at the clock on the wall told her it was 7:16.

She shouldn't have any visitors at this time, so it could either be that one of her neighbors wanted a cup of sugar, or that the government had finally caught on to her suspicions and aimed to do away with her once and for all.

Only half-weary, Erica moved toward her front door. Sourdough was asleep on his scratching post, so he wouldn't be a bother.

Knock-knock-knock.

Another series of knocks, just a little more frantic than the last. Putting aside her weird superstitions, Erica opened the door.

A massive knight wearing blood-red armor stood outside the door, a large pair of wings framing his hulking form. Erica blinked at him. In a movement so swift she could barely catch it, the knight ripped off his helmet, letting his long black hair wave freely. Beneath that helmet was Kreig. It was just his face, his normal, if slightly distraught, face. Strangely enough, the edges of his face were tinged with something red.

"Kreig?" Erica said, though her voice felt so much more far off than it should have been. "Is that you?"

In a dazzling show of light, the wings on Kreig's back dissolved into stray feathers.

"It isn't true," Kreig said. "None of it is true."

Erica smiled dishonestly. She couldn't read her own heart. "What isn't true?"

His face twisted in a grimace of exacerbation. "What they . . . The news. They are saying things."

Erica's smile worsened. "The news? I haven't watched the news tonight. Is there anything interesting on?"

Kreig gritted his teeth. Erica took a step back as he hunched down and entered the apartment. An odd smell of sweet metal touched Erica's nose. It was that strange armor Kreig wore. It smelled like blood. Blood and fresh flowers. Why was Kreig wearing that? Was he making a joke? Maybe he and Jay had collaborated to play a silly joke on her. If that was the case, it was a pretty tasteless joke.

Kreig moved through her apartment almost like a specter, his eyes falling on the turned-off radio and the dark television. And then he saw the little article that lay on her coffee table.

In one, simple movement, he fell to his knees.

"Please," he said softly. *"Don't hate me."*

Erica scoffed gently and went around to stand before him. "Why would I ever hate you?"

His eyes squeezed shut, and she could taste the blood in the air. He held out his hand and she took it. It was heavy and large. When she looked down at her hand, she found it reddened as though touched by rust.

A description of a piece of armor flitted through her mind, one that Jay had described in the article. *Reddened by the blood of countless men.*

Gulping, she retrieved her hand.

Kreig's face rose to face her, and she felt her heart lurch. She couldn't recognize him anymore. Not quite. It was almost as though she were looking at an unknown man.

The truth was staring her in the face, and yet she couldn't bear to accept it.

"I have done many things worthy of your contempt, but loving you was surely not one of them," Kreig said, almost to himself. Quietly, he continued. "What I have been through is not something I ever wished for you to truly know. I understand that. Likewise, I knew that one day, you would have had to learn of it. *But not like this.*"

Erica glanced over at the article. Her face felt numb. "Then, it's true?"

He nodded stiffly, hair falling to cover his eyes.

Quietly, Erica sat down before him, folding her legs beneath her. She laid her hands in her lap and began weeping.

His armored hand reached up to cradle her cheek and she let him, despite the way her tears absorbed the blood rust to form red stains. "Please," he said, "before you decide on how you feel, will you let me tell you my side? I do not know what the article says, and I cannot tell from which perspective it comes, but I assure you that I have in no way acted out of maliciousness or spite. For you, all I ever did was love."

"I know," Erica replied amidst the tears. "You are a good man, Kreig. I still— Despite this all . . . I still think that you are good."

His hands moved to touch her shoulders, and he brought her into his embrace. His armor was hard and the scent of blood was overwhelming. Her tears touched his chest and ran down his breastplate in great red streaks. She looked up at him again, her eyes red and large. "You're getting better, aren't you?"

Kreig nodded. "Yes."

She smiled, the edges still weighed down by her tears. "Then, that is all I need from you."

For a few minutes, they simply sat there on the floor, cradled in each other's arms. Finally, Erica wiped her tears and stood up. Kreig followed suit. They shared a look, one that agreed on every level that they would never be quite the same again. The innocence of what they were had been tarnished, but that did not mean that it was the end. In fact, it might just be the beginning.

"What happens now?"

"I don't know," Kreig admitted.

Erica slumped down on the couch, the article that started all of this held lazily in her hands. "Jay did this? Did she release her article to someone? How would this . . ." She shook her head dejectedly.

Kreig sat down next to her, the couch creaking. He slowly clasped his hands. "If it is as you say, then it is indeed the case that Jay somehow released the article across the world. Because of her . . ." He shook his head, barring any such thoughts. "What's done is done."

"Do you think Jay's in danger?"

Kreig stared at her wide-eyed. "From who?"

Erica shrugged her shoulders. "I don't know. Just . . . People will want to get her for this, right? IOCRO, the government, police . . . Something like that." For a moment, she froze in place, her eyes growing wide. "You don't think— She wouldn't try to fight, would she? Like, if they tried to arrest her, she wouldn't try to escape through the window or anything, would she?"

Frighteningly enough, Kreig couldn't be sure about that. IOCRO was, by all means, an organization with the size and power necessary to make a girl like Jay disappear. She had not been an influential girl until this moment, and her social class made her disposable. If she put up a fight, they wouldn't even hesitate to do away with her, especially if it would protect Kreig's interests.

That meant that, as bizarre as it was, Jay was in danger. She might not believe it herself, but her entrance on the world stage could very well lead to her death.

Kreig gritted his teeth. He certainly didn't want to—his old self would never—but he had to save the one who might just have doomed his one sense of normalcy.

Erica stared at him, her eyes wide and staring. "Please, we need to— She's just a girl; she doesn't understand how—"

Kreig held up a hand placatingly. "I understand. She is a good student. She shows much promise. Losing her like this . . . It would be a grave shame."

Nodding, Erica stood up, hands curling into fists. "She did this because of me. I'm the one who told her to write an article; I was—"

In a single moment, she found herself in Kreig's arms again. "You have done nothing wrong. What she has done . . . She may be young, but she still has accountability for her actions. I will help her, but she will have to face the consequences somehow."

Erica hugged him tighter.

Although Kreig hardly liked the idea of it, he knew immediately that he would have to bring Erica with him. There might still be unseen enemies about, ones that might want to use his weakness—Erica—against him. George and Sam could handle themselves, but Erica was only a girl.

If something happened and he was unable to defend her, he would never forgive himself.

Taking her hand, he led her outside.

He placed his hand on her forehead. She seemed confused at first, until he began to whisper psalms.

Aetherial Armor (II)
Blessing of Walls (X)
Blessing of Castles (IV)
Lion's Mane (X)
Protection of Gales (V)
Ogre's Hide (X)

. . .

With the wild abandonment of a lover protecting their loved one, he placed a number of protective enchantments and blessings on her, each creating a magic glow across her body. Some protected her fully from the effects of falling, others created a translucent armor across her body, protecting her from harm. All throughout, she simply watched, curious and amazed as she was granted power and defense beyond the capabilities of most professional Fighters.

"This is . . ."

"Protection." In one swift movement, he swept her off her feet and brought her into his arms.

Wings of a Dove (X)

With another whispered incantation, a pair of wings sprouted from his back.

He flapped them a few times, bringing his feet off the ground. As if suddenly terrified, he felt how Erica—still pressed against his chest—took a tight hold of his cape.

And then they were off, toward where Jay lived.

Skyscrapers and lights like stars flashed past below them. Kreig would certainly have liked to fly faster, but not with Erica in his grasp. The last time Kreig could remember flying with someone in his arms was when Peter had asked to see how it felt. At that time, Kreig had excitedly done loops and barrel rolls to make Peter scream, because it was funny. When Kreig put him down afterwards Peter didn't want to go flying again.

But Kreig felt no such desires now. Erica was still clutching him tightly, her wide eyes lapping up the stars both above and below. Going any faster than this would be uncomfortable to her, and right now, that mattered more to him than anything else.

A trembling finger stretched out in his vision, pointing to where she knew Jay lived. Kreig had forgotten to ask why she knew this, but he could imagine that she had been worried about Jay even before this whole mess.

As for Kreig . . .

He really didn't know what to feel. Off there in the distance, where Erica was pointing, a number of helicopters buzzed about a building like flies, pointing searchlights at anything that moved. A few of these concentrated on a certain apartment. That would be their best bet. If this was really what he wanted to do, that was.

Logically, he knew that this was the end of his happy days. He felt numb inside. With this, he couldn't teach at Painstone anymore. He wouldn't be able to get work anywhere else, either. He'd still have his family and he'd still have Erica, but what else?

It occurred to him that he didn't need much else.

Erica was trying to tell him something, but the rushing winds prevented her from doing so. It seemed that she was still worried about Jay.

With his wings flapping mechanically and his mind stuck in a thick fog that rendered his thoughts into silhouettes, Kreig descended toward the building. Many of the apartment doors were open, revealing nosy neighbors peeking out curiously. Several of these neighbors had exited fully, being in the middle of talking to various armor-clad soldiers. Kreig didn't care about them, though, even though many had noticed him. No, the one to whom his attention was drawn was none other than a relatively young woman, clad in a strangely revealing outfit and wearing thick makeup that only barely hid the streaks of tears running down her cheeks. And yet, despite all that, when her eyes fell on Kreig and their eyes met, a fantastic smile shone on her face and she stretched her arms toward him.

Kreig landed softly on the floor where this woman was, coming to stand right in front of her. Erica carefully stepped down from his arms. The woman didn't even glance at her.

Instead, her eyes filling anew with tears, she fell to her knees, stretching her arms to the sky again. "Oh, oh! My angel!" Then, she clasped her hands to her chest in prayer. Kreig felt his body grow stiff.

Angel? *Him?*

Erica's eyes hopped frantically between Kreig and the woman before settling on the kneeling woman. "Mrs. Crooks?" Slowly, Erica approached her. And, in a deliberate tone, she asked, "Do you know where Jay is?"

Mrs. Crooks' smile grew even wider. "Yes! Of course, of course, yes! She said—she told me, before she left, she said, '*Mother, your angel will come to you for guidance. And you shall tell him where I am. Tell him and no one else.'* And so I have done!" The poor woman was on the verge of hysteria, her eyes beaming with religious fanaticism of a kind Kreig had only seen many, many years earlier.

A few of the nearby soldiers approached warily, trading looks, gripping their weapons tightly. Among them, Kreig recognized a face.

"Craig," Kreig greeted.

"Uh," Craig replied. "Is this a bad— Erm, guys, I think . . ." Craig gestured to the rest, apparently signaling. The soldiers carefully backed off, seemingly returning their attention to the neighbors. Craig watched them with furrowed brows. When he turned back to Kreig, Craig noticed a hint of fear in them. ". . . Will you hurt the suspect?"

Kreig met his eyes. "No."

Craig shuffled his feet and glanced away. "Heh, well, that's good, because, well . . . She's only a minor, right? She doesn't . . ." Kreig made no reply while Craig fumbled for words. "Well. You know."

Sighing audibly, Craig made his exit.

Kreig turned back to Mrs. Crooks, whose eyes remained aglow with that frenzy of absolute certainty. Kreig winced at the sight of it. Maybe a hundred years before, he would have been used to being viewed with those eyes, but nowadays, he wasn't even used to being viewed with fear.

Mrs. Crooks glanced to and fro quickly before returning to Kreig, apparently assured that no one was listening. "She went out to the oak."

Erica frowned. "The oak?"

Mrs. Crooks nodded deeply, sustaining eye contact with Kreig. He really wanted to ask her to stand up. "Yes. Out by Undulat Park. A very pretty place. This time of year . . . maybe a little cold. But you should have no problem with that, my angel."

Kreig turned away from her, feeling how his mind darkened. "I am no angel."

In fact, trying to pose as a herald of God could only be considered a form of blasphemy. But she was too far gone to hear something like that.

"Does it matter?" Mrs. Crooks tilted her head. Kreig turned back to look at her. "You can part the night sky with a prayer. Does it matter if you are an angel or a demon? Regardless, you are worthy of worship."

Kreig could feel his brows pinch together. How was he supposed to understand that?

Before he could put any more thought to her cryptic words, a hand clasped his, and his eyes met with Erica's. Her lips were pulled tight in anxiety. "We need to go," she said gravely. "This isn't a matter of someone hurting her anymore."

"What do you mean?"

Erica's grasp on his hand tightened. "I think she might try to hurt *herself.*"

CHAPTER 36

WHITE EYES

It wasn't here. Not here, not there.

Her hands were red and cold and wet and freezing, and she wanted to go home, but there would be no home for her there, only men with guns who wanted to kill her and a creature that could destroy continents that wanted to kill her and everything and everyone else. Her chest ached with the cold air she had to draw in with every frantic breath. The fog of her breath clouded her vision, and she wished she'd brought a better jacket.

And still, it wasn't there.

What wasn't?

The *nook*! The cranny, the little hole for the little key! It just *wasn't there*.

She had searched all night, ever since she released the article. By now, it had to have been spread all across the world. That organization would make sure of it. That meant that her hours were limited. No, *minutes*. She told her mother to only tell Kreig, but if she told any other people . . .

Jay shook her head violently. No! Even if an army of men with guns came to attack, she could still survive!

If only she could read those files again, she might be able to formulate a plan. There were transcriptions of the observations that the therapist had made of him. Maybe, in there, she might be able to parse some new information, some weak spot that would make him spare her for fear of her releasing it. Or maybe she might find something else, or—or *anything*!

She had read those files so many times. She knew so much of it by heart. But not everything.

She had to find it; she *had to*. Otherwise, this would be the end of her. And maybe it was worth it just to get the truth out there, but she still didn't want to die. She didn't want to die.

She didn't want to die.

Her knees were soaking wet, and so were her hands and sleeves. She had gone around the tree too many times to count. But no matter how many times she ran her cold fingers over the corners of every root and hoped and wished and prayed in her heart that the little groove would present itself to her like a ray of light in the night, it never happened.

They couldn't have removed it. Why would they remove it? Would they really leave her for dead?

She gritted her teeth. They would. Didn't she come to that conclusion herself?

Yes, of course, but she still wanted to *live*!

She looked out toward the city. Countless helicopters whirled about it, their spotlights searching for something. Searching for *her*. But she was out here, and the only wretched creature that might come for her throat was *him*. He alone. Even if she had tried to escape, to leave all of this behind, it would have done her no good. He would have found her eventually. And if he somehow couldn't, then all of this would have been in vain.

She brought her freezing-cold fingers to her face and blew on them. A puff of white escaped her lips, and she wondered if she might not freeze to death before he ever arrived.

But there, in the distance, she saw it. Massive wings, shining dimly in the soft light of the crescent moon. He had arrived. He came. At that speed, he would be there within minutes.

Jay staggered to her feet. She tried to control her breathing. Maybe he would just kill her right away. Maybe he would strike her down with smiting lightning, not bothering to hear her out. Or maybe he would decapitate her in one swift slash. Or he could crush her skull with the flick of a finger. Or he might summon some form of creature to do it for him. Or he could pierce her heart with a beam of light.

Jay swallowed and balled her fists. She took a trembling breath, but she still couldn't make herself feel calm. She was supposed to be calm, damn it! How could she face him like this?

He descended from the skies with the flap of angel's wings, holding Erica in his arms as gently as a groom holds his bride. Even in the endless darkness of the night, to Jay, the both of them appeared to shine with a heavenly glow, like that of divine royalty arriving from heaven. For just a few seconds, Jay was breathless. Her hands trembled.

His eyes fell on her, and she felt the instinctual need to cower. They were white. Like snow. Like the white wings on his back. Like the depths of the sun.

Like an exposed skull.

A strange clicking noise came to her ears, but she realized it was only her teeth chattering.

Erica, her face twisted in worry, stepped toward Jay.

Jay took a step back, attempting to puff herself up with some form of pride and aggression. She had nothing to fear. It was she who held all the cards. This man—these two, they were *nothing*!

But Erica . . . Why was she there? She had read the article, hadn't she? She must have, since she was fine with being in Wiedermann's arms. And it wasn't as though she had known all this, since she would never have gotten close to him if that were the case. Then, the only possible situation was that she had read the article and accepted Wiedermann for who he was. Somehow, she had looked into the crooked and bloodied depths of Wiedermann's soul and still accepted him.

Her chest felt so cold. It was as though black bile was about to burst out of her throat. The world swayed beneath her feet.

"Jay?" Erica asked in a voice that made Jay feel like total shit. "Is everything okay? You aren't hurt, are you?" Erica took a gentle hold of Jay's hand. Her hand was so warm.

Jay slapped Erica's hand away.

Erica blinked. "Jay?"

"Shut up," Jay bit out. Her frantic gaze hopped over to Wiedermann, who stood behind like some sort of specter. Erica followed her gaze to him. She pointed an accusatory finger at Wiedermann. "Are you going to kill me now, huh? Is that it?" She felt a cocky grin tug at her lips even though Wiedermann seemed completely frozen. "You are, aren't you? Maybe with that sword, or maybe you'll just use that skill that makes stuff burn into snow. Neat skill. Have you ever tried it on a human before? A living one?"

Wiedermann didn't make a move, his eyes widening only a millimeter. Jay grinned.

"You have, haven't you?" Her grin broadened even though she wanted to run and hide and not die. "I bet you've burnt so many people, you can't even recall an example among them."

Erica approached again, her brows pinched in worry. "Jay, what are you—"

"Sh—shut up! You're not a part of this, okay? You're just . . . You're just his *flame*! Has he told you he's immortal? He's a regular grandpa, you know? In fifty years, you'll be an old grandma and he'll still look like *this*! Do you seriously want to live with a man who'll never age? After you're dead, he's sure to get himself another young little sparrow to play with for the next fifty years. Is that what you want? To be replaced like a one-use tissue wipe?"

Erica's lips pressed together into a thin white line. Jay hated to see that face on her. That face that said, *I want to slap you, but if I did, I'd no longer be allowed to teach.* So, instead, she said, "Jay, what are you saying?"

"Well?" Jay pressed, trying her best to put confidence she didn't have into her voice. "Would you?"

Erica turned away and frowned. But then her eyes fell on Wiedermann, and she smiled softly. His eyes seemed to plead to her, but he said nothing. "Yes," she said softly, barely above a whisper. "If it's him, then . . . I wouldn't mind it."

Jay ground her teeth. "Is that how you want to play? Fine."

But before she knew it, Erica's hand had fallen on her shoulder and Jay looked up at her, unsure whether to spit in her face or cry. "Please, Jay . . . It's okay. I read the article. You don't need to say anything else."

"I— You . . ." Jay glowered at the kindly smiling face in front of her. This was wrong. This wasn't how the script was supposed to go. She was making it all wrong.

Why did it have to be her?

In a movement fueled more so by desperation than anger, Jay shook off Erica's gentle hold and turned her attention back on Kreig. "What did you do to her?" His confusion shone through his blank expression. "Don't play stupid. You've got every skill and spell a man could ever dream of. You must have done *something*!"

Slowly, carefully, he shook his head. "I have done nothing."

"Or so you say," Jay growled. "You know what I think? I think you believe this all to be some sort of game. You're a godlike being, for crying out loud! That story of your fatal summoning to the otherworld? Of your friends' tragic demise? Your poor, poor life as a soldier? That's all one big lie. And this, too! I bet you really thrive off of seeing the girl you brainwashed into loving you fight for your sake while you just stand there watching like some brain-dead meaty tree. Deep inside, I'm sure you're just burning with the desire to wring my neck."

Wiedermann took a single step toward her, and she whirled on her feet to face Erica. Hysterically, she cried, "See? See? He's going to kill me! He's going to—"

What met her was a face of utter contempt. Her heart sank like a stone. Erica's face, previously so full of kindness and understanding, showed nothing but disgust. As though she was staring at a piece of roadkill. Sweat trickled down Jay's back.

"E—Erica?"

A slap cracked across her face before she realized what was happening. Trembling, Jay touched her left cheek. Her wide eyes fell on Erica.

A deep frown marred her pretty face, her eyebrows pinched together in anger. Tears pooled in the corners of her eyes. Jay's mind felt blank. What was happening? Why was Erica looking at her like that?

"How can you say that?" Erica croaked. A tear ran down her right cheek as her frown deepened. "*How can you say that about him?*"

Jay's mind ran at a hundred miles an hour, her every thought trying desperately to make sense of why Erica, the victim in this scenario, could possibly turn on *her*. Shouldn't she be happy now? Now she knew how evil Wiedermann was, right? Then, why did she continue defending him? Even now, he was just standing there! He wasn't doing any—

Their eyes met. His eyes were white. It had always seemed to Jay that he was almost blind and that there was nothing behind those white eyes. That he was only an automaton of sorts, moving stiffly in the pursuit of absolutely nothing. He barely spoke. When he spoke, it was soft, almost like a whisper. He didn't have much to say, but what he did say came from the heart.

As Jay looked at him, she slowly came to realize something.

Kreig was a timid man.

Yes, that was it. He was afraid of confrontation not because he was afraid of losing but only because he wanted to avoid hurting anyone. He was a little shy. He didn't like to make the first move or to tell someone what to do. He was open to suggestions, and he well and truly cared for his students.

In his eyes Jay saw nothing but worry.

No malice, no anger, no frustration or indignation. Only a sense of worry for one of his students.

Because she was one of his students, wasn't she? She couldn't run as fast as the guys, and she wasn't as strong as them either, but she always tried her best, and when she fell, he was always there to pick her up again.

In her little chest, her heart began to beat slower and slower. Her breathing grew steady. Her face felt hot. Even as she tried to interrogate him and get him to confess his stupid, *evil* deeds, he healed her. She could tell he had used a healing spell. Not just a band-aid.

In that old, old heart of his, he had cared enough about her to use healing magic, even though he was trying to avoid notice.

Stiffly, Jay turned back to Erica. Gone was the look of contempt on her face. Instead, what Jay found was a sympathetic smile and a pair of crystal-clear eyes that said everything she had never wanted to hear.

Her chest felt so tight and her legs felt so weak that she was sure she would fall. Her vision grew cloudy, and her eyes felt hot even in the cold evening.

She stumbled and found herself in Erica's warm arms. Streaks of hot tears ran down her face, and she felt a burning shame settle deep within her gut. Just a meter away stood Kreig, his brows pinched in worry, arms clearly ready to hold her. And still, for fear of hurting her with his armor, he had relinquished her to Erica. A fresh pang of hurt gripped Jay's chest and she felt like screaming, but instead, she could only hold Erica, trying her best to pull her as tight as was possible.

"I'm sorry," Jay gasped. "I'm sorry, I'm sorry, *I'm sorry, I'm—*"

A warm hand fell on her head. Gently, Erica stroked her hair. It felt good. Struck by a sudden tiredness, she pressed the side of her face into Erica's chest. Maybe it was okay that her tears stained it wet. "Shh," Erica cooed gently. "It's okay. You did bad, but that doesn't mean that *you're* bad. It just means that you have to work hard to make everything better again."

"Yes, yes," Jay breathed through rattling lungs. "I promise I won't do it again, I swear, never again, so please . . ." Tears and snot covered her face as she arched her neck to look at Erica. "Please, don't leave me."

Erica smiled. "We can't have that."

A lightning bolt of panic struck through Jay's mind. "C—can't have what?"

Her smile turned into a grin. "We can't have a journalist who doesn't release government secrets! I mean, come on! You're our best chance at revealing the sentient cutlery, you know? If you stop here, who'll become an awesome journalist and prove once and for all that I'm not their queen?"

"S—sentient cutlery?"

A thud made Jay turn to the right, where she saw Kreig slumped on the ground, heaving a heavy sigh. Where he sat, dejected and exhausted,

Jay couldn't help but feel a pang of sympathy. After all, looking at him, he appeared no different from any exhausted man. Jay turned back to Erica, whose expression, too, had changed to one of concern.

Gently, Jay removed herself from Erica's arms. She approached Kreig.

With him sitting and her standing, she was, for once, slightly taller than him. An hour before, she would have described his current state as *pathetic*, but now no such words came to her. Instead, letting her mind remain blank, she moved to his side and sat down. The ground was wet, but she didn't think about it. Over in the city, helicopters continued swarming.

She'd made a right big mess, hadn't she?

She almost felt like laughing, but no such sound came out. A little sob fell from her lips, and again the world grew blurry and bright.

A hand fell gently on her back. It was large and cold. She didn't need to look to know whose it was. She tried to take a breath but found herself hiccupping and trembling. Drawing her knees to her chest, she fumbled for the right words to say. But no matter how she tried, there were no words to put things right. The truth was out there, and now everything was wrong. And still, somehow, Kreig could bring himself to place one solitary hand on her back. Any more and his hard armor might hurt her.

"I—I didn't . . ." she began, but a deep breath interrupted her. She glanced at Kreig.

He was smiling.

She froze, her mind reeling and staggering.

He turned to her, and in those white eyes of his she saw great relief. "I'm only happy you are unhurt."

Tears welled up again and she broke into a great sob, and without any warning to him, she threw herself at his chest, even though it was hard and even though it was cold, because in that moment, she needed nothing more than a chest to cry on, and although he was clearly flustered and uncertain, he made no effort to remove her, and so, for a longer time than felt necessary, she stayed there, sobbing and wailing until her lungs were on fire again and her eyes felt cold and dry.

And there, right in his arms, lulled by the exhaustion of expecting death and the relief of forgiveness, she fell asleep.

Unsure of what else to do, Kreig and Erica brought her home, where she was greeted by her mother and too many soldiers to count. But at that point, she was still asleep, so before she could be interrogated or anything of that ilk, they let her go to sleep. She was tired, after all, and she would still be in the morning. Of course, the apartment remained under the impeccable watch of many IOCRO agents.

Later, she would face proper repercussions. But for now, she would rest.

EPILOGUE

It was 2 p.m. on a Saturday. The morning had been hectic and so had last night.

Kreig still hadn't quite come to understand what was happening or what the fallout of this situation would be, but for now, both of his siblings had assured him that everything would be all right. Darius had visited him, and they had talked for an hour or so. Even Gerald had shown up.

But right now, they weren't at home or anywhere else cozy. Instead, they were at Space Circle Avenue, inside the police station to the side of it. Outside the sliding glass doors of the station was a podium facing the avenue, and beyond that, a crowd mainly composed of reporters. It was amazing that so many international news representatives had been able to arrive at such short notice, but that bespoke the tenacity of journalists.

Speaking of journalists, Jay was not there. She was currently at her home, talking to a specially trained officer while being protected by a number of Fighters. According to her testimony—what Sam had told Kreig so far, at least—she had been given most of the information by an unknown organization that had somehow slipped under IOCRO's radar. But no longer. With Jay's help, they hoped to uncover it.

Jay herself remained in a state of great shame. Kreig understood her very well. After all, he, too, had made quite a few mistakes.

Mistakes that were now the main course for all those reporters out there.

Kreig felt nervous. He could be fully honest about that. He couldn't remember enjoying attention since the fall of the Theocracy. A hand squeezed his, and he looked over at one of the other people sitting in the police station's waiting area. Erica smiled reassuringly at him. He smiled back at her. "You know, you don't have to talk. It's okay to just sit here and let us do all the talking. I promise not to misrepresent your character!"

Kreig shook his head. "This is something I need to do. I cannot place all of my worries on your backs."

Erica shrugged and glanced over to the other people in the room. Darius, Sam, Gerald, Mrs. Willowgrove, Craig . . . witnesses to explain that Kreig was of no harm.

During the night, the news spread across the world in a matter of hours. The reach was impressive, though some countries chose to focus more on some celebrity, who had recently had a baby with a surprising lover. Kreig tried not to think too much about it. According to George, IOCRO would work day and night to make sure that the news published would at least retain some form of truth.

IOCRO as an organization had already made a few statements regarding Kreig's existence. For one, they had decided not to deny it. Knowing that their enemy had immense reach, the act of denying Kreig's existence would likely have immense consequences to weaken the public's trust in IOCRO. It was all pretty complex, but the situation right now was simply that those people close to Kreig would make their own statements and hope for the mercy of the crowds. People were always eager to pull down those up high, even if that height was a mirage.

And so, Kreig sat there, waiting patiently for someone to tell him to go up and talk. In all honesty, he wasn't sure what to say. He hadn't gotten any sleep yesterday. Of course, he didn't physically need it, but he had learned to—much like eating—enjoy the human act of slumber.

Outside, he saw how George spoke to the reporters, answering various questions. If Kreig strained his attention, he could make out what they were saying.

"—no reason for any sort of panic. We are currently taking every precaution and have been for six months. In this time, Kreig has made impressive improvements . . ."

Not wanting to hear people talk all that much about himself, Kreig zoned out again. Exhaustion of an old sort clawed at the back of his eyes. Just a short nap wouldn't hurt.

His eyes fell closed. In the darkness of his own mind he saw a spirit of white.

It smiled at him, but Kreig took the smile as quite wry. "Oracle," the spirit greeted.

Silently, Kreig placed his fist to his chest. "Greetings, o White One."

The spirit's smile broadened slightly, and it waved an aetherial hand. "None of that, Oracle. Let us speak as equals." Quietly, the spirit sat down cross-legged in the blackness of the dream. Following suit, Kreig sat next to it. "Of all my friends, you are the most long-lived." Kreig watched it silently, unsure what to make of it. "Indeed, I had expected your mind to end long ago. And yet, you have persevered."

"Without you, that would surely have been the case."

The spirit hummed softly. "I can't be too sure, Oracle. You seem to have a habit of surprising me." The spirit stretched out its legs comfortably. It turned to Kreig, and their eyes of white met. "You will not forget me, Oracle?"

"No," Kreig answered.

"You promise to give a thought to me from time to time?" the spirit asked quietly.

"Yes," Kreig responded.

The spirit nodded, its smile warm and content. "Then that is all I want." It placed an arm around Kreig's broad shoulders. "May your days be long and your love endless."

In the endless night of Kreig's mind, the sun rose gallantly.

Kreig opened his eyes and found Erica hunched down on the floor, looking up at him. He blinked at her and she smiled brightly. "I don't think I've ever seen you sleep before. Do divine humans sleep?"

Kreig wasn't sure how to answer. "They have no need for it, but . . ."

Erica finished the sentence for him. "—but sleep is divine, so you do it anyway?"

A spirit of white lingered in his mind. ". . . I suppose so."

An officer leaned inside the waiting room and called out. Gerald stood up, appearing suitably nervous. He flashed Darius a look, who gave him a thumbs-up and a smile. With that, Gerald seemed to have regained some form of confidence. But before he left the station to get eaten alive by reporters, he stopped by Kreig. They smiled at each other, no words needing to be exchanged.

Gerald was a good lad. One day, he would surely grow into a just and able man. If he kept this up, he would surely shrug off the shackles that Kreig had never been able to remove. But for now, all he had to deal with was the flashes of cameras and gazing cyclops eyes of video cameras.

Kreig listened absently as Gerald explained his life, from beginning to present. How he first met Kreig, how he felt at the time, and how such an accidental meeting had led him to a place such as this. Finally, baring his heart before the audience, he presented Kreig's painting of the two of them. Kreig smiled, remembering both how long it had taken him to paint the thing and how Gerald had asked him, just an hour or so before the press conference, if it would be okay for him to present it. Of course, since it was Gerald's painting, Kreig had no objections.

Toward the end, questions started being flung at him, most of which he answered courageously. Kreig hoped he might be able to act in a similarly composed manner, but knowing his own tendency to get tongue-tied, chances were that he might instead flounder on stage.

Erica pressed his hand again. When had she picked up a telepathy skill?

Gerald finished. Next was Darius, who spoke of his experiences as Kreig's therapist and observant with rigorous confidentiality. He revealed nothing unnecessary, keeping only to what he himself had felt without breaking client confidentiality. Of course, many reporters attempted to make him reveal things he had no business revealing, but he shut them down thoroughly. When the questions became too numerous, he became entirely silent and stepped away.

Since Sam had already spoken earlier, her main point being that "*He's a great cook, so please have mercy*," the next one up was Erica. She looked at the glass doors for a few seconds before turning back to Kreig. Her eyebrows were slightly pinched. A stray strand of hair lay across her face. Kreig brushed it behind her ear. She smiled and stood up.

"You'll listen closely, won't you?"

"Only if you want me to," Kreig said. Both of her hands took a gentle hold of his face. She smiled and gave him a quick little kiss.

"Bye-bye!" she said as she waved and left through the door. Kreig waved back at her, suddenly feeling desolate and alone. But as he sat there, unsure of what to do, the rest of the people in the waiting room silently moved over to sit by him. With that, he relaxed. They didn't need to say anything and he didn't need to hear anything. The only thing he wanted to listen to at that moment was Erica's sweet voice on the other side of the door.

Her voice was bright and cheerful, speaking of her experiences in a narrative sense, explaining how she had experienced this and that. Included in these little stories were jokes and dramatic reenactments of their meetings. "'*Family*,' he said, and I was like, 'How am I supposed to understand that? What does that even mean?' And since I thought he was totally a criminal or a mafia man or whatever, I led him to the police station. He gave the place one good look and then went, 'No green.' No green?! Buddy, look at all this green!"

Kreig smiled to himself. He had changed quite a bit, hadn't he? She, too, was a completely different woman.

The reporters seemed to enjoy her storytelling, as quite a few gave subdued laughter at her jokes. By the end, she excitedly answered questions, pointing broadly at whoever held up a hand or a pen. Though, of course, many questions left her quite red in the face.

And then her part ended and she left the stage, entering the waiting room again. Kreig watched her, feeling a strange emotion settle in his gut.

Erica ran to him and Kreig stood up to catch her in his arms. "I did well, right? Some of them laughed really loudly!"

Kreig nodded mechanically. "Of course. You were amazing." Unlike how he would be in a few minutes' time. Yes, as happy as he was for Erica, it simply could not overshadow his sudden feeling of dread. But it would be fine, wouldn't it? All he had to do was explain his side and answer a few questions. After that, everything would go back to normal. As normal as things could be, at least.

"Kreig Wiedermann, you're up," an officer shouted.

Erica turned back to Kreig and their eyes met. "You'll do great," she said confidently and gave him a peck on the cheek. "After all, you're Kreig Wiedermann!"

He nodded again. If she said so, then it must be true. With a heavy heart, he moved toward the door. He glanced over at the others in the room. Sam, Darius, Gerald . . . There was no doubt in their eyes. He *would* do well.

But what if he didn't?

Mouth suddenly dry, he walked to the door with slow, anxious strides.

Maybe he should just leave this to someone else. There were plenty of people who could recount his life history much better than he ever could. There was really no reason for him to do it personally.

Or, well, there was. One tiny little reason for why he *had* to do this.

It was his duty. As a man, he *had* to take responsibility for himself and who he was. A secondhand story could never be him. Only he could do this. And that was why he did it.

His heart pounded in his ears. The doors to the avenue opened and the gazes of thousands met him. When had he last been met with this many frightened eyes? It must have been six months before, the last moment in the otherworld, where an army faced him under the red skies.

The sky began to shift in color, and Kreig squeezed his eyes shut. He breathed slowly, carefully, just as Darius had taught him. And when he opened his eyes again, the red was gone. He stood on certain stone, not insidious mud. He stepped up to the podium.

You could hear a feather drop. It was completely silent. Nobody made a single movement. No, on closer inspection, a few brave souls trembled, their mouths floundering open at something unseen.

"I—" Kreig was interrupted by a nearby officer pointing toward the small mic on the podium. The crowd held their breaths. Kreig nodded and moved closer to the mic, feeling a little stupid. "I would like to greet all of those who have traveled all night. You have my sympath—" He wasn't able to finish his sentence before a camera flashed, the snap of it unnaturally loud in the inhuman silence of the crowd. Kreig tried not to react. "Wel—" Realizing he wouldn't do anything to them, a hundred cameras began snapping and flashing all at once, blinding him even though it was midday.

He felt woozy and bad. But if he just gritted his teeth and gripped the edges of the podium, then . . .

Wood splintered in his hands but he ignored it. Slowly, the snapping receded to an acceptable level. He took a deep breath. "I—I am assured that you know my name by now, but I shall repeat it regardless. My name is Kreig Wiedermann, and much like you, I am a human. Perhaps my race frightens you. Perhaps I do not appear as human to you, but I will assure you that inside, I am as human as any one of you."

A hand reached up, even though he hadn't gotten to telling his story yet. Uncertain, he glanced over to one of the many nearby officers, but none met his gaze. He gulped and pointed at the raised hand. "Yes?"

The man had to shout quite loudly to be heard, but he said, "Do you have any plans for world conquest?"

Kreig blinked slowly. "World conque— Why would I . . ." He shook his head and leaned closer to the microphone. "I have no intentions of conquering the world. Ruling never appealed to me."

A few hundred pens began scribbling on papers. Kreig had never felt so observed. Just as he was about to continue his life story, another hand flew up. He pointed at it, hoping it wasn't as weird as the last.

"Why did you return?"

Why did people come up with such weird questions? "There was no choice to be made, as I was more or less cast back here. If I had known that this had been a possibility, I would have attempted to return much sooner."

But with this, more people realized that he would accept questions. Assuming that he, therefore, had no story to tell, more and more hands flew up. Not wanting to disappoint them, Kreig let each of them ask their questions in turn. Each question was stranger than the last: "Can you drive a car?" "Why don't you wear that armor all the time?" "How does an increased level make you taller?"

Kreig answered each question as best as he could, but in many cases, it was a simple matter of yes or no.

And then, as the flashes died down and people had no more questions to ask, Kreig began to tell his side of the story. It was a tale he had told before, and not one he took joy in reliving. Especially his time in the north was a great source of unhappiness, but even then, he attempted his best to faithfully explain not only what happened but also how it felt. That latter part was important, since Jay had only written the direct recounting of his life. Only pure facts. This was what Kreig now had to supplement, as hard as it was.

Right there on stage, he opened up. His voice was clear and his back was straight.

Silence had once again descended on the crowd.

"... It is lucky I had been distracted enough not to kill him, as his death would have been a great loss for many, including myself." In the wake of his speech, silence reigned.

And then, slowly, a man began to clap. It was a meek sound that echoed dully across the room, but soon, another joined in. And yet another.

It was not applause of the sort after a concert, nor could it be called a standing ovation. Not a single person whooped or whistled or shouted. It was simply the sort of applause one received at the ceremony of being given a medal. A recognition of hardship and trial. Not one that begged for seconds but rather one that hoped no such thing would happen again.

Kreig accepted it with an open mouth and wide eyes.

Flustered, he left the stage. And that was the last appearance Kreig made before any camera. Not to say that he didn't get any requests; of course not. Over the course of a single week, he got hundreds of emails and phone calls and letters, all asking for him to appear on this or that show or the like. Some were more innocuous, young students wanting to interview Kreig Wiedermann for a better grade. Others wanted to see what he could do by putting him on a game show.

Kreig refused all such summons. He was busy winding down from the crowd of reporters.

As a matter of fact, these people were still trying to get to him. Since Jay had hoped to doxx him fully, quite a few articles included his current place of residence. Any reporter could easily get ahold of it, leading to there being quite a big crowd of reporters right outside his apartment every day.

They couldn't get in, since it was protected, but anytime Sam or George left or Erica entered, they tried to get in contact somehow. This was all in spite of IOCRO's trying to dissuade people and journalists from doing this very thing.

Kreig never had to leave the apartment, since his job at Painstone was temporarily on hold. Still, he didn't quite like it.

But as the days passed, fewer and fewer reporters stood outside. The few that attempted to remain were eventually shooed away by IOCRO officers.

Time passed. Kreig's existence was eventually overshadowed by some new, great disaster to talk about, and they couldn't keep their eyes on him forever.

Some people made an attempt to escape the city, of course, but for the most part, his presence was seen as acceptable. His sympathetic speech at the conference had won over many, but even more were swayed by what those close to him had to say. As always, there were a number of people who had everything and nothing to say about it, complaining about how he was allowed to go free or pleading that they should place him in a portal and send him back. But the tides turned, and eventually, they too grew more interested in other matters.

During that time, Painstone International High School was in a bit of an uproar. Some made a great big fuss about getting the walking nuke out of there; others simply left entirely. But the majority were largely positive to Kreig. The simple fact was that they liked him. He'd made many friends among them, and despite being quite frightening at first glance, the students had eventually warmed up to him. While the teachers and principal of Painstone ummed and aahed over the future of the school, some invested students made a petition to reinstate the beloved PE teacher. As always, a counter-petition was made, but when these two were stacked up against each other, there was a clear winner.

After two months on leave, Kreig was reinstated as PE teacher. And he was all the happier for it. Some worried parents made their students leave the school, but after a few months, things calmed down.

Kreig's life returned to normalcy.

At school, he and Erica became a known couple to the point where Erica simply couldn't work without a morning kiss from Kreig. In his free time, Kreig decided to start painting portraits. He had no interest in making money off of them, but at Erica's suggestion, he became a street artist of sorts, doing quick little paintings of anyone who bothered to sit down for a while. He would charge them an incredibly modest price, and they would leave, happy with a new heirloom.

Like this, he slowly became something of a town figure. Since his appearance was quite striking, there was no question of who had made the painting. Of course, such a situation would invariably lead to some greedy individuals buying his paintings and then selling them at exorbitant prices, but Kreig didn't mind. The vast majority of those who sat before him had only good intentions in mind.

After half a year or so, Kreig and Erica moved in together. During that same time, George Wiedermann had quickly become George Aardwyre during a wedding ceremony Kreig couldn't remember ever seeing before.

But Sam was not left alone in her little apartment. On the contrary, she found herself a little patrolman who smiled at her in the corridor, and together they became quite happy together, to the point that they even had Kreig paint their picture one bright spring morning.

On the other side of the city, Gerald lived happily with his adoptive parents. He, too, had been pestered by quite a few reporters, but his overprotective fathers had easily shooed them away, leaving him to indulge in his new favorite pastime: art. Digital art, to be precise. It was simple and it was far from the level Kreig was at, but he enjoyed it, and that was that.

Jay, on the other hand, felt quite low for a few weeks. The one who nursed her back to health was her dear mother, who stayed at her side throughout. How was this possible? Well, as it so happened, Erica was able to help Mrs. Crooks receive a bit of welfare. Not enough to support them fully, but enough to let her work at something that paid better and wasn't quite so dehumanizing. For Jay's part, she seemed to see the entire world through new eyes. And it wasn't just Kreig.

Her own mother had worked herself half to death for her. That realization hit quite hard, leaving her reeling for days. But like mothers so often do, she forgave Jay. At that moment, Jay decided that she would work hard to become a journalist that she could be proud of. One that would provide for her poor mother into elderly life.

A year passed quietly.

On the bridge where they had first met, Kreig proposed to Erica with a little ring he had made himself. They married happily in the late summer.

Jay, despite her many mistakes, slowly grew into a rigorous and determined woman. She retained her willingness to work hard and make sacrifices for what she believed in, but with a reality check that almost cost her her life, she had learned to see the world in shades of gray, making the proper decisions when they came instead of simply charging ahead. With this newfound maturity, she made up with Annie and Gerald. With a proper apology, the three became good friends again, even though they all went to different colleges.

Gerald went on to become a freelance animator, while Jay, after much trial and tribulation, became the journalist she had always wanted to be. Her mother couldn't be prouder.

Annie had followed in Gerald's footsteps as a creative person, though she chose instead to become an author and scriptwriter, happily working with Gerald on his creative projects. With Jay at their back, all of their creative efforts had great success, and they eventually chose to make their close partnership an official one.

And Mrs. Willowgrove? Well, although she had her beloved cat, she was still quite starved for social connection. And so, she formed a little group for parents who had lost their children in the portals. In this group, she made contact with a widower in a similar situation. They married shortly thereafter, and both of their cats got along great.

For Christmas, all of these people got together very happily, though each new person's first meeting with Kreig was always a little awkward. Still, once they got to know him, none could deny his charm.

And a few days after Christmas, while everyone else celebrated their things, Kreig spent a little time to give thanks to his own God, whom he never forgot.

Years passed slowly and happily. Kreig and Erica had two children, a boy and a girl. And one day, when those children were a little older, they brought them to the otherworld museum in the next city over, where they let them have a peek at their daddy's armor, kept all neat and tidy in a glass case. The armor was a pearly white, something Kreig had only achieved after washing it many, many times.

And one day, after so much time had passed, Jay would approach Kreig, and on that day, the first and last interview of Kreig Wiedermann would be done.

And through it all, there was nothing to be complained of.

Kreig had returned, and for that he was happy.

That was all he needed.

ABOUT THE AUTHOR

Palt is a Sweden-based author of isekai, short horror stories, and some fanfiction. He is currently working toward a degree in criminology. In his spare time, Palt enjoys drawing and playing the trombone.

DISCOVER
STORIES UNBOUND

PodiumAudio.com